LILY'S PLIGHT

DAUGHTERS OF HARWOOD HOUSE
Book Three

SALLY LAITY AND DIANNA CRAWFORD

BARBOUR
PUBLISHING

Print ISBN 978-1-61626-554-0

eBook Editions:
Adobe Digital Edition (.epub) 978-1-62029-662-2
Kindle and MobiPocket Edition (.prc) 978-1-62029-661-5

Cover credit: Studio Gearbox, www.studiogearbox.com

Published by Barbour Publishing, Inc., P.O. Box 719, Uhrichsville, OH 44683, www.barbourbooks.com

Our mission is to publish and distribute inspirational products offering exceptional value and biblical encouragement to the masses.

 Member of the
Evangelical Christian
Publishers Association

Printed in the United States of America.

Acknowledgments

The authors gratefully acknowledge
the generous assistance provided by:

Nathaniel Thomas MLS
Reading Public Library
Reading, Pennsylvania

Sarah Annibali
Lebanon Public Library
Lebanon, Pennsylvania

These individuals helped us gather necessary period data
and shared their extensive knowledge of various settings
used in this story. To you we express our sincere appreciation.

Special thanks to:

Delia Latham
Robin Tomlinson

Your tireless critiquing of our work in progress,
together with suggestions and comments along the way,
were an immense help. May the Lord bless you both.

Dedication

This book is lovingly dedicated to our Lord and Savior, Jesus Christ,
who blessed this magnificent nation from its founding, and to our
families, whose love and support makes our writing possible.

Chapter 1

April 1757

U rgent barking pierced the breezy solitude of the April afternoon.

Dropping corn seed into the freshly plowed trench, Lily Harwood sprang to her full height and whirled toward the sound, her heart pounding. *Please don't let it be Indians.*

Duke, the Waldons' big shaggy dog, stood poised at the edge of the porch, his huge brown eyes fixed on the path leading through the woods behind the squat four-room log cabin to the wagon road. A growl rumbled from his chest, and he barked in the direction of the forest—a kaleidoscope of spring greens and pine so thick the sunlight barely penetrated the foliage to dapple the mossy, fern-covered ground.

Lily slung the strapped seed bag to one side and pulled out the pistol weighting down the pocket of her work apron. She shrugged at the Waldon boys guiding the horse and plow. "A neighbor, most likely." Nevertheless, she positioned herself behind the workhorse.

Eleven-year-old Matthew laid their long musket across Smokey's back, its flintlock cocked and ready, while Luke, nine years old, capped the horn of black powder dangling from the gray gelding's harness.

Lily drew a nervous breath. In the three years since the invasion from the north, no French or hostile Indians had raided farmsteads along Beaver Creek. But other families a mere twenty miles away had been brutally murdered or carried off captive. One could never be too cautious in this area of Pennsylvania.

Still barking, Duke leaped from the porch and headed toward the path.

Motion at the log dwelling caught Lily's attention as towheaded Davy, the family's irresistible four-year-old bundle of energy, bolted out the door with his sister Emma hot on his heels. The redheaded girl latched on to her little brother's collar and yanked him back inside.

Matt wagged his head, muttering under his breath. "The kid's been told a hundred times not to come outside when the dog's barkin' like that."

Dragging her gaze from the path along the far side of the house, Lily glanced at her brave young helpers, both of whom had unruly hair the same light brown as their father. Freckle-faced Luke had a white-knuckled grip on his hunting knife as he peered beneath the horse's neck, while Matt stared through the sites of the musket, his finger steady on the trigger. Lily's heart crimped as she studied the lanky boy. Matt had a lot of his father in him. . .the same speculative blue eyes, the same heart-wrenching smile. Both lads looked older than their years. With their father away with the militia, they'd been forced to grow up fast.

"Remember, you only have one shot," she reminded Matt. "Don't shoot unless you absolutely must."

A grimace tweaked the older boy's mouth as he cut a shrewd glance her way.

His brother gave a huff. "Wish *I* had a gun 'stead o' just a dumb knife. I can shoot good as *he* can."

Lily slanted him a half smile. "I wish you did, too." Even more, she wished the cabin wasn't blocking her view of the path.

Suddenly Duke's barking ceased. Tail wagging, he loped up the path out of sight.

He must recognize whoever is coming. Releasing a pent-up sigh, she nodded to the boys, and they left the protection of the gelding to cut across the plowed field and greet the visitor.

A familiar figure came into view with Duke jumping playfully on him.

Lily's heart stilled. " 'Tis your father!" Her whole being warmed with relief and joy.

But the boys had already sprinted toward him, kicking up clods of dirt in their wake. "Pa! Pa!"

The cabin door slammed open. Out flew Emma and Davy, screaming their delight. All four children crashed into their papa and were swamped in a huge hug, laughing at once as the dog yipped and leaped in circles around them.

John has come home again. Drinking in the glorious reunion from some distance away, Lily feasted her eyes on the man of the house, tall and muscular in the sturdy clothing he wore for military duty. Her heart contracted. If only she could run to him and be pulled into those strong arms, too. . .feel safe and warm and deeply loved, have those penetrating blue eyes filling her with delicious shivers. But knowing it could never be stole the joy of the moment. She was not his wife. His beloved Susan, of delicate health and quiet manner, waited inside.

Just then, John looked across the field to Lily. He flashed a grand smile and raised a hand in a wave.

For one heartbeat she held his gaze. Then she forced an answering smile and wave and turned before her longing eyes betrayed her. She trudged to the horse to unhitch the gelding from the plow. The Waldons would be too excited over John's safe return to plant more seed today. As she led Smokey back to the stable, she watched the happy family go inside the cabin. . .to Susan. Without a doubt the sweet, bedridden woman of the house had heard the joyous racket and knew that her John had come home. Had his wife strength enough, she'd have run outside with their children to welcome her husband home with the same loving fervor as they had.

Closing her eyes against an ache of sadness as she entered the rough-hewn stable, Lily felt her neck and shoulders sag. She rested her cheek against Smokey's warmth. "Father, I'm in dire need of an extra measure of grace—and a *proper* love for each member of the Waldon family."

So many times over the past year she had prayed that same prayer. So many times she'd endured the same gnawing ache of hollow hope.

A rumbling neigh from the gelding reminded her she had yet to remove his harness.

Lily patted his muscled neck. "Yes, my mighty steed. You have needs that must be met, too." Filling her lungs with a deep breath laced with a hefty blend of animals and hay, she reached for a buckle and unfastened it as an ironic thought surfaced.

She could be released from her own bonds almost as easily. She only needed to contact her sister, and Mariah's generous husband would dispatch a man at once with money to buy her freedom and escort her away from the constant threat of Indian attack, away from the tiresome care of an invalid and her children, away from looking after this frontier farmstead. She could return to her family's loving bosom that quickly. The offer had been waiting for her acceptance for the past three years.

But how could she leave? She'd been a mere fourteen years of age when John Waldon had purchased her indenturement papers nearly four years ago and brought her to this cove. In that time she'd set the house to rights, harvested many a crop, and raised these children. Little Davy was but a babe in arms when she'd first arrived. As much as she struggled against feeling entitled, Lily couldn't help thinking the children and this farm belonged as much to her as they did to Susan. More, in fact. Hadn't she earned it all?

And John. . .

Her vision blurred behind hot tears. Angrily she sniffed and swiped them away as she hefted the heavy halter collar and hooked it onto the wall. All her life she'd been taught that coveting was a gross sin, and here she was, coveting Susan's family yet again. "Forgive me, Father. You know I struggle against these feelings whenever John gets leave from Fort Henry. I cannot seem to help myself."

How strange that when he was away she managed splendidly. She loved Susan Waldon like a beloved sister. Throughout the woman's lingering illness, Susan was so appreciative and long-suffering, who could fail to love her? *She needs me here desperately. Yet I betray her kindness and trust whenever John walks in the door.* A twinge of guilt snaked up Lily's spine, and she closed her eyes. *Please, please, dear Lord. Take this vile, sinful desire from me. Or find a way for me to leave this place without hurting them. Or me.*

John reveled in the sound of the children's voices, their laughter, their hugs, though those very hugs were making it nearly impossible to crowd through the doorway into the bedroom. He ached to see his dear Susan. The gaggle of youngsters, all talking at once, burst past the doorjamb as one.

His wife's faint voice penetrated the bedlam. "Welcome home, my love."

John's heart lurched at the sight that met his eyes. Susan sat propped up in bed, the colorful quilt surrounding her in marked contrast to the pallor of her skin. Had her cheeks been so sunken the last time he'd gotten furlough? Had there been dark circles underscoring those once vivid blue-green eyes? She looked so thin against the puffy pillows. Had she stopped eating entirely? His beautiful redheaded bride was a mere ghost of herself. But the sweet smile. . .that was all his beloved Susan.

Davy broke free of his siblings. "Mama! Look who's here!" His words vibrated loud as he ran to her bed and flung himself against it.

She winced as if the sudden jolt caused pain, but her smile never wavered. "Yes. I see." She reached out a frail hand to the child. "Your papa is home. . . . My Johnny."

Her use of his childhood name reminded him that he'd loved her since he was ten years old and the two of them were studying catechism at their local Anglican church. He gently pried himself free of the children and moved toward her. "Kids, would you mind leaving your mama and me alone for a few minutes?"

Davy's lips protruded in a pout. "But you just—"

Emma grabbed her little brother's arm and pulled him to the door. "Mama needs a hug from Papa, too. Without us crowding in."

John gazed after his seven-year-old daughter. The only one of the children who had a fair complexion and hair the same glorious shade of red as Susan's sounded so grown-up.

As the boys elbowed and shoved their way out of the room, Emma lagged behind long enough to bestow a treasured smile as she closed the door behind them, a long copper braid falling forward with her movement. She'd been as young as Davy when John had first signed on with the militia, and she was growing up so quickly. The children were all changing so between his leaves from the fort. He released a ragged breath.

"It's so good to have you home," Susan whispered.

"Oh, yes." He gazed lovingly at her. "I've missed you more than I can say." Easing down beside her, he carefully drew her into his arms, but instead of the comforting softness of her womanly curves, he felt the fragility of her frame in his embrace. The unthinkable could no longer be denied. Barring an outright miracle from God, if something wasn't done soon, she would die. "Oh, Susie-girl, my brave sweetheart," he murmured against hair once shiny and silky, now limp and dull. To think she'd given up the comforts of a privileged life to elope with him when he was not yet twenty. If only he could provide some of those childhood comforts for her now.

And he would!

"You've been gone too long." Her breathy whisper held little strength.

He drew her closer and kissed her temple. "I'm glad I'm here now, to hold you." One way or the other, he'd convince her to go to her family in Philadelphia. She must know it was vital for her to go. A physician there might know more about her life-draining malady than the doctors who'd examined her before they left Baltimore. This time he'd compel her to go—escort her himself, if he had to. If he was late returning to duty at Fort Henry, Captain Busse would understand.

Easing his hold on her, John looked into her eyes. "Sweetheart, we've—"

The door banged open. Pint-sized Davy burst into the room and stopped short of the bed, a frown scrunching his freckled nose. "Ain't you through huggin' yet?"

John couldn't help laughing as he gently settled Susan back against her pillows. He reached for the boy. "Come here, my boy. It'll be a long time before I'm through hugging any of you."

Lily dried her hands at the washstand by the cabin door. It would look suspicious if she stayed out in the stable any longer. Besides, John would most likely be hungry. She plastered on a welcoming smile and strode inside.

The family sat clustered around the finely crafted dining table that John, a journeyman furniture maker, had made the first year Lily came to live with them in Beaver Cove. Before the war. Davy perched on his father's lap, his wiggly hands ever in motion, and Susan sat wrapped and pillowed in the rocking chair at the warm end near the hearth.

John and Susan both wore happy smiles as they looked Lily's way.

"Come in. Come sit with us." John patted the vacant chair at the table.

"How about I get you something to eat and drink first? You must be hungry." She forced a brightness into her demeanor as she moved past the table to the fireplace. "We've beans and carrots left over from nooning."

He spoke around Davy's head. "Sounds mighty good. I haven't eaten since we left Harris's Ferry this morning."

"We?" Across from his father, Matt leaned forward. "Did the other fellas from Beaver Cove come home, too?"

"That they did. All five of us. We floated down the Susquehanna from Henry's Fort yesterday, then this morning we borrowed a canoe and paddled up the Swatara as far as Beaver Creek. Our stream was running too fast, so we walked in from there."

Davy swiveled toward him. "Did ya see any Injuns out there?"

More than interested in the answer, Lily straightened from stirring the coals under the suspended bean pot and turned.

John's jovial expression had vanished. "No, Son. Has there been sign of them in the cove?"

"Uh-huh. Last Sunday." Luke's eyes twinkled. "Micky MacBride said Pete Dunlap saw moccasin tracks in the woods behind the Bakers' old place."

"You don't say." John's worried brow matched Lily's alarm.

Matt jabbed his brother in the ribs. "Don't listen to him, Pa. Pete likes to stir things up, is all. He prob'ly was nowhere near that far upstream."

Somewhat relieved, Lily poked life into the glowing embers beneath the water kettle. "I'm sure Matt's right. Even so, we tie Duke to the porch post at night so he can't go chasing off after some raccoon."

Luke nodded. "That way Duke can warn us before any Injuns can sneak up an' shoot arrows at him. They do that, ya know, to keep dogs from warnin' folks."

Susan's plaintive voice cut in. "Boys. Please." She drew a labored breath. "Enough unpleasantness. Let's be happy your father is home— and the rest of our fine militiamen."

Poor, helpless Susan. It must be hard to be brave when one is in too much pain even to walk. Lily had watched the young woman getting weaker with each passing month, while she herself seemed powerless to do anything about it.

John leaned over and kissed his wife's cheek. "Since there hasn't been any trace of the French or Indians around the fort, Captain Busse released half the militia to come home and get our crops in. He gave us two weeks. When we return, he'll let the others go."

"Only two weeks?" Susan asked the question Lily wanted to ask. "When will this horror ever end?"

As Lily poured steaming water into the teapot, John moved closer to Susan and wrapped an arm around her. "I can't say, my love. But rather than take this time to plant, I plan to see you and the children on your way to Philadelphia. You'll all be much safer with your family, and you'll finally be under the care of a much more learned doctor."

"But we'd never see you then." Susan's voice became stronger than Lily had heard in weeks. "It's quite safe here. Truly. Folks are only a gunshot away." She swung her gaze to Lily. "Tell John how we celebrate Sundays now."

"Of course." Lily smiled and set the teapot on the table. "But first, Emma, would you please get your papa a cup and fork while I dish up his food?" Considering the fragile rein she had on her emotions, the last thing Lily wanted to do was look at John while she spoke. "The other families along the creek road have been coming here for church services for a while now. No one wants to travel more than a mile or so, since spring is so rainy."

"Roads get slick as snot after a good rain," Luke piped in.

"Slick as snot," Davy echoed, flashing a baby-toothed grin up to his father.

"*Davy.*" Frowning, Emma beat Lily to the reprimand. "You know you're not supposed to say that. And neither are you." Hands on her hips, she glared at Luke.

Lily saw John rub a hand across his mouth, but his laughing eyes couldn't hide his mirth. She continued explaining the Sabbath happenings. "We push the furniture back and set up benches. Grandfather MacBride reads from the Bible—"

"An' we sing lots an' lots of songs." Davy gave an emphatic nod. "Then we all eat till our bellies pooch out, an' I get to go out an' wrestle with Charlie an' Joseph."

After Lily set a plate heaped with beans, carrots, and bread, John picked up a fork and wolfed down a couple of bites. "That does sound like fun, and real nice for you, Susie-love." He bestowed another adoring look on his wife. "But I still want you to go to Philadelphia. There has to be a doctor there who can help you."

She shook her head. "Please, darling, don't waste this wonderful home-coming on that subject. We're all here together. Let's enjoy the moment."

"I agree. You need to eat." Lily poured John a cup of tea and met his gaze. "You're much too thin, and I've only two weeks to put some weight back on you." The words were out of her mouth before she could stop them, and her face flamed with embarrassment. She knew she should have said *we have,* not *I have.* She really must be more careful.

Chapter 2

We hoped you'd come home a few times during the winter months, John. The endless days from Christmas until now have seemed like forever."

John swallowed his mouthful of hearty spiced beans and smiled at Susan. "I know, my love. It felt like that for me also, but Captain Busse believed the French were planning a surprise attack. Turned out he'd been given false information by our Shamokin Village Indian allies. There's always more rumors and waiting than action."

"Thank the Lord for that," Lily remarked from the hearth.

John glanced up at her, surprised when she immediately averted her gaze. Odd. "It does get tiresome languishing at the fort. But you're right. We're most grateful to the Lord."

"Amen." Little Emma's affirmation was rife with feeling.

"Yes. Amen." John grinned. It felt wonderful to be home. Only why was Lily acting so shy? Perhaps she was hesitant to remind him that her indenturement would come to an end in two months. The quiet English girl had fit in so well here and been such an invaluable help to them all, he couldn't imagine what the family would do without her.

While the children chatted on about the happenings at the cove since Christmas, John tried to concentrate on his delicious, home-cooked meal. But with the troubling sound of Susan's raspy breathing beside him, he could not deny that with Lily's imminent departure approaching, it was more vital than ever to convince his wife to go to her family in Philadelphia.

His gaze meandered once again to Lily as she stirred the coals and added another log to the dwindling fire. Nothing remained of the frightened, wide-eyed waif of a bond servant who'd trembled uncertainly on the auction block in Baltimore years ago. That wisp of a girl had blossomed into an engaging young woman, her wheat-gold hair a shining halo braided about her head. The Lord had given this family a priceless gift in her. In truth, John had a few misgivings about Lily in the beginning. But she'd turned out to be quite the capable young woman. . .nursemaid to his wife, almost-mother to his children, excellent housekeeper, and willing farmhand. Hard to believe that in a mere two months the law would require him to give the winsome, golden-haired angel two pounds cash money and supplies enough to see her safely back to her sisters.

She turned her face up to his then, and for an instant he was lost in the luminous depths of her gray eyes as a flush of pink swept her delicate cheekbones.

John gathered his errant thoughts and swallowed. Two pounds. How could he spare that sum? Since being called to militia duty, he'd been unable to practice his furniture-making trade, and with his long absences, the farm barely produced enough to keep the family and livestock fed. Philadelphia was the only answer.

"Papa, you're not listening." Emma tugged his linsey-woolsey sleeve. "I said—"

"Forgive me, honey. I was enjoying being here so much my ears couldn't keep up." He reached past Davy and gave her a hug.

She shrunk away a bit, and her nose scrunched up. "You need a bath, Papa. Bad."

He could only chuckle.

"Emma!" Lily gasped. "I daresay that was hardly polite. But I'd imagine your father would appreciate a nice warm soak. I'll start heating extra water." She snatched up the water bucket and emptied it into the kettle. "Matt, would you and Luke mind taking the bucket and milk pail out to the well and filling them with water?"

"Yes, ma'am." Both boys scooted back their chairs and hastened to do her bidding.

"Lily's been such a blessing," Susan said in her thready voice. "I don't know what we'd do without her."

John released a pent-up breath and studiously avoided glancing at the lass again. How would he tell his wife their lovely helper would be gone in two months? His family simply had to leave this place—even if Susan still dreaded facing her domineering father after all these years.

Up in the loft, John tucked Davy in for the night. "Time for your prayers, boys."

The little scamp looked completely innocent as he gazed up, his blue eyes shining. "We won't have to ask Jesus to keep you safe tonight, 'cause you're here with us."

"That's right. Not tonight." John bent and kissed the child's forehead.

As his sons murmured their private pleas to the Lord, John recalled how close he'd come to losing his life the previous November when he'd been shot through his calf muscle—an injury his family knew nothing about, but one that still ached whenever it rained. He thought back on the morning when he and several of his buddies were chasing after a raiding party up the Tulpehocken Path. They hadn't seen any sign of the group since.

Although the French and their allied Indians were gone for now, John knew they'd be back, and soon. What was to stop them, as long as James Ambercrombie was commanding the English forces? Upon the newly arrived general's first and only encounter with the enemy, the pathetic excuse for a leader had set a new standard for incompetence by causing the senseless slaughter of many of his own soldiers.

John thanked God that he was stationed at Fort Henry with Captain Busse instead of with the army at Lake Champlain. Had King George dispatched an even halfway capable commander, the French would've been pushed back across the Great Lakes long ago and taken their Indian allies with them.

Now the French would be even more emboldened.

And Beaver Cove was in more danger of attack than ever before.

At the hearth, Lily stirred the huge footed pot containing the cubed potatoes and smoked ham she was preparing for tomorrow's Sabbath meal. Then, unhooking a potholder, she plucked the pressing iron from the hot metal plate sitting among more fiery coals and brought it to the worktable to iron John's finely woven white shirt for the morning church meeting. She wanted him to look his best. Smoothing a hand over the material, Lily lost herself in the memory of the smile he'd given her earlier this evening when thanking her for preparing his bath, and her heart ached with longing.

"Why are you cooking and ironing at this late hour?"

Something inside her went completely still as John descended the loft ladder. She did her best to sound casual as she spoke in low tones. "I'm cooking for tomorrow, the Sabbath." The realization struck her then that with the rest of the household now abed, the two of them were in the common room. . .*alone.*

He seemed unaware of her discomfort. "Sunday. I'd lost track of the days." Having reached the bottom, he started toward her, the chiseled lines of his face relaxing into an amiable smile.

Lily's inward struggle made her hands tremble, and she gripped the iron harder. She'd never found it hard to converse with John before. He'd been as much a friend as he was the owner of her papers. It was not his fault that her traitorous feelings had grown beyond her control. *Say something. Don't make him suspicious.* She drew a shaky breath. "We womenfolk find it easier if each of us prepares one large dish to share with everyone. And of course you'll need freshly pressed clothing, since folks wear their finest to service."

John walked past her and plucked a cup from a shelf, pouring himself a steaming cup of tea from the pot left near the fire. "You've grown up to be a very responsible young woman, Lily."

Did he have to stay so close? She put more effort into ironing.

"I doubt your sister Rose would've been so eager to help me purchase your papers if she'd known you'd end up in a remote settlement like this, where an Indian attack could happen without warning. I'm even more surprised that after your other sister married a man of wealth, she wasn't able to convince her husband to buy your papers from me." He eased down in the dining chair nearest her. "You probably don't know I thank God every day that she didn't."

Lily didn't know how to respond. To think John actually thanked God for her, thought of her every day, just as she did him! Of course, his thoughts were undoubtedly far more *proper*, she chided herself. How would his opinion of her change if he learned that Mariah's letters never failed to remind her of Colin's offer to retrieve her—or worse yet, if John discovered the depth of her yearning for him?

She filled her lungs once more and reined in her dangerous thoughts while she adjusted the fabric. Then, picking up the iron, she changed to a safer subject. "The older boys have been very good about searching the surrounding woods for signs of danger." At his appreciative nod, she continued. "While Matt and Luke were out the other day, Matt shot a buck near the creek. The boys came back for the horse to haul the buck home. Without so much as calling me to help, they managed to string up the stag and dress it out. I knew they wanted to surprise me, so I didn't let them catch me peeking out the window."

John tipped his head in thought. "And I found the three of you out planting when I arrived. You've done a great job with them, Lily. I especially appreciate your tender care of Susan."

The intrusion of his wife's name squelched the rush of tenderness

Lily felt for John. Reminding herself yet again that he was a man known for his kind words to everyone and that she had no reason to feel slighted, she forced a light note into her tone. "Well in truth, Davy can be quite the handful from time to time. But I do love watching our little Emma trying to act the grown-up young lady."

John sighed, drawing her attention to him as a wistful flash of regret creased his forehead. "I'm missing so many of their growing-up years. I know I'll never get them back."

"Perhaps. But you are putting your life at risk patrolling along the Susquehanna River. Every day you and the rest of the militiamen put yourselves between the war parties and us. That's worth a lot."

He gave a noncommittal shrug. "Sorry to say, the war's not going well at the moment. And Susan has gotten so much worse. . . . Even I can see that. I must demand this time that all of you leave here for Philadelphia."

His words troubled Lily. She shook out his still-warm shirt and draped it over a chairback as his resonant voice went on.

"If you could have the family's clothing packed by Monday morning, I'd be able to travel with you—at least as far as the mouth of the Susquehanna. I'll sign off on your bond papers, so once you get my dear ones to Susan's family, you'll be free to travel on to your sister's."

So John had also thought about her indenturement contract nearing its conclusion. She replaced the iron on its heating plate on the hearth and turned to face him. "If you're worried about me leaving before the war ends, pray be at rest. I assure you I would never abandon Susan and the children. I love them far too much."

His deep blue eyes slanted downward as a grateful grin spread across his features. "I never for a moment thought you'd abandon them. In fact, I'd planned to pay extra for your irreplaceable service to my family until the war ends. Even after that, if you're not opposed to remaining with us. But now with Susan having grown so much worse, I fear her only hope is that her father will hire the best physicians his money can afford. There's no other recourse."

Lily had to be honest with him as she met his gaze with an unwavering one of her own. "Perhaps had we gone, as you urged her, last fall, things would be different now. But I'm afraid leaving here at the moment is no longer possible. Surely you can see that."

He didn't respond right away. Lowering his head, he rubbed a hand over his face, then looked up with a kind of desperation he'd never before shown. "Her need to be under the care of a competent doctor is so urgent now. I won't accept her argument any longer, that she always wants to be here when I get leave."

"John." Lily spoke frankly, despite knowing her words would inflict unbearable pain. "I doubt Susan would survive as much as the wagon ride to the Swatara. Even if she could, there's the matter of days she'd have to spend on a damp keelboat afterward and then the trip from the mouth of the river on to Philadelphia. I understand it's at least fifty miles overland to the city, or a weeklong voyage around the Chesapeake peninsula. Such a journey in her fragile condition is out of the question. It's been three months since she's been able to endure even the brief wagon ride to the MacBrides' for church. I'm grateful everyone loves her so much they're willing to crowd in here every week so she can be part of the service."

"So am I, Lily-girl. So am I." John's attempt at a smile was a pitiful failure. He remained silent for so long, Lily was loath to intrude on his thoughts. Finally he spoke again. "I still have to believe there's a way to make this happen. I'll speak to the men tomorrow to see what can be done."

At a loss as to how to answer such blind faith, Lily turned back to the fire to check the potatoes. Susan's worst fear had now become hers. If they were all sent to Philadelphia, she'd be expected to travel on afterward to Mariah's. She would never see John again.

Chapter 3

With a mixture of pride and sadness, John helped his sons bring in boards for the neighbors to sit on during the Sabbath service. The boys had grown up so much since he'd been in the militia. Already Matt sported muscles in his upper arms, and farm chores were broadening his hands. Even his expression had a mature seriousness about it, and eyes once alight with a youthful tendency to mischief now radiated a kind of sadness in their blue depths. Would Luke also be forced to relinquish his childhood so quickly?

"That keg needs to be a couple of feet closer to the wall, Pa," his younger son commented as he hefted one end of a long board.

John grinned and complied. Today the boys were directing him, not the other way around. As they set up this last bench, he tried to envision six fairly large families occupying the eight rows facing the hearth. "Has another family moved away while I was gone?"

Matt straightened. "No. Only the Thorntons and Bakers left the cove. Everyone else is still around."

"You sure there'll be enough room for them all? Last time I counted there were forty-seven folks hereabouts."

Lily's airy, feminine voice rang out. "That was before our two new babies. We now have forty-nine."

John turned to her. He almost didn't recognize the willowy young woman standing in the doorway of the room she shared with Emma. Instead of her everyday homespun, she'd donned one of the better gowns she'd brought from England, altered now to fit her slender, womanly curves. In a shiny fabric of cornflower blue, with lace adorning the neck and dripping from elbow-length sleeves, the gown projected a delicate tinge of blue to her gray eyes. With her wheat-gold locks swept back and up into a cluster of ringlets, she looked exceptionally fetching.

"The Randalls normally listen from up in the loft." Lily glided gracefully toward the hearth and looked about, as if approving the placement of the benches.

John let out a slow breath when Matt's voice drew his attention away from their bond servant. "That's why we swung our beds crossways and moved 'em closer to the railing."

He flicked a glance up to see that the three cots now made one long bench.

Lily moved to the wooden board below the window. "Of course, with five extra men here, we'll all need to sit much closer than we usually do." She began shelving the breakfast dishes that had been left to air dry. "Mayhap we can set some of the wiggly tots like Davy on our laps."

"I'm not takin' him." Luke smirked.

Chuckling, John ruffled the boy's unruly brown locks, noting they could use a little more slicking down. "Don't worry. I'll hold the squirt."

"Good." Luke raked his hair with his fingers, trying to restore the limited order. "With you sittin' with us, maybe Robby Randall won't try to crowd in so's he can sit by Lily." He rolled his blue eyes in disgust.

Matt snickered. "Can you believe it? With old Mr. Randall off with the militia, Robby thinks he's man enough to come sniffin' around her."

Glancing over at the subject of the conversation, John caught a new flush of color pinkening the back of her slender neck. He cleared his throat and changed the subject. "What about the meal after the service? How do we set up for that?" Even as he spoke, he wondered if an English maiden with Lily's obvious beauty and refinement could be interested in a country lad a year or so younger than herself. But then, all the young men her age and older were in the militia. Even if they weren't. . .

Luke's voice cut into his musing. "Soon as the service is over, us menfolk roll in a couple a barrels to hold up some of the boards and make a long table outta them and the kitchen table. Once the ladies set out the food, us kids fill our plates and eat first so we'll have more time to go out and play."

"Yeah." Matt harrumphed. "But it galls me that Judy an' Anna MacBride an' the Randall twins got so uppity they think they're too old for the rest of us. They eat with the adults now." He gave a sarcastic shake of his head.

John managed not to reveal his surprise that Matty was already noticing the feminine sex. The lad truly was growing up. "How old are those gals? I've lost track."

"Judy's fourteen, Anna's almost thirteen, and Gracie and Patience just turned twelve."

"And actin' prim and proper as cats," Luke piped in, his freckles spreading apart with his grin. "Swishin' their skirts around like they was as old as Cissy Dunlap or Lily."

"Twelve." John did his best to maintain a straight face. "Matt, you turned eleven yourself on your last birthday, as I recall. Well, all I can say is neither of you is just *acting* older. You're *being* older. I'm proud of you both."

His boys stood a bit taller.

John couldn't help noticing that Lily wore an affectionate smile also. Her eyes sparkled with mirth as her gaze drifted to his, sharing the moment. Then her smile vanished like dew in the morning sun as she turned away and busied herself with the dishes again.

Why the sudden change? John couldn't think of anything he'd said to offend her since he'd arrived home. Or was she still embarrassed about the Robby situation? Women were difficult to figure out. He cut a glance to his sons. "Boys, with so many folks riding in, we'd best go out and fill the watering trough."

Puffy clouds scudded across the morning sky as the crunching of wagon wheels and clomping of farm horses announced the arrival of Beaver Cove's residents for the Sabbath service, the women in their very best homespun, the men spruced up with slicked-back hair and worn, but clean, attire. After trickling inside and milling about with greetings and chatter, the older folks took seats on the benches John and the boys had lugged in, while the youngest kids scrambled up the ladder to the loft.

Sandwiched between the older Waldon boys, Lily could scarcely breathe. John sat at the end next to Susan's rocking chair, with Davy on his lap and Emma snuggled close. Matt urged two of his friends to fill in the last two spaces to his right, preventing Robby Randall and younger brother Donald from monopolizing Lily. She appreciated that small distraction. John looked entirely too handsome in his burgundy frock coat and ruffled cravat, though the outfit did show wear. She didn't dare allow her gaze to linger on him.

She glanced ahead to the other families chatting happily with their neighbors. During this last period of duty, none of the valley's men had been killed, as Willard Thornton had been last year, or wounded, like Calvin Patterson two years ago. Cal's wife, Nancy, appreciated having her husband home, but his shattered knee was the heavy price paid for that privilege. Lily sneaked a glance over at John and thanked the Lord for protecting him.

"Ahem. Time to start this service." Ian MacBride, or Grampa Mac as the children called him, moved to the front of the hearth, his callused hand raised for silence. The oldest resident of the cove, at six feet he was also the tallest, and sinewy, but his grave demeanor belied a merry heart. Lacking an ordained minister within a thirty-mile radius of Beaver Creek, the grizzle-haired man with bushy whiskers had become their spiritual leader of sorts.

Lily had found the casual arrangement a touch strange at first, having grown up in Bath, England, with its magnificent cathedral, but she'd come to treasure the man's unschooled wisdom and looked forward to his scripture reading and related comments. His slight Scottish accent with its rolling *r*'s fell pleasantly on her ears.

People were still exchanging greetings with the returning soldiers, so Elder MacBride swept a slow glance around, gathering the attention of each individual in the simple log dwelling. "I ken we're all pleased to have our men back home with us again—even for just two weeks—so let's bow our heads and give thanks to the Lord for this blessed time. Father God, we thank and praise Ye for keepin' our soldiers safe and healthy despite the smallpox that ravaged the forces up in New York. Ye ken how much we missed our men, Lord. Not just because we love 'em, but with 'em bein' farmers, Ye ken the land needs 'em too. We trust Ye to see that we all have food on our tables and that the roof dunna' leak till this war ends. And if 'tis Thy will, Lord, we ask for peace to return to Pennsylvania and the other colonies. We ask this in the name of Thy Son. Amen."

Quiet *amen*s and nodding heads expressed the agreement of the gathering.

"Now," he continued, "let's stand and sing 'Praise God from Whom All Blessings Flow.' "

Lily saw John retain hold of Susan's slim hand while he stood with Davy in his other arm, and her heart ached. Susan needed her husband desperately. But heaven help her, so did Lily. Unable to endure their display of affection, she lowered her lashes.

While the rafters vibrated with song, Lily had something else to fill her mind. She basked in everyone's exuberance, enjoying the richness of extra male voices among the crowd.

Two hymns later, Elder MacBride hooked his wire-rimmed spectacles over his bulbous nose and opened his frayed Bible, a cue for everyone to sit again. "Before getting back to Ephesians chapter five, I'd like to read a few verses from Psalm 101 as a fittin' preamble for our passage. 'I will sing of mercy and judgment: unto thee, O Lord, will I sing. I will behave myself wisely in a perfect way. . . . I will set no wicked thing before mine eyes.' " Then he bowed his head. "Our Father in heaven, we offer our thanks for the Word Ye gave us for our instruction. Amen."

"I will behave myself wisely. . . . I will set no wicked thing before mine eyes." Lily shifted in her seat. Had Mr. MacBride seen the longing for John Waldon in her gaze? She looked for a sign in the Scot's expression that would expose her sin but saw none as his huge, veined hands leafed through his Bible. She shot a furtive glance past the children to John, then Susan.

Both sat placidly, paying rapt attention to the older man. Lily berated herself for her foolish fancies.

" 'Be ye therefore followers of God, as dear children; and walk in love, as Christ also hath loved us, and hath given himself for us an offering and a sacrifice to God for a sweetsmelling savour. But fornication, and all uncleanness, or covetousness, let it not be once named among you, as becometh saints. . . .' "

His voice droned on, but Lily heard nothing past those words. She knew her thoughts were unclean and covetous, just as he said. Sitting motionless between the two unsuspecting boys, she felt dirty, unworthy even to be in this house, much less a good friend of all present. Her heart contracted in abject despair.

Eventually the elder's book slammed shut, snapping Lily's attention once again to the front.

"And may our Lord bless the readin' of His holy Word."

The statement was scarcely out of the man's mouth before Emma, Davy, and the other youngsters made a mad dash outside. While everyone else clambered to their feet and began moving benches aside and constructing the long dining table in the center of the room, Lily shook off her morose mood. The Sabbath was always a gladsome day when everyone looked forward to a hearty dinner and fine fellowship. She refused to let her silly dreams steal her cheerfulness. Somehow God would help her get over the folly of untoward thoughts and forbidden longings.

As she moved out of the way to stand beside Susan's rocking chair, Matt followed her. "I s'pose you noticed Jackson Dunlap swiveling around time and again to gawk at you." A note of sarcasm colored his tone.

"Why, no. I was concentrating on Mr. MacBride's reading."

He scoffed. "Well, you better watch yourself. He's probably gonna try to get you alone the first chance he gets. He's nothin' but a rough ol' cob, even if he does think he's some kind a war hero, irresistible to females."

"Yeah. Watch him." Luke echoed his brother's advice.

Lily found her charges' protective behavior charming and gave them an affirmative nod. "I'll keep that in mind."

Luke touched her arm as she turned away. "Frank ain't no better. Watch out for him, too."

From the corner of her eye, Lily saw John come to a stop a few feet away as he watched the menfolk bustling about. Hopefully he hadn't overheard his sons' comments.

She turned to Matt and Luke. "I think your father might need assistance in helping the other men."

Just then, Susan reached up and touched Lily's hand.

Lily's heart sank. Surely the mistress had perceived her guilt during the elder's reading. She looked down at the ailing young woman, expecting to see censure in her expression.

Instead of reproach, a sweet smile rested on Susan's lips. "My little men are jealous. They don't want some strapping young fellow to whisk you away from us."

"So 'twould seem."

"Nor would I, dear Lily. I couldn't bear to lose you."

Contemplating the remark, Lily returned Susan's smile and excused herself to help the other ladies. For all their sakes, she hoped she could conjure up warm feelings for at least one of the stocky Dunlap brothers. She glanced out the open doorway, where Frank and Jackson huffed with effort as they wrestled a barrel up the steps, grinning at one another in triumph. With dark brown hair and hooded brown eyes, both had matured considerably over the past three years. Though neither bore any obvious battle wounds, the ravages of war showed on their faces and in their eyes, just as it did in John's. No doubt they'd welcome the loving affection of a gentle maiden.

The trouble was neither young man held the least appeal for her.

The only one her heart cried out for was John.

Releasing a tortured breath, she sent another desperate prayer aloft. Surely God would keep her strong. His ways were perfect. If it was His will that she leave this family and go to live with Mariah two months hence, it would be the best for all concerned.

So why did that conviction lack even the slightest comfort? Her unwitting gaze slid to John Waldon, smiling tenderly down on his wife as he gently kneaded her shoulders, and Lily's heart ached so, she pressed a hand to her breast to stop the pain.

Chapter 4

Not since Christmas had John felt as sated as he did after the delicious meal prepared by the ladies of the settlement.

When he and the other men meandered outside afterward, he noticed his best friend, Bob Randall, patting his slight paunch. A family man of medium height, with three sons and five daughters ranging in age from seventeen to nine months, Bob had sable hair; close-set hazel eyes; and a short, dark beard. John chuckled when the man emitted a loud belch. The group paused a moment to watch the youngsters, exuberant in their play as they raced along the wagon road with their hoops and sticks. Then, heading away from the melee of screams and shouts, they strolled off the porch.

Ian MacBride nodded in the direction of the furrowed Waldon land. "I see yer boys got most of your fields plowed up this week."

"Right. Them and our girl, Lily. When I came in yesterday, she was out there ankle-deep in mud helping them."

"That little miss has been worth her weight in gold," rail-thin Cal Patterson remarked as he limped along from a shot-up knee he'd gotten during a militia conflict. With sandy blond hair and light brown eyes, the father of five had two sons and three daughters. "It's a wonder how she's kept your place goin' whilst you been away. Susan, sickly as she is, has nothin' but praise for the lass." His grin gave prominence to his protruding chin.

Expecting the overeager Dunlap boys to join in the praises regarding Lily, John glanced over his shoulder. But they and a few other young lads remained behind on the porch, peeking in on her and the other girls helping the womenfolk with the dishes. John scowled.

The men halted between a cart and wagon, and a few propped a foot on a hitch or a wheel spoke while they visited.

Richard Shaw, John's closest neighbor, and the only landholder younger than he, straddled the long hitch of the cart and leaned against the front boards, pulling out a small pack of tobacco to fill his pipe. "I shore do love Sabbath dinners. 'Specially when the women serve that dried apple pie. Not that I'd allow to mention it, but my Ruthie ain't the best cook in the world." Blue eyes twinkled beneath his wavy brown hair as a sheepish smile plumped out his ruddy cheeks. His relaxed stance compressed his medium frame and height a bit.

"What with five bairns under eight, one bein' a wee newborn," MacBride commented on a wry note, "I doubt yer good wife has much time for pie makin'."

Richard warded off the Scot's words with his pipe and a grin. "Like I said, I ain't gonna mention it."

The other men chuckled, and stocky, barrel-chested Toby Dunlap removed his own tobacco pouch from a vest pocket. His deep-set eyes seemed a darker brown against balding gray hair. His family consisted of a daughter and three sons, two of whom were nearly grown.

John glanced around. "Speaking of not riling the womenfolk, while we're here, we need to talk about building a blockhouse. As Pat and Bob know, I had my mind set on taking my family down to Philadelphia during this furlough. But with Susan having deteriorated to such a low point, I fear taking such a risk."

Ian MacBride's son Patrick gave John's arm an empathetic squeeze. "I don't relish sayin', there's quite a change from the last time we was home. You have the sympathies of every man here, friend." A good, steady family man like his father, Patrick was also a fine militiaman. Lean and tall, he had the same commanding presence as the older man, and shared the same penetrating blue eyes. He'd provided Ian with two grandsons and three granddaughters.

"Ye have our nightly prayers, as well," Ian added. "From what Pat told me about how the English commanders are bunglin' their campaigns up in New York, I'm with ye. It might be wise to start takin' extra precautions. That wee line of defense you fellas have along the Susquehanna may not be sufficient this year. We dunna' want to walk off and leave everything you all have worked for. A blockhouse is a bonny solution. A solid place to hole up, if ever we need to."

"Since we're located pretty much in the middle of the settlement—and with Susan to consider—I'd like to build it over there, across the creek." John pointed down between the springhouse and the smokehouse, where several years earlier he'd built a footbridge using a broad, sturdy log that had fallen across a narrow spot of the flowing water. His neighbors from that side of the creek had used it to cross this morning, leaving their rigs on the other side.

Bob Randall kneaded his bearded chin, his hazel eyes narrowing in thought. "That would be the most likely spot. There's plenty of timber close by, and we could stock it with barrels of water, firewood, and a store of cornmeal and lard. That way, folks could stay inside till help could get there."

"We need to stock extra black powder along with the other provisions," Toby Dunlap said. "We could start buildin' tomorrow, while we have this good weather, since you boys are expectin' to leave within a fortnight."

John checked the sky. Recent rains had left the land spongy, but that would prove no hardship. "I figure we could all plant during the morning hours and spend the afternoons here this week felling trees and cleaning off the branches. Then early Saturday morning we could start raising the blockhouse. That okay with everyone?"

A collective nod made the rounds.

"It would help Ruthie be a far sight less jumpy at night." Richard swung a glance at the others. "Even though the Shamokin Village Indians have stayed loyal so far, the ones from up north prob'ly know the location of every settlement along the Swatara. They've already done their worst at the more isolated farms, especially those just below Blue Mountain."

"True. Quite true." Cal Patterson spoke on a droll note. "The redskins aren't even usin' the river. They sneak down their warrior paths. With the Bakers and Thorntons pullin' out last summer, makin' our place the last farmstead up Beaver Creek, and with that old Indian path bein' no more'n a couple miles north of us, Nancy's about to jump outta her skin every time she hears a bird call, sure it's an Indian."

Aware that the two men who'd spoken of their wives' fears weren't serving in the militia, but here at home to protect their families, John glanced back toward his cabin. No one was around to protect *his* family— or his brave Lily. Yet the delicately bred British maiden who'd lived her early years in comfort had not once voiced her fears to him. Despite the lack of protection she had every right to take for granted, she'd learned to thrive here in this rugged wilderness. In fact, she herself was all the protection his family had. She and two half-grown boys.

A smile played over his lips at the recollection of her standing out in the field yesterday with a pistol aimed at him as he emerged from the forest. Small wonder the Dunlap boys were eyeing her speculatively, the bond servant who lacked even the smallest dowry. They'd probably come around every day now to make sure she was as capable as she was soothing to the eye.

Strange, how he'd never fully noticed the incredible beauty she'd become.

"It's all settled then." Bob Randall whacked his broad-brimmed hat against his thigh, emitting a puff of dust. "Tomorrow afternoon the lot of us'll be here with our axes."

John again eyed the young bachelors lounging about on the porch of his cabin. Bob's son Robby had turned seventeen, and apparently shared

Jackson and Frank Dunlap's interest in Lily. Even now the three elbowed one another in playful rivalry to have best access to the window. Robby, with his open, honest face and manner, possessed a kind of magnetism that attracted girls, especially with that curly hair of his. . .and he'd still be here after the burly brothers returned to militia duties.

Lily stifled a yawn as she detected the rumble of an approaching wagon the following Saturday. *Oh my. They're here already—and so early.* She'd risen before dawn each morning that week to bake extra cornbread for the neighbor men hard at work felling trees. The added chore, along with cooking, washing clothes, helping plant, and seeing to the needs of her mistress, had taken its toll.

John had assured her she needn't help Matt and Luke in the fields. But Lily knew he had few precious days here, and the sooner the workers were finished each afternoon, the more time he'd have to spend with his wife. She would make every effort to see that the couple had as much time together as possible.

Today would be different, however. All the residents of Beaver Cove would come to lend a hand, and no one would leave until the structure was finished. It would be a long day.

Davy gave a high-pitched holler. "Joey's here!" Leaping down from the chair he'd stood on to peer out the window, he bolted for the door and flung it open, dashing outside to join his playmate.

"Hey, wait for me!" Emma followed in her brother's wake, coppery braids flying.

"Shut the door!" Lily's command came too late. With a resigned sigh, she ceased stirring the pot of beans simmering above the coals and went to close out the crisp morning air before the warmth of the house escaped. The cold always bothered Susan.

The arriving wagon brought the MacBrides. As it rounded the house to park in the open area between the cabin and the corncrib, Lily released a breath of relief. She dreaded having to deal with the persistent Dunlap brothers through yet another tiresome day. Or worse yet, poor lovesick Robby. The Randall lad had managed to stay in close proximity to her all week long, no matter how hard Jackson or Frank tried to crowd him out—when they weren't vying with each other for the same reason. Were it not for the fact that John would also have to depart for Fort Henry when the burly pair took their leave, she'd wish they were already gone. It was a struggle to remain polite and calm while being ogled whenever she stepped outside. The duo's dark, hooded eyes were far too penetrating.

Forgive me, Lord, for complaining. I know the day will take care of itself. Right now, Susan awaits my attention.

After fluffing the pillows in the rocking chair kept near the hearth, Lily headed for Susan's bedchamber at the cabin's far end. When she entered the room, her heart caught at the sight of the almost undetectable rise her mistress's gaunt form made beneath the blankets, but she smiled and spoke cheerily. "Emma and Davy are thrilled that all the children will be here today."

"So I heard." A slight smile accompanied Susan's murmur.

" 'Twould be quite nice if you could come out into the front room and visit with the ladies for a while."

"I'd like that."

"I'll call John, so you won't have to walk so far."

"No, please. I know he believes he helps when he carries me, but it's really quite…painful. I don't want him to know. He worries so about me."

Lily's brows drew together in sympathy. "Oh, dear. I'm sorry. I should have realized that. Well, from now on, we shall try to outsmart him." Helping Susan up to a sitting position, she gently drew the young woman's legs off the bed and put on her slippers. "Ready?"

"I think so." The statement sounded less than certain.

Slowly and cautiously, Lily brought her mistress to her feet and steadied her until Susan could support most of her own slight weight. They then made the tedious, shaky journey to the rocker. Once Susan was comfortably seated, Lily noticed beads of perspiration forming on her mistress's brow and knew her efforts had been enormously taxing.

Again came the ominous reminder that Susan Waldon was losing her battle against the mysterious ailment that had sapped her strength. She ate like a bird at mealtime and drank very little. She requested the bedpan only twice a day now. Over the years, Susan had grown so dear to Lily that the two of them were almost as close as sisters, and the thought of losing such a sweet friend was hard to bear.

"I hate to be such a bother."

Lily let out a ragged breath as she adjusted the pillows around her mistress and tucked a light quilt about her legs. "I do wish you wouldn't keep saying that. 'Tis my joy to help you. Truly it is." Threading a few loose strands of hair back into Susan's night braid, she bent to kiss her cheek. "There. Now you look quite lovely."

Susan touched Lily's hand. "Thank you, my darling girl."

Giving her friend's hand an answering pat, Lily felt a sharp twinge of guilt slice through her like a knife. She drew a pained breath and straightened. *Susan would be far less generous with her compliments if she knew the battle that raged every day inside the heart of her bondwoman.* Hating herself for being such a Judas to a helpless invalid, she turned toward the hearth.

Susan caught a fold of Lily's skirt before she could step away. "I fear I won't be able to stay out here for long today. It tires me so."

With a nod of understanding, Lily met her hollow, blue-green gaze. "Once you've greeted everyone, I shall help you back to your bed. But should you feel a need to go sooner, just raise your hand. I'll be at your side at once."

"You're far too good to me."

Movement outside the window caught Lily's attention as a familiar ruffled mobcap bobbed into view. "Oh, here comes Grandma Margaret, and I'm sure Pat's wife, Agnes, is with her as well. They're always such a comfort." Looking back at Susan, she noted the fine lines of suffering already crimping her forehead. "After things settle down, I'll send Grandma in to talk to you. I want you to be completely honest with her. She might know of a special tonic that could help you."

Please, dear Lord, let Maggie know something—anything—that can be done for Susan. There must be something else I could be doing or could have done. Please don't let her die. If she were to pass on while John is away with the militia, how would I cope? How would he? How would the children? What would become of us all?

Chapter 5

Food's on! Time to wash up!"

Hearing Lily's airy voice, John turned and saw her on the footbridge, a gentle breeze feathering a wisp of golden hair about her head and curling the hem of her long apron. He drank in the delectable picture.

"Great. I'm starved." Curly haired Robby dropped his end of the log he and John were toting to the blockhouse, and it hit the ground with a hand-jarring thud before John could let go. He shook his head as the lad sprinted toward the cabin, with the Dunlap swains right behind him, all trying to be first to catch up to the lass. Lily was of marriageable age, and John conceded it was to her advantage to be sought after. But the realization depressed him. She deserved better than any of these jackanapes. He felt a strong need to protect her from ill-suited young bumpkins.

As the other neighbors ceased working and started toward the cabin, Bob Randall came alongside John, and they headed for the log bridge. "That boy of mine ain't one bit happy to have those Dunlaps back. I reminded him they'll be goin' with us when we leave, an' Robby says he'll bide his time till they're gone."

John gave a nonchalant shrug.

"He's carvin' a real fine figurine to give Lily. He wants to make a good impression on her."

Squelching a smirk, John responded in a flat tone. "She's very kindhearted. I'm sure she'll appreciate his effort." There was no need to elaborate, but he couldn't help himself. "She was accustomed to expert craftsmanship at her home in England."

His friend's expression dimmed. "Oh yeah. I forgot about that."

Chagrined, John clapped him on the shoulder. "Hey, don't listen to me. I know she'll be pleased. She brought next to nothing with her when she came to live with us. How could she not appreciate a thoughtful gift?"

A brief silence followed, and John felt the need to amend further. "Since Robby's interested in working with wood, he might consider apprenticing with me after the war. . .when you don't need him, that is."

Bob grinned. "Mighty kind of you, John. He'll be glad for the offer. 'Specially if Lily's still on the place."

No doubt. Suspecting his friend was trying to sweeten his son's bid for the girl, John felt a touch of rancor inside. He tamped it down with a civil answer as they stepped off the bridge. "Her term of service will be up in two months, you know."

"I figured as much."

"She promised to stay on with us until the war is over, though. After that, she'll probably go live with her sister. You remember, the one who married that wealthy plantation owner back in Alexandria."

He nodded. "But there's nothin' to keep her from changin' her mind between now and then, is there? Everyone knows she's been a pure blessin' to your family, and folks around here would sure miss her sweet ways."

Not nearly as much as I would. It was all John could do to keep from shouting the thought as he and his friend stepped over a protruding root. But he knew better than to voice it. She was a mere bond servant, but she'd become much more since joining the household. She was a real part of the family, and he couldn't imagine how empty the house would seem were she not around. "Yes, and so would we—especially Susan. She'd be lost without Lily. They've grown incredibly close."

At the mention of his wife's name, guilt wrapped cold fingers around John's conscience as they neared the blend of aromas from the food-laden table. He tipped his head at Bob. "Tell the others to start eating without me. I haven't looked in on Susie all morning. Think I'll go spend some time with her." But even as he said the words, his unwitting gaze gravitated to the gentle gift that was Lily. He saw her cast a despairing look over her shoulder at the eager young bucks drooling over her as she entered the house.

A table for the noon meal had been set outside near the cabin because of the mild day. The instant Grampa Mac uttered the *amen* over the platters of roast venison, fried chicken, and fresh-baked bread that had been spread before the workers, Matt gave a shout. "Lily! Over here!"

She only half-heard him as she emerged from the house with a pewter pitcher of spring water. Her attention centered on John coming straight toward her, his expression unreadable. A tentative smile trembled on her lips.

He flashed a half smile as he paused on the steps. "Lily, my dear. You're my true blessing."

His tone had been quiet, casual, as if he'd said something as unstudied as "pass the butter." But *his dear*? *His true blessing*? She had no idea what to make of such comments.

"Lily!"

"Coming, Matty." Still staring in puzzlement after the boy's father, she collected herself and hurried to the long table where Matt and Luke sat proud and tall with the men after having worked alongside them all morning.

"Here you are." Filling the older lad's glass, she gave him a teasing smile, then did the same for Luke before moving to their friend Sam.

"Don't forget me, Miss Lily." Jackson Dunlap flashed a devilish grin from the far end of the table, a glint in his brown eyes.

Lily was grateful most of the neighbors were too busy devouring their food to notice his impropriety. "After I take care of this end." She managed not to gloat when the young man's grin lost luster. He'd been most persistent this week, cornering her with brazen stares while offering flimsy excuses for crossing the creek and coming to the cabin time and again.

But then, being twenty-two, the oldest bachelor in the valley, it was probably natural for Jackson to feel desperate. Three years of militia duty had cost him his chance to seek out marriageable young maidens from the other settlements along Swatara Creek. Lily kept that in mind as she ignored his advances.

Just then, Ian's wife, tall, bony Margaret MacBride, approached the table with another platter of chicken, the ruffled cap hiding her braided gray coronet bobbing with each step. The woman's faded blue eyes never missed a thing. Lily was relieved for Maggie's presence as she neared the Dunlap brothers, whose shameless leering made her feel undressed. She steeled her features against that discomfiting awareness and reached past Jackson to retrieve his glass, actually detecting heat radiating from him.

When she replaced the glass, his callused hand clamped over hers.

She jerked hers away in reflex, knocking over his drink. Water spilled everywhere.

"Dunlap! That'll do." John's demanding censure came from the porch.

Lily and Jackson both swung their attention to him.

"You about through there?"

"No, sir, not quite." A tiny smirk tweaked the young man's mouth as he turned back to his plate and picked up his fork, swapping a snicker with his brother as he shoveled in a chunk of venison.

Lily surmised John had been watching from the doorway, and her spirit felt lighter as she refilled Jackson's drink. John's proprietary tone made it clear that he disapproved of Jackson Dunlap's pawing. She especially liked his thinking she was *dear* and calling her *his* blessing. Not Jackson's. Never Jackson's.

Nine o'clock arrived, and tiny stars speckled the night sky as the men finished chinking the new blockhouse in the glow of lantern light. The evening had gradually cooled, with crickets and tree toads trilling in chorus.

Stretching a kink in his back at the rear of the newly completed structure, John felt as old as Ian. It had been a long, grueling week, plowing and planting till two each afternoon, then felling, stripping, and sizing trees until dark. Today had been the hardest, hoisting the ungainly logs into place, then laying the upper floor, and finally constructing the roof. Every bone in his body ached in protest when he bent to pick up a lamp in each hand.

"Pa!" Frank Dunlap's voice retained an unbelievable measure of energy as the nineteen-year-old called out to his father. "Get your fiddle and strike up a tune. I'll fetch the gals."

"Hold on there, laddie." Ian MacBride's gravelly voice threw a damper on the suggestion. "It's too late for a frolic tonight. The wee ones are all tuckered out, and I dunna' mind sayin' that includes me."

"Same here, Ian. Same here," several neighbors echoed with weary finality. A murmur of assent flowed through the group.

Donny Randall let out a huff. "But Grampa Mac. That's why we worked hard to finish up. Besides, Cissy and Judy both promised me a dance." His voice cracked on the last word, and he jammed his hands into his trouser pockets.

His father grunted. "No, Son, the reason we worked so hard was to make sure our loved ones will be safe while we men are away."

"But that's not fair," older brother Robby chimed in.

The other lads, frowning in mutinous agreement, grumbled their displeasure. The shadows cast by the scattered lanterns exaggerated their woebegone expressions.

Not to be dissuaded, MacBride raised a calming hand. "Tell ye what. After Sunday service tomorrow, and after our Sabbath meal, we'll have a wee bit of music to celebrate this occasion. What d'ye say?"

"You mean that?" A note of doubt colored Jackson's tone.

The elder's whiskers flared with his broad smile. "I dunna' reckon the Lord'll mind a little singin' and dancin'. Folks in Bible days danced with joy to the Lord from time to time, ye ken. So as long as you lads keep in mind it is the Sabbath, we'll do our celebratin' on the morrow."

Jackson jabbed his brother in the ribs and muttered under his breath. "The old goat can dance *his* way, and I'll dance *mine*. . .holdin' on to my sweet Lily."

Standing close enough to the pair to overhear the comment—and even to knock those two woodsy heads together—John clenched his fingers around the lantern handles to restrain himself. Lily came to the cove as a penniless bond servant, and he should be thrilled she was so popular, but elation over that prospect eluded him. He did have prior claim, after all. And Susan, of course. *Please, dear Lord, help me to be happy for her. . . . You know I'm not.*

After the last wagon headed off into the crisp night, John trudged across the porch and into the house. The warmth from the hearth burned his face, reminding him he hadn't been inside since visiting with Susan at noon. A small lamp and the fireplace illuminated the main room, and a quick glance about revealed it was empty except for Lily.

She sat at the hearth end of the dining table, elbows propped on its surface, her hands circling a cup. She looked up and shook her head. "You look as exhausted as the boys did when they came in. Come sit by the fire. I'll get you a cup of tea. How about some of Nancy's sweet ginger biscuits to go with it?"

"Sounds wonderful." Grasping the tails of his outerwear to lift the garment over his head, he paused, watching her go for the refreshments. A sudden wave of grief swamped him. Blinking hard against a stinging in his eyes, he turned away and stripped off his coarsely woven overshirt. A few short days and he'd leave home again. He'd sorely miss having someone care enough to wait up for him after a grueling day, offering him tea and a little sympathy. . .like sweet, lovely Lily.

He hooked the warm shirt on a spike by the door and took a calming breath before striding to a chair near the hearth. It scraped the plank floor as he tugged it out and dropped onto the seat across from hers.

"The boys didn't even have to be told to go to bed tonight," she said, bringing over his cup and a small plate of cookies. "They hardly managed a good-night before clumping up the ladder to their beds. I doubt they had enough energy to change into their nightshirts."

John watched her move gracefully around to the other side of the table and retake her seat. "They worked as hard as the rest of us. I was very proud of them." Realizing he was still gazing at her, he averted his attention to his tea and brought the steaming cup to his mouth.

"This has been a good day. So much got accomplished." Though she'd spoken quietly, her voice sounded years older than it had when she'd first come to live with them, shy and sad at being parted from her sisters. She picked up her own cup. "Being from a prosperous resort city established since Roman days, I'm always amazed at how very different these little wilderness settlements are."

Was that her way of hinting she wanted to return to England as soon as she could? John set down his mug. "I reckon they are."

She gave a nod. "The full-time residents of Bath are mostly inn-keepers and established tradesmen, you know, everyone trying to better themselves financially and socially, never wanting the taint of failure to touch them."

"It's no different in Philadelphia and Baltimore, when it comes right down to it."

"Perhaps. But here in the wilderness, folks are concerned about each other and work together helping one another out. If the people of Bath had been half as caring about the welfare of their neighbors, Papa wouldn't have felt compelled to hide the fact he'd been cheated out of a huge sum of money. People would have come to our aid and donated enough funds to pay his creditors until Papa could recoup his losses. Folks around here truly live by the Bible principle to love your neighbor as yourself." Her gaze gravitated to the ceiling. "We hold our church services in this simple abode, yet I feel closer to God here than I ever did in that magnificently ornate cathedral in Bath."

She was happy here. John relaxed and gave an offhanded shrug. "It's a wonderful place to live. . .even without all the shops you womenfolk love so much." A teasing smile tugged at his lips.

Lily chuckled. "Now, I wouldn't go so far as to say that."

Laughter bubbled up inside John, but it died as he noticed how beautifully the firelight played across her blond hair. How. . .

Coughing came from the bedroom—his and Susan's. Assaulted by guilt, he frowned and cocked an ear toward the sound.

"I spoke to Eva Shepard and Grandma Margaret about her condition today," Lily said, drawing his attention back to her. "I told them Susan eats hardly anything. Eva suggested that rather than only offering food at mealtimes, I should bring her a little something once every hour and encourage her to take a few bites. And Maggie said Susan should drink water or tea along with it. I do think that might help. I don't know why I never thought of doing so myself."

John released a slow breath. "Mayhap because you have so many other burdens. And now one more is added."

Meeting his gaze, Lily offered him a weary smile. "You forget I have the children. Sweet little Emma has taken it upon herself to brush Susan's hair every morning, and she is careful to be really gentle with her strokes. She also picks wildflowers for her." She paused in thought. "Even Davy loves to help me with his mama. He's really a tenderhearted little boy."

"Right. When he's not yelling and stomping his feet in here like a buffalo."

Her smile broadened. "He surely is the life of the house. One cannot deny that."

And you're the heart. John barely caught himself from blurting the thought aloud. How could he be thinking such a thing when his beloved wife lay at death's door? He picked up his cup and drained the last of his tea. "Well, I'd best get to bed myself. The neighbors will be back again in the morning." *Along with that randy pair, Jackson and Frank Dunlap.*

Chapter 6

Lily paused on the footbridge for a solitary moment. After the Sabbath meal, most of the other young people had hurried across to the blockhouse for its inaugural frolic. As heavy footfalls coming up behind jarred the log beneath her, Lily's spirits sank. There was no mistaking those Dunlaps.

Purposely not turning to greet them, she held on to her cheerful attitude while taking measure of the tall, square, newly completed structure. The bottom floor had only one entrance and no windows. The top half of the upper floor, however, was open all the way around, creating a roofed watchtower. "It's hard to believe you men finished that in such a short time."

"We had to." Frank craned his neck around her. "So you an' me could dance the first reel together." A rakish spark lit his dark eyes.

"Quite right. You did ask before the others." She deliberately took lively steps away from him.

"Don't forget, I get the second," Jackson reminded from behind his brother.

"And Robby is third, and Donald fourth." Though she'd spoken lightly, she thought of the younger girls and turned to face the pair. " 'Tis important to me that when you dance with the other lasses you really and truly enjoy their company. I'd hate for you to hurt any of their feelings."

"That's what I love about you." Jackson grinned. "You always think about others before yourself."

"And I love your smiling ways." Frank was not to be outdone.

Lily looked from one to the other and back. "Thank you both for your flattering comments, but we'd better hurry. I hear your father's fiddle striking up a tune."

Descending the steps cut from the large end of the log, Lily was impressed by Jackson's surprisingly mature compliment, that he considered her character rather than her appearance. Perhaps her preoccupation elsewhere had blinded her to his attributes. After all, he was part of the military, and that required a certain sense of responsibility. He likely possessed other fine qualities, as well, if given a chance. This afternoon she'd study each of her suitors with a less biased eye.

Ignoring the steps as they followed her, the brothers leaped off the log. Each grabbed one of her arms, tucking it within his.

Jackson gave her arm a squeeze. "I'm glad John's not comin'. A body'd think he was your big brother, the way he watches over you."

Lily glanced back across the creek to the house, where on the porch with the older folks, John sat next to Susan, exactly where he should be. His wife needed him so, and his visit was nearing an end. Their time together was precious. Turning forward, she warded off a swell of disappointment by trying to recall Jackson's compliment, but the words he'd said eluded her. Despite her best efforts to the contrary, thoughts of John stole them away.

Tears blurred Lily's vision as she folded the last small loaf of bread in cheesecloth and placed it in the top of John's knapsack, above the items she'd packed the previous evening. Two week's leave had passed too quickly, and any moment now, John would emerge from the bedroom, from his last good-bye with Susan.

He was leaving. How ever would she cope? Or Susan or the children?

She had to cope. They all would. Blotting the moisture from her eyes with the hem of her apron, she drew a steadying breath.

The first blush of dawn glimmered in peach-hued glory through the trees. Soon he'd be on his way. She sank onto her dining chair and poured herself another cup of strong tea as she stared at the knapsack slumped on the table. He had to realize how desperately ill Susan was, yet he was determined to report back to military duties. How could he be so callous?

A creak sounded behind her. The door at the parlor end opened, casting John in a silhouette as he stepped out of the bedroom and closed the door.

Her chest tightening, Lily came to her feet.

He crossed the room, and the flicker from the hearth fire mirrored in his clear, blue eyes as he met her gaze. Stopping directly before her, he spoke quietly. "She finally agreed."

"To what?" Surely he hadn't convinced his wife to attempt the trip to Philadelphia!

"To let us write to her father and have him send a physician here. She knows she's not strong enough to travel. The man can easily afford to send the best. . .if he will."

Elated, Lily caught his arm. "Oh, John. What a splendid idea." Then coming to her senses, she removed her hand, lest he think her forward.

He didn't seem to notice her discomfort. "Susan probably told you he wrote a letter to her soon after we eloped, saying he'd disowned her. It caused her no end of grief."

"Yes. I find it hard to believe a father could be so heartless. She can barely speak of him without tears filling her eyes. It's been a great sadness."

"Has it ever. Over the years, I've tried to convince her he'd written those words in the heat of the moment and that if he knew of her illness, he'd want her to get well again."

"Indeed. 'Tis only right."

He nodded in thought, then tipped his head. "Well, my dear girl, I'm afraid I must be on my way. If you wouldn't mind, I'd appreciate it if you would pen the letter while I saddle Smokey. I'll take the missive as far as the mouth of the Swatara and give it to someone to take downriver from there. Hopefully, Mr. Gilford will receive it within a week or so."

"Y–you're taking the horse?" Their only horse. . .

A gentle smile softened his features. "Only as far as the MacBrides'. Young Michael promised to ride him back later this morning."

Somewhat relieved at the news, Lily watched John toss on his heavy hunting shirt and walk out of the cabin. How silly she'd been to panic over an animal. It was John's departure that warranted all her angst. She would hold herself together until he actually bid her farewell and took his leave. She would get through this. After all, the man was her best friend's husband. He must never know of the improper desires of her heart. The last person who deserved to be hurt was Susan, her dearest friend in the world.

After collecting the writing materials, she could hardly concentrate on the correct words to say in her plea to Susan's father. John's departure kept intruding. She forced herself to use her finest penmanship, which did help.

Too soon his footsteps sounded on the steps, and he blew in on a rush of cold morning air.

Lily folded the hopefully sincere request then dripped wax from a nearby candle to seal it. Rising, she held it out to John. "I did my best to explain her condition and the *urgency* of her need." She hoped her emphasis on the word *urgency* would give John further pause about leaving. Surely he realized his wife's very life was draining away. How ever could he go?

"Thank you, Lily-girl. I've no doubt about that." He slipped the letter into his haversack and hooked one arm through its strap. Blinking sudden moisture from his eyes, he swallowed hard. Then he took a step closer and reached out a hand to cup her face. "Please, dear Lily, don't look so frightened. Cal Patterson and Toby Dunlap have promised to scout the Indian path every day. If they see anything suspicious, they'll fire warning shots. Don't forget to answer with a shot of your own. Then immediately reload and—"

She covered his hand with hers. "I know. You've taught me well. And get Susan to the blockhouse as soon as possible."

"Right." His eyes searched hers for an eternal moment. Then, unexpectedly, John drew her close and wrapped his arms around her. Crushing her against himself, he buried his face in her hair. "You don't know how wretched I feel having to leave you here with all this."

She felt the whisper of his breath ruffle a few stray hairs. Pressing closer, she clasped her arms about him, not daring to breathe, not daring to hope. . . .

Then, just as suddenly, he released her and averted his gaze. "Forgive me. . . . I must go." Snatching his rifle from above the door, he hurried out, leaving her bereft of his comforting warmth.

Oh, how she had reveled in that brief embrace, feeling the strong beat of his heart, inhaling the woodsy scent that was his alone, feeling for an instant that her dreams might—

Reality tore away that wayward hope. Awash in a wave of tears, Lily ran blindly to the door and flung it wide for one last glimpse of him, no longer caring if John saw her cry.

But he was already mounted and riding away.

Reaching the MacBride farmyard at the break of dawn, John spied his friend Patrick stepping off the porch of his darkened house.

"It's started."

The dreaded news gripped John as he dismounted. "Where? When?"

"A few weeks ago, up New York way. Fifteen hundred—maybe upwards of two thousand—French and Indians attacked Fort William Henry at Lake Champlain."

The concept of an attack of that magnitude was harrowing.

Patrick caught Smokey's reins and wrapped them around a fence rail. "They outnumbered the men at William Henry at least five to one." He eyed John. "Don't look so down in the mouth. It seems when the French sent Major Eyre an order to surrender, the post commander responded that he and his men would defend the fort to the last man."

"Good for him. Who wants to be taken prisoner and handed over to be tortured by bloodthirsty Indians?"

"You can't guess what happened next." Unaccountably, Patrick cracked a grin. "The French burned all the outbuildings and the fleet of sloops and whaleboats, then turned around and went back home." He clamped a hand on John's shoulder. "Can you believe it?"

John tucked his chin in disbelief. "Who told you that?"

"Ham Lister, from up the Swatara, near Fort Lebanon. He stopped here for the night yester's eve on his way home."

"Well, if what he said is true, it sounds like the French have been taking lessons in fumbling from General Ambercrombie."

Patrick hooted. "That's just what I told Lister last night."

At his friend's grin, John felt his own smile break forth. "Who knows? There may be hope for us yet."

"Ain't that what we been prayin' for?"

"Quite." John shifted his stance. "By the way, speaking of praying, I have a letter in my knapsack to post, and it needs to be well received. It's going downriver to Susan's father, asking him to send her the most learned physician in Philadelphia."

Patrick hiked a brow in understanding. "Didn't you tell me her pa had a successful brickmakin' business?"

"Right. Her family is quite prosperous." He began untying his bedroll from behind the horse's saddle. "The problem is that all of Susie's life, her father and older brother dictated her every move. And for her to marry a mere furniture-maker's apprentice was out of the question. I have to say, though, since having children of my own and knowing the powerful love I have for each one, I can't help but believe Mr. Gilford must still care for his daughter. . .enough to send a good doctor."

"What father wouldn't?" Patrick tipped his head toward John's belongings. "Put your stuff on the step with mine till the others get here."

"Will do." After setting down his gear, John spoke in all candor. "You know, if it hadn't been for Susie agreeing to have me send that letter, I doubt I could've walked out the door this morning. She's so weak. Almost helpless. It's the worst possible time for me to go away. . .only it can't be helped." He grimaced. His leaving had been imperative. Even discounting the prospect of being charged with desertion, a more important reason remained.

Lily.

Somewhere along the way, she'd become far more than just a bond servant. . .more than a young sister. . .more than a friend. He loved Susan with his whole heart, and nothing would ever change that. But he could not deny he had developed feelings for Lily, also. Feelings he had no right to have. No matter how hard he prayed for strength, one look into those pleading gray eyes of hers, and he'd caught her to him, held her close, felt her soft body pressed against his. Even now, the very breath he drew retained her warm scent. Coward that he was, he positively could not remain at home any longer. *The Bible does instruct us to flee from temptation. . .and that's what I'm doing.*

Pat's voice cut into his thoughts. "Here come those Duncans, right on time. If anybody was goin' to be draggin' his feet this mornin', I figured it'd be Jackson. That boy's sure sweet on your Lily."

My Lily. The memory of Jackson putting his hands on her infuriated John, but he restrained himself from blurting something malicious. Until now he'd always liked the lad. Time to start treating him with his due respect again. Jackson might not be educated, but he was a hard worker. Even with bullets flying all around them, he'd proved to be worth his salt as a soldier. Only last year, when John had been shot, it was Jackson who'd helped him back to the fort. He owed the kid.

All the same, John didn't want to be fielding questions about Lily. Especially not now. "I'll take my belongings to the canoe. By the time we float down past the mouth of Beaver Creek, Bob'll be there waiting."

~≈~

Gathering spring greens along the creek, Lily glanced at Emma, noting how the little girl favored Susan, with her huge blue-green eyes, delicate cheekbones, and heart-shaped face. The child somehow seemed older than she'd been herself at that age. "You truly are a big help, do you know that?"

The little redhead smiled. "I like to help, 'specially on a nice day like this."

"Me, too." But Lily couldn't help observing Emma's overly fair complexion. The child spent far too much time inside, sitting with her mother.

Emma glanced over Lily's shoulder and let out a disgusted huff. "Aww, here comes that pest."

Lily followed her helper's gaze, to see Davy running pell-mell down the bank. She gasped when he tripped and tumbled to the bottom in a shower of gravel. But undaunted by the new dirt ground into his breeches, he sprang to his feet. "What'cha doin'? Playin' in the water?"

"No, dummy. We're pickin' greens for Mama's soup." His sister flared her apron wide, displaying her bounty.

"I wanna help." He grabbed up a bunch of water grass. "See? Green!" He held up the straggle of blades with a muddy hand.

Lily responded before Emma could deride her brother again. "Why, thank you, Davy. But we're looking for special green leaves." She held out a ruffled leaf from her apron's collection. "See if you can find others like—"

Duke's barking echoed from the barnyard. Sharp. Ominous.

"Somebody's comin'!" Davy sprang like a jack-in-the-box to his feet.

Lily caught him by his shirttail before he could bolt and spoke in her no-nonsense tone. "Wait here. And be quiet. I'll go see what's wrong." The approaching supper hour was an odd time for anyone to pay a visit. Leaving the children behind, she climbed the bank and searched toward the house, where the dog remained on alert, still barking toward the wagon trail.

Matt and Luke charged out of the stable, with Matt sprinkling black powder in his musket's flashpan as he ran.

When the dog's barking became even more shrill and steady, Lily stopped and pulled out her tin of gunpowder to ready her own weapon. He'd have quieted by now if it were a neighbor approaching. Reluctant to expose herself, she sidled up against the corncrib and peered around it, while the boys sprang up the cabin steps and waited in the porch's late afternoon shadow.

The sound of several horses pricked her ears.

Fear trickled down Lily's spine. John had been gone less than three weeks. He wouldn't be coming back so soon—unless a war party was headed this way. Uneasiness spread through her.

Four mounted riders trotted up alongside the cabin and reined in, facing the front. Two wore the familiar attire of frontiersmen, and two had on tailored suits. From her position, Lily couldn't make out their faces.

She saw her brave Matt step out of the shadow, his weapon crooked in his arm, but not aimed, letting the newcomers know he was armed. "Afternoon." His brother moved to his side.

One of the frontiersmen hiked his chin. "Afternoon, lad. This the Waldon place?"

"It is."

"Thank the good Lord." One of the better-dressed men began to dismount, and the others did the same.

Deciding they seemed genuine and posed no threat, Lily moved into view, her worry escalating as she walked toward the group. "Have you brought bad news? Has something happened to John?"

As one, they turned to her. "No, miss." A distinguished, older man of medium height, with fading auburn hair and a thin mustache, tipped his hat. "Actually, we fully expected him to be here."

"I'm afraid he's not. May I be of service?"

"Allow me to introduce myself. I'm Brandon Gilford. Susan Waldon's father."

Susan's father? Lily couldn't believe her ears. He'd come! "Is the gentleman with you a physician?"

Mr. Gilford's companion, equally well dressed but more thickly built, bowed slightly. "Dr. Harold Shelby, at your service, miss."

"Praise God!" Rushing forward, she threw her arms about Mr. Gilford's neck. "Thank you! I prayed you'd come."

Clearing his throat, the man gently extracted her arms. But his mouth spread into a jovial smile. "I'd prefer it if you'd turn that pistol the other way."

"Oh. Of course." As Lily blushed in embarrassment, Matt and Luke jumped off the porch and shook hands with the visitors.

The two little ones came running out of the trees, with Davy in the lead. "How do. How do," the towhead called out on the way. "I'm Davy. What's your name?"

Lily snagged him before he slammed into the men. "Mr. Gilford, I'd like you to meet your youngest grandson, David. Right behind him is our sweet Emma, and I believe Matthew and Luke have already introduced themselves. Children, this is your grandfather."

"You mean like Grampa Mac?" Davy scrunched up his nose.

"No." Matt came to his brother's side. "This is our real grandpa. Mama's papa. He's brought a doctor to help her get better."

Mr. Gilford's smile vanished, and lines of worry furrowed his brow as he met Lily's gaze. "How is my daughter, Miss—"

Lily blanched. "Oh. Forgive me. I'm Lily Harwood. Your son-in-law hired me to take care of Susan."

He gave a nod. "The letter I received merely stated that she had a prolonged ailment which Baltimore physicians could not diagnose and that she was in dire need."

Lily endeavored to convey the situation without using words that might overly alarm the younger children. "Suffice it to say her health is most tenuous. Do come in, gentlemen. Matt and Luke, would you please see to the horses?"

As the group started inside, Davy latched on to Mr. Gilford's hand. "I like grampas."

"And I love grandsons, my boy." He chuckled.

Watching the exchange, Lily's relief was so palpable at knowing the men had come to help, she wanted to cry, but there was no time for tears. Four guests had just arrived for supper.

She only wished it could be a more joyous occasion.

Chapter 7

"This is our house." Davy puffed out his chest, jabbering with boyish pride as he led his grandfather and the other guest inside. "Our pa built it. And we have the bestest table in the whole cove. Pa made it before he went off to kill Injuns."

Preceding Lily into the cabin, Mr. Gilford shot a frown back at her.

Obviously the man had no idea that John had gone away. Afraid of what he might say, Lily squeezed Emma's hand. "Sweetheart, our guests must be awfully thirsty after their trip. Would you please run down to the springhouse for the pitcher of buttermilk?"

The child opened her mouth as if to protest, then closed it. "Yes, ma'am." She turned with a swirl of her muslin skirt and raced down the steps in an obvious rush to get back before she missed too much.

"And Davy, go out to the cellar and get four more big carrots—so we can fix supper for our company." The explanation squelched the imp's inclination to balk. With his lower lip protruding, he scampered off.

Lily gestured toward the parlor. "Do have a seat, gentlemen." Having heard from Susan about her father's finely appointed mansion, she couldn't help casting an assessing look around the simple room with its sturdy, pillowed chairs—all John and Susan's handiwork. The only embellishments were a pair of framed proverbs Susan had embroidered in her better days and hung on the walls. Even the window curtains had faded over time and showed wear. Surely a prosperous city dweller would find the abode crude indeed. But that could not be helped. Either the man would approve of his daughter's circumstances or he would not. Nothing could be done about it.

Despite her misgivings, Lily saw only deep concern on the gentleman's face as he paused in the middle of the long room. "May I see my daughter?"

"I'll take you to her, sir." But as she neared Susan's chamber, she added a warning whisper. "Please prepare yourself. Susan is extremely thin and frail. Very weak."

His golden brows shelved over his eyes in concern. "Just take me to her, Miss Harwood."

Lily hoped that after all the years that had passed, the man didn't still harbor anger toward her dear friend. "This way, please."

Reaching the bedroom door, he rushed past Lily and strode in, then stopped so suddenly, she nearly bumped into him.

"I thought I heard visitors." Lying in bed, Susan had expended the effort to sound cheery as she attempted to raise her head. "Lily, dear, would you help me sit up?"

Lily sidestepped Mr. Gilford and hurried to the bedside. Plucking an extra pillow from a nearby chair, she reached under Susan's shoulder and brought her up with very little assistance from her mistress.

Mr. Gilford, lingering near the doorway, released an audible breath and spoke in a hoarse murmur. "Susan, it's your papa. I'm here, honeybee." With a watery smile, he crossed to the bed.

"Papa? Is it really you?" Reality gave Susan's voice strength. "Papa!" She stretched out her hands to him.

With a moan, the loving father knelt beside his daughter's bed and drew her gently into his embrace, and the two wept in each other's arms.

Lily's eyes flooded at the joyous reunion she'd hardly dared hope to see. The good Lord had brought the man here, had provided a father and a daughter with a chance to erase silent years that had separated them, before it was too late. Knowing she was no longer needed, Lily slipped quietly from the bedchamber, swiping away her tears with both hands.

"Miss?" The doctor looked up as Lily closed the door behind her. "May I speak with you?" Seated in the parlor with the two bearded frontiersmen, who looked ill at ease dressed in heavy garb in the warm room, he stood to his feet. He smoothed his brocade waistcoat over the curve of his belly.

"Of course, Dr. Shelby." She sniffed, trying to regain her composure. "Please join me near the hearth, if you would. I need to check the stew." She was loath to speak of Susan's personal ailments in front of the backwoods strangers. Reaching the fireplace, she unhooked her big wooden spoon and potholder and lifted the lid from the footed kettle, giving the mixture a few stirs.

The physician stopped beside her. "Miss Harwood, the letter you wrote to Mr. Gilford was quite vague. Would you describe in detail the nature of your mistress's ailment?"

Gathering her thoughts, Lily replaced the spoon and moved past him to take a seat at the table.

He did as well, never taking his eyes from her. "Is the invalid contagious?"

Elevating her brows, Lily stared into his wide-set eyes. "No, sir. When I first entered into service for the Waldons, Mr. Gilford's daughter had recently given birth to Davy. Her joints had started to swell, causing her a good deal of pain. The physician in Baltimore suspected it was some sort of rheumatism and gave her a tonic, along with salves he felt might help. They did not."

He pursed his lips. "So. Might I ask why the Waldons left Baltimore for this remote settlement if she was unwell?" The man glanced around the rustic room, his disdain more than obvious.

Offended by his superior attitude, Lily felt her hackles rise. "They'd already purchased the land here, and since the doctor didn't know anything else to do for Susan, she insisted they not alter their plans to move here and put down their roots. Sometime later, when a skin rash developed, her husband wrote to the physician for advice."

"What was the doctor's name? Perhaps I know of him."

"A Dr. Whetsler, I believe."

He nodded. "Yes. He's considered competent enough."

"Indeed. Well, he suggested the rash might be due to something she ate. He sent more salve, which helped somewhat. After that, Susan had good days and bad as the swelling and rashes would come and go. . . up until this year, that is. Now it's as if her condition has moved deeper inside her. We've become very concerned about her breathing of late. . . and her heart."

She leaned closer and lowered her voice. "And I don't think Susan is"—hesitant to speak of such private matters, Lily searched for more delicate words—"expelling her fluids as she should."

Dr. Shelby rubbed a hand across his stubbly jaw. "I was afraid of this. So, I might add, was her father."

"What do you mean?"

"Some years ago, an older aunt of Susan's suffered from the same ailment. And its onset also came after the birth of a child."

At his words, relief surged through Lily. "Oh. Thank heavens. Then you'll know what can be done for my mistress. That's splendid."

His expression did not waver. He wagged his head and sighed. "I'm afraid it's quite the opposite, child. I tried every remedy possible. The good woman continued to waste away and finally passed on, leaving all my colleagues in Philadelphia and Boston as baffled as I was."

Alarm tightened Lily's throat. "Surely there's still hope for Susan! There must be something you can try. Some way to alleviate her condition."

"The most advice I can offer at this point is to keep Mrs. Waldon as comfortable as possible, until. . . ."

Having her hopes dashed at her feet, Lily's heart plummeted. She jumped up. "That's it? There's nothing to be done? I refuse to accept that."

Angry now, her breaths came out fast and hard as she crossed her arms in despair.

"What's happening?" Davy charged into the cabin, clutching carrots in his hand. "Are you gonna do somethin' without me?"

Schooling her features, Lily composed herself and knelt down to his level. "No, dear. We won't do a single thing without you. Thank you for fetching the carrots for our stew." She took them and stood up.

A flash of movement out the window revealed Emma coming, soft-footed and cautious as she toted the big, heavy pitcher of buttermilk.

Suddenly the dire news the doctor had uttered filled Lily with new horror. Her knees went weak, and she caught hold of the chairback. *Dear Emmy. Would the sweet child one day suffer the same terrible fate as her mother?*

Mr. Gilford spent nearly every waking moment of the next two heartrending days with his daughter. His presence lifted Susan's spirits so there seemed a slight improvement in her condition. Her smiles came more easily, and Lily often heard light laughter drifting from the bedchamber where Susan visited with her father.

But the time had come for the party to leave for Philadelphia once again. Passing by the room, Lily caught sight of Mr. Gilford sitting on the edge of Susan's bed, rocking her in his arms and kissing her. Their tearful farewell brought a lump to Lily's throat. She feared it would be their last time together.

The man's voice was husky with emotion as he murmured in his daughter's ear. "The moment I get home, honeybee, I'll make arrangements to bring your mother to visit you. It'll take awhile longer to get here next time, though, since we'll have to travel upriver."

"I know, Papa. Mama could never abide riding horseback." Susan brushed at her tears with a trembling hand. "Thank you for. . .being my papa again. I missed you so."

He buried his face in her hair and clasped her tight. "I can't believe I let my foolish pride come between us. It was unpardonable. I shall never forgive myself." Finally he eased away and stood to his feet, emitting a ragged breath as he gazed down at the wasted form of his once-healthy child. "I love you, my darling daughter," he mumbled hoarsely and rushed from the room.

Lily barely got out of his way as he stumbled toward the front door, his fists rubbing his eyes. Running after him, she nearly collided with him when he stopped short.

He swiveled on his heel, his eyes red and puffy. "I loathe having to leave my darling girl here. It's not safe." He'd expressed the sentiment several times since his arrival. "If only she could. . ."

Lily placed an empathetic hand on his arm. "I know, sir. If only."

"The French are on the move down from Lake Ontario again, you know. And with a very large force."

"Yes, so you've mentioned before. And if you're aware of that, I'm certain the commanders of our northern forts are, as well. I pray they'll be better prepared this year."

Mr. Gilford scoffed. "They would if they'd put brave fighters like our Rogers' Rangers in charge. But no—the king sends us cowards from England to lead our men. What a waste." His eyes narrowed. "John Waldon should never have abandoned my daughter here to face this danger alone. That mortician's whelp has no business—"

Lily squeezed his arm and frowned. "Please sir, do lower your voice."

He glanced toward Susan's room and drew a futile breath.

"Mr. Gilford, when John's militia was called to service, Susan was suffering only from swollen joints. And though he desperately wants to be here now, you know he would be charged with desertion were he to leave his post."

"Yes. Well. We'll see about that. The man should be here. His superior is Captain Busse, I believe you said. Rest assured, I'll be paying Governor Denny a visit as soon as I reach Philadelphia. I am not without influence, I assure you."

"In that case, I shall pray for your success. All of us would appreciate having John home where he belongs. Susan needs him now, most desperately."

His pale brows flattened as his demeanor eased, and he touched the side of her face, bringing to Lily's mind the remembrance of John's parting touch. "You are an incredibly brave lass, Lily Harwood. My daughter cannot say enough good things about you. I'd like to thank you personally for taking such wonderful care of my Susan and the children." He paused. "Speaking of the children. . ." Turning, he opened the door and strode outside.

A few yards beyond the porch, the youngsters stood waiting with Dr. Shelby and the frontiersmen. The three men sat astride their mounts. Mr. Gilford approached the group but spoke to his grandchildren. "Dear ones, my offer still stands. Any of you who would like to come with me and see where we live, I'd be more than happy to take you along. Emma?" He moved closer to the little girl. "Your Grandmother Gilford would dearly love to meet you, to see how much you look like your mama did when she was your age."

Emma shyly met his gaze. "I thought you said you were going to bring her here."

"That's true. I did say that."

"Then thank you, Grampa, but I can see her then. My mama needs me here."

"Wait!" Davy shoved between his sister and the older man. "I changed my mind. I want to go to Phila—Phila—def. I'm a good rider, you'll see. I won't fall off. I wanna go." Excitement laced his expression. "But I hafta be back for supper. Lily's makin' apple pandowdy just for me."

Mr. Gilford knelt down before the child. "I'm afraid you'd have to skip supper if you came with us, Davy. It takes three days to get to Philadelphia on horseback."

"Nights, too?" He took a step back. "I guess I shouldn't go so far. Mama and Lily'd miss me too much."

"Yes, lad." His grandfather sighed. "I suppose they would." He turned to the older boys and extended a hand to them in a firm grasp. "You're the men of the house while your father is away. I'm counting on you to take care of my dear ones." Then, looking back at Lily with a sad wag of his head, he mounted his horse, and the group rode away.

The wall clock in Captain Busse's office ticked off seconds as the man sat back in his chair, his fingers steepled over his stomach. "Look here, Waldon. If I were to allow everyone leave who says he has someone who needs him at home, there wouldn't be a—" Waving a hand uselessly in the air, he shook his head. "You know what I mean."

John tipped his head, hoping. "But sir, Bob Randall and Pat MacBride can verify what I'm saying. My wife is failing fast. I fear she won't be with us much longer." It galled him to have to beg for something that, under normal circumstances, would be a given. But he had to try.

"Might I remind you that you told me your wife was ailing over a year ago, and she hasn't passed on yet."

Rage boiled up inside John. The man was not only devoid of sensitivity, he was inferring John was a liar.

At John's stony silence, Busse came to his feet behind his desk. "I apologize, Corporal Waldon. That was a horrible thing to say. Truth is, since I was ordered to send half our men north to Fort Augusta, I simply can't spare a man. The folks in the settlements south of here are depending on us—including your own family." He shrugged. "I'm sorry. I can't give you leave."

A knock sounded on the office door.

"Come in." Busse hiked his chin at John. "That'll be all."

The orderly saluted the commander as he passed John in the doorway. "Governor Denny just rode in with a party of men, sir."

"Reinforcements?" The leader's tone held an optimistic note.

John felt renewed hope himself. Maybe he'd be given leave yet.

"Sorry, sir. Merely an escort."

Despite his disappointment, John couldn't help feeling impressed that the governor himself had come here. Had the war ended? Had he come all the way from Philadelphia to announce it personally?

Glancing out the headquarters' door John spotted a distinguished-looking man who must be the governor out on the porch, facing rapidly gathering militiamen. Obviously they, too, knew there had to be an important reason for someone in such a high position to visit this remote fort.

"Men." The gentleman in his fine attire raised a hand for order. "First of all, I wish to thank each and every one of you for your service. If not for your sacrifice, we, the citizens of Pennsylvania, would not be able to rest at night. Therefore it is vital that when your year is up, you re-enlist."

Groans of outrage came from every quarter as the enlisted men swapped dark glowers.

Flicking travel dust from his frock coat, the governor shifted his stance. "Men, our very colony is at stake. I entreat you to write to your friends and neighbors. Ask them to come and join you in this fight."

A shout came from the ranks. "What friends? What neighbors? Every settler that can be spared's already here."

Governor Denny gave a grave nod. "Then we must dig deeper. Sacrifice more to save our colony. The situation is quite dire. Last year the burning and pillaging came within thirty miles of Philadelphia."

"Then how about you give this speech to all them city fellas sleepin' safe an' sound in Philadelphia?" came from the back of the gathering. "We ain't seen hide nor hair of none of them hereabouts."

Bob Randall chimed in from the side. "And while you're at it, send back our men who got sent up to Fort Augusta. We're spread thinner than skimmed milk here. And we got a lot a territory that needs coverin' betwixt us an' the other forts."

"Hear! Hear!" shouted others in chorus.

The governor raised his hand for silence. "Again, I thank you all. I shall speak to you more formally once I've had a chance to confer with your commander." With that, he heeled around and headed for the doorway John occupied.

John quickly stepped aside, glad the men had spoken their minds.

He joined Bob as the crowd began to disperse. "In November, when my enlistment is up, it'll take a whole lot more to get me to sign up again than some glad-hander showing up with lots of words, but without a single company of reinforcements."

"Reinforcements!" Behind Bob, militiaman Fred Stuart snorted. "I overheard one of the governor's escorts admit that even New York Indian Agent William Johnson can't rally his Mohawks to fight for us anymore—and you know how they love bloodying those tomahawks of theirs."

"That doesn't sound good." Bob huffed. "I heard they think of him as one of their war chiefs. Isn't Johnson married to one of their Indian princesses?"

"I say we all just walk on outta here right now," Stuart muttered. "Go collect our families and traipse on down to Philadelphia and sit down on our behinds, like them fine city folks are doin'."

Bob sniffed in disdain. "If we did that, the Frenchies would move in and burn up everything we spent all this time breakin' our backs over."

John nodded in sad agreement. "We hoped to give our children a future they'd never have if we hadn't come out here." He sighed. "Being away from my family for months on end, it's hard sometimes to remember why I'm here." He turned to Bob. "Busse turned down my request for leave. Again."

His friend clapped him on the shoulder with a commiserating wince. "Sorry. I figured he would."

"But. . .Susan's dying, Bob. I can feel it right here." He pressed a fist to his chest. "She's dying, and I'm not there. Duty or no duty, I'd never be able to live with myself if I couldn't be with her at. . .the end." He all but choked on the last word.

Chapter 8

"Susan. . .Susan. . . Please speak to me." Leaning over the bed, Lily gently shook her friend's arm. A wave of grief washed over her like a flood. There was no denying the end was near. Susan's breathing during the night had become so labored Lily had been unable to sleep. She'd gotten up several times to check on her. Now, finding no response except that horrid rasping, Lily could only send desperate pleas heavenward, praying for strength. . .praying for her friend to live one more day. . .praying that John would come to be with his wife in her final moments. Susan deserved that much. So did he.

Scuffing and banging came from the main room as the children readied the house for the Sabbath gathering. *They don't even realize it may be their mother's last day, Lord.* A heaviness pressed on her chest, making it hard to breathe. Should she tell them before the service, or spare them? *What should I do?*

Stepping out of the bedchamber, she quietly closed the door. A quick glance revealed the older boys setting up the benches.

"Hurry up, Lily." Matt plunked his end of the board down atop a keg.

"You're not dressed for church. Folks'll be comin' any minute."

Afraid to open her mouth for fear her throat would close around the dreadful news, Lily schooled her expression to remain composed and acknowledged him with a nod. She spied Emma across the way, trying to tame Davy's cowlick with a comb as the imp squirmed beneath his sister's hand. The children were so happy, so busy. How could she steal their joy by telling them about their mother now? She propped up a smile. "Your mama doesn't feel up to joining us for the service this morning. I think it's best if we don't disturb her. We'll let her rest."

Walking into the bedroom she shared with Emma, grief gave way to anger. How could she concentrate on something so trivial as dressing? John should be here. He'd seen his wife's condition before he'd gone off almost three months ago. He had to know Susan would only continue to grow weaker. Lily had sent word relating the situation not two weeks past. Surely it had reached him.

And what of Susan's parents? Mr. Gilford had promised to return posthaste with his wife, yet where were they? Five weeks allowed them more than sufficient time to return by river. Their daughter and her children had been waiting for them, watching for them, for the past fortnight.

Dear, sweet Susan. She'd suffered more than a body should endure. How it hurt to see the pain in her eyes, and in the children's, as she grew steadily more fragile and helpless. If her parents ever did arrive, it would likely be too late.

Weary from too little sleep and already sticky from the July heat, Lily slipped into the bare minimum of petticoats and tossed on the first gown she touched. Whipping her hair up into a simple knot, she jammed enough pins in to hold it in place, hoping the dark circles under her eyes would keep Robby Randall from being such a pest today. She had no patience for his constant hovering.

She sighed and turned away from the mirror. The last thing she felt like doing was taking part in a Sabbath meeting. She swept her eyes toward the ceiling. *Father God, please fill me with Your love and charity. And please, tamp down the rage building inside me. Susan so needs Your touch now. I don't know how to pray for her. She's in Your hands. Please be merciful. . . . She's suffered for such a long time.* Drawing a calming breath only reminded her of her dear friend's constant struggle for air. Life was so unfair to the poor, abandoned wife.

Adult voices drifted from the other side of her door as neighbors began to arrive. Straightening her shoulders, Lily manufactured as much of a smile as she could and went out to greet them. Why, oh why, did this have to be the Sabbath?

"There you are, Miss Lily." Ian MacBride bobbed his white head in greeting as he strode toward her between two rows of benches. He flicked a thumb in the direction of the door. "The others are still outside, tryin' to keep cool."

" 'Tis rather close this morning, is it not?" Lily flattened her lips.

The elder held out a thick, folded paper to her. "A fella goin' upstream dropped this letter off with yer name on. From that Mr. Gilford, looks like."

She elevated a brow in scorn. "A letter? Fancy excuses, more likely." Her eyes swam as she looked up at him. "Even as we speak, their daughter is in there dying, and her father sends a useless letter."

Moved by the news, the Scot wheeled around and bolted for the door. *Men.* Lily glared after him. *All they ever want to do is escape.*

"Maggie, lass," Ian called. "Come inside, would ye? I need to speak with ye."

His wife appeared at once, as if she guessed something was amiss. Lines of concern deepened in her long, thin face as her astute, azure eyes beneath the ruffled cap looked right at Lily. "Oh, no. Has Susan passed? The children don't seem out of sorts."

"No. She's still with us. . .unless she stopped breathing while I was dressing." Unwilling to let the couple see how truly desperate she felt, Lily averted her gaze to the plank floor.

Margaret MacBride gave a commiserating squeeze to Lily's shoulder as she and her husband crossed to the sickroom.

Lily trailed behind them, feeling a pang of remorse for having misjudged them both. The older woman's presence always brought comfort, and Lily more than appreciated her patient concern, her motherly advice.

"Merciful heavens," Margaret murmured as she caught sight of Susan, gasping open-mouthed for every breath. She sank down onto the bedside chair and took Susan's limp hand. "How long has the dear child been like this?" She swung a questioning glance to Lily.

"I first heard her shortly after I retired last eve."

Margaret shook her head and met her husband's eyes. He bowed his head in prayer.

Outside, shouts erupted, aggravating Lily even more.

Ian parted the curtain to peer outside, but the window faced the opposite direction. "More folks comin', I 'spect."

His wife looked up at him. "Go ask them to be a bit more quiet, dear. Let them know this dear child isn't up to joinin' us at service, that I'll be sittin' with her. Oh, and when Eva gets here, send her in, would you?"

"I'll go wait for her." He left the sickroom in haste.

Lily felt a new rush of bitterness as he deserted them. . .one more fault she'd have to confess to the Lord along with having misjudged him earlier.

Margaret reached out with a bony hand and patted Lily's arm. "Don't you be frettin', child. Me an' Eva, we'll be stayin' here with you till our Susan passes."

"Oh, thank you." Crumbling with relief that Toby Dunlap's sweet mother-in-law would also join them in the vigil, Lily clutched onto the bedpost, her eyes brimming with tears. "You have no idea how much I'll appreciate having you both here. It's been. . .so hard."

"Don't I know it." Margaret picked up a cloth from the nightstand and gently blotted Susan's damp brow. "I been where you are more'n once in my life."

Yet again, Lily was grateful to be living among these kind people. When her own mother passed away, not one neighbor had come to lend a shred of assistance or comfort to her sister or their father except the physician. Rose had been barely thirteen at the time, and everything had fallen to her and Papa. With four younger siblings to care for and a household to run, small wonder Rose had grown into such a strong person. Lily had admired her older sister all of her life and hoped one day to emulate her.

If only Rose were here now. . .especially when the time came to break the sad news to the children. She always managed to say just the right thing.

"The young'uns don't know how bad their mama is, do they?"

Lily shook her head. "I didn't want them to see her like this. I just. . ."

"I understand." Margaret gazed down once more at Susan, her eyes soft. "You might consider sendin' Emma and Davy off to spend the night with their little friends."

"Yes, that would be best. I particularly wouldn't want sweet little Emma to see her mother's final struggle. 'Twould be something she'd carry in her memory the rest of her life. 'Tis best they remember her smiling, even in her illness." Lily paused, considering how to relate her next comment. "The doctor said there's a possibility that Emma might be stricken with this same affliction in years to come. Susan's aunt also died of it."

"Mercy me." Margaret kneaded her forehead. "What a frightful thought. Speakin' of that Philadelphia doctor, are you ever going to break the seal on the letter from Susan's pa?"

Lily glanced down to see the missive crumpled in her fist. "I forgot about it." She slid a nail beneath the edge and broke the wax seal, then unfolded the paper and read it aloud.

My dear Miss Harwood,

I cannot express the pain it causes me to be sending you this message instead of coming there personally with my wife. When I reached home, I rode to the stable to see to the needs of my horse before entering the house. I missed the quarantine sign posted on the front door. Our house servant has contracted the smallpox, and no one who enters may leave until the notice has been removed. My wife and I considered sneaking away under the cover of night. But then we thought better of it. We would never forgive ourselves were we to bring the pox to you all. We shall come as soon as we are free. Please convey this and our deepest love to our most treasured daughter and her children.

Your humble servant,

Frederick Gilford

"Now the commander at the fort will *have to* allow John to come home. You'll see." Margaret smiled, but her confidence waned after a glance at Susan. "For all the good it'll do our dear saint here."

Lily's vexation brought heat to her face.

"Our Pat sent us a message a few days back."

"You don't say." The realization that the post was getting through, just not to *her*, made Lily clench her teeth. She hadn't received a word from John in weeks.

The older woman droned on, oblivious to Lily's anger. "Mail's been real slow comin' from the fort. But Pat's been sent south to the fort at Harris's Ferry, and he found somebody comin' our way. He wrote that with the threat of them blasted Frenchies, river traffic upstream of the ferry has purty much stopped altogether."

"And?" Lily wasn't interested in excuses.

"Pat's surprised John hasn't up and deserted. John *is* that worried about his dear Susan. But the captain ain't givin' nobody leave. I was gonna tell Susan that today an' let her know her husband's itchin' to get to her."

"He should have deserted." Lily no longer tried to conceal her bitterness.

Margaret offered a droll smile. "If he did that, honey, they'd just come an' get him, lock him up for Lord only knows how long. They could even hang him."

In her heart, Lily knew that was true. John was not a heartless lout, but a loving, caring husband and father who loved his family deeply. He'd have moved heaven and earth for the opportunity to come home to them had it been possible. Her anguish spilled over into self-pity, and a wrenching sob burst from deep inside. Clapping a hand over her mouth, she swung away from Maggie.

In an instant, the older woman rose and drew Lily into her comforting arms. "I know, child, I know. It's been powerful hard for you here alone. But we're here with you now."

A Sabbath service, somewhat subdued, went on without a hitch, though spiritual leader MacBride did cut it short out of respect for Susan. No one made mention of the inevitable, yet folks seemed to sense the unspoken fate looming over the household, and the adults were considerate enough to keep their voices quiet.

That did not extend to the children. Lily detected Davy's squeal above the racket of the other children as they played blind man's bluff outside after the meal. Glancing out a small loft window, she saw little Harry Shaw spinning blindfolded Davy round and round amid peals of laughter.

Emma stood in the circle with the other children, but she wasn't laughing along with them. Her eyes remained focused on the house. Despite everyone's efforts to act as if this Sabbath was the same as all the others, Lily's little darling sensed something was terribly wrong with her mother. Never before had she and her brothers been barred from Susan's room for so long a time.

Emma, especially, needed to be away from here, and so did Davy. Lily knew it was imperative for the little ones to leave for at least a day or two. She stuffed the last article of Davy's clothing into a pillowcase and climbed down the loft ladder. Then, collecting a second pillowcase holding Emma's things, she ambled out the door.

The sound of splintering wood caught her attention. The older boys were occupied with throwing hatchets and knives at the bull's-eye painted on the side of John's abandoned carpentry shop.

She paused for a moment, studying Matt and Luke, both of whom wore grim expressions. Her explanation that their mother was sleeping and shouldn't be disturbed could not fool two such bright lads. They knew the truth. Lily felt their eyes on her as she passed by the adults speaking in hushed voices around the outdoor table.

"Lily, child." Ian MacBride, seated at the head, crooked a finger at her.

She turned back to him, hoping he wasn't expecting another report on Susan.

A kind sparkle lit his watery eyes. "Cal, here, has volunteered to ride to the fort and fetch John as soon as he gets his family home. The commander's sure to let John come now."

Having had her hopes dashed too many times already, Lily barely restrained herself from spewing her mounting exasperation. Somehow she managed to utter something trite but acceptable. "That would be a kindness." Then before she could blurt anything further, she turned on her heel and continued on to her young charges.

She waited until Davy had tagged one of the other teasing, dodging children and gleefully ripped off his blindfold before stepping up to her little towhead. "I've a most splendid surprise for you, Davy."

"For me?" His eyes rounded with delight.

"Yes. You're going to go play at Joey's house today."

"I am?" He swung his gaze to his five-year-old MacBride friend. "Hear that, Joey?"

"And his mama said you could even sleep in his bed with him tonight. Is that not marvelous?"

Davy grabbed hold of Joseph and the pair jumped up and down together. Then he stopped, his grin turning to a frown. "You mean I can stay all night? Till morning?"

Lily knelt before him. "Yes, for this one special night. Your mama and I want you to have lots and lots of fun. And just so you won't get lonely"— she opened his pillowcase and drew out his stuffed lamb that had been his sleeping partner since babyhood—"Wooly is going with you."

The boy's mouth dropped open. "Wooly! You get to go, too!" He snatched the stuffed animal from Lily's grasp and caught Joey's hand.

"Let's go climb in your wagon right now!"

From behind, Lily felt tugging on her skirt. She turned around to her Emmy.

Tears filled the little girl's blue-green eyes as she stared despondently at the second pillowcase. "You're sendin' me away, too, aren't you?"

Lily tugged the child into her arms and cradled her head. "I'm so very sorry, sweetheart. It's best."

"My mama's dyin', isn't she?"

Lily couldn't bring herself to lie to the child. "I'm afraid so."

"Doesn't she want to see me?"

"I'm sure she would, if only she were able, honey." She blotted Emma's tears with her apron. "But she can't now. She's no longer awake. I'm thinking the Lord wants to take her away gently while she's asleep."

"Up to heaven, where she won't hurt anymore." Emma's chin began to tremble as new tears spilled over her lashes and down her fair cheeks.

Lily's heart crimped with an ache beyond words. "Yes, darling, where she won't hurt anymore."

"Will the angels brush her hair for her so she looks pretty? And bring her flowers?"

A soft smile tugged at Lily's lips even as her own eyes swam. "I'm sure they will. They'll take special care of her because she's been sick such a long time. And the Lord will take care of all of us, too. But right now, it's best if you go visiting."

Emma released a shuddering breath. "All right. I'll go. But if mama wakes up again, tell her I love her. I want her to know that."

"I'll surely tell her for you."

"Am I goin' with the MacBrides, too?"

"No. I thought you'd rather stay at the Pattersons' with Mary. Her father is going to ride to Fort Henry to fetch your papa home."

"He is?" A glimmer of hope glistened in Emma's moist eyes. "I'll tell Mr. Patterson to hurry 'cause it's real important." Resigned to her fate, the child took the pillowcase of belongings from Lily and started for the Pattersons' cart.

Already missing her little ones, Lily turned to see that everyone had climbed aboard their wagons. This Sabbath that had seemed so interminably long had ended earlier than usual. It couldn't be past two. Watching the families leave, she mustered a smile and waved at Davy as the wagon wheels crunched over the trail.

The last wagon had barely disappeared into the trees when Matt and Luke approached her, their demeanors gloomy and despondent. "Where do you want us to start digging?" Matt asked in a dull voice.

"What?"

"Mama's grave."

Her little men stared at her, their arms akimbo, ready to do what needed to be done. Lily reached out and pulled their unwieldy bodies close. "Your mother is still alive, but she's no longer conscious. Grandma Margaret and Eva Shepard are sitting with her. I'll let you know when it's time."

"We want to start on it now," Luke said, his voice wavering.

His brother nodded. "We don't want no one else doin' it."

Lily looked from one to the other, seeing their determination, knowing their need to be doing something—anything. She realized their being outside, working through their feelings of helplessness was far better than waiting in the house. She could hardly face going back inside herself and breathed a silent prayer of thankfulness that Margaret and Eva had stayed behind to wait with her.

"Well, I believe your mama was partial to that pretty little knoll behind the pasture, where the first spring flowers always bloom. I think that would be a fine spot."

With a solemn nod, the lads walked, shoulders sagging, to the shed where the tools were stored.

Lily watched after them, feeling their despondency. *Please, dear God, bring John home quickly. Not for me, but for the children. They need him now.*

Yet even as she prayed, she couldn't keep from desperately needing him herself.

Chapter 9

Susan never regained consciousness. Approaching the midnight hour, she drew one last, gurgling gasp, and her soul took flight. The features so recently pinched with suffering relaxed, and an almost-smile settled over her lips. The death watch had finally, mercifully, come to an end.

Silver-haired Eva Shepard's generous bosom rose and fell as her faded blue eyes darted from Lily to Margaret; then she got up from her chair and drew the sheet over Susan's face.

Lily's own heart seemed to stop as she swallowed a huge lump in her throat and stared at the still form beneath the quilt.

With a sigh, Margaret reached out and touched her arm. "Go fetch the family Bible, child. You need to write down the date of her passing."

"Oh. Of course." Walking out into the cabin's darkened main room, Lily lit a table lamp, then collected a quill and ink jar and brought them to the dining table. The Bible still lay open to 1 Corinthians, where she'd been reading earlier. She flipped to the beginning of the volume, to the page where family records were listed.

Scanning down the contents, she sank onto the nearest chair. The facts of the Waldons' life together were all there—their births, the date of their marriage, the day each child had been born. Now Lily would make this unhappy recording. She dipped the quill into the ink and tried to steady her hand as she wrote: *Susan Gilford Waldon died on Sunday, the tenth day of July, 1757.*

Finished scribing the words, she closed her eyes against stinging tears. Dear, sweet Susan had died at such a young age. She'd lived a scant thirty-one years, five months, and two days, far too many of which had been spent under unspeakable suffering. It was so unfair. So senseless.

Lily blew on the wet ink. *Oh, Lord, please don't let this cup of suffering visit our little Emmy, too. . . . I beg of You.*

Closing the Bible, she glanced up at the loft, where the boys lay sleeping. Tomorrow morning would be soon enough to tell them about their loss.

By the time the sun passed its zenith, much had been accomplished. Ian MacBride had come by shortly after dawn to check on Susan's condition. Upon hearing the sad news, he rode across the creek and asked Richard Shaw to build a coffin; then he rode on to inform the rest of the families in the cove. Because of the hot, sultry weather, he scheduled the funeral service for the following evening, figuring that if Cal Patterson didn't run into trouble, he'd be back with John by tomorrow afternoon.

John. . .here. . .tomorrow. Try as she might, Lily couldn't keep the thought out of her mind. How would he deal with having missed his wife's final moments?

Washing the dishes after the noon meal, she noticed that the pounding of hammers in the workshop had become sporadic. She looked across to the squat building. Mr. Shaw and the boys must be almost finished with their task. The boys. As before, they wanted to keep busy away from the house while Lily helped the older women prepare their mother's body for burial.

The dog started barking, and a different sort of pounding drifted her way now—but not from the shop. She pushed the window open wider. Hoofbeats. Someone was coming. Fast. Wiping her hands on her apron, she hurried out the open door. It couldn't possibly be John coming so soon.

She reached the edge of the porch just as the rider rounded the building. *Ian MacBride.* The older man's mount skidded to a stop before her, lathered and panting hard.

Ian swung a frantic glance about. "Richard! Where's Richard?"

"In the shop."

Having heard the commotion, Mr. Shaw, Matt, and Luke exited the building with weapons in hand and approached Ian with questioning frowns.

"Matt!" Ian ordered. "Ride over to the Shaws' and on to my place. Tell the women to bring the children here to the blockhouse while we're gone. You, too, Lily. Richard, mount up. We've no time to spare!"

Lily's heartbeat quickened. Something was amiss. "Where are you going?"

Even as Mr. Shaw bolted for the hitching rail and his horse, Lily leaped from the porch and captured Ian's mount's bridle. "What's happened?"

His wife echoed Lily's question from the porch. "Yes, Ian. What's wrong? Are we bein' attacked? We need to know."

"We didn't hear no warnin' shots," frizzy-haired Eva piped in as she came alongside Margaret.

"There weren't any." Ian stared at them momentarily, then dismounted. He stepped up to Lily and took her by the shoulders, his demeanor grave.

A dreadful foreboding tightened her chest. Whatever the trouble was, it couldn't be good.

The old man's eyes softened as he gazed down at her. "Now, I dunna' want ye to be frettin', lass. There was only three of 'em, near as we could tell."

"Three of whom?" Lily felt her panic rising.

"We're thinkin' Indians. They was most likely sent ahead to scout out the cove. When Mary and Emma dinna' come back from takin' leftovers to the springhouse, Nancy sent her Henry to fetch them. He come runnin' back alone, just as I rode in."

Lily clutched his arms. "Are you telling me Indians took Emma and Mary?"

He gave a guilty shrug. "Dunna' be worryin'. They're afoot and canna' have much of a lead. That's why I dinna shoot off a warnin'. Dinna want 'em knowin' we was onto 'em so quick."

"Quick!" Lily all but spat. "Why on earth did you ride all the way back here?"

"I come for Richard. With most our men gone, there's only me, Toby, and Richard. Robby'll come with us, but he's young." Ian swung up into his saddle. "That's why we want you womenfolk to go the blockhouse, just in case."

Eva fisted her plump hands on her hips and leveled a stern glare. "You're sayin' they might be usin' this to pull you men away from the cove."

Before he offered a response, Lily saw that Mr. Shaw had mounted and started toward them, but in his own good-natured time. She whacked Ian's horse on the rump. "Go! Now! Both of you. Get those little girls back!" Her knees almost gave way as she imagined her sweet angel in peril.

As the pair galloped off, Matt and Luke raced out of the stable, dragging unsaddled Smokey by the reins. "The Indians have Emma?" Matt yelled. "Luke, run in and get the musket."

His brother sprinted for the house.

"No!" Lily shouted. "You were given another important job. Go tell Ruthie and Agnes. Now. And hurry back. Bring Davy with you."

"Wait, Matt," Luke called from the porch. "I'm goin', too."

The older lad held up a hand, taking charge as he scrambled up on the big-footed farm horse. "You're needed here. Help Lily carry food and supplies to the blockhouse." Ramming his heels into the horse's flanks, he galloped toward the creek and the Shaw place a quarter mile away.

As Lily watched Matt ride confidently away, past the springhouse and beyond, the possibility of what could happen to poor little Emma flooded her mind. . .the tortures. . .the unspeakable horrors. Her little girl was so young, so tender.

'Tis my fault. I was the one who insisted she go to the Pattersons'.

Only the night before, Lily had pleaded with God for Emma. Surely the Lord would not answer her prayer in such a cruel, heartless way!

She started for the porch steps, but her shaking legs would not cooperate. She collapsed onto the bottom one, all pretense of control gone. Burying her face in her hands, she convulsed into wracking sobs. How much could a person bear? Susan lay dead in the house, and Emma— *"Emma!"*

⌒

John readjusted the knapsack strap gouging his shoulder and trudged with his scouting party through the gates of the stone fort. Weary after having searched the far side of the river as far as the Tuscarora Indian Path for the past three days, he was gratified there'd been no sign of the French. He shrugged off his gear and leaned his musket against the inside wall, then strode toward headquarters to report. As he walked, he pulled a rag from his belt to wipe the sweat and grime from his face.

"Waldon! Wait up!" Pat MacBride cut across the parade ground toward him.

John paused long enough for his neighbor to fall into step with him.

"How'd it go out there?" Pat asked.

"We didn't see a sign of danger. What about the Juniata Path? Spot anything suspicious along there?"

"Nope, nary a thing. Who knows? Maybe the French are gettin' stopped by our boys up north."

"Or better yet, pushed all the way back to Canada. Wouldn't that be great?" Swiping again at his damp forehead, John hiked a brow. "Any dispatch riders come in from up New York way while we were out?"

Pat wagged his head. "Just one checkin' in from Fort Augusta. Here it is already July, an' we're still just hangin' around, waitin.'"

"Yeah." John clenched his teeth as he and his friend neared headquarters. He could've been to Beaver Cove and back half-a-dozen times by now, spent time with Susan and the rest of the family, checked on how Lily was coping with things. . . .

"Rider comin'!" The shout came from the south watchtower.

Captain Busse and his orderly stepped outside headquarters and focused their attention on the gate. Then the commander spotted John and came down the steps. "Corporal Waldon. See any movement between the river and the Tuscarora Path?"

Stiffening his posture, John saluted his superior. "No, sir. Not a sign."

The captain grunted and returned his attention to the gate as the rapid thud of hoofbeats grew nearer.

John also turned toward the sound as a rider came through the gate. Slowing his mount to a walk, the newcomer whipped off his hat.

Cal! Recognizing his neighbor, John wondered if the man had decided to reenlist even with his bad knee.

Cal rode straight for headquarters and reined in, but without bothering to greet the captain, he lowered his gaze to John. "Thank the good Lord you're here an' not out on patrol."

Dread gripped John. Only one thing could have brought his friend here right now. *Susan.*

"I rode hard to get here, John. Your wife took a turn for the worse." He moistened his lips and averted his eyes to the ground. "She's been real bad. I hate to say this, but it wouldn't surprise me none if she already passed on."

Before John could process the information, Busse stepped around him. "You're Private Patterson, aren't you?"

A frown drew his bushy eyebrows together. "I was, sir."

"Which way did you come, perchance?"

Hearing their voices as if from far away, John gaped at the commander's audacity to butt in where he wasn't wanted. Still, stunned by the dire news Cal had delivered, he stood silently by while his friend answered.

"I cut across from Beaver Cove to the Susquehanna, an' took the trace north from there."

"Did you see any sign of the French? Any scouting parties?"

"Just some of your men, sir."

Having had quite enough of Busse's questions, John spoke up forcefully. "*Captain.* Permission to speak, *sir.*"

The commander reluctantly shifted his gaze. "Permission granted."

"I'm sure you heard Patterson's news. I must go home. If not for my wife," he railed bitterly, "I have four young children there and must see to their welfare."

The captain had the grace to look a bit guilty as he inhaled a deep breath and shifted his stance. "I. . .uh. . .am sorry about your wife, Waldon. Go see to your family. I'll give you five days to take care of things. Take extra mounts so you'll get there faster. But go home by the Tulpehocken Path and watch for Indian sign along the way."

John couldn't believe the man's gall—expecting him to take time to scout on the way home to his dying wife!

Busse edged closer to John and spoke for his ears only. "A large war party has been sighted north of Fort Augusta. Godspeed."

The frogs and insects along the creek kept up a steady racket punctuated by the occasional hoot of an owl. This long night refused to end. Too stressed to sleep, Lily shared sentinel duty on the top floor of the blockhouse with Cal's grief-stricken wife. Nancy Patterson, known as the cove's most fervent worrier, idly twisted a strand of her light blond hair within an inch of its life as she and Lily slowly, silently circled opposite sides of the perimeter, staring beyond the moonlit clearing into the inky blackness of the woods. As they watched and waited, they prayed fervently, ceaselessly, for the men to return with their girls. . .their little girls who'd been dragged off, frightened, helpless in the foul hands of savages.

"Think they'll be all right?" Nancy's whisper barely broke the silence as she turned her swollen blue eyes to Lily.

I don't know! How could I know? Lily wanted to wail. But she forced herself to remain calm, recalling how her sister Rose might answer a senseless question. "We must trust the Lord," she finally murmured. "Little ones are very precious to Him. I'm sure He'll send angels to protect them. We have to believe that."

"I know. I do. But it shore is a hard thing." Nancy drew a ragged breath and turned her attention outward once again, her slender profile gilded by moonlight.

It was a hard thing for Lily, too. She'd had no words of comfort for the boys, especially Davy. She wondered if she truly had the kind of faith it took to trust God's providence when it came to someone she loved so dearly. Her faith had done precious little for Susan Waldon. Even now the young woman's ravaged body lay inside the cabin, waiting its final commitment to the earth. At least she would never know her little daughter had been captured and perhaps—

Unable to finish the unthinkable possibility, Lily struggled against feeling resentment against Nancy for allowing the little girls to go down to that creek alone. She should have kept them inside, safe. The Patterson farmstead was the farthest one upstream. Nancy had to know her place was the most vulnerable to attack. Why hadn't she worried about that when it mattered?

The bouts of anger inevitably gave way to self-condemnation. Lily knew she should have had the foresight to send Emma home with the Shaws to play with their Lizzie. But the Shaws lived no more than a quarter mile away, and she feared Emma might take the notion to run home if she were that close.

Utterly spent, Lily sighed. It was no one's fault. . . . It was everyone's fault. *Why on earth are any of us still here? We should have left a year and a half ago.*

Coming again to the side of the structure facing her farm, Lily paused as she'd done every circuit since climbing the ladder from the windowless room below. The cabin's outline was barely discernable through the growth along the creek. And over there, Susan lay in her room in the inky darkness, still in death, all alone.

Would this night never end?

Steps sounded on the ladder. Lily moved to the hatch to assist the person up onto the deck.

"Sure is stuffy down there." Patrick's wife, short, plump Agnes MacBride, took in a deep breath. "Thank goodness, the children are all finally sleepin' sound." She tipped her auburn head as her small hazel eyes met Lily's gaze.

"Even Davy?" Lily asked.

"Aye. He's sleepin' betwixt his brothers."

Nancy came to join them. "What about mine?" Worry drew her golden eyebrows into a V above her pert nose.

"Your boys was real good about playin' with li'l Sally till she drifted off."

A sudden twinge of envy gripped Lily. Even if Mary were never found, Nancy would still have baby Sally to love and cuddle. Emma was the only little girl Lily had. The only one. She ground her teeth and glanced up-creek again. "Where are those men? Ian said the Indians didn't have much of a lead. *Where are they? What's taking them so long?*"

Chapter 10

The afternoon dragged on as John and Cal Patterson rode their mounts along the Blue Mountain trail. As if sensing John's heaviness of heart, his friend refrained from needless chatter. But inside, rage and resentment toward a commander who would order them to go miles out of their way at such a pressing time all but consumed John. Only prayer helped him to get beyond the anger.

Oh, God, if my precious Susie is to be taken away from me, please let her passing be a gentle one. She's been so patient in her suffering, so brave, with thoughts only of me, of the children, and Lily. She told me she didn't want us to be angry or sad, but to dwell on the happy times. He swallowed, and his shoulders slumped. *How I wish there could have been more of the joyous times. She deserved a happy life, but I failed her. Lord, be close to our little ones. Help them to accept Your will quietly and go on as their mother would have wanted. She was so proud of them all.*

John had to admit that Busse hadn't been completely heartless. The man had provided two extra horses for the trip, making it possible for him and Cal to reach Beaver Cove in the same amount of time the more direct route would have taken with only two mounts. A pity the river had too many twists and turns for a swift canoe trip.

His thoughts drifted again to Susan, and he recalled a beautiful bride in filmy lace, her red-gold curls a glorious tumble beneath a crown of field daisies, her turquoise eyes alight with hope. She'd been so filled with dreams. He hoped she'd seen some of them fulfilled along the way. She'd made a wonderful mother, doting on each baby yet never allowing the older children to feel slighted. *Oh, Susie-girl. How can I face life without you?* He bowed his head once more in prayer.

When darkness descended on the already shadowy forest, they plodded cautiously onward, not chancing the lighting of torches to illuminate the trail, but relying on the horses to carry them along the centuries-old Indian path. According to the captain, the enemy had been spotted a few miles to the north. They could easily be closer.

After several hours, they came to a small clearing bathed in the subtle light of the moon.

Calvin moved alongside John and muttered the first words he'd said in quite a spell. "The horses should get some rest."

John nodded and veered off into the grassy meadow where their mounts could graze while the two of them caught whatever sleep they could. While they unsaddled, hobbled, and rubbed down the horses, he longed to question his friend about Susan, the children, and Lily. But voices carried easily on the night air.

After laying their saddles beneath the outer edge of a tree's low-slung branches, they crawled inside the shadowed haven and rolled out their bedding.

A few yards away John's horse nickered.

Then Cal's.

John grabbed his musket and lunged forward, snatching his powder horn loose. Cal followed suit, and they uncorked their black powder, pouring a smidgen of the grainy substance into their flashpans. John marveled that his neighbor's stiff leg hadn't slowed him down a bit.

Up the wooded trail, a horse returned the greeting of the hobbled mounts, and a lone rider came out of the trees at a slow gait.

John rose to his knees. Shoulders tense, he raised his musket and took aim, cocking an ear for sounds of others approaching. Hearing none, he spoke just loud enough to be heard. "Who goes there?"

The rider jerked on his reins. "Robby Randall, from Beaver Cove."

"Fool kid," Cal muttered. "What are you doin' all the way out here, ridin' through the night?" He accepted John's help to get up.

"That you, Mr. Patterson?" Robby asked.

"Aye."

"Thank the good Lord." The lad kneed his mount toward them.

John met him halfway across the clearing. "What are you doing this far north all by yourself in the middle of the night?"

"I'm headin' for Fort Henry."

Puzzled, John shook his head. "Why would you come this way? Are you being chased?"

"Nope."

"Don't tell me the cove was attacked!" Cal piped in.

"Nope. If you two'll stop askin' questions, I'll tell you. Me an' the other men are after Injuns what took our little girls. We think there's only three of 'em, but they'll prob'ly meet up with others, so Grampa Mac sent me to get help."

"Which of your sisters did the varmints steal?" Cal asked, his voice deadly quiet.

"None of mine." The lad hesitated, then looked down at Calvin. "I'm real sorry, Mr. Patterson, but your little Mary was one of 'em."

Cal gasped and grabbed hold of John, his fingers biting into John's flesh. "My Mary. They took my Mary."

"She ain't the only one." Robby turned to John. "They took Emma, too."

The news punched into John like a fist. "That can't be. We live more than a mile downriver from the Pattersons, past several other farms."

" 'Fraid it's true. Lily sent Emma to stay with the Pattersons for the night. She, uh, didn't want her there, watchin'. . .you know. . .your wife takin' her last breaths."

His legs starting to give way, John leaned hard on his musket for support. "Susan's dead, and my baby girl's been carried off." He could hardly choke out the words.

Cal's big hand clamped on to John's shoulder and shook it. "We gotta saddle up. Go after 'em."

The urgency in his friend's voice jerked John into action. He glanced at Robby as he wheeled toward the spot where he'd left his gear. "How far back did you leave the others?"

"A couple a hours back. It's been real hard, you know, the redskins on foot, cuttin' through thickets an' up rocky cliffs. We had to get off our horses an' drag 'em after us lots of times. Once the Injuns hit this trail, we thought we'd have 'em for sure. But they must'a got wind of us, 'cause they cut off into the woods again, headin' north. That's why Grampa Mac sent me to get help. When I left 'em, they was tryin' to track them sneaky savages by torchlight."

Calvin yanked Robby's sleeve. "You sure they still got our girls?"

"Last I seen. The girls ain't got no shoes on."

Slinging his saddle onto the back of the nearest horse, John prayed out loud. "I don't even know what to say, Lord. Those heathen savages are dragging our frightened little barefooted girls through brambles and thorny bushes and across roots and rocks, cutting their feet all up." He stopped as a more terrifying thought chilled his blood. "If they haven't already slit their little throats and cast them aside. Please help them, Father. Send Your angels to be with my Emma; be with Mary. Keep them safe. Please, God, it would be more than I could bear to lose my wife and my daughter on the same day."

⌐───

Lily jerked awake as a shaft of light hit her eyes. Sitting up, she realized she was in the windowless blockhouse, and the beam came from the square opening in the ceiling. All the horror came rushing back. "Emma!"

She scrambled to her feet. The day must be half gone. Surely the men would've been back by now if they'd rescued her darling and Mary.

Her insides tightened around the unthinkable. *What if none of them return?*

No! She would not dwell on that unspeakable possibility. The men would find the girls and bring them both home, safe and sound.

Looking around, she realized she was alone in the bottom floor of the blockhouse, with its crude dirt floor. Where was everyone? They couldn't all be up above, or she'd hear them. Climbing the ladder rungs, she reached the opening and searched the deck.

Bob Randall's petite wife, Edith, stood on one side, frowning as she idly twisted an errant mousy brown curl around a finger. Hearing Lily, she flashed a worried smile. Her son Robby had ridden out with the men. "Did you get any sleep?" she asked in her quiet way, concern softening her light brown eyes.

Lily only grimaced.

"Nancy woke up about half an hour ago. The two of you shouldn't have taken the entire night watch. You should'a woke me an' Ruthie up."

"We couldn't sleep. Where is everyone?"

"Down there." Edith nodded below. "They're havin' a picnic outside. We told them not to get too noisy."

Joining her neighbor at the rail, Lily gazed down on the scene. It looked so pastoral with everyone gathered on several quilts in the shade of the structure. The women chatted, and the little ones giggled as they ate from wooden trenchers or tin plates. Her little Davy, being his usual busy self, was using his spoon to sword fight with his friend Joey.

Nancy, however, stood off by herself, looking northward, anguish frozen on her face.

Knowing exactly how her neighbor felt, Lily focused across at the cabin. Susan's body still lay over there. . .a day and a half in this relentless summer heat. Something must be done. Now. Today.

Exiting the building, she walked around to its shady east side.

"Lily, girl." Margaret waved her over. "Come and have something to eat, child. Sit with us a spell."

Even though she hadn't eaten since the night before last, Lily had no appetite. She did force herself to swallow a few bites before Davy came running, full of questions.

"Did my mama really go to heaven, like Socks? Where's Emmy? When's she comin' back?" He dropped down on his knees before her.

Before Lily could answer, Matt plucked his little brother up and whisked him away. His own expression hard-set, he carried the child up to the watchtower.

Luke, fighting tears, ran after them.

Not having dealt with her own grief as yet, Lily would have liked nothing more than to collapse and weep until she had no tears left. But she knew if she gave in, she would never stop crying. Better to remain strong for the children. There'd be time enough for sorrow in days to come. She turned back to her meal, picking up the only thing that looked remotely appealing, a cup of tea. As she took a swallow of the hot liquid, she glanced around at the other women. Their expressions were not so much sympathetic as they were wrought with tension. They knew any of the other children could have been taken as easily as Mary and Emma. Any of their homes could have been burned to the ground and the residents massacred by the savages, as had happened at other settlements.

Every woman here had a loved one away, either at Fort Henry, manning a line of defense, or out tracking the kidnapping Indians. Not a wife among them could be certain her husband would come home alive.

But. . .they were men. Not two helpless little girls.

Lily caught herself before she sank into that pit of despair. Her fears would have to wait. There was something more immediate to tend to. She swept a glance up to the fifteen-year-old Randall lad. "Donald, I need you, Sammy, Jimmy, and Pete to come with me back to the house."

All eyes turned to her.

"Why?" Jimmy Patterson's youthful face contorted with puzzlement, then smoothed out again. "Sure 'nough, Lily. Whatever needs doin', we'll help you with it."

All the lads were having to take up their manhood too soon. When would this madness come to an end? She set down her empty cup and rose to her feet. "Shall we go?"

—————

"We lay this dear young woman's body to rest," Grandma Margaret droned in a sympathetic tone, her back to the grave as she faced Lily and the other women and children clustered in a semicircle about her. Rays from the slanting sun filtered through the trees on the knoll, casting long shadows over the scene. "And we thank Thee, Lord, that our Susan is free of her pain and suffering and is now basking in the light of Thy glory. We ask Thee to comfort each of her children and fill them with the assurance that they are loved as much as ever."

She paused and centered her attention on Lily, who stood with Davy tucked against her to keep him still as the older boys flanked her, all huddled together. Then she resumed speaking, this time with force. "And Father, we beseech Thee to bring our precious baby girls home safe and sound. . .our girls and our men."

"Amen" resounded from every woman and child in the circle.

"Most gracious God," Margaret continued, her tone gentle once more, "we look forward to the day when we will see Susan again in heaven, see her wonderful smile, hear her sweet laugh. We express our deepest thanks that our sister is now at peace in Thy loving arms. We praise and worship Thee for Thy goodness and care, and we beseech Thee most fervently to keep little Emma and Mary safe, in the name of our blessed Lord Jesus. Amen."

As everyone looked up at the close of the prayer, Margaret turned to the grave. "We commit the body of Susan Gilford Waldon to the earth from whence it came, to await the glorious day when we will all be raised to meet our blessed Jesus in the sky. Ashes to ashes. . .dust to dust." She reached for the shovel in the waiting pile of dirt and emptied its contents atop the wooden casket.

Lily's heart thudded at the hollow sound of clods falling atop the few little wildflowers the children had picked and laid along the lid. She'd thought she'd be ready to face this moment, but the depth of emptiness that filled her stole her very breath.

The older woman handed the shovel to Matt.

He stared at it, then turned his swollen, red-rimmed eyes up to Lily.

She gave him a nod, barely holding back her own tears as he filled the shovel and emptied it in the grave, then handed the tool past her and Davy to Luke.

The nine-year-old wiped his sleeve across his eyes and followed suit, but as he attempted to hand the shovel on to the next person, Davy jerked free. "Me, too. Mama needs my dirt, too."

Reluctantly, Lily nodded her assent, hoping the child understood enough to carry out the task with respect.

The tyke jammed his foot down on the iron edge of the shovel's scoop, and with his hands halfway down the handle, he brought up the dirt and let it trickle into the grave. He looked up at the sky with a triumphant smile. "See, Mama? I help real good." Then the little big man handed the shovel to Lily. "Your turn."

Despite her sadness, Lily's heart swelled with joy. Davy understood. He knew his mother wasn't lying in that grave, but in heaven with God. She drew a steadying breath and added her own shovelful of earth.

Moments later, as the others took turns filling in the grave, Agnes MacBride moved alongside and wrapped an arm around her. "I'm sure John would've been here by now, if he could've."

Lily barely managed a nod as her fury at the fort's commander flared again. And though she knew it was irrational, her anger at John resurfaced. And at Mr. Gilford. Most of all, she condemned herself for sending Emma to the Patterson farm. She'd known Calvin was leaving to go fetch John home, that no man would be on the place to guard the family.

She glanced across the gathering to where Nancy Patterson had been standing with her toddler.

Nancy was gone.

Turning on her heel, Lily spotted her. Carrying little Sally, her neighbor had left the wooded knoll and started across the footbridge on her way back to the blockhouse. No doubt Nancy would climb up to the watchtower and continue searching the forest beyond—not for Indians, but for the return of the men. . .her Cal and John. She'd be watching even more intently for those who'd gone after their girls.

It would be dark soon. The little ones had already been out there one night. *Please, dear God, bring our children home to us. Please.*

"Lily."

She pulled her gaze back to the knoll, to Matt. "Yes?"

"Me an' the rest of the boys are gonna tend to the animals."

Lily glanced toward the pasture, filled now with the extra livestock brought in from the other farms.

"You women need to take the young'uns back to the blockhouse while we're gone."

"Quite right." She laid a palm alongside his smooth cheek, tipping her head as she let her eyes roam her young man's face. "I hadn't noticed. You're almost as tall as I am now."

Matt gave her hand a squeeze. "I know." A half-smile tweaked his mouth. "Better go along."

Lily turned away before he could see the tears she could no longer restrain. Matt. Matt, who'd been only seven when she first arrived to look after the children, was now looking after her.

Chapter 11

The late afternoon breeze feathered over the clearing, ruffling the edge of Lily's muslin gown and toying with her hair. She caught a wisp that blew into her eyes and tucked it behind her ear as Davy's chatter broke into her thoughts.

"When folks die, people bury 'em real deep."

"Is that right?" She did her best to sound interested.

"Uh-huh. That's so dogs and wolves can't dig 'em up." He looked down at the mound of earth Lily, Agnes, and Ruth were patting with the flat of their shovels to smooth out the grave. "I wish Mama wasn't so deep, though. I miss her a lot."

Agnes stopped to wipe perspiration dripping into her eyes. "When your pa gets home, he can make your mama a fine-lookin' cross, what with all them nice tools he's got an' all."

"Maybe he'll let me help." The little boy puffed out his chest. "I'm good at helpin'. Mr. Pat-a-son went to bring Pa home, didn't he, Lily?" His huge blue eyes sparkled. "When's he gonna get here?"

Agnes answered for her. "We're not sure, little man. Soon, we hope."

Just then a wild, piercing shriek came from the blockhouse beyond the trees. Lily froze. *Indians?*

Musket fire erupted from the upper floor.

Duke and the other families' dogs took up a cacophony of growls and yapping.

Alarmed, Lily glanced about her. Half the people were scattered hither and yon. She and the two neighbor women—and Davy—were still here on the wooded knoll. The older boys were off tending livestock. Not one of her own was at the blockhouse!

Answering shots blasted from farther away, followed by a scream from the log structure.

Snatching Davy's hand, Lily reached for the pistol she'd tucked in the crutch of a nearby maple tree.

Beside her, Ruth clutched the handle of her shovel in a white-knuckled grip, visibly shaking. *"Oh, Lord, we're gonna die!"*

Agnes, musket now in hand, rushed to Ruthie and gave her a sound slap across her sallow face. "No time for hysterics, gal." She then snagged the young woman's hand and pulled her down behind a tree. "Stay put."

Lily dragged Davy along as she ran to a break in the trees. She could see riders—not Indians, at least—coming down the trail on the other side of the creek, but she couldn't make them out in the lengthening shadows.

When the horsemen emerged out of the woods and into the clearing, Lily released the breath she'd been holding. "It's our men!" Racing off the knoll, dodging trees and brush, she headed for the creek. *Please, Lord, let Emma be with them. Bring her back to us.*

Matt, Luke, and the older boys reached the fallen log first and let out a gleeful hoot. "They're back!"

Davy jerked free and sprinted for the footbridge ahead of Lily. His little legs working hard, he scrambled across with her on his heels. Lily desperately needed to see the riders clearly.

Ahead of her, the boys veered to the right as they reached the clearing. Lily followed. Panting for breath, she stopped, her eyes widening at the sight before her. Two little girls—*Praise be to God!*—Emma! Her little one rode double behind one of the men.

A cry tore from deep inside as Lily bolted straight for the approaching horse, her eyes filled with one small person. "Emma!"

Leaning out to peer around her rescuer, Emma reached out a hand to her. "Lily!" Then she burst into tears.

Reaching her, Lily pulled her darling off the still-moving horse. A tearful Emma collapsed into her waiting arms, then clung so hard, Lily could scarcely draw breath. She smothered the little girl with kisses. Emmy, her precious child, was home again.

Lily breathed a wordless prayer of thankfulness as she hugged the filthy little angel to her breast. Emma's braids had come loose, and her pretty red hair was dull and matted. Scratches and bruises covered her arms and legs, her neck bore definite rope burns, and one little eye was black and swollen. Lily's heart wrenched as her own eyes brimmed with tears. "Oh, my darling Emmy." She drew her close again.

Matt, Luke, and Davy crowded around them, crooning sympathetically as they reached out, needing to touch their sister. "Glad to have you back, Sissy." Then Davy's voice rang out above the rest. "Pa!"

John? Lily followed the child's gaze, and her heart skipped a beat. John was home! She'd been so absorbed in the joy of Emma's return, she hadn't noticed her rescuer! And at his weary smile, all the anger she'd harbored during his absence evaporated.

As John beheld the joyous, tearful reunion of his daughter and Lily, he easily identified with the lass's emotion when she tugged Emma off the horse. He'd felt the same way the moment he'd had his daughter safe in his arms. Fully aware that Indians wouldn't hesitate to murder little captives if they got wind of an impending attack, he, Calvin, and Robby had approached the camp with stealth. They waited long after dark, after the children had been cruelly bound to trees and the three young braves finally fell asleep, before they unsheathed their hunting knives and made their move.

The sleeping girls never heard the gruesome deed, but woke to two elated fathers who swiftly cut away their bonds and smothered them in hugs before whisking them away. Having Emma in his arms once more had been the most joyful, yet painful, moment of John's life. He knew exactly how relieved Lily felt to have the child back.

When Lily looked up and saw him, her lips parted and she stared for a brief heartbeat. Then she gave a cry of joy and rushed with Emma right past the boys and into his waiting arms.

He enveloped them both, near tears himself, as the boys charged over and grabbed on. Davy jumped up and down. "Up! Up! I want up, too!"

Reaching down, John lifted the little tyke into the embrace, immediately finding himself in a stranglehold around his neck as his son peppered him with kisses.

"Hey, ever'body!" Davy hollered. "My papa's back!"

His son's words brought John up short. The captain had given him a mere five days, and he'd used a costly chunk of that to rescue Emma. How could he possibly desert them all again the day after tomorrow?

⌐⌐

John trudged up the hill alone. The sultry gust of evening air rustled the leaves and carried the scent of fresh dirt—dirt covering his long-suffering wife's final resting place. With heavy heart, he picked up a clod and crushed it in his hand, watching it dribble through his fingers, just as Susan's life had. It was so senseless. A soft-spoken woman, she'd never had an unkind word for anyone. She shouldn't have had to endure that debilitating ailment.

According to Cal, she'd been in a coma even before he left for the fort, so there was little hope John could have reached her before she drew her last breath. If only Busse had allowed him to come home weeks ago, when he'd begged for leave. His and Susan's marriage had been a good one. They'd loved each other since they were the same age as Matt and Luke, and it crushed him to think how brief her time on earth had been. How would he live with the knowledge he hadn't been with her at the end, holding her hand?

He should have pestered Captain Busse ceaselessly until the man let him go. . . . But the truth was a small part of him abhorred the idea of watching the love of his life take her final breath.

No. I left that to Lily and the children.

John sank to his knees. "I'm sorry, Susie-girl. So sorry I'm such a coward."

"Papa!"

Davy's cry brought John to his feet. He swung around to see his little boy scampering up the rise.

"Son." He shook his head in exasperation. "I told everybody I wanted a few minutes alone with your mother."

"That's why I had to come." Davy huffed, out of breath. "I runned as fast as I could."

The statement made no sense. John knelt before the boy. "Davy—"

"Mama 'splained it to me. So's I wouldn't worry."

"What are you talking about? What exactly did she tell you?"

"She said the body she was wearin' wasn't no good no more, that it hurt all the time. So she was goin' up to heaven to get a new one. She said Jesus would give her a brand new one up there. Lots better than this one. An' she said she'll be right there waitin' for us. Soon as my body don't work no more, she's gonna make sure I get the bestest new one they got in all of heaven." He stretched his arms apart to add emphasis.

Even with his heavy heart, John felt the twitch of a smile. "Did Mama really tell you that? The last part, I mean."

"Well"—Davy scrunched up his face—"not a'zackly. But that's what she meant. I know it." He studied his feet for a second, then looked up again. "Mama always told me she loves me better than anything. So you'll see. She'll get me the best one they got."

John did smile then. He pulled his little scamp into a hug.

Davy eased back enough to look straight at him. "So anyway, you don't need to be frettin' about Lily's red eyes or Matt's or Luke's. They was just cryin' because they was scared them mean Injuns was hurtin' our Emmy. An' they was right about that, huh? She gots bad marks all over." Easing out of John's grasp, he raised a clenched fist. "If I ever see them bad Injuns, they'll be sorry."

Reaching out, John took hold of his son's little fist and peeled back the fingers. "The Indians who took Emma are already sorry for what they did, Son." He tousled the towhead's hair. He knew he should say the righteous words: *forgive them as we would want to be forgiven, leave the vengeance to the Lord.* But even though they lay dead, he still hadn't been able to forgive them himself. Maybe in time, once his little girl's scratches and bruises healed. . . . He released a ragged breath.

Rising to his feet, he took Davy's hand. "Well, my little man, if your mama's not here, I reckon there's no sense in us hanging around, is there?" He started toward the cabin.

"Nope." His son skipped along at his side. "But it sure will be differ'nt, not havin' her to take care of no more."

"I know what you mean." John cast a backward glance at the sad-looking grave, strewn with a fading rainbow of wilted flowers. His childhood sweetheart, too fragile to live on earth any longer, had gone on without him.

"Oh no! Ever'body's leavin'!" Davy wrenched free of John's hand and bolted across the meadow. "Don't go! I still wanna play!"

But the neighbors never slowed. John knew it was natural for them to load up and return to their homes. There'd been no evidence of a war party in the area, merely the three scouts who'd taken the children. And those varmints would never report to their chiefs again. Still, a very real threat remained. Captain Busse had relayed the sighting of an approaching force, and no one could be certain whether they'd come south or follow the trail east along Blue Mountain and continue down through the "Hole" and on toward Reading. Would they descend on a larger town this time?

Regardless, it was too dangerous for his family to remain at Beaver Cove without him any longer. He'd see them on their way before he left for the fort. His beloved Susan was gone—to get her new body. John couldn't help smiling when he thought about Davy's remark.

He climbed through the pasture fence just in time to see the last wagon heading out, carting with it a lamb, a calf, crates of chickens, and children. Worn-out Ian MacBride, slumped in his saddle, herded the larger livestock behind. Chasing after Indians for two days had taken a lot of starch out of the old fellow. But thank God, he and the others had never given up. John would be indebted to them for the rest of his life.

He scanned his farmstead, the piece of land where he'd invested all his hopes and dreams for himself and his children, the place he'd built with his own hands. Now it may have been for naught: the cabin he'd planned to expand one day into a bigger, nicer home filled with fine furnishings he fashioned himself; the stable already roomy enough to house six large animals; the corncrib; his workshop; and the springhouse, smokehouse, and sheds. He'd practically broken his back digging the cellar. Then there were the fields and orchard, the fencing—all in jeopardy. If everything were burned out, would he have the heart to start over?

He exhaled a harsh breath. Tonight he'd put aside his worries and enjoy his family. His time with them would be much too short.

Watching his dear ones waving to the MacBrides from the porch, he noticed that Emmy had on a fresh dress. Lily must have bathed her and tended her wounds and now had his daughter tucked close to her side. If ever he'd doubted the love the British girl had for his children, he never would again. She certainly was God's blessing to them all.

He increased his pace to reach them, then slowed a bit as he noticed Eva Shepard, Toby's mother-in-law, standing with them. Why hadn't the woman gone home with her family? What possible reason could she have for remaining behind?

Of course. *Lily.*

Could the woman possibly have seen the way he'd looked at the lass the last time he was home? A familiar twinge of guilt waylaid him. Surely he'd managed to hide that forbidden yearning.

Or was it the way he'd drawn Lily close to him today, held on to her. When he'd been bestowing kisses on all the children, had he inadvertently kissed her, too? He might have. He wasn't sure. He'd been so happy to see them all.

One thing was certain. From the way Eva was eyeing him, her arms crossed as he approached, she wasn't here merely to help out. She was here to chaperone Lily.

Chapter 12

Lily listened through the open kitchen window while her family washed up for breakfast. Their laughter and good-natured banter was a welcome change from the heavy sadness that had enveloped the household since last spring, when John had gone off with the militia and Susan's health had waned. Now that the man of the house was back, the light chatter fell on her ears like music from the cathedral choir at Bath. But even though the family was acting as if nothing had happened, Lily knew that soon enough the finality of their loss would sink in, and they'd all be forced to face their grief.

Silver-haired Eva came up behind her. "This'll be a fine homecomin' breakfast."

"So I'm hoping." Reluctantly, Lily left the window. "Thank you for making the blackberry syrup. Everyone will love it on the flapjacks."

"Aye, lass. We'll have us a good stick-to-the-ribs meal." She brushed flecks of loose flour from her generous bosom. "Then later, I think you an' me need to have a little talk."

"Oh? Did I forget to do something?" Lily thought she'd taken care of everything concerning Susan's burial the day before.

The older woman wagged her mobcapped head with a smile. "Nothin' to fret about. Right now, I'm so hungry I could eat a horse."

"So sorry, then." Quirking a teasing smile, Lily picked up the platter of sliced salt pork and took it to the table. "You'll have to settle for a hog."

Eva chuckled.

Still, Lily couldn't help wondering what her neighbor had on her mind. She hoped the woman hadn't caught her gazing in an unseemly way at John at supper last night, especially after having put so much effort into not looking at him. But she could not have related the joy Mr. Gilford's visit had brought Susan, or the letter the man had posted to them, without looking in his direction.

Unless. . .Eva wanted to lecture her about that telling moment when she'd first glimpsed John and literally thrown herself at him. She hadn't made the slightest attempt not to appear inordinately glad to see him. Oh, mercy.

"Mmm. Can I have more syrup?" Fork clutched in his fist and wearing as much of the sticky sweet as he'd eaten, Davy besought Lily.

Luke cocked a grin and pointed his own smeared finger. "Just let him wipe his flapjack down his shirt."

"Oh, give the boy all he wants," Eva said, positioned a generous distance away from the messy pair.

Lily wasn't quite so invulnerable, seated next to Davy. On her other side, Emma sat in silence, toying with the food on her plate. The child had hardly uttered a word since her return. Whenever she wasn't glued to Lily or her pa, she huddled curled up in a corner or under the table, often crying without a sound. Lily mourned for the child, wondering—but dreading to know—what unspeakable abuse she'd endured. She eased away from the little girl enough to pour more syrup on Davy's already soggy flapjack.

At the end of the table, John set down his fork. "Now that we're about finished. . ."

Lily shot him a glance. The happy expression he'd worn when the family gathered for breakfast had turned serious. Did he, like Eva Shepard, have something to say she didn't want to hear?

The jovial banter between the older boys ceased as Matt and Luke slid wary glances at their father.

Wiping his mouth on his napkin, John laid the cloth down and cleared his throat. "First of all, I'd like to thank you ladies for this wonderful breakfast—the best I've had since last I was home."

Lily smiled but remained quiet.

Eva, however, stood and began clearing the table. "Shucks, John. It's a special day. Your family wants to celebrate your homecomin'."

"Yes. Well, speaking of that, there's something you all need to know. I was given only a few days' leave. As much as I hate to say it, I'm duty-bound to start back to the fort. . .tomorrow."

Davy's fork clattered to his plate. "Papa! No! It's not fair."

His brothers grimaced and exchanged incredulous looks.

Emma's little hand slowly moved across Lily's lap and found hers.

Lily swallowed the lump forming in her throat and fought back tears already trembling on her lashes. John's children had suffered the loss of their mother only three days past. They needed him more than ever before. How could he leave them again so soon? What sort of love could be so cruel?

As if oblivious to the sullen mood that descended on the room like a smothering blanket, John continued. "After much consideration, I've come to a decision, Lily. I want you to pack everyone's clothing today while the boys and I drive our stock over to the MacBrides'. Then first thing tomorrow morning, I'll take you all down to the Swatara and hire a canoe. I'm sure Matt and Luke will be able to handle paddling it as far as the Susquehanna. Then you're to secure passage on a keelboat the rest of the way."

"The rest of the way?" Lily's voice emerged in a hoarse whisper. It was finally happening. He was dismissing her. "But—"

He held up a hand. "Please, let me finish."

With an aching heart, she pressed her lips together.

"I know you promised to stay and look after the children until I return for good. But in the light of Susan's passing and the current potential for an Indian attack, I won't hold you to that any longer. You told me Mr. Gilford has expressed a desire for his grandchildren to come and stay with him, so that's what they'll do. I have every confidence the man will see to their needs, but I'd be pleased if you'd consent to remain with them—at least until they're settled and comfortable. Once this ugly business with the French is over, I'll reimburse you generously. You have my word."

No one spoke for an instant.

"I ain't leavin' here." Matt slapped the table, rattling the utensils. "Mama always said our future was on this land. We don't have nothin' back in Philadelphia. I'm not goin' off an' leavin' the corn an' beans an' the sorghum we planted for somebody else to harvest."

"Me neither." Luke sat up straighter.

Lily had never heard them defy their father before. Shocked, she swung her attention to John.

"I understand how you feel, boys," he said evenly. "But I need to know you're all safe. It's as simple as that."

"Hmph. We'd like to know *you're* safe, too, Pa," Matt retorted. "But that ain't stoppin' you from goin' back to that blasted fort, is it."

John slowly shook his head. "You know I have no choice."

"Well, neither do *we*. Luke an' me have to stay here. Keep the place goin.'"

His younger sibling nodded in assent.

Lily marveled that the two had become a force of one. More amazing, they'd rarely had an argument during the past year and truly had worked hard on the place. In the ensuing silence, she turned again to gauge their father's reaction.

Eva finally chimed in from the side. "You know, John, if the boys stay here, me 'n Maggie'll check in on 'em from time to time. So will the other neighbors, I'm sure."

John looked over at her. "So you folks are all planning to stay? Even knowing there's a war party coming down out of New York and heading this way?"

"That's right." She hiked her chin, blue eyes flashing. "Like your lad said, we done worked too hard to just cut out an' run. 'Sides, you militia boys are up there ready to stop 'em, ain't 'cha?"

He gave a conceding nod. "We'll do our best." Returning his focus to his sons, he stared at them a few seconds, then huffed out a breath. "Very well. Against my better judgment, I'll agree to let you stay here. . .if Ian MacBride will consent to accompany Lily and the little ones on the canoe trip as far as the mouth of the Susquehanna." He turned to her, his eyes pleading. "Would you be willing to go with my children? I'd do it myself, except I have extra horses I'm obliged to return to the fort."

Lily felt battered little Emma's hand still clinging to hers. She couldn't bear the thought of parting with the sweet angel again so soon, nor could she subject her to the possibility of being recaptured by savages. She filled her lungs with a shaky breath and moistened her lips. "Emma would be much safer in Philadelphia, that is true, and so would Davy. Their grandfather Gilford appeared to be a kind, loving man. I'm sure he'd be elated to house them until it's safe to come home. No doubt the quarantine has been lifted by now. I agree to take them. But"—she added force to her words—"then I'll return here and look after Matt and Luke. I'll not leave them by themselves with no one to cook or wash for them and see they get their lessons."

"No. That is out of the question." John tightened his lips.

He truly meant to send her away. Her heart sank with a sickening thud.

"You'd be alone on the river then. It's far too risky."

Lily strengthened her case. "I'm sure Mr. Gilford would provide an escort for my return. Perhaps the frontiersmen who guided him here to the farm. I'd prefer coming back overland anyway. 'Tis much faster than a slow, cumbersome journey upstream."

"Lily. . ." John looked from her to Eva Shepard and back. "Once you deliver the children and remember how wonderful it is to feel safe again, you may decide not to return to Beaver Cove."

"Oh, I'll be back. You can be certain of that." She gently disengaged Emma's hand and picked up the milk pitcher. "Would anyone care for more?"

"Me. Me." Davy squirmed in his chair. "We haveta hurry up and eat, Lily. We hafta pack my stuff. I'm gonna get to go on a boat all the way to Phila—Phila—"

"Delphia," Emma whispered, the first word she'd spoken in hours. But a tear spilled over her swollen eye and trickled down her cheek.

Lily filled Davy's glass half full, then set down the pitcher and wrapped her arm around Emma. If no one else needed a safe haven, this baby girl had to leave here to feel safe again. . .no matter how empty the house would be without her.

She raised her lashes and met John's gaze, seeing there a tender look that said he was aware of her concern, that he shared it as well. Then he averted his eyes, increasing the awkward silence filled with words unspoken. It was like her heart was being winched.

What might he have said to her if Eva Shepard wasn't hovering nearby? She didn't dare allow her imaginings to drift in that dangerous direction. But at least the forthcoming trip would eliminate the need for the older woman to lecture her.

⌒⌒

Lily could hardly bear to think back on John's emotional farewell to his two older sons when she and the little ones had waited with their luggage to begin their journey. Even now, soaking in warm, silky luxury in a tub filled with sudsy water at a travelers' inn, she could still envision him barely managing to contain his tears. Matt and Luke had tried so hard to be brave and manly, promising to work hard and keep the place in order as the threesome hugged and kissed, administering awkward thumps on each other's backs.

Downstairs, a hotel maid was looking after Emma and Davy in the front parlor of Stevenson's Tavern while the pair watched travelers ride by on the post road between Baltimore and Philadelphia. The sights enthralled Davy, who had rarely seen a stranger before embarking on the trip downriver. He couldn't wait until tomorrow when the three of them would board another vehicle—not so fancy as one of the stylish carriages that made the little fellow's eyes widen like saucers, but a stage wagon. Lily herself felt a niggle of excitement about going to a city she understood to be even larger than Baltimore.

If only something would put a smile on Emmy's face.

A pity there hadn't been time to stitch some proper clothing for the children before they left, instead of their plain homespun. Lily could have salvaged enough material from one of her fine gowns or an old waistcoat of John's. She glanced down the lace front of the day gown she'd laid out to wear when she and the children would go for supper. Thank goodness she hadn't grown any taller since sailing across the sea from England or grown overly buxom. Mayhap she wouldn't be too out of fashion.

Out of fashion! A laugh bubbled out of her. To think being fashionable had been one of her greatest concerns before coming to the colonies. Such a foolish, naive lass she'd been then. At Beaver Cove she'd hesitated about wearing her lovely gowns, since most of her neighbors usually wore homespun garments. But a tiny part of her wondered if John would think she looked pretty tonight, had he come with them.

Dear, considerate John. Here she was soaking in a tub, anticipating supper in the public room, while he was stuck at a primitive fort that lacked even the simplest of comforts.

John. . . She recalled his expression of relief when Ian and young Michael both volunteered to canoe with her and the children down to the Susquehanna and see them aboard a flatboat. He had given each child a hug, a kiss, and a promise to come for them in November, when his enlistment was up. A wailing Emma clung so tightly to her pa it had taken the combined efforts of Lily and the MacBrides to peel her away. Only Davy bubbled with joyous anticipation.

Without attempting to unravel the tangled feelings the bittersweet memory gave her, Lily relaxed in the water up to her neck. One would expect she'd be quite good at good-byes by now, after being ripped away from her own father, two sisters, her dearest friend—and John— numerous times. She would survive this parting, too. She forced herself to concentrate on the present. It had been a lifetime since she'd bathed in water she didn't have to haul in and heat. Basking in the privilege, she smiled as a whiff from the briny Chesapeake Bay teased her nose.

In her deepest heart, Lily wished John had rendered the same kind of farewell to her as he had to Davy and Emma. His handsome features relaxed when he turned to her, and his eyes softened. An ocean of words they might have said, had they been alone, lay between them. Lily knew he still loved Susan, and she accepted it because it was only right. But still, there was that invisible cord of shared heartache, shared longings, that bound them together. No use trying to deny it.

But gentleman that he was, he only enclosed her hand in his much larger one and spoke words that still echoed in her heart. "My dear Lily, once you reach civilization and the children are settled, you may very well realize all you've been missing. You're a beautiful young woman, you know, and your sisters must be concerned for your safety. I'm certain they'd endeavor to see you pleasantly situated in an advantageous marriage. I, too, care very much what happens to you, and desire—" He glanced away, then took a breath and continued, his voice husky. "I'm already so utterly in your debt I shall think no less of you should you choose to travel on to the Barclay Plantation in Virginia. You are so very deserving."

"As I told you before—"

He touched a finger to her lips, stopping her words. "Please, lass, do what's best for you." Sweeping her up into his arms, he waded into the water and set her down in the canoe. "May God always keep you in the palm of His hand."

Despite the MacBrides' presence, Lily would have liked him to kiss her good-bye. He did not. But something in his gaze told her he had to leave right then, or he never would.

"Godspeed, my dear ones," he breathed.

Blowing soap bubbles away from her mouth, Lily struggled to contain stinging tears as she recalled John's compliment. *You're a beautiful young woman.* She let the memory linger at the edges of her mind, drawing from it what little comfort she could.

Just then, Davy, with his typical exuberance, burst into the room.

She'd forgotten to bolt the door! Lily gasped and grabbed a towel from the stack on the nearby chair, slapping it over her.

"Lily! Quick!" The imp flew past her to the window. "The biggest horses you ever saw!" Glancing over his shoulder, he widened his eyes. "Oops! I forgot. You're takin' a bath."

She arched an eyebrow and gave him a stern look. "Quite right. Now be a gentleman and go back out. And close the door behind you."

"But, Lily." He turned again to the window. "They're giant horses, and they're pullin' a giant wagon. You gotta see."

She let out an exasperated breath. "Emma wanted to bathe next. But since you're here, I suppose you—"

"*Huh? No!*" He backed toward the door. "I haf ta go back downstairs now. I'll go get Emmy."

As he made his escape, Lily pressed a hand over her mouth to muffle her laughter. There was no faster way to get rid of that scamp than to mention a bath. She only hoped Emma would relax enough to enjoy her time in the tub. Lifting the sopping towel out of the water, Lily wrung it out and draped it over the back of the chair to dry.

Most of Emma's bruises were fading away, and now that the journey had taken them far from danger, Lily hoped her darling's fears would fade as well. The child had sat close and still on the boat trip, but her eyes constantly scanned the wooded shorelines, as if expecting a painted savage to leap out of the forest and snatch her out of the canoe. *Dear Father in heaven, please relieve those fears. Replace them with Your love. Help her to feel safe again.*

By the time Lily rose from the tub, dried off, and donned fresh undergarments, Emma had slipped into the room, her black eye now a sickly yellow.

"I hear you and your brother have been having fun watching the travelers pass by." She dropped her day gown over her head and threaded her arms through the elbow-length sleeves.

"We shouldn't a come here." The little girl's voice sounded thin, trembly. "Nobody has a musket or pistol or nothin'. Indians could sneak in here an' grab anybody they want."

Dismayed, Lily settled the gown over her petticoats and snugged the front lacings a bit as she sat down on the bed. She held out her arms to the wisp of a girl.

Emma moved into them, calming immediately.

Lily raised Emma's dainty chin with the edge of her forefinger. "Sweetheart, there's a very good reason why no one is carrying a weapon. There's no need. We're several days away from the nearest Indian."

"But they could come down the river, like we did, real easy. Pa said they came all the way down from New York, and that's far."

Drawing her closer, Lily hugged her tight. "Listen carefully, Emmy. Thousands and thousands of people live here along the seacoast. They have entire armories filled with guns and cannons if they ever have need of them, and the Indians know that. Believe me when I say you are completely safe here. No Indian will ever, ever take you away from us again."

Emma's little arms moved up to wrap Lily's neck, her nose all but touching Lily's as she peered deep into her eyes. "Promise?"

"Promise." Lily smiled gently. "Remember how, back at home, I always took the pistol when I went very far from the house?"

She nodded.

"Well, I'm far, far from our house now, and I didn't even bother to bring it. That's how sure I am that we're safe. Now, how about running down to the kitchen and asking them to bring your bathwater upstairs. Oh, and see if you can find out what they'll be serving for supper this eve." She eased out of Emma's grasp. "Just think, Emmy. Supper without us having to cook it or clean up afterward. Won't that be marvelous?"

A hint of a smile tickled the little girl's mouth, the first Lily had glimpsed since the ordeal. "Really and truly? We just get up and walk away? We don't clear the table or nothin'?"

"Really and truly. Today you and I are young ladies of leisure."

"Hm. Ladies of leisure." Her smile broadening, she scampered away.

Watching after her, Lily knew her little angel would soon be Davy's rather serious, bossy older sister again. *Thank You, Father.*

The closing door emitted a whiff of baking bread. . .bread someone else had made for their pleasure. Breathing in the aroma, Lily wondered if mayhap the niceties of civilization would prove to be too tempting to resist, after all. What really awaited her back in Beaver Cove? Could she—or John—ever betray Susan's memory? He'd all but ordered her not to return. Yet there'd been something in the low timbre of his voice, the tender touch of his hand, the way he'd scooped her up and gently deposited her in the canoe. And that yearning look. . .

Or was it all merely her overactive imagination?

Still, he had said she was beautiful.

Stop it, you silly goose! Lily lurched to her feet and grabbed for her day gown's ties, tightening them so hard she was almost afraid to breathe. *The poor man's wife just died.*

Chapter 13

Is this Grandpa's house?" Holding on to Lily's hand, Davy stared wide-eyed at the gambrel-roofed brick dwelling with its generous dormers and large Palladian window above the columned portico. Black shutters adorned the first-floor windows, and manicured shrubs bracketed the entrance. "It's as big as the tavern where we stayed last night."

" 'Tis the home the gentleman at the corner indicated." Lily's body ached from the long, bumpy stage ride to Philadelphia, and her feet hurt from the hour they'd spent walking the cobblestone streets searching for the Gilford residence. But the lovely garden enclosed by a wrought-iron fence was a refreshing sight to her eyes. Taking advantage of the chance to drink in the lavish array of pastel roses, she filled her nostrils with their heady perfume.

Emma squeezed Lily's other hand and pointed. "Look at the door. It's blue and as shiny as glass."

"Yes, it is." Of far more import, no quarantine sign remained posted. "Come along." Letting go of the little girl's hand, she unlatched the scroll-worked gate. John had not exaggerated when he said Susan's father ran a very prosperous enterprise. This substantial home was proof. It wasn't as breathtakingly grand as Mariah's mansion, but it was a far cry from the cabins at Beaver Cove.

As they neared the porch steps, both children began to lag behind.

Lily paused. "There's nothing to fear. Remember what a nice man your grandfather is? How much he loved your mama? He loves the two of you just as much."

A worried look crimped Emma's face. "But what if Davy breaks something?"

The imp had the grace to look guilty.

Lily fought a smile. "Let's just hope he doesn't." Taking him by the shoulders, she gave him a warning glare. "No one is happy when something special is broken, but that doesn't stop people from loving each other. Let's do our best to mind our manners and be especially careful. Now, come along." She started up the neatly painted steps, and her charges followed.

As they approached the door with its brass lion's head knocker, Emma tugged on Lily's skirt. "Look how clean the porch is. Maybe we should take off our shoes."

"Yeah. My feet hurt." Davy stooped down.

Lily pulled him back up. "You need to keep them on." The children hadn't worn shoes since early spring, and likely their feet hurt even more than hers. She reached for the knocker and rapped twice.

"Oh, let me!" Davy jumped up, trying to reach it.

"If no one answers our first summons, I'll pick you up and let you knock again, how's that?"

He shrugged. After a few seconds, he stretched his arms up to her. "Now?"

As Lily reached down for him, the door opened. An unsmiling, middle-aged woman wearing a mobcap, starched white apron, and black service dress swept a glance of appraisal over Lily and the children. One eyebrow arched. "If you're looking for a handout, you need to go around to the kitchen." She started to close the door.

Lily quickly stepped within the portal. "We've come to see Mr. Gilford. These are his grandchildren."

The woman eyed them more critically. "They aren't any grandchildren I've ever seen."

"That's 'cause we live in Beaver Cove," Davy announced.

A visible change came over the servant's demeanor. She quickly stepped back to allow them entry. "The master and mistress are upstairs dressing for supper. If you would kindly wait in the parlor. . ." She gestured toward an archway to the right of the tastefully appointed entry. But rushing up the wide staircase, she glanced back with that same expression of doubt.

Again, Lily wished she'd had time and funds to have had the children properly clothed. Far worse, she dreaded having to be the one to bear the sad news of Susan's passing.

Walking into the parlor, Lily noted that the furnishings would have been respectable even in a cosmopolitan city like Bath. Susan's father had done remarkably well for himself in his trade. Her gaze assessed the sapphire velvet drapes with sheer underpanels; the upholstered settee with its matching Queen Anne chairs, done in satiny stripes of blue and silver; and lamp tables in dark wood. The same rich wood capped the fireplace with a mantel that held porcelain figurines and an intricately carved clock.

"Wow." Standing openmouthed with her brother in the archway, Emma grabbed Davy's hand. "Don't touch anything. Come with me." She led him to the settee and perched gingerly on the edge, tugging him onto the seat beside her.

The blessed sight of Emmy becoming her old self again, mothering Davy, almost brought tears to Lily's eyes. She smiled and crossed to one of the companion chairs. But before she could sit down, she heard a door bang open on the upper floor. Rapid footsteps descended the staircase.

"Where are they?" Auburn-haired Mr. Gilford rushed into the room and went straight for the children, his thin mustache spreading wide with his smile. "Emma. Davy." He gathered them into his arms and kissed each in turn. Then he turned to Lily, and his joyful expression fell as the reason for her presence dawned on him.

She nodded gravely. "I'm so very sorry, sir."

A surge of grief brought moisture to his eyes, and he rubbed a hand down his face.

Lily waited for him to regain his composure before uttering the words she'd prepared ahead of time. "I want you to know our dear Susan's passing was made so much more peaceful because of your visit. She spoke of little else afterward, and some of her last words expressed how happy she'd been to see you again. She loved you very much."

It took a brief span before he could respond as he tried to come to terms with his daughter's loss. Then he drew a fortifying breath. "But for that blasted quarantine, her mother would have been able to visit her as well," he muttered, still holding the little ones. "The city official came only yesterday to remove it. I went immediately to the stage office and purchased our fares to the Susquehanna. Olivia and I would have set out for Beaver Cove in the morning."

Lily stepped closer to the stricken man and laid an empathetic hand on his sleeve. "I can only imagine how hard the waiting was for you both."

He nodded and hugged the children close again.

"I realize our coming was not announced, sir, but you had offered to have Emma and Davy come visit. . . ."

"Absolutely." His enthusiasm returned. "Thank you for bringing them to us. It will mean so much to their grandmother." With the children still clinging, he wheeled around and strode out to the entry. "Olivia!" he shouted up the stairwell. "Forget your state of dress! Come down at once. I have a wonderful surprise!"

Lily had thought she'd been pampered at the travelers' inn merely because she'd been able to bathe in a real tub. But for three days after she and the children arrived at their grandparents' home, they'd been treated to a whirlwind of luxuries. Mistress Gilford proved to be a tireless shopper, scouring the bookseller's for picture books, the toy shop for playthings, and arranging for her seamstress to provide wardrobes for her grandbabies and Lily. And once the older couple learned of Emma's ordeal, they both lavished extra love on her.

"Look what Grandma bought me, Lily." Lying in bed next to Emma, Davy pointed to a stool in the corner of the nursery, where an assortment of lead soldiers stood in a row. "I have this many." He held up all his fingers. "And Grandpa said if I go straight to sleep, he'll help me build them a fort tomorrow, just like Papa's."

Lily gave him a pleased smile.

"The one on the littler horse. . .that's Captain Busse. I'm gonna make Papa the general. The general's the captain's boss. That way, Papa can come home anytime he wants."

"Aren't you the clever lad." Lily tapped his nose with her finger.

On his other side, Emma propped herself up on an elbow. "Grandma's seamstress is making a dress just like mine for my new dolly."

"That's marvelous, sweetheart." Lily shifted her gaze to the porcelain doll that lay on the pillow on Emma's far side. "You couldn't ask for more generous or kinder grandparents." Had they been otherwise, she'd never be able to leave her little ones in their care. "I hope you remembered to thank them."

"We did," they said in unison.

"Good. Now it's time to say your prayers."

"Me first." Always wanting to be first at everything, Davy pressed his palms together and bowed his head. "Dear heavenly Father, thank You for the food, for the soft feather bed, for my new clothes, an' for my new whip-an'-top an' the bag of marbles. But most of all, for my lead soldiers. Amen."

Emma tucked her chin and glared at him, then looked at Lily with a long-suffering shake of the head. "I'll do it right. Dear heavenly Father, thank You for taking care of us even when we think You can't. . . ."

Lily's heart melted over Emma's having to learn such a hard lesson at such a tender age.

"Thank You for Grandma and Grandpa and all the pretty things they bought us. Bless everybody here and back home in Beaver Cove. And please keep Papa safe till he comes to get us. *In Jesus' name,*" she added with emphasis as she peered at Davy. "Amen."

"Well done." Leaning across the bed, Lily kissed each of them again. "Sweet dreams. See you in the morning." Then, after blowing out the bedside lamp, she left the room and headed downstairs to have supper with the adults. She wished the little ones were coming with her, but she'd been reminded that in polite society, children were fed and put to bed before the evening meal was served. How unfortunate that folks would allow stiff rules to deprive them of some of life's most precious times. She had so enjoyed meals with the family all together—even if they could get loud and rather messy on occasion.

Reaching the bottom landing, she heard voices coming from the dining room and recalled that the Gilfords' eldest son and his wife had been invited to dine with them. Lily stopped before the gilt-framed mirror to check for any out-of-place curls or a twisted tucker. Assessing herself in her lovely new gown of ruffled ivory dimity, she decided if not for her work-hardened hands and newly tanned face, she'd have looked quite presentable. No bonnet had been able to shield her from the reflection coming off that mile-wide river.

Well, nothing could be done about that now. She plastered on a pleasant smile and glided toward the dining room, just as she'd been taught by her sisters so long ago, to meet the older brother Susan had often talked about with fondness.

A tempting array of delicious aromas greeted her as she entered. The sideboard displayed a wider variety of items than it had the two previous evenings.

At the head of the table, Susan's father rose, and his son, a man of equal height, but less breadth, did as well. He, too, had a mustache, and bore a marked resemblance to his sire. "Lily, dear, I'd like you to meet Warren and his lovely wife, Veronica."

As Warren nodded politely, the overhead candlelight cast a warm glow on his auburn hair, a few shades richer than his father's. Beside him, his sable-haired wife also nodded as he reclaimed his chair. Their gazes lingered a touch overlong as they took the measure of Lily.

"I'm pleased to meet you," Lily breathed as Mr. Gilford drew out the chair next to his and seated her. She settled her skirts around her.

At the foot of the table, Mistress Gilford, looking regal in an emerald satin gown, her salt-and-pepper hair in an elegant upsweep, plucked a silver bell from beside her and rang for service.

The younger Gilford mistress leaned forward, her ice-blue eyes cool as they focused on Lily. "Mother Olivia tells me you're from Bath, England, that you're the daughter of a jeweler." She blinked as she elevated her little pointed chin.

Lily caught the hint of skepticism in the woman's voice. "That is correct."

"Your family must have had an enormous reversal of fortune for you to be sold into bondage." She took a dainty sip from her water goblet, looking quite pleased with herself.

"Veronica." Mistress Gilford silenced her daughter-in-law with an arch of the brow.

" 'Tis quite all right," Lily replied. "I don't mind answering." She leveled a languid gaze at the impertinent young woman. "My father did not sell me. After he'd been swindled by an unscrupulous aristocrat, my eldest sister took it upon herself to pay our father's debtors by selling our furniture as well as herself to a sea captain sailing for America. Though my father did all he could to cancel the contract, he was not successful. I did not want my sister to undertake such a journey alone, so I convinced him to allow me to sign on as well. Unfortunately, and contrary to the sea captain's promise, we were separated and bonded to different individuals after we disembarked the ship. For some time now, another sister and my father have both offered to buy back my papers. But with Susan's poor health to consider, I could not find it in my heart to leave her or the children."

"I see." Veronica Gilford's comment still sounded dubious as a maid set a plate of food before her.

Lily retained her syrupy sweet tone. "Fact of the matter is, my term of indenturement ended weeks ago. When I leave here, I must decide whether to return to Beaver Cove to look after the older Waldon boys or travel on to my sister's, as Susan's husband urged. He fears for my safety as he does that of all his children. My sister, by the by, is wed to Colin Barclay, of Barclay Bay Plantation in Virginia. Perhaps you've heard of it. They are reputed to grow some of the finest quality tobacco in the colonies. Lovely mansion, and such restful grounds. I attended my sister's wedding there not three years ago."

"You traveled while you were still indentured to the Waldons?" Veronica gave a snide half smile.

"Quite right." By now everyone had been served. Lily felt compelled to direct her next words to Susan's mother. "Your daughter always treated me as if I were her little sister, a beloved member of the family. We became the very best of friends. I shall miss her sorely."

"That would be so like her." Sadness filled Mistress Gilford's eyes, and she lowered her lashes. "My greatest regret is that I was unable to be at her side when she needed me most."

Lily wished she'd have been seated near enough to the older woman to comfort her, but she had to rely on spoken words. "Susan understood. Truly. She asked me to send you her deepest love." Lily hadn't the heart to tell them their letter regarding the quarantine had arrived too late.

Thankfully, Mr. Gilford changed the subject. "Shall we bow our heads?"

As he led the family in prayer over the meal, Lily emitted a silent breath of relief. How very much she missed the simple, genuine folk of Beaver Cove.

Chapter 14

Riders comin'!"

Standing in the long, slow line of militiamen waiting in the dusty compound for another tasteless supper of beans and cornbread, John glanced up to the watchtower, where the announcement had initiated.

"Sure hope they're bringin' better food," someone behind him muttered.

"I hope they're bringin' good news," Patrick MacBride said.

A sarcastic chuckle issued from the back of the line. "Like the war's over."

Pat nudged John. "We could use some news like that about now."

Within moments, a pair of frontiersmen rode into the fort and reined their mounts straight for headquarters. Neither wore a smile.

John spotted Captain Busse buttoning his red jacket as he came out of his office. Still resentful of the officer, the sight of him filled John with rage. His eyes narrowed and his fingers dug into his wooden trencher.

Stepping closer, Pat squeezed his shoulder. "You need to get past that, John."

"I've tried, believe me. I just can't. Every time I see the man I'm reminded that I wasn't there for my wife in her last hours because of him."

"Perhaps the Lord thought it more important for you to leave here at the perfect moment to save your daughter," Pat said quietly. "Ever think of that?"

John slid him a glare. "Yeah. The last time you mentioned it. But had I been home, Emma probably wouldn't have gone to the Pattersons' in the first place."

"Then again. . ." Pat shrugged. "She might have. You can't keep tryin' to second-guess what might have happened. You need to ask the Lord to help you forgive. That's the only way you're gonna find peace." A gap opened in the line, and Pat moved forward, then turned back to John. "Pray about it."

Pray about it. If only it were that easy. John gave a bitter smirk. "Right now, the only thing I can think about is my boys. Matt and Luke are at home. *Alone.* Matt had a birthday this week. He's only twelve. Just a kid."

"Aye."

"Another birthday I missed. And as much as I appreciate Lily and want her to be there for the boys, that may not happen. If she gives any serious thought to herself, she'll go to her sister's place in Virginia where she'll be safe—and looked after, for a change. She's carried far more responsibilities than any lass should have to bear, and for a family that isn't even hers."

Reaching the serving table, John held out his trencher. After the unappetizing fare was plunked onto it, he and Pat found an empty wall to lean against.

As he sat down with the stone wall cooling his back, the last rays of sunshine gilded the fort with golden light, reminding John of Lily the morning they parted. He'd never forget the pain in her face as she floated away in the canoe. The early morning sun glistened on the tears in her eyes. The memory made it hard for him to breathe whenever he thought of it. Of her. He was a first-class heel. His wife was barely cold in the grave, and he couldn't stop thinking about Lily. What he really needed to pray about was for God to forgive his untoward thoughts.

"And we ask Your blessin' on our food an' the rest of the evenin', as well."

Becoming conscious of his friend's voice, John added his own silent plea. *Dear Lord, do what You will with me, but please don't allow my children or Lily to suffer because of my unwillingness to forgive Captain Busse—or for my unholy thoughts about her.*

While Mr. Gilford, at the head of the table, offered a blessing for the food, Lily sent her own unspoken prayer heavenward. *Father, for almost a fortnight, I've asked for Your guidance but have received no answer. Where would You have me go? Should I stay here with the little ones, go on to Mariah's, or return to Beaver Cove? I need an answer. Please.*

She knew such a prayer was presumptuous, but what else could she do? There was no one to advise her, and she didn't dare base her decision on her desire to see John again. That would be terribly wrong.

Becoming aware of the scrape of soupspoons on china, Lily raised her head, realizing that the others had started to eat.

Veronica Gilford's cool gaze focused on her as the haughty woman daintily lifted a spoon to her mouth.

Lily moistened her lips. Warren's wife had been hostile from the moment Lily had entered the dining room. And though Lily had received an invitation from the elder Gilfords to stay on as the children's governess, now that she'd met Susan's older brother and his wife, she had no intention of subjecting herself to further snobbish treatment. When she'd visited the Barclay plantation, Mariah's in-laws had treated her like family. Despite knowing she was a bond servant, they'd bestowed their love upon her.

Warren's voice brought her out of her reverie. "Father, you'll never believe what I heard at the newspaper office today."

"Oh?" His father blotted his mouth on his napkin.

"I'm beginning to wonder if it's wise to trust these so-called generals the Crown sends over from England. They haven't the foggiest idea how to wage war in America."

"Get to the point, Warren. What happened?"

Yes, Lily urged silently. *Are John or his boys in danger?*

Warren gave a droll huff. "Remember that huge army that gathered in New York, heading up to Lake Champlain under General Ambercrombie? They were to retake Fort Ticonderoga and the lake."

Lily relaxed. He wasn't talking about Pennsylvania.

"There he was," the younger man continued, "with all those men and all those cannons, going against a fort reported to be undermanned. And after dragging those fool cannons across that long distance to batter down the stone walls, he was so stupid he didn't wait for them to be brought from the rear. Instead, Ambercrombie ordered a frontal assault. Sent thousands of foot soldiers—mostly New Hampshire militiamen—with nothing but muskets to charge a stone fortification with a battery of cannons pointed at them."

Mr. Gilford leaned forward, his hands gripping the table edge. "What was the idiot thinking?"

Warren's voice took on a bitter note. "After eighteen hundred colonial men were senselessly slaughtered, not British regulars, mind you, the general panicked and ordered a hasty retreat, leaving those unused cannons behind."

Stunned, Lily stared in disbelief. *Eighteen hundred men.* Thank the Lord John was stationed farther south, under the general command of a more sensible officer, Colonel Weiser, who was in charge of the string of forts in Pennsylvania. If such mishandling were to continue, all the backcountry could be lost to the French. No wonder John had been so adamant about her and the children leaving. Perhaps this was God's answer. She should travel on to Mariah's.

"Warren, darling," Veronica said, slightly agitated. "You must have a talk with Warren Junior. Before we left home"—she switched her attention to her mother-in-law—"I overheard him tell his friend Willy he's going to run off to join the militia the day he turns fifteen."

"Oh, la," Mistress Gilford commiserated.

Lily remembered that Warren and his wife had two lads older than Matt and Luke.

Veronica returned her attention to her husband. "I'll not have any sons of mine slaughtered over some backwoods territorial nonsense."

"Yes, dear. We've already discussed this at length." Warren switched his gaze to Lily. "We were disappointed you hadn't brought Susan's older sons with you. I'd like to have met my nephews."

She angled her head and shrugged. "They refused to come, and it was hard for their father to argue with them so soon after. . ." She chose not to mention the recent death. "Both Susan and John always impressed upon the boys that their future was there on the land."

"Nonsense." Mr. Gilford shook his head. "We could easily bring them into our business."

Warren flashed a stern glance at his father before turning again to Lily with a benign smile. "Yes. I'm certain we could find work for them at the brickyard, stacking and loading. Perhaps making deliveries."

Lily fully understood the young man's look of disapproval. Warren's sons were in line to inherit the business, and he didn't want them to have any competition. His wife, of course, would be of the same mind. No wayward sister's offspring would get in the way of *their* children's inheritance.

Matthew and Luke, young as they were, had been right to remain on their land. Hopefully, General Ambercrombie would soon be replaced by a more competent commander, and the farmstead she and the Waldons had worked so hard to develop would once again be secure. Instead of a lifetime of stacking someone else's bricks, the boys would one day be making beautiful furniture with their father, furniture to grace all the homes that would be sprinkled throughout the Susquehanna and Swatara Valleys in years to come.

The Lord's direction suddenly became crystal clear, and a peace flowed through her. She would go back to Beaver Cove. If she didn't, Matt and Luke might find staying at the farm too difficult, too lonely.

They might give up and come to Philadelphia only to labor in some lowly position for their uncle.

Her boys needed her there to cook and wash, to help bring in the harvest. And for their future, they needed her to give them their schooling. Her own future would have to wait.

⁓

"Peaches should be ripening at my place about now." With a sigh, John picked up his pewter cup and washed down the last of his cornbread with weak tea. The thought of the plump, sweet fruit on his tongue caused him to yearn for juicy peaches smothered in rich cream and honey. He hadn't enjoyed such a delicious treat in ages.

"Aye." Pat shifted his weight against the stone wall. "My ma makes mouth-waterin' peach pie. What I'd give for a hunk of that now."

"Or maybe I'd have them sliced thin over a sweet biscuit. Lily makes biscuits lighter than air." John closed his eyes, envisioning the delectable golden brown scones hot from the dutch oven.

Abruptly, Pat elbowed him and motioned with his head. "Looks like we got company. Them two long hunters that rode in a couple a minutes ago are comin' straight for us."

John groaned and turned his attention toward the approaching frontiersmen. Surely Captain Busse wasn't sending him and Pat out roving again! They'd just come in from scouting this afternoon.

Blast it all! The woodsy pair didn't veer off anywhere but stopped right in front of him and Pat.

"One of you happen to be John Waldon?" The larger of the two, a strapping figure with dark brown hair beneath a coonskin cap, nodded in greeting. Merry hazel eyes flicked from John to Pat and back.

Already harboring considerable anger toward Busse, John didn't bother to get up. He responded in a flat tone. "That's me."

The man dismounted and stretched out a hand. "Well now. I'm plumb pleased to finally meet up with you, man. Nate Kinyon, husband to Rose Harwood."

"You don't say!" Breaking into a grin, John put down his trencher and grasped Kinyon's huge hand. "Glad to meet you—and to know you've still got your hair."

A chuckle rumbled from the man's chest. "Same here."

Belatedly, John remembered his manners. "Pat, I'd like you to meet Lily's brother-in-law. He lives to the south of us, along the Potomac River."

They exchanged nods, and Kinyon gestured toward his companion, whose darker complexion and almost black eyes hinted at possible Indian heritage. "This here's my partner, Bob Bloom."

The man swung down from his tall black horse.

At the conclusion of greetings, handshakes, and light banter, Pat left the group to fetch food for the visitors.

John met Nate's gaze. "So, how are Rose and your little ones?"

The smile evaporated from Kinyon's face. "Sorry to say, Bob an' me ain't seen our families since the thaw."

His partner spoke up. "An' if a serious offensive ain't mounted against Fort Duquesne soon, I ain't gonna be signin' on again, neither."

"I feel the same way," John agreed. "I can't believe nothing's been done about that French fort. The Indians attacking the Pennsylvania frontier come from there."

"Down along the Potomac and Maryland's backcountry, too," Kinyon supplied. "The French are givin' 'em presents hand over fist to keep 'em fightin' us."

"So I heard." John wagged his head. "They've been ravaging west of the Susquehanna for more than two years now. Not so much our side, though. I thank God every day I settled to the east. I expect you've heard what happened to the folks over near Fort Granville last year."

"Aye." Bob Bloom flipped a long braid over his shoulder. "The best the governor of Maryland has managed is to build a fort a bit west of our farm. They finally finished it this year."

"Your people do know not to surrender, right?" John asked.

Kinyon's expression turned grave. "Sure hope so. Better a quick death than one at the hands of them Shawnee, with them bone-chillin' torturous habits of theirs."

"I thought you boys were with the Virginia militia."

"We are, but we live on the Maryland side of the river."

"What brings you to our neighborhood?"

"Me an' Bob come across the tracks of a sizable war party headin' this way, so we followed 'em. Before they got to the Susquehanna, though, they turned north. We figgered they was gonna cross somewheres above Fort Augusta, so we cut across to give fair warnin' to you folks here before headin' up to Augusta. We suspected they'd try to bypass that fort an' go east along Blue Mountain, then sneak down through the Swatara Hole, where the creek cuts through. Raise havoc down the Schuylkill River."

"You two must be the ones who brought the news by a couple weeks back."

"Aye." Kinyon nodded. "But we got to Augusta too late. Instead of stayin' together, the Indians split up into smaller parties an' headed in different directions. Folks in Berks County got attacked. That ain't far from Reading."

"We heard about that." Pat walked up with trenchers of food for the longhunters. "They say that last week Indians caught some children outside at one of them German settlements an' hacked 'em to death." He handed the men the victuals, then dropped down beside them with a troubled frown.

"At another place," John added, "families staying at one house while their men were out picking fruit were set upon by Indians. The women put up a fight, but before their men could get to them, three of the children were carried off."

"Speakin' of kids bein' snatched away," Pat piped in, "same thing happened to John's Emma an' another little girl from Beaver Cove. But thank the good Lord, the men were able to catch up to them red devils an' get their daughters back."

Nate paused in eating, and his dark brows rose in alarm. "Your Emma? What about Lily an' the rest of your family?"

Even though he'd surmised the subject would eventually turn to his family, it was still difficult for John to speak about them. He exhaled a breath. "Emma had gone to our neighbors, the Pattersons, to spend the night at their place when some Indian braves grabbed her. I was on my way home for my wife's funeral when we crossed paths with men going after Emmy and the Patterson girl. Thankfully, the Lord led us to them before the little ones were hurt too bad."

A sympathetic tone softened Kinyon's boisterous voice. "God was with you for sure. I'm glad you was able to find Emma in time. But. . .you say your wife passed on? I'm right sorry to hear that. I know you've had a run of bad luck. Lily's letters to Rose never failed to mention Mistress Waldon's sufferin'." He bit off a chunk of bread.

John could only manage a nod. "At my urging, Lily took Emma and Davy to my wife's family in Philadelphia. She had it in mind to return to the place to stay with my older boys, but considering the danger, I told her that once the youngsters were settled, she should travel on to her sister Mariah's. She'll most certainly be safe there."

"Aye." The hint of a smile tweaked Nate's lips. "That'll save Rose a pile of frettin'. But ain't those boys of yours a mite young to stay on the place alone? They should'a gone to Philly, too."

John shrugged. "Matt's twelve now, and Luke will turn ten next month. But you're right. Even though Pat and I have fine, caring neighbors and have built us a solid blockhouse, it would've eased my mind considerably if my sons had gone with Lily. The thing is, if I forced them to leave, they threatened to jump out of the canoe and go right back."

Pat laughed. "Knowin' those two, they would'a done it, too."

"They'd put a lot of hard work and sweat into our farm," John elaborated with a mixture of pride and angst. "They refused to leave their harvest there to rot. Those boys of mine have been working the place like men ever since I've been in the militia."

"Sounds like you got kids a man can be proud of," Bob Bloom inserted with a knowing nod. "Hope mine grow up to be just like 'em. May the good Lord look after 'em an' keep 'em safe till you get back home."

Having finished his meal, Nate set the trencher on the ground. "I'd say from the letters Lily wrote to my Rose, she'll make some farmer a real fine wife."

"That she will." The begrudging statement sank in John's heart like a stone.

" 'Course, she could end up weddin' a plantation heir, like Mariah did." Then a wary grimace colored Nate's demeanor. "Considerin' the passel of Injuns roamin' this area, a trip through the wilderness back to your place would be mighty risky at this point. I'm purely glad to know Lily's out of harm's way."

And likely out of my life forever. John's chest banded painfully at the thought.

Chapter 15

Lily's eyes sprang open. Again.

Her anticipation—or more accurately, anxiety—had interrupted her sleep several times throughout the night. This morning she was scheduled to leave for home on horseback. She glanced out the open window, where the beginnings of dawn had barely started lifting the curtain of night.

Tossing back the sheet, she left the dreamy comfort of the feather bed and padded across the woven-thrush summer carpeting to look outside. A faint glow silhouetted the brick dwelling across the street. She'd never get back to sleep now. She might as well get dressed.

Feeling around in the darkness for the flint-striker on her nightstand, Lily found it and lit the wick of her bedside lamp. Her gaze immediately fell upon the letters she'd written to her sisters before retiring last eve. They had yet to be sealed. Reaching in the drawer for a piece of candle, she paused and opened the message she'd penned to Rose. She read over her explanation for returning to Beaver Cove instead of going on to the Barclays in Virginia:

No doubt Mariah will feel I should give thought to my future, now that my time of indenturement has ended. But I cannot. Not yet. You, dearest Rose, have always been my example, and I have always admired your integrity. You sacrificed your marrying years to stay at home and take care of us. Then, here in America, the Lord brought a marvelous and loving husband into your life and blessed you with sweet little ones. I do long to see how they have grown, but I cannot, until I know my own dear charges are all safe and sound. I truly believe the Lord is sending me back to look after the boys. I join you in constant, fervent prayer that the Lord will return your husband to you just as I pray for John and our other brave Beaver Cove men.

With a sigh, Lily skipped over the rest and folded the heavy paper before putting flame to the candle and allowing a dollop of wax to drip on the outer edge and create a seal. She then stacked the missive atop the letter to Mariah.

Even as she lifted her night rail over her head, she lacked the absolute certainty that returning to the farm was God's leading. Part of her felt assured that she'd made the right decision, but the other part of her questioned whether the choice to go was merely her own willful desire. She wished the Lord would speak audibly to her as He had to Moses and Samuel in the Bible.

She dropped to her knees and spoke softly. "Father, if I'm not supposed to go back to Beaver Cove, please create a circumstance that will prevent me from making that mistake. I truly desire Your will, and not my own. But if I am to go, please, give the Gilfords the kind of tender love for Emma and Davy the children desperately need. I know I've asked this before, but"— she shrugged—"perhaps I should ask You to give me peace about leaving them here. I shall miss them terribly. And I needn't mention how nervous I am about riding a horse on such a long trip. You know my experience has been limited to short jaunts on my brother Tommy's pony in England and our gentle workhorse at the farmstead."

Lily paused and raised her gaze heavenward. "One more thing, Father. . . the men who will be escorting me are not the ones who accompanied Mr. Gilford. He says they come highly recommended, but still, a lone miss traveling with two total strangers. . ."

Huffing out a worried breath, Lily came to her feet. Surely the Lord was weary of hearing those same requests over and over. Time to get dressed.

Why, oh why, had she given in to her weakness? Lily knew she should have slipped out before the children woke up. But no, she'd had to have a last hug and kiss from each of them before departing. Now two whining, teary-eyed darlings tore at her heart as they begged her not to go.

"Please stay with us. . .please." Still in nightclothes and barefoot, Emma and Davy trailed Lily down the stairs and out the door. They stayed on her heels all the way to the gate.

Lily slid an apologetic glance to Mr. Gilford, who waited in the street with the two longhunters he'd hired to escort her. Beside them, three mounts and a packhorse raised tiny bursts of dust as their hooves pawed the cobblestone street in impatience.

Emma latched on to Lily's hand, tugging her backward. "Matt and Luke are bigger. They told you and Papa they could take care of themselves."

"I'm big, too." Davy pouted, his lower lip protruding. "I wanna go with you." He yanked on her dark gray skirt and elevated his voice to neighborhood pitch. "I wanna ride the horsies!"

"No, silly!" His sister jerked him away. "I want her to stay here with us, where it's safe."

Lily knelt and drew the little girl close, smoothing down her rumpled hair. "Matt and Luke can do the farm work well, but they don't know how to cook or do women's work. They've surely got the kitchen in a horrid mess by now."

"I—wanna—go!" Davy threw himself at Lily and clutched her shoulders, nearly toppling her.

She managed to disentangle him and tugged him around to the front to include him in the embrace. "There's a fine cook here, sweetie, and servants. And you have your grandma and grandpa to look after you and give you lots of hugs and kisses and read you stories until it's safe for you to come home. We'll all be together again soon. I promise."

The towhead squirmed free. "I ain't scared a no Injuns. I'll get a sword like my lead soldiers, an' stab 'em an' cut their heads off."

Rendered speechless by his tirade, Lily breathed with relief as Susan's father stepped in and scooped the boy up. "Davy, my boy, I do believe you need a few sword-fighting lessons first before you go charging off to fight, don't you think? How about you and I make us some practice swords? I've got just the right pieces of wood in my workshop." With a wink at Lily, he toted the diverted little fellow away.

Emma, however, clung all the tighter. "Please don't leave me. . . . Please. . ."

Lily's heart cinched as she kissed her darling's little red head. "Sweetheart, you know I have to go. And the only reason I feel it's right for me to leave is because I know you and Davy will be safe and loved here." She gently removed Emma's arms from around her and stood to her feet. "You know I'd rather stay here with you. But your other brothers also need someone to look after them and keep *them* safe."

Steeling herself against the tears rolling down Emma's fair, freckled cheeks, she strode to a long-legged dun and took the reins from the hand of one of the silent frontiersmen. His frizzy red beard hitched up on one side as he smirked at his hook-nosed partner. Neither hunter looked happy, and Lily wondered whether their displeasure stemmed from dissatisfaction over the price they'd agreed upon, their distaste at having a woman along on an arduous journey, or worse—concern about the Indians reportedly raiding farmsteads in Berks County.

She had concerns of her own—especially since she'd never ridden sidesaddle. Before she could voice any doubts, however, the red-bearded man rolled his hooded eyes to the sky and grunted as he hoisted her up onto the contraption.

Hooking a leg around the tall pommel, Lily had second and third thoughts about her decision to set off into the wilderness with the swarthy, rumpled pair. Nevertheless, she determined not to let it show. She would conquer this fear. She would.

Gazing down from that lofty height, her eyes misted at the sight of the shattered little girl sitting on the hard stones, arms about her drawn-up knees, weeping as she rocked to and fro.

"I love you, sweet Emmy," Lily somehow choked out. "We'll come back for you as soon as it's safe. Now go back in the house. There's a good dear." Without waiting for the men to mount, she clucked her tongue, starting the horse down the street before they could see her tears. Emma was still emotionally fragile, but right now, Matt and Luke needed her more.

Plodding along after the shaggy duo, Lily ground her teeth in vexation. The rawboned guides rode with their jaws hard-set, not even talking to each other as they led the way out of Philadelphia. All they'd done since setting eyes on her was look her up and down with ill-concealed disdain and then ignore her as if she didn't exist. She could only surmise that the two considered her a soft, silly female who had not the slightest inkling of what she was getting herself into. On the other hand, she decided as she emitted a spiritless breath, she *was* riding sidesaddle in a fashionable riding costume of summer wool trimmed with emerald velvet and a matching hat with a feathery plume. Perhaps they needed no further reason for their opinion.

The city buildings and mansions gradually gave way as the road led out of town toward Reading, and passing the last dwelling, Lily decided to make an attempt to dispel some of the men's misconceptions. She guided her docile mare up between them. "I don't believe we've introduced ourselves. I'm Lily Harwood, from Beaver Cove."

They both grunted and continued to stare straight ahead.

She tried again. "How might I address you gentlemen?"

The red-bearded one, obviously the spokesman, emptied his lungs and turned to her. "The name's Hap Reynolds. That there's Virgil Stewart." He indicated his cohort with a crook of his thumb.

"Mr. Reynolds and Mr. Stewart." She offered a polite smile to one, then the other. "I'm pleased to make your acquaintance."

"We don't much cotton to that *mister* stuff. Call us Reynolds an' Stewart, or Hap an' Virge. Yer choice."

She gave a hesitant nod, not quite ready to comply with such familiarity as first names. "Reynolds and Stewart, then. Well, could you give me some idea of how long it will take us to reach Beaver Cove overland?"

"Depends." The frizzled beard hitched again as Reynolds smirked at his buddy.

"On what?" It appeared she would have to drag information out of him a word at a time. She struggled for patience.

"The weather, the cricks, an' streams."

"An' the Lenape." Hook-nosed Stewart snickered. He flashed a gap-toothed grin at his pal and nudged his broad-brimmed hat a fraction higher.

Lily had no idea what a Lenape happened to be. "Is that a lake or a mountain?"

Reynolds chuckled at her naïveté. "Not *what*, missy. *Who*. They're the Injuns you folks insist on callin' the Delaware, after that river."

Despite the heat of the day, Lily felt a cold shiver. The Delaware and Shawnee tribes had been attacking from Fort Duquesne with the French. "Have there been more massacres between Reading on the Schuylkill and the Susquehanna?"

He shrugged. "Couldn't say. We just come south from the council meetin' Indian Agent Johnson in New York called. The man's doin his best to keep the friendlier tribes fightin' with us. Considerin' the mess them Brit generals is makin' of things, our allied Injuns is becomin' real standoffish."

A low chuckle rumbled from Stewart.

Lily did not consider that information particularly humorous. "I presume, then, that you're also rather reluctant scouts for the British. Is that correct?"

"More or less." Reynolds cocked his head. "We git our orders from the governor of Pennsylvania."

"I see. Then what Mr. Gilford told me is quite true. He must be a personal friend of the esteemed gentleman to be able to acquire your services."

"Don't know about that. But I never shy away from makin' a little extra coin on the side."

"Oh?" Lily wondered what sum Susan's father had paid them.

"Aye. The governor's sendin' us out to check on Fort Augusta, an' yer kinda' on our way."

"I was told it will take us two days to get to Reading."

Reynolds grunted with a nod.

"An' that's the last feather tick you'll be sleepin' on." The grin Virgil Stewart slanted her way made Lily uneasy. "Sure ya wouldn't rather take a nice easy riverboat trip up the Susquehanna?"

She refused to be scared off by his words—or his leer. "That would be nice, Mr. Stewart, but I cannot spare the time. Mr. Gilford's young grandsons are all alone on our farm." She paused. "Speaking of which, I noticed there's no extra musket for my use. Perhaps when we get to Reading you might help me purchase one that shoots true."

Four bushy eyebrows rose high as the scraggly pair eyed her with dubious expressions. Then Reynolds spoke up. "Those're awful big an' loud, missy. Ya sure ya want one?"

He seemed to enjoy having fun at her expense. Lily leveled a glare at him. "I will also require a horn of black powder. Enough so I can make a sufficient supply of cartridges before we start into the wilderness. It always helps to be prepared, would you not agree?"

Neither longhunter uttered another disparaging remark after that. She might be dressed like a simpering lady, but she refused to be treated like one. Still, she knew she'd be quite sore after riding on this silly female contraption all day. In all likelihood, tomorrow would find it difficult for her to walk. "By the by." She addressed Mr. Reynolds. "I should like to trade this useless sidesaddle for a regular one as soon as possible."

At that, the two sour-faced guides burst into a belly laugh.

"My pleasure." Reynolds's beard widened with his grin. "A good sensible saddle."

Lily surmised she'd finally earned a bit of respect in their eyes, but she still hadn't appreciated that suggestive leer from Virgil Stewart. She changed the subject. "I know the wilderness is vast, but is either of you acquainted, perchance, with Nate Kinyon?"

"Kinyon! That backwoods scalawag?" Reynolds tucked his scruffy chin. "We crossed paths now and ag'in, back when trappin' an' tradin' didn't guarantee a scalpin'. Once Virge 'n' me helped him out when he was in a tight spot with them heathens, too."

The news cheered Lily considerably. "Nate is my sister's husband. Mayhap you've met her as well, out along the Ohio. Rose Harwood."

Hap Reynolds whacked his knee and turned to his buddy. "Well, I'll be hornswaggled. This here gal's sister to that bondwoman ol' Eustice Smith took back to his tradin' post, rest his ornery soul." He switched his attention to Lily. "How's that purty Rose doin'—her an' that li'l orphaned babe she was a'motherin'?"

Lily smiled. "She and Nate married. They now live along the Potomac, where Nate and Black Horse Bob have adjoining farms, and are doing splendidly, as far as I know."

"Well, li'l missy." Reynolds nodded. "Since yer kin to Nate an' that li'l Rosie gal, Virge an' me'll be takin' extra care to git you home safe."

"I'd be most grateful for that." She relaxed a few degrees. "You two are a true godsend."

Virgil Stewart snorted through his nose, parting his droopy mustache. "I ain't never been called that b'fore."

But noting the pair's rather embarrassed, closed-mouthed grins, Lily knew she'd now be in good hands. She sent up a silent prayer of thanks to the Lord.

Chapter 16

Throughout the hard day's ride out of Reading along the Tulpehocken Creek Trail, the lanky guides spoke scant words to one another, and only then in whispers. Fearing a possible Indian attack, Lily spent so much time peering into the dense brush and trees crowding the path on either side that her head began to throb.

At last they reached a sheltered spot along the trail where they could camp for the night. But as wary as she'd felt earlier that day, matters worsened after a cold supper of jerked beef and biscuits when the men started drinking something that smelled suspiciously like rum. Fortunately neither of them had eyed her suggestively, but her fears doubled nonetheless. The confidence she'd felt three days ago after bringing Nate Kinyon's name into the conversation dwindled, and for the first time since departing from Philadelphia, she worried about her safety with these supposed protectors. Despite her exhaustion, she remained awake under her oiled canvas tarp until long after she heard snoring coming from both hunters.

Lily felt a smidgen of relief the following morning when the men appeared to have no lingering effects from their drinking, but it took her a number of steps after rising for her legs to lose their stiffness. She wished they could build a fire, since the glow would not be easily seen in the dense forest. But the guides chose not to.

Stewart handed her a biscuit from a grubby canvas sack and whispered into her ear. "The smell of smoke's a dead giveaway if any hostiles is about."

Hostiles! In close proximity? The fact that the man resorted to whispering increased her fears. Lily washed down the hard biscuit with cold water, trying not to compare the limited fare with the sumptuous breakfasts she had enjoyed at the Gilford house.

She untied the tarp shelter and folded it, noting that the covering was damp from sprinkles during the night. Her belongings and gear, however, remained dry. She encouraged herself with the reminder that God was with her. Recalling some of the experiences her sister Rose had laughingly related about her life in the wilds, Lily had to admit the Lord had definitely kept His hand on her sister through far worse circumstances than these. Rose was convinced that God always looked after those who belonged to Him. Lily focused on that thought.

She grabbed up the mare's bridle and blanket and strode through the trees to where the hobbled dun had wandered. She slipped the bridle over the horse's ears.

Hap Stewart came alongside and spoke again in that worrisome, soft rumble he'd used earlier. "After a spell, we'll be leavin' the crick trail and cuttin' south toward Fort Lebanon. We should git there sometime after high noon. We could stay there for the night, if ya like."

Lily continued to work, readying her mount for another day of travel. "Thank you, no. I'd rather keep going. I need to get home to the boys." More than a fortnight had passed since she'd left John and his sons, and she had no idea if any of them was still safe. There seemed no end of things to fret about, and she could only trust the Lord to look after them. *Please, Father, look after us all. Take this gnawing worry from me. Help me to feel Your peace.*

They broke camp and traveled onward. After a few hours, whenever they happened to break out of a stand of woods, they came upon cleared fields and farmsteads dotting the gentle hills and vales. Lily was especially heartened by the distant sight of a man driving a hay wagon. . .the first person she'd seen since leaving Reading yesterday morn.

Ahead of her, Reynolds nudged his chestnut gelding into a faster gait, and Lily and Stewart followed with the packhorse.

The wagon driver tipped his head politely when he reached them. *"Guten tag."* Obviously one of the German settlers who purchased land in the backcountry along with the English-speaking people, he drew his sturdy farm team to a halt.

Hap Reynolds touched his hat brim. "Folks hereabouts have any trouble with Injuns lately?"

The farmer rattled off something in German, then with a curt nod, slapped the reins over his team's backs and rumbled by with no more than a quick glance.

Lily had heard the Germans kept to themselves for the most part, though Indians attacked their settlements as often as they did those of the English. She looked over at Reynolds. "Did you understand anything he said?"

"No. We'll come up on the fort purty soon. If anybody knows anything, the militiamen posted there will."

The prediction proved to be true. But as Lily rode with her escorts into a large clearing a short time later, the fort's appearance came as a disappointment. In the center, a stockade of sharpened poles surrounded a blockhouse similar to the one her neighbors had built at Beaver Cove. In comparison to how John had described Fort Henry, this fortification was far less substantial. Fort Henry was built of stone. Still, riding toward the gates, she felt a sense of relief. Unlike their own blockhouse, this one housed militia, at least.

Glancing about, she saw several uniformed men out in the meadow, digging a trench. Another, just outside the gate, worked with a colt on a rope. Short and stocky, with the beginnings of light stubble emphasizing a pronounced underbite, he raised a hand to stop them, then strode in their direction, bringing the young horse along. "Where'd you folks come from? See any sign of a war party?"

Reynolds reined in. "Nope. We're comin' from Reading."

"Along the Tulpehocken Creek?"

"Aye."

The man shook his head. "A farmer and his wife were killed and scalped up that way four days ago."

"What about to the west?" Virgil Stewart asked. "Hear tell of any trouble out thataway?"

The soldier shrugged. "Can't say for sure. Whoever's still left between here and the Susquehanna ain't travelin' much. Leastwise, not in this direction. Some of our men are out rovin' that way now."

"No word a'tall? That don't sound good." Reynolds met his pal's gaze then turned to Lily. "Ya sure ya wouldn't rather stay here where it's safe, lass?"

"Are you and Stewart going on?"

"Aye. But we got orders."

"Well, so have I." The Lord did want her to keep going, didn't He?

⌒

The afternoon waned as the trail grew perceptively more narrow. Lily again rode single file between Reynolds and Stewart, while the packhorse brought up the rear. They'd passed the last cutoff to a farmstead a quarter hour ago, and an uneasy feeling began gnawing at her. She tried to fix her mind on more pleasant subjects.

When a cool breeze found its way through the thick undergrowth, Lily gladly turned her damp, sticky face into it, recalling the glorious, lavender-scented bath she'd had at the travelers' inn. The first thing she'd do when she reached home was fill the tub with tepid water and soak away her tired muscles.

"Hold up!" Stewart's order came from behind. . .and not in a whisper.

Hap Reynolds whipped his horse around and eased past Lily to reach his partner.

Lily's heart pounded as a strong, acrid smell assaulted her nostrils. Smoke. She searched forward through the tree growth to where thick clouds of smoke billowed upward—much more than would issue from a chimney.

"Stay here with the gal." Without another word, Reynolds circled his pal and the packhorse. Within seconds the dense forest swallowed him up.

"Might as well rest the horses," Stewart muttered, dismounting.

Grateful for the chance to rest her backside as well, Lily swung to the ground. When she saw Virgil Stewart pull his musket from its scabbard, she did the same and stepped back into the brush. The two of them stood on alert, waiting, listening, expecting Hap Reynolds to return with news. Minutes stretched like hours, but peering up at the sky, Lily saw that the sun had moved very little.

The clatter of fast-moving hoofbeats announced Reynolds's return back up the forest trail. He pulled hard on the reins, bringing his panting, lathered horse to a stop. "Got there too late. The man an' his wife are dead." He grimaced and wagged his head. "Them murderin' savages took off on foot with what looked like the tracks of two young'uns. No more'n four or five years old, I'd say."

Davy's age. Lily gulped past a lump in her throat.

"They must'a just left. The corpses was still warm an' seepin'." He shot a look to his partner. "Hand off that packhorse to the gal, Virge. We can catch 'em easy a'fore it gets too dark."

Lily's blood turned cold. They were leaving her here? Alone?

Stewart untied the packhorse from his saddle. "How many is there, ya 'spect?"

"Four, near as I could figger." He turned to Lily. "Take them horses off the trail far 'nough so's you can't be seen. Unload 'em best ya can."

Her insides trembling, she wanted to beg them to stay with her. But. . . little ones. How could they not try to save innocent children?

"If we ain't back by mornin', head on into the Palmyra settlement. It's only a couple a miles ahead." He pointed in the direction they'd been traveling.

Lily had no choice but to tamp down her panic and tug her dun and the packhorse between two matted spreads of berry bushes.

The longhunters snatched up fallen fir limbs and brushed over her tracks, then mounted and rode farther down the trail a short distance before cutting off on the other side.

Watching after them through the branches of her haven, Lily appreciated their having taken that small precaution on her behalf. She did her best to ignore her fear and stripped the gear and supplies from both animals then hobbled them. In all likelihood, the men wouldn't return for hours. She decided it might be prudent to find a safer, more secluded spot to hide, some distance away from the horses. No matter how well hidden the animals were from the trail, they could easily give away her position by making rustling noises or whinnying.

After filling her pockets with hard buns and dried meat, she slung a blanket over her shoulders and strapped on her water flask, cartridge pouch, and powder horn. Then, hefting the tall, awkward musket to one shoulder, she plucked a fallen fir branch from nearby and began the painstaking job of wiping clean any footprints she'd made backing away from the horses.

By the time she came upon a hemlock with low-hanging limbs skirting the ground, her whole body ached from trying to keep the musket aloft while sweeping away the traces of her presence. She swished debris back across the bared earth and stretched to loosen the kinks from her spine. With a backward glance in the fading light, she was fairly sure she'd left no readable sign.

She hunkered down into a crawl and backed herself and the six-foot-long weapon beneath the limbs, brushing away the last of the evidence. When she bumped into the tree trunk, a nervous giggle erupted. She slapped a grimy hand over her mouth to stifle the sound. If Mistress Gilford could see her now. The woman had been so adamant that she have just the perfect bonnet to go with her fancy riding costume. . .and here she sat in dirty homespun on old, dusty pine needles with cobwebs in her hair.

Her mirth vanished when the reason she'd been left here hit her full force. Two people lay dead among the ashes of their home, and their little ones had been kidnapped. What horrors had those dear children witnessed before the savages hauled them away? *Dear Lord, look after those babies. Take care of them. They must be so frightened, like my sweet Emmy was. And please bring Mr. Reynolds and Mr. Stewart back safely. I cannot imagine traveling on without them.*

Hours dragged by. Lily had long since eaten from the food in her pockets and watched darkness descend until she could no longer see her hand before her face. She'd never felt so alone in her life. Where were her guides?

A distant gunshot echoed through the woods. And another. Three more followed in close succession. The frontiersmen had only a single-shot weapon apiece. Had they been wounded? Killed?

Please, dear God, don't leave me out here alone. . . .

Chapter 17

Something crawled across her nose. Lily groggily brushed it away and opened her eyes. *A spider!* She lurched up, fully awake, banging her head on the branch right above her. Dust rained down, probably bringing more of the hairy pests with it. Scurrying out from under her shelter, she dusted herself off, head and body, shuddering all the time.

Rays of sunshine peeked down through the canopy of forest leaves from a rather high angle. Lily realized that after catching only fitful snatches of sleep during the night and waking at every noise, she had finally fallen into a deep slumber.

But. . .she glanced around. The men. They never came back.

She reached cautiously beneath a pine limb for the musket and its fixings, then started moving slowly, silently through the thicket toward the spot where she'd hobbled the horses. After only a few steps, she caught a whiff of smoke. Her guides would not have lit a fire. Renewed panic surged through her. No. She must not give in to fear. She had to stay calm. There might be a farmstead nearby.

The breeze appeared to be blowing from the other direction this morning and could have carried the smell from the Palmyra settlement. But like yesterday's smoke, this was far too strong and heavy to be from a mere fireplace.

Lily stepped gingerly out into a tiny clearing and glanced overhead. Billows of thick smoke crawled toward her from not very far away.

What should she do? Yestereve, a farmstead to the east of her had burned to the ground. Now one from the west had met the same fate. For all she knew, Indians might have passed right by her on the trail during the night. Another shudder rocked her being.

A few yards off to the side, a sudden fluttering of feathers almost stopped her heart as a covey of ground birds took flight. What—or who— had flushed them out?

A horse neighed in the distance. Then another. Lily prayed it was the longhunters returning. She stopped and cocked an ear, waiting for an answering neigh from the men's mounts.

None came.

Backing toward the fir tree again, she used her free hand to brush away her footprints until she and the weapon were again within its shelter. The single shot from her musket would do little good.

Seconds passed. Having heard nothing else, Lily felt foolish, huddled here with the spiders. She used the rifle to move a branch aside.

The rumble of low voices came from where she'd left the horses. Hopefully Reynolds and Stewart had come back for her. But. . .on foot? She hadn't heard hoofbeats.

Lily strained to gain sight of her guides, but with all the trees and underbrush she'd put between herself and the animals, it was impossible to see anything. The frontiersmen would have no idea where she was. Surely they'd call out to her. She waited. . .and waited.

When she detected the snap of twigs and the clomp of horse hooves, Lily surmised that the animals were being led back onto the trail. Surely the longhunters wouldn't go off and leave her.

But what if the pair assumed she'd gone on to Palmyra? After all, she'd carefully covered her tracks.

Unless these were Indians. . .the ones who'd set the farms ablaze!

Slowly, noiselessly, she crawled from beneath the branches. Keeping below the undergrowth, she inched toward the small meadow and raised her head for a peek.

No one was there.

She could still hear sounds coming from the direction they'd taken, so she rose cautiously to her feet. A dire realization came to her. Whoever it was had crossed the trail and headed north!

Sprinting to the place where she'd left the mare and the packhorse, she stopped and checked the ground. A multitude of footprints met her gaze—too many to have been made by Reynolds and Stewart. And all of them were from moccasins!

Overwhelmed at how close the Indians had been to her, Lily's knees began to give way. Only the support provided by her musket kept her from sinking to the ground. As strength slowly flowed back into her, she inhaled another strong breath of smoky air. *She* might be safe for the moment, but what about the folks who lived in that house? Had they been warned? She didn't recall hearing any gunshots. *I pray, Lord, that they got safely away before the savages got to their farm.*

And what about children! Had any more been captured? Mr. Reynolds had told her that Indians sometimes stole youngsters to hold for ransom. Lily scanned the footprints more closely, looking for small ones. When she found none, she nearly cried with relief. But what if she had? What could she have done? She'd never felt more helpless in her life. *Dear Father, please tell me what to do, which way to go. I have no idea.*

No matter how much she dreaded it, she knew she had to go to the burning farm. Someone there might still be alive and in desperate need of help.

⌒

About half a mile to the west of her haven, Lily came upon a clearing where an assortment of buildings smoldered. During her trek through the woods, she'd hoped and prayed neighbors in the vicinity would have seen the smoke and hastened to help. But to her great disappointment, no horse or wagon team sat parked in the barnyard. No one had come.

Taking full measure of the scene, Lily realized the farm lacked even its own wagon, nor was there any livestock in the pens. The family must have fled after spotting smoke issuing from the neighboring farm.

She stared forlornly at the smoking ruins, knowing the same could happen to the Waldon farmstead. Even if this family had not suffered the vicious attack, they'd lost their home and all their worldly goods. It was almost September. Many of the crops were already harvested and would have been stored to see them through the long winter. It was a huge loss.

Whatever had possessed her to leave Matthew and Luke alone at the farm? She should have insisted that John hog-tie his sons and toss them into the canoe. Filled with renewed urgency, she purposed to get to the boys before the Indians did. She would get them safely out of there.

But another chilling thought gave her pause. John had said the Palmyra settlements lay no more than ten miles south of Beaver Cove—and the Indians were even now cutting through the woods and heading in that direction!

Dear God, I beg of You. Keep my boys safe until I get to them.

Shoving the musket through a tangle of thorny bushes, Lily would have given anything to feel safe enough to travel on the trail, but she had no idea where the small raiding party was headed. They could have changed direction. Worse, they could be a part of a larger group sent by the French to ravage the countryside.

By staying close to the trail, she'd reach whatever fortification might exist at the Palmyra settlement. There she hoped to find someone to guide her across the hills to the Swatara Creek and Beaver Cove.

The ever-present stench of smoke lacing the air gradually diminished as she distanced herself from the burning farm, but the smell grew powerful again a short time later. Perhaps the wind had shifted. Wiping her grimy finger on a fold of her skirt, she licked it and held it aloft. The wind had not changed. Another place up ahead of her must have been set ablaze.

Lily felt utterly defeated. Tears stung her eyes and blurred her vision. Savagely she swiped them away, loathing her weakness. She would not give up. She would head north on her own. She had no other choice.

Checking her pockets, she found she still had a hard biscuit and two pieces of dried beef. She'd save it for supper. And if she didn't get back to the cove before dark, she'd survive one more night in the woods. She'd done it before. At least it was still summer. Thank heaven for that.

She filled her lungs with air. Turning toward the trail, she listened for several seconds, then crossed it, brushing away her footprints as she went. She was now on the north side—the same side taken by the Indians who stole her horses. And the same side as the last burning farm.

Determined to keep her eyes and ears alert, she dodged through the thick forest growth, keeping the source of light filtering through the trees to her right. She didn't know if she would reach the Swatara above or below Beaver Creek, but she'd worry about that detail once she came to the river.

The sun had risen high in the sky by the time Lily hiked down a rocky gully and into a small glen with an inviting spring. She stopped to fill her water flask and take a short rest. The small pool edged by water grass and a few reeds looked enticingly cool. As she filled the drinking container, she took a precious moment to enjoy the commonplace sounds of birds twittering overhead. A squirrel chattering as it watched her from a tree branch made her smile.

Once she'd corked the flask, she splashed water over her face to clean off the accumulation of perspiration and dust. It felt incredibly refreshing. She realized her feet needed attention as well and quickly stripped off her shoes and stockings, then sat down on a mossy boulder and lowered her ankles into the cool pond.

Eyes closed, she reveled in this small luxury as her feet began to lose their pain, only to be replaced by the aching of her shoulders and arms from lugging the heavy musket and using the awkward weapon to clear the way before her. She'd gotten so little sleep, it was hard to resist the temptation to take a nap in the cool grass.

That would have to wait for another day. With a sigh, she pulled one of the pieces of meat from her skirt pocket and bit into it.

A twig snapped behind her!

Chills shot through Lily as she whirled toward the sound.

No more than twenty feet away, a stag stared at her through some ferns. Vastly relieved, she sighed. She'd invaded his watering hole. But how easily it could have been savages. Chiding herself for having become careless, she stuffed the dried meat back into her pocket and raised her feet out of the water. She patted them dry with her skirt and replaced her footwear.

Suddenly the deer bounded away through the trees and the squirrel above stopped chattering. The sound of breaking twigs and slapping brush made its way down into the gully. Something big was coming!

Grabbing her musket, Lily dove off the rock and into a stand of ferns among the trees. Would a bear sniff her out? She certainly smelled ripe enough. It took only seconds to realize the noise was not being made by a large animal, but by men moving swiftly as they splashed through the small brook below her and up the other side of the hill.

She cautiously raised her head enough to have a look. Through the smattering of tree trunks, she spied several nearly naked Indian braves. One pulled the packhorse still loaded with the food and blankets and other necessities that would have provided sustenance for her homeward journey. She ducked back down immediately, her heart pounding. Likely the raiding party had done its worst and was now heading northeastward, toward the Swatara Hole, where the creek cut through Blue Mountain to the north.

Lily hoped they were the only raiders in the area. She'd wait here a little longer, then travel on.

When she again set out for home, the close call gave wings to her feet. But before an hour passed, heavy clouds rolled in, and the sky darkened. The faint scent of rain carried on the breeze. Without the sun to guide her she could no longer be sure which way north lay. Didn't moss grow on the north side of trees? She searched about but couldn't see moss anywhere.

Then she remembered something John had once told her. The Swatara Creek was the watershed all the little brooks and streams of the area fed into. All she had to do was follow any one of them, and she'd eventually come to the creek. *Thank You, dear Lord. You truly are looking after me.*

Feeling more encouraged than she had all day, Lily walked down a slope that led to a tiny streamlet. If she followed it and hurried, she might reach Swatara Creek before the rain let loose.

She did not. Not more than an hour or two later, the clouds opened up and great dollops of water splashed down onto the tree leaves, dripping off branches. Lily desperately yearned to go on, but she loathed getting drenched with night approaching. She looked around for the nearest big tree with thick branches and huddled against its trunk, tucking her legs and damp hem as close as she could.

Daylight faded without the rain slowing down, and morose thoughts filled Lily's mind. Here she sat under a tree again, this time wet from head to toe. Shivers wracked her body. What if she never made it home? What if she were captured and hacked to death, or mauled and eaten by some wild animal? No one would ever know what became of her. The little ones, Davy and Emma. How would they fare if they lost both their "mothers" in the same month? And the boys. They could be under attack at this very minute. *John, your children need you to come home. I need you.* She hugged herself all the tighter. *I need you so desperately to hold me close, to tell me everything will be all right.*

Sloshing and crunching sounds coming across the debris and fallen leaves overpowered the sounds of rain.

Lily snatched up her musket. Had someone come across her tracks? Had she been followed?

Chapter 18

"That's my boy yonder!" A big grin splashed across Patrick's face.

John followed his friend's gaze and saw young Michael MacBride on the opposite side of the Swatara, waving his arms and jumping up and down.

With a gleeful shout, the lad swung around and ran back to the house, likely to fetch his grandfather so the raft could be brought across the water.

John was relieved to see the MacBride farmstead still standing. Several militia rovers had reported recent attacks on homes a few miles away on the outskirts of the Palmyra settlement. After he and Pat passed a particularly gruesome scene where all the buildings lay in ashes and bodies had been left to rot after being hacked and scalped, they were glad to hear that remaining families in the area had sought shelter within the stockade. John and Pat were frantic to get home and check on their own dear ones.

Even with Nate Kinyon and Black Horse Bob tracking for them, it seemed John and his roving party had only been chasing ghosts. The

Delaware war party sneaked past the Swatara Fort in the Hole, then split up and split again. For the past three days, John's group, along with Nate and Bob Bloom, had tracked one small band of raiders. But just when they thought they were closing in on the savages, the trail vanished in a stream. The Indians had sent off a packhorse to throw the searchers off track. John's group found the decoy but never discerned the point where the war party had emerged from the water.

The loose packhorse was minus all goods except tied-on haversacks. John figured its owner must be lying dead somewhere. The gravity of the situation compelled their leader, Sergeant Forbes, to allow Nate and the Beaver Creek men to travel on to their cove, while Bob and others continued the search for the war party.

John ground his teeth. If Fort Duquesne wasn't taken from the French soon, vicious raids could go on forever—and Beaver Cove would inevitably be targeted. Sloughing off his frustration, he dredged up a grin at the cheerful greetings from the other side of the broad creek as Ian MacBride and his grandson hauled the raft they had rigged with a ferry rope over to fetch them.

Jackson Dunlap moved to John's side, a sullen glower darkening his brown eyes. "Sure wish you didn't send Lily away." The stocky young man had voiced that comment at least a dozen times over the past weeks. "Me an' Frank's enlistments is up the first of September. Near as I can reckon, that was yesterday. We won't be goin' back. Neither of us."

"So you've said." John kept his eye on the raft.

"An' like I tol' ya, I was plannin' on takin' her to wife now that she ain't bound to you no more."

John nodded a response. He'd already explained his reasoning to the persistent upstart till he was blue in the face.

Jackson droned on. "Soon as I see my folks, I'm headin' on out to fetch that li'l gal back here. Her sister lives on one of them tobacco farms on the Potomac, don't she?"

John cut a glance to Nate Kinyon. Being a backwoodsman himself, Nate didn't seem to have a problem with this jackanapes courting Lily.

But John did, and he detested being trapped in this same conversation with Jackson yet again. "Her sister lives on a *very prosperous plantation*." He hoped the emphasis on the Barclays' prosperity would dampen the guy's enthusiasm a bit.

It didn't.

"Aw, that don't matter none to Lily. I heard her say a dozen times she placed more value on friends she has here than she would any amount of silver or gold. An' I figger she values *me* a whole lot more'n any of that truck."

John couldn't recall a single instance when Lily had brought that young buck's name into a conversation, nor had he ever caught her stealing a glance at the burly lad. If she'd expressed the slightest interest in Jackson Dunlap—or any other young man in the settlement—John was certain he'd have noticed.

As thoughts of Lily danced across his mind, he envisioned her tearful farewell, the desperate look that tugged at his heart. The tears she'd shed had not been for the Dunlap kid or that brother of his. They'd been for—

Well, maybe not for himself directly, but certainly for his boys and for the farm they'd built together.

The raft thudded against the bank. Ian and Michael jumped ashore and went to hug Patrick. John and the others waded in to help hold the craft steady so Jackson and Frank could load the packhorse onto it.

Once everyone was aboard, eager hands grabbed hold of the ferrying rope while Ian poled the raft away from the bank. Then the older man set the pole down and stepped cautiously across the lashed logs to John.

"I kinda hoped to see Lily-girl with ye."

"With us? Why would you expect that?"

The raft lurched a bit, and the Scotsman clutched John's arm for support. "Ye dinna' hear, then? We rafted a couple backwoods fellas across the crick 'bout an hour ago. They was escortin' her back here an' lost track of her."

"*Lost track of her!*" Shocked, John used his musket to steady himself on the rocking conveyance. "What do you mean, *lost track of her*?"

Frank Dunlap's hooded eyes grew wide. "Ya talkin' about Lily? She's missin'?"

Ahead of them, Nate, Jackson, and Pat stopped tugging on the ferry rope.

Ian scanned the group with his shrewd blue eyes. "A pair of frontiersmen escortin' Lily back here to the cove rode into John's place awhile ago, hopin' the lass made it back on her own."

His jaw set like granite, John thrust his musket into the older man's hands and snatched hold of the rope, pulling the clumsy raft across the creek as hard as he could with the help of the other three men. The instant it banged against the bank, he, Nate, and the Dunlap boys grabbed their weapons and took off along the wagon trail to his farmstead.

Please, dear God, let her be there. I promise never to be jealous again. If she has a mind to marry Jack or Frank or to go live with her sister, I won't try to stop her. Just let her be safe. That's all I ask.

Despite being completely winded by the time he and the others reached his cutoff, John kept going. He turned down the wooded path to the farm, pressing a fist to the hitch in his side as he ran down his lane.

Duke, ever on alert in the distance, started barking.

Before John broke completely out of the trees, his sons rounded the house and raced to meet him.

"Pa!" Matt slammed into him. "Come quick! Lily's missing!"

All strength left John. Panting, he struggled to regain his footing. "She's not. . .here, then."

Luke tugged on his arm. "We gotta go find her, Pa, before somethin' bad happens to her."

The rest of the group arrived, breathing hard, and surrounded the boys.

"Where are those worthless maggots who lost track of Lily?" Jackson grated out, his eyes angry slits. "Let me at 'em."

Matthew gestured toward the cabin. "Back there. At the house."

The words barely left his mouth before John and the others charged toward the place. Rounding the corner, John saw two tall, lanky men in hunter's clothes sitting on the porch *like they'd come to tea*!

The strangers both rose. One had his arm in a sling. "Kinyon!" one of them hollered.

"Reynolds?" Gasping for breath, Nate frowned. "Thought you was up New York way at that Indian council, you old scapegrace."

"We was. Till we reported to Governor Denny. He tol' us—"

"Quit yer blasted jawin'!" Jackson spat. "Where's Lily?"

The red beard on the longhunter's jaw hiked upward with his scowl as he shot Jackson a surly glare. He returned his attention to Nate and clambered down the porch steps. "I know the gal's yer kin, an' all, an' we was takin' real special care of her. But when we seen some Lenape braves carryin' off two young'uns, we tol' the lass to hide whilst we went to fetch 'em back."

His cohort stood on the porch, favoring his injured arm. "The varmints heared us comin' on them dad-gum horses of ourn an' started shootin' at us. We was lucky to escape with our scalps. Winged me good, they did." He indicated his shoulder with a tip of his grizzled head, then reclaimed his chair.

"Aye." Reynolds elaborated a bit more. "We made some fast tracks outta there. Figgered they might follow us, so's we went the opposite direction from where we left yer little gal. When we finally shed 'em an' got back there, she was gone, an' so was the packhorses."

"A whole passel of moccasin tracks was all over them horse prints, too," his buddy said. "But strange 'nough, there wasn't none of hers. I never heared tell of no savage wipin' away tracks of no victim, neither."

At the end of his patience, John latched on to the nearest frontiersman. "Well, she couldn't just disappear."

Reynolds peered down his nose at his captured arm, then eyed John. "We figger she must'a heared 'em comin' an' covered her own tracks." He paused. "Would the gal know to do that, ya think?"

"Our Lily sure would." Matt took John's hand. "She ain't no stupid city girl. Let's go, Pa. We gotta find her and bring her home."

Even as he and Matt turned to head out, Reynolds raised a hand to stop them. "Hold yer horses, boy. I ain't finished. Me an' Stewart made a wide circle around where we left the little gal, an' the only sign we come across was from them Lenapes. We lit out for the Palmyra stockade, hopin' she found her way there. But nobody seen her. So we rode on back to Fort Lebanon. No luck there, neither. Then we come here, hopin' the gal'd come home."

"Pa." Matt tugged John's sleeve. "I was just goin' out to saddle up Smokey. We gotta go find her."

John turned to frontiersman Reynolds. "Are you willing to take us back there? Show us where you left Lily?"

"Don't see as how it kin help, but we'll give it a try."

"Frank." Jackson elbowed his brother. "Run over to the Shaw place. Borrow his two horses while I round us up some extra food."

As irritating as the young militiaman could be at times, John was grateful the lad and his brother weren't hesitating to help with the search.

"You can take along that packhorse we found," Nate suggested.

"An' mine." Stewart rose to his feet again. "Ya kin take my horse. My arm's achin' somethin' fierce. I'll stay here an' look after the livestock for ya."

Reynolds glanced at Nate. "Did I hear you mention a packhorse?"

"Aye. Some Injuns we was chasin' used him for a decoy. Threw us off their trail."

The longhunter wagged his head. "Prob'ly ours. Did the beast still have our gear on him?"

" 'Fraid not."

"Well, let's go." Leaping off the porch, John sprinted to the stable. Who cared about some worthless horse when Lily was who knew where?

━━━

Within the hour, John, Matt, Nate, and the Dunlaps were again unloading horses with frontiersman Reynolds on the south side of the Swatara. A disappointed Luke had been left at home with the wounded longhunter.

Nate looked at Reynolds. "Why don't you take the Dunlap boys with you? Spread out and backtrack to where you left Lily. I'll take John and Matt and head upstream. No matter what, she'll have to cross the Swatara."

Matt gave a decisive nod as John hoisted him up onto the big pack-horse. "Lily knows the Palmyra settlements are south of us. Right, Pa?"

"I'm pretty sure she does, Son." *South, southeast. Would she be able to tell the difference?* It was easy to lose one's direction in these dense woods, especially when overcast and raining, as it had been yesterday. He hefted himself up onto Smokey's broad gray back. *Please be alive, Lily. Be alive.*

Nate cocked his head at Matt as they headed upstream along a narrow trace. "Boy, stay close to your pa. I'll search a ways up the first gully, then cross over to the second. You two ride up the trace an' track across from the second to the third, then I'll take the next, and so on. We'll cover more ground that way. An' remember to keep your eyes open an' your mouth shut. We think them war parties're headed outta here, but we ain't sure." He switched to John. "If you find Lily, shoot off a ball."

"Pa." Matt reined his mount alongside. "Would it be all right if I go with Mr. Kinyon? Maybe learn somethin' more about trackin'?"

The idea didn't appeal much to John. He'd just gotten home again. Besides, it was a couple of frontiersmen who had somehow managed to lose Lily.

"I'll see the boy comes to no harm," Nate said.

"All right. But, Matt, do exactly what Nate tells you, you hear?" With that, John heeled his mount into a trot ahead of them. The sooner he reached the second brook, the sooner he could start searching in earnest for Lily. Still, he couldn't deny that, in this vast wilderness, the chances of finding her were slim. She could be anywhere.

Setting his jaw with determination, he vowed to maintain hope. No one had spoken the words, but he refused even to venture anywhere near the thought that Indians had captured her. Not his sweet Lily. He would find her. . .or die trying.

Chapter 19

J ohn reined Smokey to a stop when he reached the Swatara. The tall trees edging the far shore were outlined with waning sunlight, and their shadows stretched across the water, making a deceptively beautiful scene. But this was not a time to appreciate God's handiwork. The sun would soon set, and Lily was still out there somewhere. He'd searched through the woods and along the creek trace for hours and hadn't found a single footprint that wasn't pocked by yesterday's rain. This area north of Beaver Creek was too rugged for settling. He had yet to pass a farmstead, so there was no place Lily might have gone for help if she was wandering lost out here. The weight of his discouragement pressed hard upon him.

Where was she?

He tried to fortify himself with the possibility that Reynolds and the Dunlaps might have already found her and were returning with her to the cove.

The sound of distant hoofbeats coming at a trot from along the trace fell on his ears. Nate and Matt must have finished searching their section and were on their way to the next one. Nate probably wanted to scour one more area before darkness set in. John waited for the pair, eager to find out if they'd come across any sign of Lily.

Within seconds the two came into view around a curve.

John waved, and his son returned a smile and a happy wave. The bittersweet sight was one more reminder of how much he had missed his children, missed being there to share their joys and triumphs, their hurts and sorrows. Two more months, and his enlistment would be up. He'd come home to them for good then—providing they still had a home left to come home to.

Despite the optimism in Matt's expression, John could tell by Nate's demeanor they'd found nothing. He spread his arms with a disappointed shrug.

Nate halted next to John's mount and spoke in a quiet tone. "How far d'ya think we covered?"

"Eight, maybe nine miles. Sound about right to you?"

"Hard to tell. Thought me an' Matt would go up an' over one more hill then call it a night. We'll meet ya at the next stream an' camp there—unless you'd rather head on home. I'll leave it to you."

John had never felt so helpless or defeated, but he couldn't give up yet. "I want to keep going for a while."

Nate reached over a big hand and gave his shoulder an encouraging squeeze. "I'm sure Lily couldn't vanish into thin air. Either Reynolds or us'll find somethin' soon."

An unwanted mental picture of Lily lying dead, her body broken and bleeding, tore at John's mind. "I told her not to come back. I *told* her."

"That's all right, Pa." Matt edged his horse nearer. "Lily's as brave as the rest of us. She learned to shoot real straight, and she never backed down at strange noises. Fact is, when me an' Luke was out away from the house doin' chores, she liked callin' us the Rogers' Rangers of Waldon Place. You know, after them rangers up in New York. They really know how to fight the Indians."

John nodded, knowing those men fighting with the English against the French and Indians had provided the bulk of the colonies' paltry victories.

"If we had more fightin' units like them," Nate added, "this war would'a been over a long time ago, 'stead a draggin' on like it is. Worst of all, it's us folks along the frontiers payin' the price, while them English generals dally around cozy an' safe, surrounded by thousands of soldiers." He popped a curious grin. "I say after we run them Frenchies outta here, let's do the same with them useless Brits."

John slanted a gaze his way. It was a radical idea, but it might make for an interesting conversation some other day. He exhaled a tired breath. "Well, reckon I'll ride up to the next stream and check it out. See you there in a while."

Moments later, as John skirted the outside of a large bend in the creek edged by a sizable hill, he realized he had yet to pass an inlet. With Nate and Matt taking a roundabout route, they wouldn't reach the next section till well after dark. He slowed Smokey almost to a stop. Maybe he should ride back and find them. The spot where they'd met awhile ago would do for the night.

"John?"

Startled, he peered up the wooded rise. Nate couldn't have caught up so soon.

"John, is that you?"

His heart jolted. A woman's voice!

Lily! Suddenly there she was, breaking past some brush high above him, half running, half sliding, as she scurried down the steep incline to him. Relief engulfed John. He leaped off his mount and started to climb up to her—then remembered the signal. He stopped and turned back, yanking his weapon from its scabbard. Hands shaking, he sprinkled black powder in the flashpan and fired the ball into the air—the loud, joyous announcement echoing across the river and back.

By the time he jammed the rifle back into its sheath and turned around, Lily, crying and laughing at once, ran into his arms.

He caught hold of her so quickly he banged his head on her musket barrel. But he couldn't have cared less. She was here, and she was. . . unharmed?

Easing her to arm's length and looking through a sheen of moisture blurring his vision, he took an assessing look. Her hair, matted and tangled, lacked its usual golden highlights. Her tattered gown was a pitiful mess of wrinkles and stains and soils. Her arms, dirtier than he'd ever seen them, were a map of scratches, scabs, and insect bites—and she'd never looked more heart-stoppingly beautiful. Noticing the muddy traces her tears were carving down her face, he took out his kerchief and dabbed at them. "I was so worried. Thank God I found you."

Then with an unexpected flash of anger, he tightened his hold on her shoulders and gave her a shake. "Why did you have to come back? I told you it was too dangerous."

"I. . ." She swallowed hard and gazed up at him, all hurt and helpless, dissolving away all his ire.

He cupped her sweet face in his palms and searched deeply into her eyes. "You had me worried out of my mind," he murmured. He brushed his lips across a nasty scratch on her cheek, then kissed another. Then he kissed her eyes with their tear-spiked lashes, tasting her salty tears. "I could've lost you, too."

"I had to come back."

Her voice was so choked with emotion, it ripped at his heart. He drew her closer, and his lips found hers. He felt her meld to him, and he couldn't help himself. He cupped the back of her head and deepened the kiss.

Lily emitted a throaty moan, and her weapon dropped to the ground as she wrapped her arms around him, making his heart ache with profound joy.

She was here.

He tightened his embrace. Vaguely, the pounding of horse hooves knocked at the edges of his mind.

"What the blazes is goin' on here!" Nate shouted. He skidded his mount to a halt.

Lily gave a shuddering breath and pushed away from John, her eyes flaring wide.

He didn't completely release her but heeled around.

Nate glared down at him from atop his tall horse. "I hope you ain't been toyin' around with my sister-in-law all this time."

Mortified beyond words, Lily stepped away from John and almost tripped over her fallen musket, compounding her embarrassment. Quickly she snatched it up. How could she have taken such gross advantage of him by turning his welcoming kiss into one of her deep passion for him!

And to think Rose's husband had witnessed her disgraceful conduct! She felt her face redden.

"Lily! You're alive!" Matt hopped down from his horse, the presence of the lad adding even more misery. He had to have seen it all as well. But he threw his arms around her with the same fervor his father had done. "Nobody said it, but we were all afraid you was dead." He gave her a smacking kiss on her cheek. "We been prayin' our heads off that we'd find you safe. Right, Pa?"

"Yes, Son. We sure have." John's words came from right behind her as he stepped close again.

"Enough chit-chat." Nate cleared his throat. "I still want an answer. What's been goin' on betwixt the two of ya?"

John rested a hand softly on her shoulder. "There is nothing going on, and no fault to be found in this wonderful lass. She's never been anything but pure and true. I was just so glad to find her, to know the Indians hadn't dragged her off to. . ." His face heated, and he lowered his gaze to the ground.

The dear man was defending her, taking the blame for her inexcusable actions. Mustering her courage, Lily raised her gaze to her brother-in-law. "If there's any blame here, Nate, it is rightfully mine. I was so overwhelmed and thrilled to be rescued, I'm afraid I lost all sense of decorum. I assure you, I shall not thrust myself on poor John in that fashion again."

Rose's husband looked from her to John and back and broke into a grin. He spread his arms. "Then come here an' give this ol' hunter a hug. I been mighty worried about ya myself."

Vastly relieved he was willing to overlook her indiscretion, Lily gladly accepted his welcoming embrace. Then he held her away a bit and regarded her. "Ya come mighty close to getting caught by them Delaware, ya know."

She nodded. "Three times. There were two groups of them. When I thought I was safe from the ones who took the horses, another bunch ran past. Thank God they never noticed my tracks. I truly believe the Lord blinded their eyes, because they crossed right over my footprints without stopping to search for me. And then to stumble upon John. . ."

Having remained behind her, John put an arm around her again and drew her close. "Well, you're safe now. We'll have you home in a couple hours."

Her expression flattened. "You mean I'm still two hours away? By horseback? I thought once I finally reached the creek I wouldn't have far to go."

A gentle smile curved his lips. "The Swatara starts turning more to the north up this way. Makes it a longer hike."

With a resigned nod, Lily looked at Matthew and smiled. "I see you brought Matt along. But where's Luke? Is he safe?"

Nate answered. "The boy's stayin' with Virge Stewart at your place."

"Mr. Stewart is at the cabin?" Lily stepped out of John's hold. "God is so good. I thought for sure my frontier guides had been killed. What about Mr. Reynolds?"

"He's fine," John said from behind her.

Matt sidled up to her. "Him an' the Dunlap boys headed back to where they left you, hopin' you'd made it to the Palmyra stockade by now. Him an' Stewart never could pick up your trail. You covered your tracks real good."

Cupping his face, Lily tipped her head and drank in the sight of him. "I did my best, just like you taught me." She then lifted her gaze to Nate. "By the by, I don't suppose any of you happened to bring along any food. I've had nothing to eat since yesterday."

"Sure did." Matt ran to Smokey's saddlebag and pulled out something wrapped in cloth. He handed it to her. "I cooked this last night for supper. Hope it's not too dried out."

Even before she unfolded the cloth, she could smell the delicious meat through the fabric. At least half a chicken lay in her hands. She squealed and barely managed to thank him before biting into a drumstick.

"Well. . ." Nate peered up at the darkening sky. "Best we git goin'. Lily can eat on the way. An' she should ride up behind the boy, to even out the weight on the horses." He darted a meaningful glance at John.

Lily realized the man was still blaming John for the kiss that was so passionate her lips still tingled. Perhaps she should divert him. After her brother-in-law hoisted her up behind Matt she turned to him. "By what miracle are you and John here?"

John hooked the bar that held the kettle of boiling water over the flames and swung it within reach as his sons brought in two more buckets of water. Using a pad, he lifted the kettle off the heat and trailed after them to Lily's room. It had been after nine when they'd arrived at the cabin, but Lily said she couldn't possibly go to bed filthy. These last batches of water should be enough.

For himself, he'd go down to the creek with Matt and Luke. Neither of them smelled any better than he did. He wondered if they'd bothered to bathe even once since Lily left for Philadelphia.

As the two emerged from her bedchamber with the empty buckets, John carried the kettle in. He found her standing before the looking glass, brushing the twigs and tangles from her surprisingly long tresses.

She glanced briefly at his reflection. "I'm such a horrid mess."

He wanted to tell her she was the most beautiful mess he'd ever seen.

She hadn't worn her hair down for years, so he had no idea it flowed so far down her back. He resisted blurting out the compliment and substituted one less personal. "A warm soak and a good night's rest will put you to rights again, I'm sure."

"John?"

He met her image in the glass.

"Thank you." Having spoken quietly, she continued to occupy herself with her hair.

He noticed that a bar of the perfumed soap she used lay on a chair next to the tub, along with some towels. The items sent his mind in a dangerous direction. Heat from the kettle's handle began to radiate through the cloth, reminding him he had yet to empty the contents into the waiting tub. Steam billowed upward as he quickly dispensed the hot water. "I'll be taking the boys with me down to the creek for a good scrubbing. That way we'll all smell like roses in the morning."

Lily turned toward him. "One doesn't realize how dear the little niceties are until one is without them."

"Them and food," he teased, grinning. He remembered how she'd devoured the chicken they'd brought with them.

She treated him to a bit of a smile. "Yes. And food."

Her smile, her eyes, her presence gave his heart a jolt. Time to get out of here. Reluctantly he started backing out of the room. "Well, I'd best get after those boys of mine." Stepping across the threshold, he closed the door. Closing himself out.

Seconds passed before it dawned on him he was just standing there staring at the door. He turned away, only to find Nate glowering at him from across the room.

"Me an' you need to talk," the big man said.

Chapter 20

Not a sound issued from the loft after Matt and Luke, bathed and utterly spent, climbed into their beds. Virgil Stewart apparently had no such leanings toward cleanliness. He used his injured arm as an excuse to avoid washing his rank self in the creek. Even now he lay in John's bed, smelling up the entire room.

John was disgusted that Lily would have to rewash the bedding she'd left clean for his use. But with her kind spirit, she'd always do what needed to be done. In any event, there was no need for anyone in the house—particularly her—to hear whatever Nate had to say to him. He handed Lily's brother-in-law a cup of tea. "Why don't we go sit on the porch?"

"Sounds good to me." Nate led the way outside and took the far chair, stretching his long legs out before him as he sipped from his mug. "It's September already. Won't be havin' too many more porch-sittin' nights this year, I 'spect."

"No, reckon not."

Not far away, a pair of bullfrogs croaked back and forth, joined by sporadic hoots from an owl and the rhythmic chirping of crickets.

It seemed Nate was going to start with pleasantries, so John took a moment to gaze up at the brilliant stars sparkling like diamonds against the blue velvet sky.

"Me an' Bob Bloom, we been gone from home since April. We've run for our lives out there more'n once. Sure hate the thought of never getting to see my little ones again, or my own Rose of Sharon."

Studying Nate's profile in the starlight, John sighed. "I know. It's stone-hard. I wish we could make a separate peace with the Indians, separate from the British, I mean."

"Won't happen. Not as long as the French keep dolin' out goodies to the tribes. The Indians want easy access to European trade goods, an' if they have to spill a little blood to get 'em, they will. The tribes been raidin' one another for supplies an' slaves for centuries. It's a way of life with 'em."

John mulled over the words and nodded. "Well then, I hope the British navy is doing a better job of blocking the mouth of the St. Lawrence River than our English generals are doing out in the field. Looks like our best hope is in stopping French supplies from coming in altogether."

Nate huffed through his nose. "Some inglorious way that'd be to win a war."

Taking a sip of tea, John grunted his agreement. "All I know is I'll do my family far more good by leaving Fort Henry in November. I was wrong to leave them here alone."

"Speakin' of that. . ." Nate turned to John. The inquisition was about to start. "No self-respectin' man would go off an' leave his wife's baby sister here in a situation like ya have here these days, neither."

"You're absolutely right." John suddenly refused to let the man continue on to where he was headed. The subject was far too painful. "I've decided to send Lily *and my boys* downriver this time. It's obvious I can't protect them from a distance."

"Glad to hear that. Then Lily'll have no obligations to come back here. Once she delivers your lads to their grandparents, she can go on to the Potomac. I know Rose'd love the company. She always set such store by young Lily."

The man was talking as if John had nothing to say about the matter. Still, he didn't want Nate to know how much this conversation gnawed at his insides. He kept his tone casual. "From what you said earlier, your place is just as vulnerable to attack as mine is. It'd be better for Lily to stay with her sister Mariah. I'm set on that."

Nate gave a slow tip of his head. "I reckon that'd be best. I been after Rose to take our children and go there, too. But she's too attached to her little yellow house, an' it's like pullin' teeth to get her to go someplace else."

"It is hard, leaving everything behind." *And everyone. Lily.* John stood, his heart aching sorely, and tossed the remnants of his tea out in the yard. He was in no mood to sit out here any longer with this accuser. "I'm done in. I'm going up to the loft to sleep with my sons. You're welcome to share my quarters with Stewart."

Nate chuckled. "If you don't mind, I'll bed down out here where it's cool—an' the air's a whole lot fresher."

<hr />

Lily awakened with the melody of a hymn in her thoughts. She mouthed the words silently as the familiar tune swirled through her mind. *"O God, our help in ages past, our hope for years to come. Our shelter from the stormy blast, and our eternal home!"* She smiled, remembering how God had sheltered her when savages passed close by her not once, but thrice. And He'd sent John to bring her back here. Home.

This morning she felt anything but guilty about a kiss she probably would have given *any* rescuer—even Rose's husband had he been the one to find her.

Stretching away her stiffness, she glanced out the open window to where birds already trilled the glorious morning, even though it was nowhere near full daylight. All the better. It would give her extra time. Her men deserved a hearty breakfast after all they'd been through on her behalf.

She bounded out of bed to dress while whisper-singing another stanza of the song. *"O God, our help in ages past, Our hope for years to come; be Thou my guide while life shall last, and our eternal home."* God had been her faithful guide through the dark and dangerous woods. She'd never again doubt He was watching over her, even in these perilous times.

Remembering the two small children the war party had snatched from their home, she dropped to her knees beside her bed. "Father, forgive me for not praying for them last night. I am trusting You to take care of them as You did me. Please, keep them as safe as if they were in Your own hand. In Jesus' most precious name, amen. Oh, and thank You for bringing me home."

She finished dressing, quickly twisted her night braid into a knot, and pinned it in place. Then, grabbing her apron from a spike by her door, she hurried out to the hearth. She wanted desperately to glance up to the loft, where John slept with the boys, but she fought that desire and refrained from even the slightest peek.

But how nice it would be if he woke before the others and we could enjoy a cup of tea together. . . .

No one stirred while she got a fire going and put water on to boil. Recalling how John always bragged about her biscuits, she quietly got out a mixing bowl and all the makings and in no time at all had a batch baking in the dutch oven. Then she stepped outside to get some side pork from the smokehouse and eggs from the coop.

Closing the door quietly behind her, she spied her brother-in-law asleep at the far end of the porch. She cringed, knowing he'd caught her kissing John square on the mouth, and guilt made her cheeks burn again— as they were prone to do every time she saw him. After leaving the porch on tiptoe, she ran all the way down near the creek to the smokehouse. Maybe she'd even milk the cow before collecting the first laid eggs of the day, since the coop could be easily seen from Nate's position.

By the time Lily took the milk down to the springhouse and filled a pitcher of the creamy liquid for breakfast, Rose's husband was nowhere to be seen. She did spot Matt and Luke, however, on their way across the yard to tend to morning chores.

The younger boy caught her eye and waved. "The biscuits sure smell grand. We ain't had much of anything good since you went off."

Stopping before the duo, she grinned, knowing Luke could devour three or four biscuits with no help from anyone. "Remember, we have guests this morning. You'll need to share."

He nodded, his eyes as bright as sunshine. "How soon'll breakfast be ready?"

Lily chuckled, tempted to ruffle that shaggy mane of his. Had her hands been free, she wouldn't have resisted the impulse. "As soon as I get this side pork sliced and cooked." She held the slab aloft for them to see. "If one of you would collect the eggs for me."

"I'll get 'em." A smile splashed across half-grown Matt's face. "Soon as I let the livestock out to graze."

"Thank you. I'd appreciate that."

The boys headed toward the stable, and Lily turned back for the house. If those two were up, likely the rest of the men had risen. And no matter how much she'd lectured herself, her heart tripped over itself at the thought of facing John and her brother-in-law together at the same time. But the biscuits did need to come out of the oven before they burned. Taking a calming breath, she walked purposefully to the house.

The door swung open before she reached it.

"Good morning." John smiled and stepped back for her to enter.

"Good morning." Her voice came out in a whisper as she passed him.

"Mornin', Lily."

Her eyes widened at the sight of Nate actually setting the table. "Them biscuits smell powerful good."

Having lost her voice a second ago, she acknowledged his greeting with a quick smile and a nod, then hurried with the milk and side pork to the worktable.

John followed her. "I'll slice it for you."

He'd done that chore for her a number of times in the past, but this morning his kindness felt considerably more intimate. "Why, thank you." Glad to have recovered her voice, she hurried on to the hearth. She scanned the room. "Mr. Stewart is still asleep?"

"I reckon." Nate plunked down a plate. "It's hard to get rested up with a shoulder wound."

"I see." She stooped to haul the dutch oven out of the embers with a poker.

"We need to have us a talk, Lily, b'fore John's boys come back in."

The serious note in her brother-in-law's voice set her on edge. "Very well. As soon as I get the biscuits on the table."

To her dismay, she accomplished the task far sooner than she'd hoped.

Both men had taken seats and now stared at her.

"Sit down a moment," John urged.

She looked from one to the other. Whatever they had to say, she wasn't going to like it.

"Please." John gestured toward an empty chair.

Reluctantly, she did as he bid.

He glanced from her to Nate. "Nate and I have decided you and the boys will be leaving here tomorrow morning. And this time I mean it. You need to stay where it's safe."

"Aye." Her brother-in-law nodded. "We decided the best place for you is with your sister Mariah."

They decided. *They decided?* Lily sprang to her feet. "And *I've* decided I'm staying right here—at least until John's enlistment is up. I'm certain the boys will side with me."

"No." Raking a hand through his hair, John stood up. "Not this time. The way the Indians have started breaking into small groups and moving fast, they can strike anywhere, anytime."

"You're quite correct in that regard." She retook her seat, pulling him down as well. Then, realizing she had hold of his hand, she quickly let go.

"I'm glad ya come to yer senses," Kinyon said.

At his gloating expression, Lily hiked her chin. "I never lost them." She switched her attention to John. "I've witnessed myself how and where this group of Indians strike. They don't attack anywhere near a stockade or a populated neighborhood like ours. They sneak up like cowards on outlying farms before the families know what's going to happen, do their worst, then hightail it back into the woods. Well, the boys and I do not live off by ourselves. We'll be quite safe here. After all, we have the blockhouse just across the creek. And you did say the Dunlap brothers aren't returning to Fort Henry. That's two veteran fighters we'll have at the very next farm."

John opened his mouth as if to respond, then closed it.

Lily continued before he could utter a word. "So, as you see, I, too, have been weighing the danger. Matt and Luke want to stay and protect their inheritance, and I'll not abandon them. After seeing the sort of life they'd have in Philadelphia—and considering the life they'd be relinquishing for one less worthy—I can do no less."

Nate whacked a hand on the table so hard, the plates rattled. "By George, Waldon, this gal has spunk. An' she does make sense. Lily, girl, if you wanna stay on here, I won't be one to stand in yer way." He cocked his head. " 'Course, come the first of November, I 'spect ya to go on to yer sister's. What d'ya say, Waldon?"

Lily felt her cheeks catch fire again. She couldn't bring herself to look John directly in his eyes.

"I don't like it." He paused and heaved a defeated breath. "But you didn't mind me when I told you not to come back. I shouldn't be surprised that you won't listen now. One thing I will have your word on, though."

Her gaze slid up to his.

"If those Dunlaps start trying to get too cozy, I want you to spend your nights at the MacBride place."

"You don't have to worry none about Jackson or Frank as long as I'm here, Pa."

Lily swiveled in her chair.

There stood Matt, his shirt cradling the eggs, her young, rustic knight in shining armor. She could not have been more proud of him.

Chapter 21

Later that morning, Ian MacBride and neighbor Richard Shaw volunteered to ride to the Palmyra settlement to track down Hap Reynolds and the Dunlap brothers and let them know Lily had been found.

With her presence on the farmstead for the next two months settled, Lily was happy John and Nate had decided to wait for Mr. Reynolds's return before reporting to their duties at Fort Henry. Facing another stretch of time without her most wonderful of men around to do the heavy work and ensure protection, she harbored the hope it would take days for Grampa MacBride and Mr. Shaw to find Mr. Reynolds.

As the day waned, she sat on the porch shucking corn for supper. She glanced past the men's laundry flapping in the breeze and beyond to the orchard, where John, Nate, and the boys plucked peaches from the fruit-laden trees.

The heart-gladdening sound of John's laughter could be heard in the distance. Lily watched as he hoisted Luke up into a tree and handed him a bucket. A tender smile tugged at her lips. How marvelous it was to see him enjoying time with his sons. His last homecoming had been dreadful, with Emma captured by Indians and Susan's demise.

Her gaze gravitated toward the wooded rise, where grass had only begun to cover Susan's final resting place. Susan and John had loved each other since childhood, and Lily knew John still grieved for his wife. She often saw him glance in the direction of the grave, and sadness would cloud his features. Then he would fill his lungs and assume a pleasant expression.

Tearing off a handful of corn husk, Lily wondered how she could ever presume John would care for her in that way. She had not the slightest doubt he loved her, but it was the kind of love one would have for a beloved little sister, not the romantic kind that would lead to marriage and endure for a lifetime. High time she faced that fact and began thinking about another future for herself. November was a mere two months hence.

She peered down at the ears of corn still to be shucked and forced her mind onto an entirely different subject: the sweet, juicy peaches the men would soon bring in. This was the first year of a bountiful crop from the trees the Waldons had planted when they'd first arrived. Envisioning a dessert of peaches smothered in sweet cream, Lily felt her mouth water. Next month the apples and pears would be ripe, along with the bright orange pumpkins. It would be a bountiful harvest, God willing.

Having grown up in a city where folks shopped for food on market day and farmers loudly hawked their fruits and vegetables, Lily had never given thought to much else besides whether or not Rose would make a good bargain. The transfer of money had taken precedence. But there was something wonderful and fulfilling about eating the bounty from one's own labors, one's own harvest.

She could understand why ever-so-proper Rose had chosen to live on a small farm. Naturally, her sister's love for that stalwart frontiersman had played a large part in her decision, but farm work was never-ending. If the war hadn't torn Nate away, he and Rose would be laboring together to make a future for their children—working side by side, always together, laughing, loving. . . .

Suddenly Lily's mind flooded with the memory of John kissing her face, her eyes, her lips, and her heart skipped a beat. How her lips had tingled then, how her whole being seemed to come to life.

Catching herself venturing to that forbidden place again, she ripped at a corn husk with renewed fervor. Far better to think about Mariah, the black-haired, violet-eyed beauty of the family who had arrived in America determined to use her stunning appearance to attract a wealthy husband. She had done just that. But not until the Lord taught her that true beauty came from within, that knowing the everlasting love of God and showing charity for others far outweighed the importance of having an easy life. The once vain, self-centered girl had blossomed into a sensitive, loving woman, after all.

A rasping snort behind Lily drew her back to the present. Virgil Stewart was slumped in a chair at the opposite end of the porch, napping as he'd done most of the day. She smirked as another nasal rumble emitted from the dozing frontiersman.

She bundled the stripped corn in her apron and took it into the house, where earlier she'd set a big pot over the hot coals to boil. Supper needed to be ready in time to allow a nice long visit this eve. Tomorrow or the next day the men would be leaving.

John would be leaving. She heaved a morose sigh.

$\backsim$

Midmorning the next day, John glanced out the window of his workshop and groaned in disgust as Hap Reynolds and Jackson Dunlap cantered in. With those two back, he'd have no excuse to remain at the farmstead another day. Even the wooden stock he'd been working on to replace the cracked one on Nate's musket was finished, except for the varnish that had yet to dry.

He shifted his gaze to the open doorway and spied Lily at the well, drawing up a bucket of water.

She went still, holding the handle, looking as distraught over the return of the men as John felt. *She hadn't brightened at all upon seeing*

Jackson! A gloating smirk pulled at his lips.

Abruptly she swung her gaze to his shop.

John quickly stepped back into the shadows so she wouldn't see him mooning over her. What would she think if she knew her dear Susan's husband couldn't keep his eyes—or his thoughts—off her? Especially not after having kissed her with such fierce passion. His chest still swelled as he recalled the taste of her sweet lips. With a hopeless wag of his head, he wiped the varnish from his hands and strode out to greet the men.

He stopped dead in his tracks when Jackson flew off his mount before it came to a full stop and grabbed Lily—*and kissed her right on the mouth!* John's hands curled into fists.

Nate, having emerged from the house, reached Dunlap before John got there. He jerked the upstart backward.

Angry though he was, John's main concern was Lily. To his overwhelming relief, she did not look at all pleased with the young man. She swiped at her mouth with her apron, rubbing away Jackson's kiss. She hadn't done that when *he* kissed her. He squelched the smidgen of a smile.

"That happens to be my little sister," Nate grated between clenched teeth. "An' she's not to be manhandled."

The young man looked only slightly repentant as he returned his attention to Lily. " 'Scuse me. I was just so happy to see you. We looked everywhere. We thought the Injuns took you for sure."

She planted her hands on her hips. "Well, as you can see, I'm perfectly fine. I've nothing more than a few scratches and blisters." Relaxing a bit, she glanced past him. "Where's your brother? Did he go on home?"

A lazy grin spread across Jackson's face. "Frank'll be along in a couple days. A lass at the Palmyra stockade caught his fancy. He didn't even mind that she spoke no more'n a smatterin' of English. He volunteered to stay an' help raise some cabins for the burnt-out folks."

Lily's demeanor softened. "Young lass or not, that was quite generous of him, especially since you boys haven't been home in months."

"Didn't John tell you? My enlistment's up. I'm home for good." He puffed out his chest.

Her slender brows rose, but she responded in a pleasant tone. "I'm sure your family will be most pleased to hear that."

Watching the exchange, John reminded himself that even though Jackson had just kissed her, Lily treated him with only polite regard. Nothing more.

Nate changed the subject. "Don't tell me more cabins have been set afire."

Not bothering to answer, the young man continued to stare boldly at Lily.

Hap Reynolds responded. "No. A couple a men searched the woods b'fore we got back, hopin' to pick up the trail of the little boys that got carted off. But with the rain. . ." He shrugged. "They're purty sure them raidin' parties headed back toward the Swatara Hole. Leastwise, that's what they're prayin' for."

The pleasant expression on Lily's face wilted at the news. "Those little boys. How old are they, do you know?"

"Six an' four, miss."

John watched her shoulders sag. She turned troubled eyes to him. "How horrid. Our Davy's age. We must pray for their safety every day."

Nate gave a solemn nod. "After noonin', ya feel up to headin' out again, Hap?"

The question tore John's attention from Lily.

"Sure do." The bearded hunter directed his next words to her, and he whipped off his worn hat, his face contrite. "I know we promised to keep ya safe, missy. We let ya down, an' I'm real sorry about that."

She offered him a pleasant smile. "You've no need to apologize. I don't fault you at all. You had to try to save those little ones. Anyone would've done the same. God took good care of me."

Awed by Lily's gentle response, John was dumbfounded. Heaven help him, he loved every word that came out of her mouth.

Obviously, so did Jackson Dunlap. John could see it in the young man's eyes when she turned to him.

"Jackson, I want to thank you from my deepest heart for spending so many days searching for me when you could have gone home to your family. They've missed you boys so, especially your mother. I refuse to be the cause of any further delay. So get back on that horse of yours, and don't keep the poor woman waiting any longer."

He tipped his dark head at her with an uncharacteristically tender smile. "For you. . .and Ma, I'll go. But rest assured, pretty gal, I'll be checkin' back with you real soon."

John knew that was no lightly given promise. He also knew he wouldn't be there to stop the lad.

"Pa!"

Turning toward Matt's call, John saw his boys running up from the creek with their poles and a string of fish, Duke bounding along after them. "The men. They're back already?" Panting, Matt came to a stop in front of John, with Luke a mere step or two behind. "You'll be leavin' now, won't you?"

At the pained looks on their young faces, John pulled his sons into a fervent hug and looked up at Lily.

Her eyes swam with tears.

How desperately he wanted her to stay on when he returned, stay with him and his children. But unlike that bold Dunlap rogue, he had no right to ask anything of her, no right to take advantage of her kind heart and her love for his children. After four long years of ministering to Susan and taking on the care of his children and everything else he'd thrust on the girl's slender shoulders, she deserved the chance to find a love of her own. To have her own little ones. There was only one right thing he could say. "I'll be back come November."

The cabin felt indescribably lonely when Lily rose the next morning. There'd be no sound of John's solid footsteps, no echo of his rich voice or laughter, no tender whisper after the kids were in bed. She tugged her wrapper tighter against the morning chill and pulled the bedroom window closed. The men must have taken the warmth with them when they left.

Not even Virgil Stewart, with his touch of fever, had stayed behind. "Don't like bein' closed in by jabberin' walls," he'd said. But Lily suspected it was the jabbering kids the longhunter wanted to escape. He'd turned out to be nothing but an old grumbler.

On the other hand, she was just as happy he'd taken his smelly self out of the house and out of Susan's bed. . .John's bed.

No! She could not allow her mind to dwell on that subject. Lily stopped halfway out of her bedchamber and closed her eyes. *Father in heaven, I beg you to take this awful yearning away. Help me to redirect my inappropriate feelings for John Waldon to some other man, a godly one I can love freely as my sisters do their husbands. I know You can do this. If You could blind the eyes of Indians to my footprints, surely You can blind the eyes of my heart to this man who can never belong to me.*

Slowly, gradually, a warm, gentle peace flowed through her. God loved her despite her weakness. "Thank You. . .so much," she whispered.

Realizing she could easily have been overheard, she darted a glance up to the loft, but the boys hadn't awakened. She smiled and padded to the hearth. They'd been so happy to have their papa home, even if it was for only that short time. Just two more months, and they'd have him home again for good.

At the thought, Lily's moment of peace vanished. Two months, and she'd have to leave not only John Waldon, but also the boys whom she'd grown to love. And sweet Emmy and her little scamp, Davy. How would she ever part with them all?

A Bible verse floated across the pages of her mind: *"Take therefore no thought for the morrow; for the morrow shall take thought for the things of itself."*

She sighed. Yes. Let tomorrow take care of itself.

That sweet sense of peace came flooding back.

Lily stirred the embers of the backlog to life and added a few small splits of wood, then reached for the empty water bucket. Walking outside with it, she felt a chill breeze sweep her face as she hastened toward the well. The woodshed, she noticed on the way, was already half empty.

She'd best get the boys started on filling it today. Winter could easily come early this year.

A sudden strong whiff of smoke wafted past her nose, and Lily froze. *Someone's cabin!*

She sprinted out to the center of the clearing and whirled around, trying to determine the direction of the blaze. Then, realizing the smoke issued from her own chimney, she felt utterly silly and went back to the well. Obviously, as little Emma had experienced, it would take awhile for her own terrors from the past week to fade away. But with God's help, she would overcome those frightful memories.

Still, lowering the well bucket down into the water, she couldn't help searching the woods for any sign of movement, any strange sound.

Chapter 22

Matthew and Luke moaned when Lily rousted them to feed and water the stock, but it didn't bother her. Every time they had to part with their pa, it had the same effect on them, and she knew it would take awhile for the pain to go away. Soon enough they'd turn back into the jovial helpers she knew and loved.

As she bent down at the hearth to flip the pancakes in the iron skillet, she recalled how a hymn had lifted her spirits earlier and determined to raise theirs as well. She lifted her voice to sing. "See Israel's gentle Shepherd stand with all engaging charms; Hark! How He calls the tender lambs, and folds them in His arms."

How wonderful it would have been to serve her brave lads a big helping of eggs, too. But the small flock of laying hens had failed to keep up with the demand of all the voracious eaters she'd had. At least there was plenty of butter and some peach jam she'd made yesterday after the men left. Walking outside, Lily clanged the bar around the triangle, calling the boys in to breakfast, then hurried back to pile the golden-brown flapjacks onto a platter.

Loud tromping issued from the porch. Never one to be late for a meal, Luke burst inside ahead of his brother. "What's for breakfast?"

"Pancakes, fried fish, and peach jam."

"Great! I'm starved." He flew to the table. "Sure am glad you're back."

Matt, still under a cloud, trudged behind the younger boy and plopped down at the table, his forearms resting on the surface, his shoulders slumped.

Lily's heart went out to him. "I hope you both remembered to wash up," she said brightly.

"Sure did." Luke displayed a pair of drippy hands.

"Better dry them on your napkin." Moving beside him, she forked a stack of hotcakes onto his trencher then moved to Matt's and filled his. She couldn't resist giving him a kiss on the cheek and softening her tone. " 'Tis hard, I know. But this time we can be assured he'll be back come November."

"You really believe that?" He cast a despondent glance up at her, his blue eyes dull.

"Of course I do. Your pa promised not to sign on again, didn't he?" Setting the platter down, she pulled out the chair beside him and sank onto it. "The good Lord tells us not to borrow trouble. He says we should only concern ourselves with the worries of the day."

He let out a huff. "Well, that's my worry today. An' you should be worried, too. Our Emma got took by redskins, an' then you had to run from 'em yourself, hidin' lost for days. An' Pa—he's probably out there right now chasin' after them wild savages. Anything could happen to him."

"Dear, dear Matty." Lily placed a hand on his. "It's wonderful that you care so deeply about things. It shows you're becoming a young man. But if you recall, your pa and the others were going directly back to the fort to report in."

"Aye, an' there's a whole lot of forest between here an' there where those heathens could be skulkin' around, waitin' to pounce."

"Well then, the thing to do is pray for him. Right now, while we ask the blessing for the food. Let's bow our heads." She paused. "Thank You, heavenly Father, for the bounty You provided for us this day. We lift up a special prayer for John and Nate and the two longhunters. Please surround them with angels and shield them from danger as they travel to the fort. And, again, look after the two little boys who were captured. Keep Your hand upon them while they're with the Indians and bring them safely home. We ask these things in the name of Your Son. Amen."

Matt grunted and reached for his glass of milk.

"Don't you believe God listens to our prayers?" Lily asked quietly.

"He might be listenin', but that don't mean He's gonna do nothin'."

Reaching over to him, Lily took him by the shoulders and turned him to face her. "We prayed for Emma, Matt, and God brought her back to us, didn't He? I prayed the Indians wouldn't find me, and they didn't. Surely that proves the Lord hears prayer."

"Oh yeah? I'll wager the mama and papa of them little boys prayed mornin' and night that the Injuns wouldn't come an' burn 'em out an' kill 'em an' take their little ones. But it still happened, didn't it? An' what about Mama? We prayed and prayed for her all the time, an' she still died. All them prayers didn't change nothin'."

Lily had no answer. What he said was true. Why *had* God saved her and Emma and not that other family? Still, she couldn't leave the subject there. "Tomorrow's the Sabbath. When Grampa Mac comes, we'll ask him those questions. I'm sure he'll know the reason why bad things happen to some people and not others."

Unimpressed, Matt scoffed. "He'll come up with somethin'. Probably the usual pretty words that sound good. He always comes up with those."

⁓

The day wore on, and Lily could not get Matt's words out of her mind. Added to that, the sweet peace she'd found early that morning had vanished. *Did God truly care about His children as much as the Bible said?* She ran the iron over the back of Luke's Sunday shirt. *Did prayer actually make a difference. . .or was it time and chance that affected the outcome of situations?*

A splintering sound broke into her thoughts, and she went to the window to check on the boys. For more than an hour now, they'd been taking turns splitting logs at the chopping stump and stacking the wood in the shed. As always, Matt's musket leaned against the wall of the woodshed, while old, shaggy Duke lay with his head on his paws, watching from nearby with his chocolate eyes at half-staff.

John's sons were good boys. Lily hoped old Mr. MacBride would have a satisfactory answer for Matt. And for her. Strange how a day could begin with such promise and then end with such doubt. It even looked like rain was headed their way. Perhaps it would be best to call the boys inside so they could work a few sums on their slates before supper.

After lifting the shirt off the workboard, she carefully folded it and set it atop Matt's, then carried the hot iron to its plate on the hearth. Unhooking the big spoon, she stirred the bubbling kettle of beans. She, Matt, and Luke would have some this eve; the rest would be shared with the neighbors tomorrow. It would be a treat to see everyone again. Lily was particularly anxious to learn how little Mary was faring now, after having been rescued with Emma. She replaced the spoon and went to summon the boys.

Suddenly, Duke's barking shattered the stillness.

Lily told herself not to be frightened. She reached above the door and took down the musket and powder horn, then poured gunpowder into the flashpan. She opened the door.

Matt and Luke were striding toward the path with Duke still barking as he loped beside them. Matt had his musket tucked under one arm, his gaze trained in the direction the dog had sensed alarm. Luke was armed now with the pistol, since Lily had purchased a musket for herself in Reading.

"Quit yapping, Duke, you mangy mutt," came a male voice in the distance.

Obviously someone they knew. Lily stepped out onto the porch to have a look.

A lone rider emerged from the dark forest.

"Aw, it's just Robby!" Matt called, tossing a glance over his shoulder to her. He jabbed a finger at the dog. "Pipe down, boy."

Robby! Why would he come here this evening, when the whole cove will attend the Sabbath service tomorrow? And with rain coming!

"Halloo the house!" Robby plodded around the corner on his old roan workhorse.

Matt and Luke went to meet him then walked alongside him until he reached the front of the cabin.

"What's up?" Matt frowned. "Somethin' wrong?"

"Sure is." Robby caught sight of Lily just then, and his whole face lit up with a smile. "I just heard you was back, Lily. I sure did miss you—I mean—*we* sure missed you. Ever'body did."

She offered him a genuine smile, though she remained on the porch. "I'm pleased to hear that. I missed all of you, too."

"Jackson Dunlap said you was all scratched up an' I shouldn't bother you yet." He swung down and casually let the reins drop to the ground as he walked toward her. He tipped his head, scrutinizing her with those big hazel eyes of his. " 'Cept for that little scratch on your cheek, you look plumb purty."

Matt cut in before she could respond. "Well, she's real wore out. Not up to a whole lot of company this evenin.'"

Robby's happy expression wavered, and he ran a hand through the short, sandy curls all the cove girls went dreamy-eyed over. "That's what Jackson said, but I needed to see for myself. I won't be stayin.'" He shuffled back toward the roan.

Lily couldn't help feeling sorry for the lad. "Since you took the time to ride down here, please, do come inside. I was just about to call the boys in. I baked two peach cobblers for tomorrow. I don't believe folks would mind if we sampled some now, while it's warm."

His grin came back full force. "Thanks. That sounds real pleasuresome."

Glancing past him to glowering Matt and Luke, however, Lily could tell that, peach cobbler or not, they didn't appreciate her invitation to Robby Randall. It would appear her young roosters didn't like anyone sniffing around their henhouse.

This was the first Sabbath Lily had spent at home since Susan died. Strange, how much faster she'd been able to finish the preparations for the service without the young ones underfoot and Susan to get ready. But the house felt empty without Davy scampering in and out and Emma helping wherever she could. Even in her weakest moments, Susan had loved to have company and always looked forward to catching up on everyone's news. Her blue-green eyes would sparkle against her pale skin. Emma had those same beautiful eyes. How were she and Davy faring now? Sadness started creeping in.

Lily swallowed against the hard knot in her throat and glanced out the bedroom window. The morning had dawned bright and sunny with not a single storm cloud in sight. A lovely day lay ahead.

Tightening the front laces of a rather ordinary day gown, she bemoaned the loss of the more stylish clothes she'd taken to Philadelphia. Likely some Indian woman was strutting about in the elaborate riding costume Mistress Gilford had given her, the scarf and bonnet plume trailing behind in the breeze. Lily sighed. No sense dwelling on what was lost.

She strode to the mirror and began dressing her hair in the simple upsweep she often wore on Sundays. She must remember to arrange a few moments alone with Elder MacBride so she and Matt could hear their much-needed explanation for why God chose to allow undeserved horrors to befall on so many good Christian people. In her four years in Beaver Cove, she hadn't met a single farmsteader who didn't attend services every Sunday. They all gladly offered a hand in Christian charity to anyone with a need.

Lily knew that actually finding a private moment with their pastor would be difficult. The neighbors would be eager to hear the latest news from Philadelphia and about her own harrowing adventure in the wilds. And if Robby Randall's attention yestereve was any indication, he'd be hovering at her side all the while he was here. So would Jackson Dunlap.

Lily still felt appalled over that bold kiss he'd planted on her in front of the men.

Well, none of that could take precedence. She'd simply have to find a way to get time alone with Mr. MacBride somehow. She pushed the last hairpin in place then pulled a few shorter tendrils loose at her temples to soften the look. Finished with her toilette, she went out into the front room, where benches already formed rows and scuffling sounds issued from the loft. "Are you two ready yet?"

Luke leaned over the railing. "Just gotta comb my hair."

"Shoes good and shiny?" *How like a mother I sound!* She rolled her eyes.

"Uh-huh." He nonchalantly rubbed the toe of one on the stockinged calf of his other leg.

Matt moved into view. "*My* shoes are clean and—"

Rapid barking interrupted his statement.

Lily shot a glance to the mantel clock. "No one should be arriving for another half hour." *And Duke gave up barking at friends and neighbors months ago.* Whirling around, she went for her weapon.

The boys scrambled down the ladder and ran for theirs as she opened the door and stepped outside.

The dog stood in the middle of the wagon lane, growling in that direction and baring his teeth. He barked again toward pounding hoofbeats.

Jackson Dunlap emerged at a canter from the dense trees.

"Quiet!" she ordered from the top step.

Duke closed his jaws and plodded back to a shady spot near the cabin.

Reaching the yard, Jackson caught sight of Lily and reined in his mount. He tipped his tricorn with a cocky grin. "You're lookin' purtier than a spring mornin', Miss Lily."

"Thank you." She kept her tone polite.

In one fluid motion, he swung his leg over the saddle and came down from the horse. A tiny cloud of dust puffed out as his boots made contact with the ground. Lily couldn't deny he was a rather good-looking young man. Months in the military had honed his formerly flabby build into one more trim and muscled. The forest-green waistcoat he wore over copper britches complemented his brown eyes, and his dark brown hair was neatly slicked back into a queue.

This was not a lad who needed mothering, like Robby. Fact was, Lily always felt in need of a mother herself whenever Jackson came close, for a chaperone. It was not a feeling she particularly appreciated, but if she had any hope of staying near the Waldon children after November, she'd do well to consider at least one of those young men as a potential suitor.

Jackson strode with assurance toward the porch. "Thought I'd come a little early, in case you needed help settin' up."

"How thoughtful." Lily tilted her head with a little smile. "However, everything's ready."

Matthew and Luke came outside just then.

The visitor eyed them up and down and laughed. "The three of you thinkin' on goin' huntin' before church?"

Suddenly remembering the musket she held, Lily smiled with chagrin.

Matt didn't seem inclined to share their mirth as he moved up beside her. "A body never knows what kinda varmint might come ridin' in."

"Right." Luke came to her other side. "Never can tell."

Lily didn't dare laugh. To think mere seconds ago she'd imagined needing a mother, when she had Matt and Luke around to protect her!

Undaunted, Jackson and his grin didn't lose any luster. He raised his hands, palms open. "No worries here, boys. I'm harmless."

"We'll see," Matt muttered.

Again, Lily felt like laughing. How would she ever be able to choose between her suitors with those boys making sure she was never left alone? Throughout Robby's visit last eve, both of them stayed glued to her side, unsmiling, listening to every word that came out of the young man's mouth.

She switched her attention to Dunlap. "Would you care to join us, Jackson? We were about to enjoy a cup of tea on the porch while we wait for the others." Anything to keep him seated and his hands occupied.

"Be my pleasure."

Once she had served them from the worktable, she led the way past the rows of benches and out to the porch. Matt and Luke dodged rudely past her, leaping over curious Duke, to take seats that would separate Jackson from her.

He outwitted them. As Lily took the chair at the far end, he picked up an empty chair and hefted it with one hand while juggling his tea in the other. He set it down facing her.

Matt's eyes narrowed to slits.

Lily cut him a stern glance then turned to their visitor. "Lovely morning, is it not?"

"Aye." He leaned forward. "Almost as lovely as yourself. Some people admire a gal who stays inside to keep her skin lily-white, but I'm kinda partial to the way that sun-kissed skin of yours makes your eyes look all the purtier."

Matt tucked his chin with a grunt of disgust.

Lily hoped Jackson didn't notice. "Such flattery." She smiled and sipped her tea.

"No such thing," he said, seemingly unfazed by the scowling boys. "I've long since admired you an' all you done to keep this place goin.'"

"Well, Matt and Luke have been a tremendous help." She glanced at her young chaperones, sitting rigid on the edge of their seats, their tea obviously forgotten.

"Mebbe. But you're gonna make one fine settler's wife." His jovial smile didn't diminish a fraction. "Oh, I plumb forgot. Y'all are invited to a cabin raisin' at our place Saturday after next."

"You're adding rooms to your place?"

"No." He cleared his throat, sidling a bit closer. "I been thinkin' for some time now on havin' my own place. I chose myself a real nice spot. Purt' near flat with a couple a big maple trees to shade the porch on summer afternoons."

"That does sound pleasant." Lily kept her tone light, but was beginning to feel like prey. Jackson was definitely a man on the hunt. He was already building a house to bring his bride to. To bring *her* to.

"You prob'ly know that spot betwixt this place an' ours, where the crick makes that half-moon bend an' there's that nice sandy beach? That's where I'm gonna build."

Duke lunged to his feet, his tail wagging, and Lily began to detect the faint rattles and creaks of approaching wagons.

Matt, too, sprang up from his chair, sloshing untouched tea onto the porch boards. "Folks are comin'. It's about time." Luke stood and stretched to peer toward the wagon trail.

Expecting the pair to follow the dog out to greet their new guests, as always, Lily was surprised when they both sat back down and resumed glaring at Jackson with thunderous faces.

Jackson rushed back into his topic. "Like I was sayin', that's where my place'll be, betwixt my folks' and this one." His dark eyes sparked as he met Lily's, as if gauging her reaction.

She knew he wanted a response. "That's quite near your property marker, is it not? That's a really nice spot." Averting her gaze, she rose. "I'd better go greet the neighbors."

He got up and followed close behind her. She sensed the young man hoped his decision to build a place of his own would be far more enticing to her than the thought of living with Robby's family among that big brood of Randall children. She'd heard John say more than once the reason their father joined the militia was to get a little peace.

But was Jackson Dunlap the Lord's choice for her? She'd prayed that God would redirect her affections away from John Waldon. Perhaps this was His way of allowing her to stay within easy walking distance of the children after John returned.

On the other hand, could she ever be a proper wife to Jackson Dunlap when all the while she yearned for a man who lived a mere ten-minute walk away?

Chapter 23

Acool breeze wafted by as John sat among the rows of benches at the fort, waiting for the church service to begin. He mentally reviewed his arrival the night before, when he, Nate, and the longhunters rode in and reported for duty. John had informed Captain Busse about the Indians' change of tactics, how the war party had broken up into small raiding groups that swooped in on vulnerable cabins, then moved quickly on to others.

The commander found the news disturbing. The timing could not have been worse. Farmers needed to be on their properties to harvest their crops and preserve food for the winter. Cognizant of that need, he ordered Hap Reynolds and Virgil Stewart to leave the fort as soon as they were rested and ride through the settlements to instruct people to seek shelter at their fortifications. Armed work parties would then be sent out to take care of the harvest.

Glancing around the orderly grounds, John wondered how safe this fort was at the moment. Less than a quarter of the garrison remained here. Half of the militiamen had yet to return from Fort Augusta, and those

John had roved with had not come back yet. Would this fortification, understaffed as it was, withstand a serious assault?

The bench jolted as Bob Randall dropped down beside him. "I sure appreciate you stoppin' by my place on your way here, lettin' my family know I was safe at the fort and not out rovin'."

John chuckled at his bearded neighbor. "With you on guard duty last night, I couldn't go into detail. After I fought my way through that herd of youngsters of yours and found Edith, she didn't look too pleased to hear you were just sitting around out here."

"You don't say." A frown knitted Bob's thick brows. "I thought she'd be glad to know I wasn't in danger."

"Hardly. If anything, she's jealous. She said it's high time you came home and started helping out instead of lazing around at the fort. She feels Robby's old enough to take your place."

His friend gave a sheepish grin, but his eyes retained a spark. "Sounded put out, did she? Well, if them raidin' parties ain't left the Swatara by the time our rovers report back in, I may have to do what she wants. 'Course, with the Dunlap boys home now, I can't see as how Robby'd want to give up the courtin' field to them two. From what Edith wrote in her last letter, he's set on marryin' your Lily."

John barely had time to assimilate that disconcerting news before the chaplain's voice issued from the front of the sparse gathering.

"Let us open with prayer."

Since Bob had hit a sore spot, John heard hardly a word of the chaplain's prayer. Thoughts of Robby and those pushy Dunlap brothers nagged at him. He had no right to feel possessive, but what did any of them have to offer a gently bred and educated young lady such as Lily? If he, a man born and educated in Philadelphia, couldn't have her, why should those young jackanapes have a chance with her? As her long-time employer, he deeply appreciated the years of unselfish labor she'd provided as Susan's caretaker and second mother to his children. He couldn't justify taking advantage of her sacrificial goodness that way any longer, not when she could do much better. She deserved the best.

She must go to Mariah's.

With the chaplain's voice droning steadily in the background, John caught himself sighing. If he never had anything else, at least there was one memory he'd always treasure. Lily's beautiful image filled his mind as he reflected on that one astonishingly wonderful moment when he'd kissed her and she'd melted into him. Even now he recalled the sweet taste of her soft lips, the look of complete adoration in those gorgeous eyes, and his heart ached with yearning. But he knew that stolen moment of bliss was all they would ever have. His breath came out on a ragged rush of air, his shoulders sagged, and he closed his eyes.

"Oh, marvelous." Lily stepped around Jackson. "It's the MacBrides. I need to speak with Mr. MacBride."

"I'll go with you." Dunlap followed her off the porch.

Matt and Luke fell right in behind him, not missing a step.

Before the older man reined the team to a stop, Lily intercepted the wagon. "So nice to see you all." She included the entire family in her smiling greeting and added an extra wave for Maggie MacBride's namesake, little Margaret Rose, whose infectious grin displayed every one of her tiny teeth. "Hop down, and my boys will help Michael unhitch the horses. You'll be staying the whole day, will you not?"

Patrick's wife, Agnes, handed the toddler down to Lily, her hazel eyes shining. "We sure are. I want to hear all about Philadelphia." She tucked a strand of auburn hair her daughter had tugged free back into place beneath her lace-edged bonnet.

Moving from behind Lily as she set the wiggling tot on her feet, Jackson surprised her by helping Agnes down. Lily had never thought of him having gentlemanly tendencies, and wondered if the two years he'd spent in the militia had matured him more than she realized.

While he reached up to lift the older Maggie out of the wagon, Lily circled to the back, where Ian MacBride was helping his brunette granddaughters, Judy and Anna. Their brothers had already jumped off.

Lily relinquished Margaret Rose to big sister Judy then met the elder's gaze. "If you have a moment, I'd like a private word with you."

He set twelve-year-old Anna on her feet and turned. "Lead the way, lass."

Much to her dismay, Jackson chose that moment to join them. She managed a polite smile. "If you don't mind, I'd like to speak to the pastor a moment."

A frown furrowed his solid features. "If there's somethin' you need, I'd be happy to—"

She stilled him with a hand on his arm. "It's kind of you to offer, Jackson, but my question is of a theological nature."

He looked puzzled.

"About somethin' in the Bible," Mr. MacBride clarified.

"Oh." Somewhat stunned, the young man backed away, then quickly recouped. "After, would you do me the honor of sittin' with me durin' the service?"

Lily had little choice. "Yes. Thank you for your kind invitation. Now, if you'll excuse us. . ."

Knowing no one else would venture into Susan's room, Lily invited the pastor there for their conversation and gestured toward the chair. "Please, have a seat." She then sat on the bed across from it.

He sat down and leaned forward, resting his elbows on his knees. "Did some problem arise while ye were away, lass?"

"No. Yes. Well, not exactly." Lily felt heat rising to her cheeks under his scrutiny. "Matt asked me a question I was unable to answer, and it's been bothering me." She hesitated and gave careful consideration to her next words. "As you know, our family has had a number of, shall we say, trying events this summer."

"Aye. Ye have. We've been keepin' yer family in our evenin' prayers."

Lily smiled inwardly at the pleasant sound of r's rolling from the Scot's tongue. "I do thank you. We appreciate your prayers, truly we do. But in a way, my question has to do with that very subject."

"How do ye mean, child?"

"I was telling Matthew how God answered my prayers at the time a party of Indians crossed my path only a few feet from where I was hiding. They didn't notice my tracks, even though they crossed right over them. It was as if the Lord had blinded them momentarily."

The elder's face beamed as he straightened in the chair. "That's wonderful news. It had to be the hand of the Almighty protectin' ye."

"I thought so, too." Lily paused and moistened her lips. "But then Matt made a very disturbing point. We—all of us—prayed for Susan's healing for years. And the parents of those little boys in Palmyra who were captured most likely had prayed for their children's safety, as well. But it would appear all those prayers were for naught."

Clasping his big hands together, MacBride dipped his head with a solemn nod. "I can see where you and the lad might have a problem. For now, I'll just say the Bible tells us that it rains on the just as well as the unjust. This life isna' so much about what happens to us as it is about how we choose to respond. Then, so's we dunna' get too discouraged, God gifts us with a little miracle every now an' then, like he done for you. But now that ye've mentioned it, I'll study up on prayer an' do a whole sermon on that subject next week, if ye like. Point ye toward some scriptures that'll help."

"That would be most appreciated." She rose from the bed. "Life is really a lot harder than I thought when I was a little girl. I think my papa and older sister sheltered me from most of what went on."

"That's what we parents always want to do for our children. Ye'd be surprised how often the good Lord shelters each of His children—most of the time without us even noticin'." He stood up. "Well, lass, if ye dunna mind, I'd like to stay here a wee moment longer an' go over me thoughts for this mornin'."

"Not at all." Lily smiled. "By the by, have I ever told you how very much I appreciate you and your dear family?"

"Now and again, but it's always good to hear." He gave her a jovial wink.

Lily found Jackson *and Robby* waiting outside the bedchamber when she came out. Both stood rigid and humorless.

"Good morning, Robby." She peered past him to the open front door. "Your family's not with you?"

He edged a step ahead of Jackson. "No. They won't leave till the twins stop fussin' with their hair. Donald'll be drivin' 'em when they do come. Could I help you with somethin'?"

Jackson nudged him aside slightly. "I already asked her. She don't need nothin'."

"She might not need help, but I do." Agnes MacBride's voice came from the hearth, as she and Maggie placed their food offerings in front of the fire to keep them warm. Agnes straightened and plucked a covered bowl from the worktable. "If you wouldn't mind, Robby, I need you to tote this down to the springhouse to keep cool till we eat."

The lad shot Lily a wounded look, then turned to Agnes. "Glad to."

As he followed her bidding, Lily caught a sparkle of triumph in Jackson's dark eyes.

"And Jackson," Maggie said, "if you plan on stayin' here with the rest of us, you might wanna put that horse of yours away. He's just wanderin' around out there."

The gleam in his eye dimmed considerably. Jaw muscles working, he gave Lily a slight bow. "Be back directly." He pivoted on his heel and hastened outside.

Snickers sputtered into laughter as soon as the door closed behind him. Lily couldn't help but join in with the MacBride women.

Maggie untied her apron and slipped it off. "Methinks maybe me an' Eva Shepard better start takin' turns stayin' here for a while again. I'll have Ian go home an' fetch some of my things afore the shootin' starts."

"Shooting?" A chill skittered along Lily's spine. "Have Indians been sighted?"

The older woman snorted. "Not that kind of shootin'. I'm talking about them two bucks out there. With Jackson home, I need to be here to see him an' Robby don't kill each other off. An' Frank. Ian said somethin' about him helpin' out them Dutch folk over to the Palmyra settlement for a few days. When he comes home, there'll be three of 'em trippin' over each other's feet to win your attention."

Lily's cheeks turned scarlet with embarrassment.

"Mayhap Frank won't be a problem." Agnes took Maggie's discarded apron and hung it over Lily's on the hook. "I heared tell Frank took a fancy to a young gal over that way. But then, I can't imagine that lastin' very long, with them not bein' able to talk to each other. They don't speak the same language."

The old woman gave her daughter-in-law a hug. "Agnes, girl, don't you know young folks spoonin' don't need to talk much? They say it all with their eyes. The eyes is what you gotta watch."

Suddenly Lily became keenly self-conscious and stooped down to stir a pot that didn't need stirring. How much talking did her eyes do when John was around? Undoubtedly, more than she knew. After all, the last time Maggie had seen the two of them together, the wise old woman had insisted on staying here as chaperone. Now she was planning to do that again.

La, what must Maggie think of me? Had she perceived that I was mooning hopelessly over a man who'd just laid his beloved wife to rest?

Chapter 24

If any child present had asked a question about Elder MacBride's sermon, Lily couldn't have given an answer. With Jackson on one side of her, Matt and Luke on the other, and Robby and his clan seated behind, she'd been unable to concentrate. Even the air she breathed seemed rife with hostility. . .and that during a church service! Worse yet, even though Jackson had never actually touched her, she felt as if he surrounded her. She made a solemn promise to herself not to be trapped like this again next week. She'd make sure her self-appointed chaperone, Maggie, would be sitting right beside her.

At last the final *amen* sounded. Lily sprang to her feet. "Matt, Luke, would you please help the men move the benches out while I help with the food?" She tossed the question over her shoulder as she hurried to the hearth, leaving the two rutting bulls behind to help with the chore. Not until the last child ran outside laughing and squealing and the clatter of the benches ceased did she turn to look behind her.

She grabbed some potholders and hefted up her pot of ham and potatoes, then turned to cart it to the table.

A row of women stood gawking and grinning at her.

" 'Tis not at all funny."

"Oh, but it can be so much fun." Nancy Patterson's pale eyebrows arched over her twinkling blue eyes.

"Aye," Richard Shaw's slender wife, Ruth, added, the levity of the moment adding color to her sallow complexion as she flicked a blond curl from her eyes. "Particularly now that your indenturement is over and you're free to choose whoever you wish." Puzzlement narrowed her azure eyes. "Which one *do* you fancy most?"

The last thing Lily wanted to do was keep this particular conversation alive, but her friends waited for a response. "That's a touch premature. Now that Robby's brother Donald's taken an interest in Cissy Dunlap, I'm the only unbespoken female around. Once all this war business is over, the lads will be able to look farther afield."

Robby's mother, Edith, spoke up with surprising force, considering her normally reticent personality. "My boy won't be lookin' beyond the cove. He's had his heart set on you for more'n a year now. And I'd be plumb tickled to have you on the place. I could use an extra pair of hands as capable as yours."

Millie Dunlap, Toby's wife, pursed her lips and planted her knuckles on one plump hip. "I'm afraid your boy'll have a time gettin' past mine. Jackson's so set on you, Lily, he's already choppin' down trees for your honeymoon house." A satisfied glint lit her blue eyes as she tucked a few errant strands of hair into her salt-and-pepper bun.

"I. . .uh. . .thank you both for considering me, a bond servant, with very little to bring to a marriage. But I've promised Mr. Waldon I'd remain here with his sons until he returns in November."

"I'd forgotten about the indenturement." Edith Randall tapped a forefinger on her lips in thought. "John will owe you what your contract says you're due. How much is that, anyway?"

The nosy question coming from a normally reticent woman irked Lily. She didn't appreciate anyone prying into her personal affairs. Nevertheless, she answered in an even tone. "I believe it's two pounds sterling."

"You aren't sure?"

Lily tamped down her growing anger. "Our arrangement has never been based on money. From the beginning, John and Susan treated me like family, and that's how I think of all the Waldons."

"And that's why we all love you, dear." Millie Dunlap nodded to the other ladies. "Now, I think we'd best get the food out to the servin' table a'fore it gets cold."

Utterly grateful for the reprieve, Lily lagged behind as the others walked out with their pots and platters. She'd been mistress of this household for so long, she'd never thought about living under the thumb of a prospective mother-in-law. Robby had always seemed a rather gentle young man, but his mother certainly was not. She was looking for an extra pair of hands to help her with her brood.

Then there was Jackson who had that brash way about him. His mother, though, had always been quite congenial, and so was his grandmother, Eva. Was there perhaps hidden somewhere in that young man a gentle spirit as well?

"Come along, darlin'." Maggie MacBride had remained behind. "An' stop that frettin'. I ain't gonna let nobody push you into somethin' you ain't ready for. I promise you that."

Lily was profoundly grateful to the older woman. The grandmother had shooed Jackson and Robby away and made a place for Lily at her dinner table. Now she could eat in peace between Maggie and Ian. Still, she could feel the tension between the two eager swains even after they'd taken seats at different tables.

Spearing a fat chicken breast, she spotted Matt and Luke sitting with their friends. Both sported triumphant grins. They'd managed to interrupt any attempt by Jackson or Robby to get her alone and were enjoying their meal.

But what if she *did* want some suitor's attention? Had she not asked the Lord to redirect her affections? Biting into the meat, she dismissed that thought as inconsequential. There was only one person's attention she craved, and he wasn't here.

Agnes MacBride reached across the table and touched Lily's arm. "I know Robby and Jackson are being somewhat boorish. But we all hope you'll choose one of the Beaver Cove lads and remain here with us. We already lost Susan. To lose you now would be a great sadness, indeed. Everyone here is so fond of you."

"Why, thank you." Auburn-haired Agnes was a dear, as were all the MacBrides. Lily had always been grateful that they were her nearest neighbors. "I've grown to love everyone in the cove, as well. But my own family wants me near them. I'm really quite torn." Her eyes misted lightly, and she blinked the moisture away.

Nancy Patterson's slender form leaned forward as she peered around Agnes. "It sure would be a lot safer, livin' near the coast."

"Yes, it would." Lily gave her a companionable smile. "Speaking of that, how is your little Mary faring?" She glanced at the table occupied by the younger children. "She seems a tad quieter than the other youngsters."

Nancy's light blue eyes drifted to her six-year-old. "She's still having nightmares, sad to say. We've had to take her into our bed most nights. An' durin' the daytime, she follows me like a shadow every step I take. But considerin' what happened. . ." She shrugged. "My heart cries for her. I only wish. . . ." Her golden eyebrows arched upward.

Agnes caught her hand and gave it a comforting squeeze.

Ian laid down his fork. "I'll speak to wee Mary a'fore we all leave here today, see if I can coax her to give her fears to the Lord."

Lily shot him a glance. Had he not told her more than two hours ago that the rain fell on the just and the unjust alike? He could not assure that little girl that the Indians wouldn't attack her parents' place. It did happen to be the farthest inhabited farmstead up the creek.

The dog suddenly charged out from under the children's table and bounded toward the lane, barking as he went.

Instantly everyone began untangling legs from benches to get to their feet. Men sprinted for their wagons to retrieve their weapons.

Mary ran wailing to her mother's arms.

A familiar horseman came trotting in. Frank Dunlap reined in his mount as his father and brother strode to meet him. "Looks like I made it in time for dinner. I could smell that lip-smackin' food a mile away." He swung down to the ground.

Lily's heartbeat returned to normal, and she started back to her seat.

"Thought you was gonna stay an' help with them cabin raisin's." Jackson sounded a bit accusing.

"I was. But news came that I figgered you'd wanna know. Fort William Henry surrendered to the French. An' most of the soldiers stationed there got massacred."

The strength went out of Lily. She grabbed hold of the table for support.

"What are you sayin', boy?" Toby Dunlap latched on to his younger son's shoulders.

"I'm talkin' about Fort William Henry, up in New York, Pa. The one on Lake George."

Sounds of relief drifted to Lily as the folks began to relax. It wasn't John's fort. On shaky legs, she eased down onto the nearby bench, her hand over her pounding heart, as Frank elaborated.

"Seems General Monroe was forced to surrender. The French told him he could take his soldiers an' their families on to Fort Edward, but them vicious savages killed most of 'em along the way. Worst of all, it didn't have to happen. General Webb at Fort Edward, only a few miles away, refused to send reinforcements to save the fort. The coward just sat safe behind his walls, no matter what William Johnson or anybody else told him. The dispatch rider said bodies were strung out all along the trail."

Little Mary's frightened crying grew louder.

Her mother scooped her up and carried her to the cabin. Nancy's three-year-old Sally ran after them.

"Just like last year." Cal Patterson's pained gaze followed his wife and babies to the porch.

Ian raised a hand. "Folks, let's sit down an' finish our Sabbath meal. This tragedy took place hundreds of miles away. Frank, get yourself a plate of food an' join us. But a'fore we get settled again, I'd like to say a prayer for those poor souls an' their loved ones."

After all that had just transpired, Lily found it impossible to give her attention to his words. Her insides continued to tremble, and she could still hear Mary's hysterical sobs. To think the very same horror could happen to John's fort!

Calvin Patterson stood to his feet and brushed crumbs from his trousers. "Men, whilst the womenfolk clean up, what say we walk on over to the blockhouse an' check out our supplies?"

Busy clearing her table, Lily stopped and set down the trenchers in her hand. Cal had been in the militia until he was shot in the knee, and he had the respect of all the other men. Lily was pretty sure they weren't going across the creek just to take inventory. She turned to Agnes. "Would you mind finishing here? I'm going with them."

"*Lily!*" Shock clouded Agnes' hazel eyes. "They're going to be talking about the protection of our valley. Man talk."

"That's why I'm going. I happen to be the man on my place."

"Lily—"

But she didn't wait to hear more. Ripping off her apron, she started after the men. She spotted Jackson near the front of the group. When it came to war talk, even her most determined suitor hadn't lagged behind.

No one noticed her until after they'd crossed the bridge and moved to the shade of a tree.

"Sorry, Lily-girl." Ian raised a calloused hand to ward her off. "Us men need to talk."

"As you should." She did not slow down.

"He means away from you women," Cal added as the men gathered together.

"And I would normally agree." Undaunted, Lily joined the circle. "But since I have no man on my place to speak for me, I've come to speak for myself."

Jackson came to her side. "You go on back now. I'll see to your interests."

"That's kind of you, but you don't know what I want to say."

Ian released a resigned breath. "Very well, lass. Say your piece, then shoo yourself on back."

Men. They always acted as if matters like this didn't concern anyone but themselves, when women and children were in every bit as much danger as they were. Lily stretched to her full height and mustered every ounce of authority she could into her airy voice. "Since there's been no word about our military moving against Fort Duquesne to the west any time soon, we'll continue to be under constant threat of raiding parties. If you make no other decision this day, I earnestly request that the Pattersons come and stay here with me." She turned to Cal. "I'm sure I can make room for you and your family. Your children—and most especially little Mary—need to feel safe again."

Cal eyed her momentarily and slowly shook his head. "I hate the thought of bein' run off my own place."

"You can still look after your place and get your harvest in. Please, do this for Mary."

Jackson opened his mouth as if to speak, then shut it. He obviously didn't like the idea either, and probably for his own reasons.

"I'll give it some thought," Cal finally conceded.

"That's all I ask. Now, gentlemen, I'll not hinder your *man talk* any longer." She clutched handfuls of her skirt and turned to leave, but stopped and swung back. "Except, you might consider building a stockade around the blockhouse. We do seem to be pretty much on our own." With a tilt of her head, she curtsied, as any polite woman should.

As she took her leave, she overheard Calvin muttering something. She cocked an ear, trying to make out the words.

"You lads sure you wanna wed up with somebody as bullheaded as her?"

The comment caused Lily to take an assessing look at herself. Long gone was the frightened, helpless, young gentlewoman from the genteel city of Bath. This lass had survived years of hardship and tragedy and the dangers of days alone in the wilderness. That other young girl had been replaced by a strong, capable woman who could load and shoot a musket as fast as any man.

Yes, she'd become a real frontier woman, and she liked what she saw.

Chapter 25

I t was a wondrous feeling, this sense of confidence, of having worth in one's self. As Lily strolled past the springhouse, she knew she'd have to pray about her lack of humility this eve during her prayer time. For now, however, she felt marvelous.

Matt and Luke, awaiting their turn in the rope-ring tossing game of quoits, broke away from their friends and jogged toward her, intercepting her by the smelly hog pen. "What's goin' on?" Matt's stony expression did not soften. The lad rarely smiled anymore.

"The men refused to let me stay."

Luke quirked a wry face. "I'll be glad when Pa gets back so us Waldons can have a say in things, like everybody else."

Lily returned his smirk with a rather satisfied one of her own. "Actually, I did have my say before I left. By the by, I think 'twould be prudent for Mrs. Patterson and her little ones to come and stay with us for the time being, even if her husband and their older boys do not come. I figured you two wouldn't mind extra people around while things are so unsettled."

Matt met her gaze. "It'd be better if Mrs. Patterson could take Mary east to stay with family, like we did with Emma."

"That would be ideal, had they someone to go to."

An unruly lock of brown hair fell in front of Luke's eyes with his emphatic nod. A toss of his head flicked it out of the way. "That Mary is a scared little rabbit. Did you hear the way she screamed when Frank come ridin' in?"

Stepping between her two caring boys, Lily draped an arm over their shoulders and started away from the ripe animal pen. "Let's pray her papa makes the right decision, shall we?"

Matt stopped. "Speakin' of prayin', what did Grampa Ian say about... what I asked?"

His hair, too, looked sadly in need of a good trimming. Lily brushed aside a hank bordering his nose and tucked it behind his ear. "He wanted to study up on it a bit. He said he'd preach a whole sermon on it next week."

"Better be a good one." Matt pressed his lips into a flat line.

"I'm sure it will be." Unable to resist the impulse, she ruffled his dark brown thatch. "You need a haircut. Both of you."

Luke hiked his chin. "I like mine long, like those hunters have theirs."

Eyeing her freckled charge, Lily cocked a brow. "So, you think those longhunters look good with their hair dirty and stringing down." With a teasing laugh and a disbelieving shake of her head, she started forward again. "Come to the house with me and help me take our food over to the springhouse, would you?"

"All right if we finish playin' quoits first?" Luke asked. "So far I've made more ringers than anybody."

"You have not." Matt gave a huff.

"Well, then, my ever-so-skilled lads, I believe you need to get back to the game. You wouldn't want to lose your turn." Watching after the pair as they sprinted back to their friends, Lily felt a wave of sadness that she had to keep reminding herself they were still only children.

While the men were meeting across the creek, Lily noticed that each of the women paused at least once in clearing the table, storing leftovers, or washing dishes, to peer out the window. With no concern for her Sunday frock, flighty Cissy Dunlap even volunteered to take the slop down to the pigs. But strangest of all, these normally jabbery women spoke no more than necessary. Obviously they were all worried.

Suddenly Ruth Shaw's fears got the best of her. "I can't take it anymore. I'm plumb scared all the time. It's just me and Richard and our little ones, you know. . .and we only have that one musket. I've begged him time and again to take me back home to New Castle. But he keeps telling me to wait till harvest is over." Anxiety clouded her light blue eyes. "Seems he cares more about his precious corn than he does about me and my babies. And we all know the savages are out there. Lily saw them. Saw what they did to folks. They could be out there right now, skulking about, waiting for the right moment to swoop in here and murder us all, just like they did that family across the Swatara."

Grandma Margaret moved to her side and put an arm around her. "I know it's hard, lass, but you need to keep your voice down. Nancy's in the bedroom tryin' to get little Mary to sleep."

Ruth tightened her lips and swung a gaze to Susan's bedroom door.

"Ruthie, dear," Lily said, balancing a stack of trenchers in her hands, "the Indians are in small groups. If we all stick together—"

The young wife elevated her voice again. "So you're saying they'll only be able to scalp a couple of us before the rest of the cove's men come running!" She burst into tears.

"Shh, Ruth. Shh." Maggie nodded to Agnes, and they each took an arm and led her to the table, where they sat her down in a chair.

Eva, Jackson's grandmother, took a seat beside Ruth, and the neighbors gathered around, their expressions laced with understanding.

Lily placed the trenchers on their shelf and turned to the others. "Mayhap we shouldn't wait for the men to make our decision for us. I'd be pleased to have all of you women and your children living here with me. I've only the boys, and I'm certain we could make room." She arched her brows hopefully. "We could make a big party out of preserving our food for the winter together, peeling and pressing our apples. . ."

Jackson's mother nodded in agreement. "We could stay here until we know for sure the heathens have gone back to their villages for the winter. An' all our little ones would love bein' able to play together every day. It'd be a real treat for them."

"Please, could we do that?" Ruth's emotion-filled voice rang out as she dabbed at her eyes with the edge of her apron.

Maggie placed a comforting hand on the woman's shoulder. "What do the rest of you gals say?"

"I'm all for it." Edith Randall looked around the group. "I don't even have a grown man on my place." She shot a quick glance at Lily. "That's not to say my Robby's not holdin' his own. He is, sure enough."

Lily squelched a grin. The lad's mother wasn't about to demean her son in front of a prospective daughter-in-law and her oh-so-capable hands.

Maggie stood to her feet so quickly her mobcap went askew. "Then it's settled. When the men slack off jawin' and get back over here, we'll tell 'em what we decided."

Hearing the old woman speaking so confidently helped Lily to settle another matter in her mind. No matter how much pressure she received from any quarter, she would not allow herself to be rushed into marrying anyone. Not by Robby or his mother—and especially not by Jackson, no matter how many honeymoon cabins he built in her honor.

Upon hearing what their wives had to say, the men were less than thrilled the women had taken matters into their own hands. But by the time the neighborhood wagons started rolling out, smiles reined in abundance. Even young Mary sported a tremulous smile. The decision had been made and approved. The women would pack their necessities and, together with their little ones, would move to Lily's farmstead during the week. The men and boys would work together harvesting crops from place to place.

After she and Maggie bid the last family Godspeed and strolled back to the house, Lily noticed Jackson lounging in the shade of the porch with his legs stretched out and ankles crossed as if he lived there. Tamping down her irritation, she resolved once more that she had no intention of being pressured into a situation she didn't want. Besides, Maggie was staying the night. Confident in her assertion, she squelched a smug smile.

John's boys emerged from the house with their fishing poles. Both slanted a glare at interloper Jackson.

"Sure is nice of you, Grandma Maggie, to stay with us awhile an' keep us company," Matt said with added meaning as Lily and the older woman mounted the steps. "Okay if Luke an' me go fishin', Lily?" He cut another glower at the would-be suitor.

"That'd be fine." She tilted her head at Maggie. "I hope some fried rainbow trout sounds good to you for breakfast in the morning." Even Jackson could recognize the less-than-subtle hint that the older woman wouldn't be going away anytime soon.

"Nothin' I like more. I'll fix us up some fried taters an' biscuits to go with 'em."

"Sounds delicious." Lily nodded to the boys. "Don't stay out after dark, and don't forget your weapons." She motioned toward the firearms they'd left on the porch.

Grinning, the pair snatched up the musket and pistol and took off.

Lily gestured toward vacant chairs. "Let's sit down and rest for a while, Maggie. It's been a long day. And I do believe a nice cup of tea would be most refreshing. I'll brew some. Would you care for any, Jackson?"

"Don't mind if I do." He started to get up.

"Just relax." Lily stayed him with a hand. "I'll only be a moment."

His shrewd eyes flicked to Maggie, and he eased back down without a smile. Obviously the evening wasn't going according to his plans. Nor had the earlier part of the day, since his attempts to catch Lily alone had been to no avail.

Inside the cabin, Lily chuckled to herself as she pulled out a tray from a shelf and loaded it with cups and a few scones left over from the Sabbath get-together. Through the open window, she could hear Maggie speaking to their persistent visitor.

"I take it you got yourself set on that lass in there."

Lily paused to listen.

"That's right, ma'am. Don't want no other but her."

"She ain't no peach a body can just pluck off a tree, you know."

"She sure ain't."

There was no lack of determination in the young man's tone. Lily recognized it whenever he spoke about her or to her, and it rankled her.

Thankfully, Maggie's tenacity matched his. "I'd say you'd best trim your sails a mite, boy, if you're really serious about her. Just 'cause Lily was a bond servant, that don't mean she ain't without a lovin' family that wants her. Her folks tried to buy back her papers the first year she come to us. If it hadn't been for her carin' so much for poor sick Susan, she would'a lit out from here a long time ago."

Lily couldn't help herself. She inched closer to the window.

"Well," Jackson drawled, "she said herself she likes livin' at the cove. I'm purty sure I can talk her into stayin'. Besides, I'm a hard worker. I'll take good care of her."

His confidence made Lily's eyebrows hike upward. The guy actually believed he could make her dance to whatever tune he played! She shook her head as Maggie's voice came back into play.

"You must'a noticed them fancy duds she come here with. That gal was used to fine things, lots better than the rest of us. Her pa had a bad run of luck is all, or she wouldn't be here in the first place. An' you do know she can read an' write. That's more'n half the folks around here can do."

A span of silence followed, stretching long enough for Lily to feel sorry for Jackson. After all, it was not his fault he hadn't been schooled. Still. . .

"My pa's the best tanner and harness maker twixt here an' Reading," he finally said, force returning to his tone. "A good livin' can always be made from workin' leather. Pa learnt me a lot before the war. When it's all over, I'll be able to do right by Lily. See if I won't."

"Mm-hmm." The chair creaked as Maggie shifted her weight. "That's right good to hear. But then there *is* that quick temper of yours. I heared tell about lots of them whoppers you an' Frank got into. You two boys're known for flyin' off the hook at the least little thing."

Lily clamped a hand over her mouth to keep from laughing out loud. Bless her heart, the old woman was relentless.

But Jackson didn't back down. "Aw, that's just me an' Frank bein' brothers. But when it comes to defendin' myself an' what's mine, I ain't ashamed to say I can hold my own." He paused and spoke again in a more gentle voice. "You can ask my ma. I wouldn't harm a hair on Lily's head... or any other gal's. I know womenfolk are...delicate-like."

His statement pierced Lily's heart, and she felt ashamed to have thought ill of Jackson. He was a touch rough around the edges, but inside, he had a soft heart. She poured water into the pot and added some tea leaves.

"I have just one more question for you, boy," Maggie said.

About to pick up the prepared tray, Lily stopped again.

"Yes'm?"

"Have you prayed about this? Courtin' Lily, I mean."

He gave a snort. "Ain't no need to. I don't see Robby Randall's much competition. The lad's still wet behind the ears."

No need to pray about something as important as choosing a wife? A lifetime partner? Lily had heard more than enough. Plastering on a smile, she hastened toward the door and strode outside to join Maggie and *His Arrogance.*

Chapter 26

Neither Jackson nor Maggie wore a smile when Lily stepped out the door with the refreshments.

Jackson, however, brightened when he saw her. He sprang to his feet. "Let me help." He whisked the tea tray from her hands.

"Thank you. Put it on the side table." She indicated the one next to Maggie, then sat opposite her.

The young man plopped onto the seat next to Lily's.

His nearness irritated Lily, but she maintained her composure. She turned to the older woman. "What would you like in your tea, dear?"

"Plain'll do fine. I'm still full from that big meal we had this afternoon."

Lily dispensed some of the hot brew into a cup and handed it to her, aware of Jackson's gaze hot upon her. She reminded herself of her resolve to be strong and confident as she turned to him. "And how would you like yours, Jackson?"

"I like mine sweet an' creamy." The words sounded innocent enough, but his eyes said a whole lot more.

Once she'd handed him his tea, she poured her own plain drink and sat back, hoping to enjoy it for a moment. Alas, mere seconds passed before Jackson spoke again.

"Lily?" Balancing his cup and saucer on one knee, he leaned forward. "If you don't mind, when we finish our tea, I'd like a private word with you."

"How about now? The sun will be down soon. You can walk with me while I go shut the chickens inside their coop for the night." She set down her cup and looked at Maggie. "Would you excuse us for a few moments?"

At the woman's nod, she exited the porch, with Jackson right behind her. The coop was out of Maggie's line of view, but not so far that Lily couldn't summon her if need be.

Several fat fowl sought their roosts as Lily approached, and others came running when they saw her. Watching them scramble up the board ramp to their little house on stilts, she chuckled.

Jackson wasted no time coming to his point. "I ain't thought about nothin' but you since I was here last spring. I want you for my wife."

That was it? His proposal of marriage? Lily was tempted to give him a flat no. But what if the young man was actually God's choice for her? "I must say, that was an odd proposal." She switched her attention from the chicks to him. "Why do you want to marry me, Jackson?"

He frowned, as if that was the dumbest question he'd ever heard. "Why not? I can't keep waitin' for this lousy excuse of a war to get over. It's past time I started thinkin' on my future, an' you'd make a real fine wife. Besides. . ." He leaned closer, his breath feathering the fine hairs on her neck. "There's no other way to say it. I want you in my bed. *Real bad.*"

The intensity in his voice almost compelled Lily to holler for Maggie. She took a step back to put distance between them as she weighed her response. The young man was only being honest, and his reasoning regarding the war was logical. "Jackson, I'm honored that you would consider me for your wife. Truly I am. But before I answer you, I must spend some time in prayer and seek God's will. This is a momentous decision that would affect the rest of my life. My family expects me to join them once my indenturement is over. But even though I'll no longer be his bond servant, I promised Mr. Waldon I'd stay with his sons until he returns in November."

Jackson captured her shoulders. "You belong here with us, Lily. With me. You know you do."

"Perhaps." She reached up and gently removed his hands from her person. "Nevertheless, I believe we both need to pray about it. November is only two months hence. John will be home then."

He scoffed, and a corner of his mouth quirked upward. "We don't need to pray *or* wait. It's obvious. Who d'ya think God put you here for, anyway? Me. We could up an' marry now, an' I could stay here with you till Waldon gets home."

Lily couldn't squelch a droll smile. "You and me, honeymooning here with all the women and children from the cove? I think not. Besides, I have no intention of being rushed into the most important decision of my life. I will say this much. I will never marry a man who doesn't pray."

"Okay, okay." He took a step back and spread his hands. "If that's what you want, I'll do some prayin'. But it won't change a thing."

The following week proved to be a whirlwind of activity. By Tuesday, every entire family, not merely the women and children, took up residence in the farmhouse, the workshop, and the blockhouse. Crude canvas coverings also shrouded the wagons scattered about the Waldon clearing. The paddock was filled with milk cows. Inside the cabin, sleeping pallets were everywhere, and after bedtime, it was nearly impossible to step between them.

At dawn each morning, the men and older boys split into two groups and took their leave. One group headed downriver, the other upriver, to tend the remainder of the cove's livestock and to harvest whatever crops were ready. Lily and the neighbor women picked the last of the vegetables from her garden and began cooking them down for preserves, or drying what couldn't be stored in her root cellar. She didn't want to think about the pears and apples that soon would be ripe for picking.

By the end of the week, wagonloads of corn and vegetables from the other farms arrived to be dealt with. Lily wondered where they would put it all. The boys had cut the hay while she'd been in Philadelphia, and it was dry now and needed to be raked up and brought in.

And the corn! On Saturday evening, a weary Lily stopped with her pail of milk to stare at the bulging corn crib. Even with all she and the others had already done, tons of corn still needed to be shucked and dried and hulled. Some would need to be ground into meal at Cal's watermill. Then there was sorghum cane to be cut, pressed, and boiled down for molasses. Chestnuts and walnuts would be ready to gather soon, and then it would be hog-killing time.

Agnes, toting her toddler Margaret Rose, came to her side. "It's been a good week."

"Yes." Lily managed a smile. "Tiring, but 'tis nice to have company while we work. Lots of helping hands."

"Extra ladies help things go a lot faster. This evening, though, we have the biggest job of all to take care of."

Lily wanted to sink down to the ground and curl herself into a ball. "What are you saying?"

"Baths. You tell me how we're gonna get all them young'uns cleaned up tonight and keep 'em clean for the Sabbath."

Shoulders drooping, Lily turned toward the house and saw the Patterson twins toting water buckets to three tubs heating over fires, while Cissy Dunlap hauled more from the well for other tubs waiting to be filled. "I'm just glad Davy's not here. He'd be impossible." She laughed lightly, then sobered. "No, I wouldn't care at all. I miss him and Emmy terribly."

"So does my Joey. But soon the Indians will leave for the winter, and the children will be able to come back. Never expected I'd be looking forward to the cold months." She shook her head in disbelief.

Lily nodded in agreement. "When Jackson and Frank went out scouting, they said they didn't see any sign of war parties lurking about."

Having mentioned her persistent suitor, she had another thought. "We'll need to string up some blankets around those tubs. We womenfolk will need some privacy when our turn comes."

Agnes chuckled. "Especially you. Between Jackson and Robby, one of 'em seems to always be watching you. Personally, I think that Robby is a real charmer. And so handsome, with those cute curls and that smile of his. Don't you think?"

Knowing her friend was teasing, Lily just tucked her chin. "I think 'tis time I take this milk to the springhouse and rustle up whatever blankets I can find."

Moments later, on her return trip from the springhouse, the sight of a wagon drawing to a stop made her sigh. More work for her and the other ladies. Would it ever end? Thankfully tomorrow was the Sabbath, a most needed day of rest.

Ian, holding the reins, set the brake. Richard Shaw occupied the other half of the seat. His son Michael rode in back atop another load of corn with Matt and Luke, both of whom sported big smiles. It was good for her boys to have older men to rely on for a change, since their father was absent. At least John would return soon. Too soon, in a way, yet not soon enough for her longing heart. She knew the decision regarding her future would have to be made then.

As she walked toward them, her two lads hopped off the wagon bed. Matt waved something in his hand that looked suspiciously like. . .a *letter*! "We found some mail and a notice hooked on the nail at MacBride's dock on the river. This one has your name on." He held it out to her.

Lily took the missive and scanned the writing. *John!* Her heart leaped with joy. " 'Tis from your father."

"Thought so." Luke grinned. "The notice came from Fort Henry, so we figgered the letter prob'ly did, too."

Her joy dimmed. "Did the notice say anything of importance?"

Matt scoffed. "Nothin' much. Just that we should all do what we already done."

"Which is. . . ?"

"Gather together at one place an' harvest the fields, like we been doin'. Now open the letter, would ya? I wanna hear what Pa has to say." He tapped his foot impatiently.

Glancing down at the smudged paper, Lily only hoped the news was good. But according to the notice the boys had seen, nothing had changed, so what good could there be? She broke the wax seal and unfolded the rough, heavy paper, then read aloud:

> *My dearest Lily, Matt, and Luke,*
>
> *You are always on my mind and in my prayers. Nothing is more important to me than my children. I deeply regret that duty keeps me away from home during these dangerous times. Captain Busse has posted a notice throughout the surrounding settlements for folks to gather together for safety. I fear the people at the cove will refuse to abide by his orders, so I most urgently demand that you take the livestock to Ian MacBride's place and leave the area at once. Everything we possess at the cove can be replaced, but I could never replace you. Please do as I ask. I love all of you very, very much.*
>
> > *Your loving Papa, and, to Lily, your most loving friend,*
> > *J. Waldon*

Lily wished she'd been alone when she read the letter. Seeing the words penned by John's hand, she'd come very close to pressing the missive to her heart. He loved her. He said it in writing.

Matt's voice interrupted her thoughts. "Well, at least we don't have to go anywheres. The cove folks already did what the notice told us to do."

Looking at the lad's dirty, dusty self, Lily smiled. "No, we don't have to leave just yet. But *I* have a demand for you two. As soon as you finish tending the livestock, I want you to go down to the creek and take a bath. Tomorrow's the Sabbath."

"Aww. . ." Luke whined. "Do we have to? I'm tuckered out."

"And be sure to take soap."

As the disappointed pair grumbled and trudged off toward the stable, Lily sought the solace of a nearby tree for a private moment. She unfolded John's letter again and drank in the message: *I love you all very, very much. . . . Your most loving friend. . .*

She ran her fingers over the treasured words. He loved her more than a mere friend. He said he was her *most loving friend.* When he'd written *I love you all very, very much,* he was trying to tell her more. For the briefest of moments, her heart flooded with joy.

Then reality set in.

It could not be. It could *never* be. John had loved Susan, had cared for her with his whole heart. It would be wise to remember that whenever thoughts of him drifted to mind. How unseemly to think anything else. John was exactly as he'd set it down on the paper, a most loved *friend.* Had it been otherwise, he'd have stated it in a way that would've left no doubt.

Still, that kiss he'd given her hadn't been that of a friend. Dared she hope it meant more? Heaven help her, she wanted desperately to cling to the hope that it did.

Chapter 27

An overnight shower brought the cool breath of autumn, but Sunday dawned bright and sparkling with fat droplets of moisture falling from the trees into puddles below. Lily smiled with chagrin at having insisted Matt and Luke bathe in the stream last eve in such brisk weather. But they looked ever so nice in their Sabbath best, their hair slicked back, as they sang with the rest of the congregation.

She appreciated having her two lads flanking her. It effectively prevented Jackson and Robby from grabbing those seats. Elder MacBride would bring a message regarding the concerns she and Matt had expressed about the Lord's supposed care of His people. She hoped the wise, older man would give the matter a perspective she could understand and accept.

The lyrics of "Hail Thou Once-Despised Jesus!" spoke to Lily's heart as she joined the other folks in the third verse: " 'There for sinners Thou art pleading, there Thou dost our place prepare; Ever for us interceding, till in glory we appear.' " While the others continued on to the next verse, she prayed those weren't merely empty words.

The song came to an end, and Brother MacBride offered a brief prayer then motioned for everyone to be seated.

Lily reached beside her and gave Matt an encouraging smile as she took his hand, then Luke's.

The elder gazed over the congregation. "Ye've all heard that the Lord is our Shepherd, an' that we're the sheep of His pasture. So in light of recent happenings, some of ye might be wonderin' where our Good Shepherd is, that He's permittin' wolves to snatch away some of His own sheep outta the fold."

Lily squeezed Matt's hand.

"We pray for His protection, yet the wolves still circle. We're bein' stalked like animals, an' it dunna' fit with our conception of God's holy promise to be with us an' look after us. When Jesus was in the Garden of Gethsemane, he prayed"—he glanced down at the open Bible he held— " 'O my Father, if it be possible, let this cup pass from me: Nevertheless, not as I will, but as thou wilt.' Our Father in heaven allowed His own Son to die a violent death. It has often troubled me that a father would ask somethin' like that of his son. But God had a great and grand purpose beyond that death. Because of His Son's sacrifice, those who believe in Him are assured an eternal life of love an' great joy."

His faded blue eyes focused on Lily. " 'Tis a fact that all but one of the twelve disciples were martyred for preachin' the Gospel, yet their message of salvation dinna' die with them. It's been carried forth through the centuries and to every continent. The apostles fulfilled God's purpose for them in this life an' are now enjoyin' great rewards in heaven."

The elder's words far from soothed Lily's unrest. She had expected comforting words for this life, not the next.

"Now we have the privilege of piercin' the darkness of this continent with that same glorious news, the Gospel of Christ. As Christians, that is our commission while we dwell on this earth. The Lord never promised we'd all pass away gently in the midnight of our old age. The sudden death of a loved one or friend takes us by surprise, but it dunna' take God by surprise. Every death comes at its appointed time. The Bible says the

Almighty's ways are higher than our ways, an' His thoughts are higher than our thoughts. Even though we canna' understand some of the hard things, we must trust that He knows best."

Elder MacBride thumbed through the worn pages of his Bible. "I'd like to read now from Romans, chapter eight, startin' with verse thirty-five: 'Who shall separate us from the love of Christ? Shall tribulation, or distress, or persecution, or famine, or nakedness, or peril, or sword? As it is written, For thy sake we are killed all the day long; we are accounted as sheep for the slaughter. Nay, in all these things we are more than conquerors through him that loved us. For I am persuaded, that neither death, nor life, nor angels, nor principalities, nor powers, nor things present, nor things to come, nor height, nor depth, nor any other creature, shall be able to separate us from the love of God, which is in Christ Jesus our Lord.' "

Ian's voice droned on. "I'll read a few verses from chapter eight that I pray will answer more of your questions." He met Lily's gaze over his spectacles. " 'Likewise, the Spirit also helpeth our infirmities: for we know not what we should pray for as we ought: but the Spirit itself maketh intercession for us with groanings which cannot be uttered. And he that searcheth the hearts knoweth what is in the mind of the Spirit, because he maketh intercession for the saints according to the will of God. And we know that all things work together for good to them that love God, to them who are the called according to his purpose."

He closed his Bible. "Consider those last words. Are ye livin' yer life accordin' to His purpose for ye? Do ye start each mornin' askin' the Lord to guide ye through the day? Are ye servin' the Lord in whatever He asks of you? Are ye lovin' the Lord thy God with all thy heart and with all thy soul, and with all thy mind, as the Bible requires? An' are ye lovin' yer neighbor as yerself? Do ye pray for the salvation of yer enemies as well as yer friends? If ye do those things, the Lord will give ye peace in the midst of doubt and chaos."

As their spiritual leader continued reading related passages, a heavy burden of guilt pressed on Lily. Had she been praying for God's message to be sent forth? Had she even considered anything beyond her own household? No, all her thoughts had been for herself and her family, her desires and the needs of her loved ones. She'd tried to be a good servant to John and Susan, but it was all for naught unless her first purpose had been to serve the Lord. Never once had she asked God what He wanted of her on a particular day. Her prayers had always been personal wants and pleas. What an incredibly unworthy person she was. It was amazing that the Lord had bothered to save her from the Indians!

Thoroughly humiliated, she bowed her head. *Lord God, thank You for all You've done for me. I beg forgiveness for my selfishness. My mind has been cluttered with my secret hopes and desires that do nothing but war with my decision about whom I should marry, when all the time I should be seeking what You want of me. From now on I shall try to seek Your will alone. Thank You for a father and sister who tried to train me in the way I should go. And thank You for being my heavenly Father even though I've been a silly, wayward child. I pray this in Jesus' precious name. Amen.*

Lily could hardly wait for the rest of the service to end so she could find out how Matt reacted to the pastor's message. But Robby descended upon her before she had the chance.

"May I have a private moment with you, Lily?"

"Before dinner?" Lily dreaded another proposal.

He nodded. "Could we step into a side room?"

"Very well." From the corner of her eye, she saw Jackson looking daggers at Robby as she preceded him into the bedroom she now shared with several of the women.

He closed the door behind them. "Cissy overheard Jackson tell his pa he asked you to marry him."

Not appreciating being the latest topic bandied about, Lily grimaced. "I'd hoped that would remain a private matter until if and when there'd be a public announcement."

Her words did not deter Robby. "Well, did you say yea or nay?"

"I've not yet given Jackson an answer. After hearing the sermon this morning, I don't feel it's an answer I can give, as yet. Not unless the Lord directs me to do so."

He looked puzzled momentarily; then he grinned. "Whew. At least you didn't say yes. I hope that means you'd rather marry me. You must know I'd be a more pleasant fellow to live with. I'm real slow to anger, and I'd build us our own cabin just like Jackson's doin'. Far 'nough away so's you wouldn't have to listen to all the screamin' young'uns. Mr. Waldon says he's gonna let me apprentice with him, you know, so I'll be able to make us some fine furniture real soon. What d'you say?"

Lily took his hand and did her best to smile. "I must say, that was a fine proposal of marriage, Robby. However, my answer to you must be the same as it was to Jackson. I shall not marry anyone until I feel the Lord is leading me to do so." She tilted her head and searched his eyes. "Did the Lord direct you to come and propose to me?"

His gaze faltered. "I. . .uh. . .I guess not. I mean, I told God how much I want you, but I never asked if He wants me to have you."

She gave him a reassuring nod. "Well, if we're both praying for God's leading, it shouldn't take long to receive an answer. Now, if you'll excuse me, I need to help get our Sabbath dinner on the table." With a polite smile, she took her leave.

Several people stared at her when she exited the room. Lily knew it was most uncommon for an unmarried couple to go into a bedchamber alone. There was sure to be more talk.

She spied Jackson leaning against the wall by the front door, his expression morose. Thankfully, Matt and Luke were closer. She headed straight to her boys and pulled them into a hug. "Nothing's changed," she whispered. They relaxed, and their fisted hands uncoiled. "Better get these benches out to the tables now. We'll be having sweet potatoes to go with that tasty ham you boys were turning on the spit all morning."

Glancing up, Lily saw Jackson shift his attention to Robby, who carried a bench board in the direction of his seething rival.

"Jackson," she called out, hoping to forestall more fodder for gossip. "May I speak to you a moment?"

He eased his angry stance and moved away from the wall, starting toward her.

Much to Lily's relief, Robby walked on out.

She accompanied her dark-haired suitor to the relative shelter of the loft above. "I thought I should be the one to tell you Robby has asked me to marry him."

He shot a glare toward the door.

Lily caught his arm. "But I told him what I told you. If and when I marry, it will be to the person the Lord chooses for me. Especially after hearing Grampa MacBride's sermon this morning, I've no right to take matters into my own hands."

Jackson's eyes dulled with puzzlement. "God ain't talked out loud to nobody since Bible days. How d'ya expect to know for sure?"

Lily realized this young man was as confused about God and His power as Matt was. "I don't want to tell you what to do, but I believe you need to talk to Mr. MacBride about what you just asked me. Perhaps he can help you see how truly awe-inspiring our God is."

He opened his mouth to speak but apparently thought better of it and just looked at her momentarily. "If that's what you want me to do, I'll do it. But I'm gonna feel downright silly doin ' it."

"You'll not regret it. I promise."

Chapter 28

Bits of hay and yellow dust drifted down from the boards overhead where Matt and Luke raked a wagonload of hay the other lads had pitched up to the hayloft. Below them, Lily sat hunched over on the milking stool. After stripping the last of the creamy milk, she draped her apron over the pail to protect the contents from the falling debris. Then she brought the bucket out from under the cow and stretched out a kink in her back.

The boys started down the ladder. Lily had wanted to get Matthew alone ever since Sunday to ask him what he thought about Elder MacBride's sermon. She was thankful she and John's sons were no longer alone on the farmstead and vulnerable to Indian raiders, but she'd never felt so smothered in her life. People were everywhere, and they seemed to be watching her more than usual, since she'd received two marriage proposals in the same week. Everyone wondered which suitor she'd accept.

When her lads reached the bottom, Lily smiled at them. "Mercy, but you two are covered in straw." She finger-brushed bits of hay from the younger boy's hair while he and his brother dusted themselves off. "Would you mind if Matt and I had a minute to talk alone, Luke?"

His brows dipped. "Are you keepin' somethin' from me?"

"No, not at all. It has to do with a question your brother had last week about prayer. But you're welcome to stay, if you like."

"Naw, that's all right." He took the bucket from her and backed away. "I'll take this to the springhouse." Swiveling on his heel, he dashed off.

Lily had to laugh. "Next time I want to get rid of him, I'll know what to say."

Matt grinned. "Well, your talkin' about prayin' has kept Robby and that bossy *Jackson* away, that's for sure."

From his gritty utterance of Jackson's name, Lily could tell Matt was still not fond of him. But that was a topic for another day. "You may be right about them. At least they've stopped bristling every time they see each other. But getting back to that question you had regarding prayer, did Grampa Mac answer you sufficiently last Sunday?"

His expression flattened. "Imagine him wantin' us to love our enemies. *An' pray for 'em*, yet. I'll tell you how I'm gonna love any Injun that comes sneakin' in here. I'll shoot him right between his beady eyes, like I would some bobcat tryin' to get our chickens."

Placing a hand on his forearm, Lily met his gaze. "Matt, dear, 'tis right and proper to protect ourselves. But we still should pray that our enemies find the Lord. Think about it—if they came to know God, they'd realize that what they're doing is wrong. Sinful. And hopefully they'd stop doing it."

Matt's eyes narrowed to slits. "I ain't wastin' one minute of prayin' on them murderin' heathens. They deserve to go to hell." Before Lily had a chance to respond, he turned and darted out of the stable.

Watching after him, Lily wondered how to find the words that would make him understand, when many of the grown men felt exactly the same way. Yestereve, she'd overheard Cal and Richard saying they'd relish the chance to wipe out every Delaware this side of the Appalachians. She swept a look skyward. "Lord, please give me the right words and the right moment."

She strolled outside and noticed people gathering around two horsemen. She recognized the taller one as Jess Thomas, the post rider who used to come riding through with mail every three or four weeks. With the current unrest, the cove was fortunate if he arrived every two or three months. Usually jovial and quick to relate a humorous incident encountered during his travels, his light brown eyes were somber, and there were added furrows on his forehead. His partner, a short, stocky fellow with small eyes, looked equally pensive. Both men carried muskets and a brace of pistols.

Drawing closer, she could hear folks peppering the visitors with questions. The tall post rider raised a hand for quiet and waited for the chatter to subside. "Let me hand out the letters, folks. Then if you have no objections, me an' my partner'd like to stay the night. We'll have plenty of time this evenin' for swappin' news." He pulled a bundle of mail from his leather pouch and began calling out names. By the time he got to Lily's, most of the neighbors had dispersed to read their missives. Matt and Luke joined her as the rider handed her two pieces of mail.

"Is one from Pa?" Luke peered over her shoulder, trying to see as Lily studied the writing.

Matt huffed. " 'Course not, dummy. That post rider come from Reading, not from the fort."

"One's from Philadelphia," Lily answered, "the other is postmarked Alexandria. That will be from my sister. Let's go sit under the maple tree to read them, since all the chairs on the porch are occupied."

Luke grabbed her hand to hurry her along. "Let's hear about Emma and Davy first."

The boys plopped eagerly to the ground. Lily handed the letter from the Gilfords to Matt. "You read it."

He broke the seal and unfolded the paper:

Dear Lily, Matt, and Luke,

All is well here. The children are doing fine. We pray nightly that you are all equally well. Your grandfather and I want you to know you are always welcome. Please reconsider joining us here until after the war is over. Emma is afraid for you and misses you terribly. Davy says Matt and Luke can stay in the room with him, and Emma will sleep with Lily, the same as at home. They have the details worked out quite nicely.

I dearly long to meet you, Matthew and Luke, and hope you will come.

Your loving grandmother,
Olivia Gilford

"She's a lovely woman," Lily said. "You'll adore her when you meet her. She has that same gentle spirit your mother had."

"Really?" Luke's eyes clouded. "Let me see that letter."

As Matt handed it to him, Lily opened the one from Mariah. Knowing how blunt her sister could be, she debated whether to read it aloud. "Perhaps you two aren't interested in this one. It's probably girl talk."

"Sure we are. Anything that concerns you concerns us." Matt slanted a glance to the pasture gate, where Jackson was unhitching a team of oxen.

"Very well. But I must warn you, Mariah always says exactly what she thinks." Several pound notes fell out of the letter when Lily unfolded it. Ironically, it was more than John had paid for her indenturement papers four years ago. Lily tucked the funds inside her apron pocket and began reading:

My dear baby sister,

I am most upset with you. I cannot believe you would willingly put yourself in danger again. If those Waldon boys were too stubborn to go to Philadelphia with you, they should reap their own reckless consequences. You should not have to suffer with them. I insist you leave that perilous place at once and come to us. I understand this letter may take weeks to reach you. But if you do not walk through my front door within the next two months, I shall

send men to fetch you, with or without your consent. I refuse to
celebrate another Christmas season without you.

Your very worried sister,
Mariah

"She's right, you know," Matt commented, his eyes soulful. "You took an awful risk comin' back here. It almost got you killed. You should go to her."

"Not without you. If I were to leave here, would you and Luke come with me?"

Luke didn't wait for his older brother to answer. "Pa will be back in a couple weeks. I wanna stay here for him. We're safe now, even if I do have to share my loft with a passel of noisy fellas."

Lily ruffled his hair, shaking more bits of hay loose. "Then I reckon we'll all stay here and wait for your pa. He should arrive before Mariah's hired men. I don't have to decide what I'm going to do until after he comes home."

"Right." Matt's gloomy demeanor matched his response. "Like which one of them two jaspers you're gonna marry."

Lily inhaled a calming breath. She and the boys could have sat here the rest of the evening without that reminder.

Lily drew her shawl tighter before taking the last bite of her supper. Not only were the evenings growing steadily colder for outdoor eating, but her nerves were constantly on edge. She suspected the news from Philadelphia wouldn't be good. Both newcomers had avoided questions during the meal, promising to convey what information they had after supper. Post riders garnered more tidbits than any newspaper or broadside reported, so the air crackled with anticipation.

Seated with the adult MacBrides and the Shaws, Lily noticed the women's conversations centered on the contents of the letters they'd received, while the men were ominously quiet. She also noted that most everyone had finished eating as quickly as she had. The children had already scurried off to play hide-and-seek.

The post riders, however, were taking their sweet time eating. Seated at the next table, with the Dunlaps and Pattersons, the horsemen shoveled in food as if it were their last meal. But considering the dangers of their occupation, one never knew when it might very well be.

Too anxious to sit and wait any longer, Lily untangled her limbs from the bench and rose to her feet, straightening her skirts. "I'll go prepare more tea."

She returned a few moments later with a large pewter pitcher in each hand and handed one to Agnes, then approached the cove's guests. "More tea, gentlemen?"

"That would be nice." Jess Thomas and his companion held up their mugs. "Mighty fine spread you womenfolk laid out."

"Thank you."

Lily filled their cups and mustered a pleasant expression as she moved on to Jackson. "And you?"

"Sure thing, purty lady." He didn't hold his mug up for filling, so Lily reached past him to retrieve it. Hearing his intake of breath and feeling his eyes on her, she quickly moved on, assuring herself the Lord would never expect her to marry someone so bold.

As she moved to the next table, she realized that had it been John drawing her near and looking at her the way Jackson had, she'd have been thrilled. The only thing wrong with Jackson Dunlap was her and her wayward feelings.

Cal's voice cut into her musings. "If you men would care to join us down by the crick for a smoke. . . ."

The post riders immediately rose to their feet.

They want to bring the men up to date privately! "Please!" Lily blurted out. "We women want to hear the news, too."

"That's right." Oftentimes prickly Edith Randall nodded emphatically. "Some of us don't have our husbands at home."

The stocky visitor glanced around at the men, as if seeking their consent. "You sure about this?"

Ian shook his head wearily. "Might's well tell the womenfolk. Otherwise us men won't get a lick of sleep tonight for all their badgerin'."

"If you say so." Brown-eyed Jess Thomas took a position between the adult tables. "First off, you folks are doin' the wise thing by bandin' together. The redskins are still rovin' both sides of Blue Mountain. They come in fast, burn and kill, then disappear again into the woods. One thing, though. . .you should be storin' all your harvests here where you can best protect it."

Toby Dunlap nodded. "We been storin' some of it in the blockhouse yonder, but we don't have time to build nothin' else right now. It's all we can do to git our harvest in. Mebbe in a few weeks. . ."

"Just lettin' you know, them heathens know burnin' you out before winter sets in is as easy a way of getting you out as killin' ya. Me an' Fritch here figger that's why they ain't started back to Fort Duquesne yet. They wanna destroy your food supply first."

"The only run-ins we've had here was a couple months back," Richard Shaw said, "when they snatched away two of our children. We got 'em back, though." He glanced at his anxious wife and gave her a confident tip of his head as muttering assents made the rounds.

The post rider raised a hand. "Well, you picked a lucky spot for your settlement. What with the string of forts and blockhouses guardin' along the Susquehanna not far to the west, the Injuns ain't been comin' this way. They're crossin' upriver of Fort Augusta and Shamokin an' comin' down through the Swatara and Schuylkill passes, which puts 'em quite a ways to the east of here. An' even though the Indians at Shamokin say they're loyal to us, we think some of 'em are guidin' the Delaware in."

Jackson came to his feet. "We know all that. What we wanna know now is why aren't there more militia comin' out here from Philadelphia to help? An' where are the troops from England? Why ain't them generals tryin' to take Fort Duquesne? Me an' my brother refused to reenlist this year 'cause we can do more good here protectin' our cove, since nobody else can—or will."

"I understand how you feel, lad. I did hear talk in Philadelphia that they're still considerin' takin' that fort this year."

"Considerin'?" He spat on the ground. "It's October, man. If they ain't started out by now, they ain't goin' to." Shaking his head in disgust, Jackson reclaimed his seat.

"Can't help but agree with you," Thomas said in a flat tone. "There's another rumor floatin' around that's a mite crazy. Folks are sayin' the governor wants to declare Pennsylvania its own republic and petition France to let us be under their protection. In exchange we would agree to let the Injuns freely pass through on their way to Virginia."

"Yer right about one thing," Ian said. "That *is* crazy talk."

"I wouldn't be too sure," Cal injected. "Last summer, folks on t'other side of the Susquehanna were talkin' about doin' somethin' like that. 'Course, it's too late for them. There ain't too many people left over there. Not anymore."

Jess Thomas scanned the group. "Well, like I said, your forts along the Susquehanna have been the biggest help."

"Fort Henry is pathetically undermanned." Jackson rolled his eyes. "Governor Denny won't give the order to bring our men back from Fort Augusta."

The post rider eyed him steadily. "That bein' the case, I'm surprised you an' your brother left the militia."

That raised Jackson's hackles. "We ain't cowards. But month after month we was out there chasin' ghosts. We hardly ever caught up to the marauders. We do better here, protectin' what's ours. An' me an' Frank ain't the only ones. John Waldon an' Bob Randall from here in the cove are both comin' home in November to stay. We're through havin' our families out here with no protection."

Listening to Jackson, Lily found herself impressed with the strength of his conviction. He was a much more responsible, levelheaded person than she gave him credit for. He might be a touch clumsy about courting, but if an Indian raid did come, she'd feel much safer knowing she had his protection than Robby Randall's. Jackson was militia-trained and truly cared about his family. Besides, he *was* rather nice looking, and strong. . . .

Chapter 29

"Nineteen more days," Bob Randall commented. He and John scanned from beyond the fort's clearing to the forest as they slowly walked the perimeter of the watchtower.

"Soon we'll be counting the hours." John had been doing that for some time already. He prayed constantly that Lily and his sons had done as he'd pleaded in his letter and left the cove. The French and Indians had taken particular interest of late in the area between the Susquehanna and the Schuylkill Rivers.

Bob nodded. "I've been away so long, baby Laurie's cryin' will be like music to these poor ol' ears. Did I tell you she's been walkin' for months now?"

"Only about a hundred times." John quashed a wry grin.

"Sure hope Edith didn't cut off those pretty curls of hers. They're cute as anythin'."

John shifted his stance and peered more closely at the woods. "That's right. I forgot she cut off little Charlie's when he turned one."

"Well, he *was* startin' to look like a girl. He'll be four in a couple a

days. I've sure missed a lot. Don't think I'll ever want to leave home ag—"
He stared hard into the distance. "Hey, somethin's out there." He pointed
toward the edge of the clearing.

John wheeled around.

A figure attired in French blue stood silhouetted against the trees, a
hundred yards or so away!

John peered through the spyglass. "I see him. A man in uniform."
Quickly he scanned the forest shadows on either side of the enemy
soldier, but saw no one else. Of all the times for Captain Busse to be
downriver at the fort at Harris's Ferry. For days, the man had been too
sick to make the return trip to Fort Henry.

He handed the telescope to Bob. "Watch him. If others show up, give
a holler. I'll go report."

He descended the ladder and hastily covered the ground to headquarters. Reaching the open doorway, he saw Ensign Biddle, now
in command, at Busse's desk. A couple of other men stood in front.
"Corporal Waldon reporting, sir. We spotted a French soldier out there.
Seems to be alone."

"Where?" Biddle's chair scraped back as the stocky man lunged to
his feet.

"At the edge of the forest, sir. In the southeast."

Several soldiers who'd come onto the porch after John flew by now
blocked the entrance. One spoke up. "You think the bloke's come to ask
us to surrender? Are we surrounded? I knew it was dumb to let 'em order
so many of our men up to Fort Augusta."

"We won't have a chance," another muttered. "Not with so many of
our guys out rovin' right now."

John was amazed at the outburst. Captain Busse would never abide
such disrespectful conduct.

The ensign broke past the mouthy pair without a word and charged
for the watchtower with John at his heels.

Once they reached the platform, Bob handed the spyglass to the
commander and pointed toward the forest. "Over there, sir. Must be lost

or somethin'. He just stood there watchin' the fort, then plunked hisself down. Been right there ever since."

"I see." Biddle's face scrunched up as he squinted into the spyglass. "He's armed. He's got a musket across his lap."

John prompted the ensign to issue an order. "What do you think Captain Busse would want us to do?"

"Uh—yes." Biddle returned the spyglass to Bob. "You two stay here and keep checking all around. I'll send two or three men out to learn why he's there." He shook his head. "We can't afford to weaken the fort any more than it already is." With a last glance at the French solder, he hurried back down to headquarters.

John saw Ensign Craighead and two other men dispatched in short order. From his vantage point, he could tell they weren't anxious to be going out there alone. Striding a number of feet apart, they held their weapons at the ready as they scanned the forest edge.

No one else appeared.

The Frenchman rose and strode forward, his musket held crossways above his head.

"He's surrenderin'. Don't that beat all?" Bob frowned in confusion.

"Keep watching. It could be a trick."

But it wasn't. The soldier relinquished his weapon and came quietly along with the militiamen.

Once safely inside the gates, the enemy soldier began jabbering in French. From time to time he would put his fingers to his mouth, indicating he needed food.

Militiamen converged as the soldier in the light blue coat was escorted to headquarters. One snatched away the Frenchman's tricorn, affording John a better view. Even from the watchtower, he could see the feared enemy was nothing but a shaggy-haired lad of sixteen or seventeen. Still, if he'd been wandering out there so near the fort, there could be others close by. How many? Would there be a full-scale attack?

John's heart plunged. Why now, with only nineteen days to go?

Nineteen days before he was to leave for home to be with his boys and his darling Lily, if they were still there. Once again he sent pleas heavenward for their safety and for Fort Henry.

An hour had passed since the French soldier was escorted to headquarters. In the tower, John and Bob continued to survey the surrounding woods, all the while vitally interested in the information the lad was giving the officers.

John knew everyone at the fort shared his concern. Whenever he glanced down into the fort grounds, he saw fellow militiamen keeping close watch as they waited outside the building to hear what was transpiring in that room.

Suddenly the door opened, and company clerk Carson hurried out. He dashed over to the cook tent, then ran back with a trencher of food without a word to the waiting men.

Unable to hear the conversation being bandied about on the grounds, John surmised from the way the other soldiers milled around that their anxiety matched his. Everyone itched to know if an enemy force lurked nearby ready to launch an attack.

From across the platform, Bob hiked his chin. "That lad may not be so hungry once he tastes that slop we eat."

John grinned at his friend's dry humor.

He caught a movement in the distance. Placing the spyglass to his eye, John zeroed in on the spot. Just a deer. He relaxed.

Then Carson came out the headquarters' door again. "Anybody here speak French?" he yelled from the porch.

No one stepped forward.

The ensign turned on his heel and returned inside.

Bob snorted. "Well, we got ourselves a prisoner, for all the good it's doin' us."

"Too bad we don't have any English regulars here." John's gaze continued to rake the edge of the clearing. "Some of them might know that language, with England being off the French coast."

"Far as I'm concerned, the Brits an' the Frenchies should be fightin' the whole blamed war by themselves. Us colonials shouldn't have ta risk our lives over some tree-munchin' beavers across mountains you an' me'll prob'ly never cross just so's them two greedy kings over the water can fill their treasure chests."

John cocked his head in thought. "Must be hard, trying to keep hold of so much territory. But there is a bright spot. Did you read the broadside the dispatch rider posted on the board yesterday?"

"Naw. I don't work my brain that hard 'less I have to. 'Sides, if there was anything worth tellin', you would'a already told me."

"Ha! Well, there was something you might consider interesting. Seems the English have whipped the French in Bengal. Maybe some of those soldiers will now be sent here."

"Bengal? Where's that? Up north somewheres?"

"No. India."

"*India.* Are you tellin' me they're fightin' over land in India, too?"

John nodded. "And someplace in Africa called Senegal."

"Well, now. Ain't they the busy ones." Bob's tone sharpened as he studied something in the distance. "Hand me the spyglass."

John tossed it across the deck to his friend then came alongside. He strained to see what had drawn Bob's attention.

His friend lowered the telescope with a sheepish grin. "Just some leaves on one of the trees wavin'. Thought mebbe somebody might'a climbed up it. But it was just a bear scratchin' its behind."

Moments later, their relief for sentinel duty climbed up the ladder.

"You fellas heard anythin' yet?" Bob asked.

The first one to reach the platform answered. "Yep. Finally. Since nobody could understand that lad's jibberish, it took awhile to find out he was with thirty-three Indians, Delaware and Shawnee. Somehow he got separated from them."

John gave a huff. "Sounds to me like they lost him. Deliberately. They probably didn't relish taking orders from some green kid."

"Likely they won't wanna head back out without plenty of scalps, neither," Bob added.

The second man rested an elbow on the watchtower's rail. "One thing, at least. We here at the fort can relax. No thirty-three Indians would ever try to take this fortification."

John nodded and headed for the ladder. But he knew that breaking up into armed parties of five or six, those thirty-three savages could do a lot of damage, roaming the area. His urgency to return to his family intensified. Nineteen more days.

The delicious aroma of baking bread permeated the air, and now that the nights had grown chilly, the glorious colors of autumn filled the countryside. Breathing deeply of the fresh, crisp air, Lily was glad to be outdoors, despite her icy hands. Wash day had become a huge undertaking, and she appreciated sixteen-year-old Cissy Dunlap's help as the two of them pinned up the last load of wet laundry.

A wisp of light brown hair wafted over Cissy's shoulder as she peered from around a sheet flapping sluggishly in the breeze. "I really wish you'd marry up with Jackson. If you don't, he'll probably go looking for a wife somewheres else, like Frank did. He don't hardly ever come home no more since he found his Hildy."

Lily rolled her eyes. At least once a day, someone provided her with a reason why she should choose either Robby or Jackson. "The Lord hasn't nudged me in that direction as yet." She loved giving that answer, since it usually put an end to the topic.

"Well, just so's you know," Cissy persisted, jamming a pin over the draped sheet, "Jackson don't show his best side when he's out and about. When we're home, he's always good about bringin' in water and fillin' the woodbox without bein' asked. He's like that. If he sees something needs doin', he up and does it."

"That's an admirable trait." Lily shook out a dish towel to hang and changed the subject. "How are you and Donald getting along?"

Cissy's face pinkened as she brushed her bangs out of her eyes. "Oh, he can be so silly. Yesterday he gave me a bouquet. At least, that's what he called it."

"A bouquet? Where would he find flowers this time of year?"

"Aw, it was just some tree branches with pretty colored leaves. But he arranged 'em real nice. If we was at home, I could a put 'em in our blue china vase and set it on the table to look fine."

Lily averted her gaze into the distance. "I know how anxious everyone is to return to their own homes. 'Tis so crowded now that we all stay inside at night, with only the cabin, the carpenter's shop, and the blockhouse for shelter."

"You know, if I was to home, Donald could come callin' proper-like, like the fellas did for my older sisters before they married up." Cissy pulled another piece from the basket on the ground and came up with a sigh. "That's another thing that makes me sad. Esther and Betsy wed before we came out here, and I ain't seen 'em since. They both got young'uns already, too. Just think, me, an auntie." Turning to pin up the towel, she froze, and her eyes widened. She pointed with the wet article in her hand. "Look! Smoke!"

Lily spun around. A huge black cloud climbed the northern sky.

"Oh, no. Do you think it's our place?" Cissy cried.

"Call in the children. Quick!" Leaping over the basket, Lily ran to the house and bounded through the door. "Quick, everyone, grab what food you can and get to the blockhouse."

"What is it?" Edith came from the hearth, a large wooden spoon in her hand.

"Smoke. To the north."

The women dodged past each other as Ruth bolted to the bedroom for her baby then ran outside screaming for her other children.

"Stop!" Millie Dunlap hollered above the chaos, her hands on her hips. "Ever'body stop. The men are workin' at our place today, boilin' down sorghum. Remember?"

"There's far too much smoke," Lily countered. "Dear Lord in heaven, my boys are with those men. Grab all the food and bedding you can."

She lifted down her musket and hastened outside. Quickly pouring powder into the flashpan of the weapon she always kept loaded, she fired a signal round. She prayed that the Randall twins and MacBride girls would hear it. They were supposed to stay close while out picking up wild walnuts. After reloading as fast as she could, she rammed the wad down the barrel, then dashed back inside, propped the rifle against the wall, and climbed up to the loft.

Lily scooped up an armful of blankets littering the floor and threw them over the railing to the floor below. "Grab some and go to the blockhouse," she yelled to anyone still about.

Descending the ladder, she saw that the large cauldrons of food the women had been cooking for supper were already gone. She hurried to the corner by the hearth and slung a sack of cornmeal over her shoulder. Then, with a last glance around, she grabbed the musket and ran after the others, who were already disappearing beyond the springhouse.

A sudden eerie feeling made the fine hairs on her arms stand on end. She cast a glance behind her. Seeing no one, she took off again, the heavy canvas bag bouncing against her spine with every step.

She'd just crossed the creek bridge when she heard a distant gunshot. Then another. Two more. Desperate to know what was happening, she stopped, gasping for breath, as she strained to hear any others. *Matt and Luke are out there!* The thought was too much to bear.

Why, oh why hadn't she made the boys leave when she had the chance? John had been very explicit in his letter. If anything happened to them, she'd never forgive herself.

And neither would John.

"Hurry up, Lily." Edith Randall called from the blockhouse. "We need to bar the door."

Chapter 30

"Is everyone here?" Lily glanced around the shadowy blockhouse as the door closed behind her.

"Yes," Agnes MacBride said. "Ever'body's been counted."

Ruth started bawling along with her baby as she cowered in a corner, her whimpering children pulled close around her.

Others huddled in family groups, murmuring concerns to one another.

Lily's heart went out to Nancy, who held her little Mary tight. The child shook uncontrollably, her eyes huge with fright. Mary especially shouldn't have to be here.

Fifteen-year-old Judy MacBride held up hands stained with walnut hull. "Mama, how will I ever get the stain off? Did you bring the lye soap?"

Agnes ignored her whining daughter and went for the ladder in the center, hauling her ungainly weapon with her.

Slipping the sack of meal off her shoulder, Lily followed her neighbor to the top deck. Millie and Cissy Dunlap were already there, staring intently at the smoke to the north.

"It's comin' from two places now." Never taking her eyes from the sight, Millie gestured with her head. "I can't rightly be sure, but I don't think it's our place. The smoke seems to be comin' from the farmsteads the Thorntons an' the Bakers abandoned last year."

Lily joined them to stare at the two distinct and ominous black clouds billowing above the trees beyond the clearing.

"That means ours'll be next," Cissy murmured just above a whisper.

A mental image filled Lily's mind, of everything her neighbors owned being reduced to ashes. . .including the blue china vase the girl had mentioned such a short time ago. *And even my boys, if the men haven't stopped those Indians.* She squeezed her eyes shut, trying to keep them from flooding. *God in heaven, please bring back my dear boys soon. . . .*

Edith shoved her musket onto the deck and climbed up through the hole. "Any sign of our men yet? Robby and Donald's with 'em. *Not Bob, of course,*" she grated bitterly. "Duty-bound to that blasted fort, an' all."

"Donald. . . ." Cissy swung around to Edith, tears pooling.

Lily's eyes also swam.

"Ain't no time for cryin'," Edith scolded. "We gotta keep watch, make sure them heathens don't sneak up on us." She reached for Cissy and gave her a quick hug. "Our menfolk need a safe place to come back to."

"And pray." Lily used her sleeve to wipe away the moisture in her eyes. "I'll take the east side."

Millie suddenly turned around. "Did you hear that?"

"What?" Agnes stiffened.

"Another shot."

<hr />

Time seemed to stand still as the sun slowly inched toward the west. Gunshots no longer echoed through the thick woods. The night air turned cold. Lily had goose bumps up and down her arms, but she wouldn't take a minute to go down and fetch a blanket as she willed the men—Matt and Luke in particular—to return. Visions of them scalped and sprawled on the ground in pools of blood, their sightless eyes staring at nothing, their mouths gaping in soundless cries, flashed through her mind. The single hope she could cling to was that the Dunlap place had not been set ablaze. Yet.

Most of the women and children had gathered on the platform and now lined the railing, quietly watching. Rarely did anyone utter a word.

Finally, as the sun disappeared behind the tallest trees, Edith slammed the butt of her musket against the deck in a resounding crack. "I'm through waitin'. I'm goin' down to saddle me a horse."

"I'll go with you." Lily headed for the ladder. Anything was better than not knowing.

"Wait!" One of the twins pointed toward the bridge. "Somebody's comin' across."

Friend or foe? Lily flew back to the creek-side edge, along with everyone else. She positioned her musket across the railing and took aim.

Breaking past the foliage, someone waved his arms as he raced across the clearing.

Luke! The boy was unharmed! *But was he being chased?*

Seconds behind him came Pete Dunlap and Michael MacBride.

Lily held her breath. *Let Matt be next, Lord. Please!*

As John's older son did indeed come into view, the sight of him brought such relief, Lily nearly dropped her weapon. He came more slowly, at a steady jog, his musket bouncing on his shoulder.

Tears streamed down her cheeks. Her knees buckled, and she sank down to the floor of the deck. Her boys were safe. Safe.

While she struggled to regain her composure, the other women scrambled down the ladder. One resolution took shape in Lily's mind. No matter how the boys felt about it, the three of them were going to take the MacBride canoe and leave this cove as soon as she could gather the needed supplies together.

Inhaling a strengthening breath, Lily rose and moved across the deck to the spot above the blockhouse entrance, waving to Matt and Luke as they neared.

People were already streaming out the heavy door. But where were the rest of the men? Surely those lads weren't the only survivors!

In the distance, Jackson and Donald emerged into view, carrying someone between them. Someone had been injured, but who was it? She couldn't see past Jackson. She could see, however, that Jackson wore no shirt, and his chest was smeared with blood. Had he been hurt as well?

Below, Edith screamed and ran toward her son.

Across the clearing, Richard appeared next. Ruthie ran to him, sobbing loudly, her baby bobbing in her arms.

Then, one by one, Toby and Ian came into sight, and finally Cal, limping awkwardly on his bad leg.

Lily could finally make out the person being carried. *Robby! Kind, gentle Robby.* Across the lad's middle, a wide leather belt held a wad of bloody cloth in place.

She propped her musket against the half-wall and scurried down the ladder. Before she reached the lower floor, Matt and Luke were already inside, reaching for her.

Sweat streaked Matt's dirty face. "We prayed all the way back that you were safe. We were afraid other Injuns would attack here while we were off chasin' the ones that burned those two empty farmsteads."

Lily tugged them both close and held them tight, weapons and all. "What happened to poor Robby?"

"He got shot." Matt's expression was hard with rage, but his voice sounded cool and steady. "We'd been chasin' them painted devils for near an hour when one of them leaped out from behind a tree and shot him. Jackson got that savage good, though. And we took care of two others back at the Thornton cabin whilst they was still torchin' the place."

Lily couldn't help noticing Luke remained silent, and he had more than just sweaty streaks down his face. He had tear tracks as well. "Are you all right, Luke?"

He buried his face against her shoulder and nodded, his breath catching as he tried to be brave. The handle of her much-too-young warrior's pistol gouged into her, but she didn't care. She held on all the tighter. She was absolutely determined to take the boys away from here as soon as she could. What a fool she'd been to insist on staying in this perilous cove.

Shadows filled the open doorway as Jackson and Donald carried Robby inside the blockhouse. His mother already had a blanket laid out. His teary-eyed twin sisters, Gracie and Patience, trailed behind, their troubled gazes fixed on their brother.

"Fetch some water an' clean rags," Edith ordered, her eyes wild as she crouched beside her fallen son.

Lily grabbed the bucket sitting atop a water barrel and partially filled it. She carried it to Edith and dropped down beside her.

Robby, barely conscious, moaned with pain. With his bloodied fingers he reached for Lily's hand. "Lily—" He started coughing and grimaced as a spasm made him gasp for breath.

"Don't talk, boy." His mother unbuckled the belt holding the makeshift bandage. Lily recognized the item as Jackson's shirt. "Gracie, where are them rags?"

"Here, Mama." She turned her head away as she handed them down to her mother.

Robby squeezed Lily's hand, drawing her back to him. Blood seeped from one corner of his mouth. "I. . .killed an Indian." He gulped. "You think. . .God will. . .forgive me?"

Lily leaned closer and brushed the hair from his pale brow as she did her best to smile. "Oh, Robby, I know He will. He loves you so—"

Robby's chest sagged as a final breath emerged. His eyes seemed to freeze in place, and his hand fell away.

He's dead. Lily swallowed hard.

Jackson plopped down beside her and grabbed Robby's shoulders. "Not now, man. You're home. You're safe." He shook the lad. "Robby! Wake up! Wake up!"

"Let him go." Edith clawed away his fingers. "Let go of my boy."

As quickly as he'd knelt down, Jackson sprang to his feet again. "I'm real sorry. I just—" He pivoted on his heel and bolted out.

Grace and Patience began crying audibly, and Donald, who had carried his injured brother in, draped an arm about each of his sisters and wept with them.

As Lily quietly moved out of the way, she noticed Matt and Luke staring at Edith, who sat crooning to her dead son as she brushed damp curls from his forehead. "Let's give the Randalls a moment of privacy." She took their hands in hers and drew them away. The stark realization that John's precious lads could as easily have been killed closed her throat till she could scarcely draw breath.

They strode out into the late afternoon light, not bothering to talk. Lily realized the sun had moved very little since she last checked the sky.

Her neighbors stood in clusters all about, the younger ones clinging to their parents, staring mutely into the blockhouse. Even the babies seemed to sense it was not a time to fuss.

Lily offered a fleeting prayer, thanking the Lord that Emma and Davy weren't there to witness this horrid occurrence.

"I brung him out as fast as I could." Still bare-chested and smeared with blood, Jackson fixed his gaze on her. "I know I always gave him a hard time about you, but I did ever'thing I could for him. You believe me, don't you?"

She nodded and attempted a smile. "Of course I believe you." All anyone had to do was look at the anguish on his face to know he spoke the truth. She took a step toward him.

His father, Toby, came to his side, looking equally distressed. "Son, you did more for Robby than any of the rest of us could. You carried him all that long way back to the wagon."

"I should'a got him there sooner. Mebbe if I had—"

Toby took him by the shoulders and looked him in the eye. "Listen to me, Son. Nothin' anybody could'a done was gonna save that boy. He was gut-shot an' bleedin' out. It was God's mercy he didn't suffer very long. Now, let's go down to the crick an' get you cleaned up a bit."

"Huh?" Jackson glanced down at his hands, then his body, as if he hadn't noticed he was covered with Robby's blood.

Lily untied her apron. "Here. Take this with you. I'll see about getting another shirt for Jackson."

She watched them stride toward the creek—the usually powerful Jackson stumbling along with his father, still staring at the blood on his hands. Obviously his guilt stemmed from the rivalry he and Robby shared, not his efforts on this most terrible of days.

Jackson's mother came up to Lily. "I'll go fetch my son a shirt." Then Millie wagged her head. "I'm startin' to believe no piece of bottom land is worth all this sufferin', no matter how rich it might be."

As Millie walked away, Lily's gaze gravitated back to the Randalls inside the blockhouse, weeping quietly and consoling each other. She drew Matt and Luke close. "She's right, boys. No land is worth a single hair on either of your heads."

Chapter 31

No sense all of us crowdin' together in that blockhouse." Cal swept a glance over Lily and the others who stood waiting for the Randall family to come out. "We run them red devils off good an' proper. They won't tangle with us again anytime soon." His light brown eyes grew soft as they gravitated to his little, golden-haired Mary. "Let's take the young'uns back to the cabin so's they can warm up."

Ian gave a decisive nod. "Cal's right. Go on back. I'll stay here awhile longer."

One by one, the women trickled inside the blockhouse and gave Edith a hug or an empathetic squeeze to her shoulder. No one seemed able to think of anything to say to comfort their grieving friend. Each neighbor emerged with a kettle or skillet of food that had been cooked earlier. Watching through the doorway, Lily wondered if Edith even noticed their presence.

Lily went in last for the sack of cornmeal. She ran a soothing palm across the heads of Robby's siblings as they sat in a circle around his body, watching tearfully as their mother worked at bandaging the unfortunate boy's wound. The lad had been the kind of son and brother any family would have been proud to have.

Backing out of the structure with the sack in one hand and an armful of blankets, Lily knew Robby would have made a wonderful husband, too.

The loaves of bread in the outdoor oven the men had constructed weeks ago had burned to black lumps during the crisis. The women quickly whipped up some less-tasty johnnycakes, and the somber neighbors gathered at two long, makeshift tables stretching almost the length of the cabin's common room. The air crackled with tension as everyone waited for Ian to fetch the Randalls for supper.

Realizing she was fiddling with her fork, Lily placed it on the table and slid a glance across to Jackson, several seats away.

Flanked by his mother and grandmother, each of whom held one of his big hands, the young man wore a clean linsey-woolsey shirt. Not a speck of blood remained on him, and his hair looked darker than usual, damp and slicked back. His eyes were downcast, but bright blotches on his face bore evidence of recent weeping.

Sudden, loud footsteps pounded on the porch.

Lily's attention flew to the door.

Edith Randall burst in, auburn curls all askew. She gulped in air as if she'd run all the way from the blockhouse.

Lily's blood turned cold. Had the Indians come back?

The woman took several gasping breaths, then let the air out in a whoosh. "I want one of you men to go get that shiftless husband of mine. You get him back here so's he can see what he let happen to my boy."

Jackson wrenched up from his seat. "I'll go fetch him right now." He threw a leg over the bench.

"No, Son," his father ordered from across the table. "Sit down. It's too late to go tonight." Toby turned his sympathetic gaze to the distraught mother. "We'd spend all our time out there just wanderin' around, Edith, lost in the dark. First light, me an' my boy'll start out." He switched his attention back to his son. "Sit down, Jackson. We'll make better time in the mornin.'"

Jackson eyed his father momentarily, then cut a glance to Robby's mother. His shoulders sagged, and he slumped back down, staring right through his trencher as if it wasn't there.

Lily's heart ached. Toby was close to sixty years old, and the trip would be hard on him. But she didn't doubt his wisdom. In Jackson's present state of mind, he'd probably run his horse near to death.

Edith glared wildly at Toby for a few moments, then as suddenly as she'd come, she charged outside again, bumping past her returning children and Grampa MacBride.

Cissy Dunlap flew to Donald's side as soon as the lad entered the room. "Come sit with me, Donald." She took his hand.

He pulled his fingers from her grasp. "Not tonight, Cis. I need to sit with my family."

"Oh. Of course." Inching back, Cissy's sad blue eyes misted as she watched him follow his siblings to vacant seats at the far end of the table. . .the same lad who'd brought her a carefully selected autumn bouquet just the day before.

At times like these, the comfort of family overshadowed the pangs of young love. Lily was utterly grateful she had Matt and Luke next to her.

If only John were here, too.

Even as that longing surfaced, so did the hope that if Bob actually were to come back, the commander would release John also. Only twelve days remained of his enlistment.

Ian's voice spoke out from between the two tables. "Let's ask God's blessing on this food and pray for Almighty God's comfort at this sad time."

Edith never left the blockhouse that night, and Lily knew that in the woman's present state, she'd have been no comfort to her other children.

The only time anyone caught a glimpse of her the next day was at dawn, when Toby and Jackson rode their mounts out of the stable. She ran up the path from the creek just as Lily and Millie brought a last cup of tea and food to the men for their trip.

Edith looked like a wild woman, her hair tangled and flying every whichway, her eyes red and swollen, bloodstains spattering the front of her day gown. Vapor clouds spewed from her mouth in the chilly air when she spoke. "Just makin' sure." She came to a stop several feet in front of the men. "You get that useless man back here right quick." Then, whirling around, she marched down the path again.

"Don't let it get to you." Millie handed the food up to her husband, then the steaming cup. "She just don't know where to put all her pain."

Lily realized Jackson could easily read something extra in her being there, and wondered if it would have been wiser to have his grandmother bring the food to him. Wishing she had awakened Eva, she gave him the cinched bag of leftover johnnycakes and sausage before passing the tea up to him.

But as he took the mug, Jackson didn't offer his usual over-confident grin. His lips moved into a merely grateful smile. He took a couple of large gulps and handed the cup back. "Tell Mistress Randall we'll bring Bob back as quick as humanly possible." Then he reined his mount around and nudged him forward. His father bent down and gave Millie a peck on the top of her head then followed their son.

⌒

The ominous, dreadful sound of nails being hammered into a coffin echoed from the workshop. With Ian busy at the chore, Lily sought a task that would take her away from the noise.

Out back in the vegetable garden, digging up potatoes with Ruth, she spied Richard and Cal rumbling away in the Dunlaps' wagon.

Ruth dropped her shovel and bolted after them. "Where you goin'?" Fear heightened her voice. Aside from Ian, these were the only two grown men left in the valley.

"We're gonna fetch the sorghum molasses from Toby's place. We left it there when—" He stopped abruptly. No one needed a reminder about the Indian attack. "Don't worry. I promise we'll be back."

Cal leaned around him. "Might be a little while. We're gonna look around a bit, too." Snatching the reins from Richard's grip, he snapped them over the horses' backs before Ruth could utter a protest.

Lily could hardly blame the man. Ruth's tendency to be hysterical was no secret. And now poor Edith. Lily gazed across the barnyard and down toward the creek. How long would she stay inside the blockhouse, secluded like that?

Only after Ian had finished the coffin and taken Donald and Michael with him to get Robby's remains did Edith leave the blockhouse. Her eyes fixed on the blanket-wrapped body, she followed as they carried the lad to the workshop. As she approached the door, her two youngest ones ran to her, but she pushed them away. Both immediately started wailing.

Gracie and Patience ran to the children and scooped them up. The twins did their best to comfort them, since their mother had nothing to offer.

The sound of more nails being hammered shattered the quiet as Ian fastened the lid in place. There would be no last viewing.

Maggie walked up between Lily and Agnes. "It's best this way. For her own good, Edith needs to be separated from the boy's body now."

But a mere closed coffin did little to deter Edith from her son. The second Ian and the lads left the building, the grieving mother shut herself inside and locked the door.

She did not come out for the rest of the day.

Calvin and Richard returned at midafternoon with the assurance that the Indians had left the area. The news provided Ruth much-needed relief. She'd gone into the house with her brood as soon as the men drove away and kept the little ones on the floor beside her stool while seven-year-old Lizzie helped at the spinning wheel. Ruth sat rigid, working fast, her flintlock pistol in her lap.

That evening, Maggie took a trencher of food and a small pot of tea out to Edith. The woman had remained sequestered in the workshop all day and wouldn't open the door to anyone, not even Maggie. Ian's wife finally sighed and left the offering on the doorstep.

Had it not been for the funeral, Lily would have taken the boys that day and left Beaver Cove.

At the close of the supper meal, Grampa MacBride picked up his Bible and motioned for everyone to remain seated. "I was hopin' Edith would be here for the readin', but I'm sure the scriptures will edify the rest of us. We all share our neighbors' great sadness."

Lily glanced along the table to Donald and the Randall children. Cissy sat beside Donald now with baby Laurie on her lap. That family needed all the comfort and help anyone could give.

"I'll be readin' from the first chapter of Philippians."

As the elder's voice filled the room, Lily put her arms around Matt and Luke. They'd done their chores without any reminders today and then found extra work to keep busy, just as she had. She hoped they'd be tired enough to get a good night's sleep.

" 'I am in a strait betwixt two,' " Ian read, " 'having a desire to depart, and to be with Christ; which is far better: Nevertheless to abide in the flesh is more needful for you.' "

A sense of peace infused Lily, that the moment Robby's soul left his body, he'd received the answer to his final question. The young man knew instantly that he'd been forgiven by God and deeply loved. He was now in the very presence of the Lord.

Ian's voice drew her back to the present. " 'And in nothing terrified by your adversaries: which is to them an evident token of perdition, but to you of salvation and that of God. For unto you it is given in the behalf of Christ, not only to believe on him, but also to suffer for his sake.' "

That last statement struck Lily. Was God calling her or any of these people to suffer here for the sake of Christ? Or should she and everyone else in the cove stop acting like fools and leave? Cal and Richard may not have found any sign of the Indians, but war parties were noted for hitting and running, attacking anywhere, anytime, at will. Any day they could all be killed. Had Robby's death furthered the kingdom of God?

She folded her arms. She would stay two more days, no more. Long enough for Bob to get here and Robby to be laid to rest. And should John return with Bob, she prayed he'd allow the boys to leave with her. She couldn't pray for anything more than that. . .not even for John.

No matter what else occupied her thoughts, they always came back to her desire for John Waldon, her dearest friend's husband. Most likely that was why she had yet to receive assurance from the Lord regarding Jackson's proposal of marriage. She'd left the poor young man dangling.

The sight of the half-moon-shaped fort came as a relief to John after the long, hard march from Tolihaio Gap. His feet felt raw and could use a few days' rest within the safety of those stone walls.

Again, as during the last ranging, all the moccasin tracks not washed away by the recent rains were days or weeks old. And all pointed eastward. The Indians always managed to slip past the patrols. John wrapped his knitted scarf tighter against the cold breeze. Would they *never* leave for the winter?

Walking a few feet from him as their roving party crossed the clearing in a wide spread, Pat gestured with his head. "Ain't that Jackson Dunlap comin' this way?" He immediately raced toward Dunlap, spurring John and Bob to follow suit. By the time they converged, John had imagined all manner of horrors. Had his family left, like he'd asked them to? Or had they stayed, been murdered, or carried off?

Pat grabbed hold of Jackson. "What happened, son? Is it my family?"

Jackson's terrible gaze slid past Pat and John, stopping at Bob.

Bob latched on to John's arm.

"It's Robby," Jackson blurted. "He's been killed. Indians."

John felt a surge of relief that it hadn't been Lily or the boys. *May God forgive me.*

"No. Please, God. No." Bob would have collapsed in grief had John and Pat not been supporting him. "I should'a stayed home." He shook his head over and over as they turned and headed back to the fort, bringing him along. "Edith's been wantin' me an' him to trade places, an' I was gonna do it. I was. A couple a more weeks, an' he would'a been here. Safe. This fort ain't once been attacked. I'd a had them make him a cook's helper or somethin' that would keep him inside. Oh, Robby, Robby." He rambled on in a flat tone the entire way back to the fort.

As they neared the gates, Toby Dunlap came out and strode up to Bob. "We're all real sorry. Just want you to know your boy weren't no coward. He shot one of them murderers before they got him."

While Toby administered comforting thumps on the grieving man's back, John sidled over to Jackson. "I need to know, lad. Are Lily and my boys still at the cove?"

He nodded. "Aye. But they're fine. All the families have been stayin' at your place for weeks. Us men took the Injuns by surprise whilst they was torchin' the old Thornton place."

"Was my pa with you?" Pat asked, leaving Bob with Toby.

"An' your Michael. We was at our place boilin' down sorghum cane."

John's breath caught. "What about my sons?"

"They was there, too. You got a real steady boy, in Matt. He shot and loaded that musket of his 'most as good as the rest of us."

John's head almost exploded with rage. His little twelve-year-old son, having to fight off Indians like a man! "I'm going home with you. And I dare Captain Busse to try and stop me this time."

Chapter 32

At the bend in the river, the silhouette of Harris's stockade and the ferry dock came as a welcome sight after a grueling day's ride from Fort Henry. The sun had set some time ago, and John had wondered if he and the others would make it there before dark.

Harris's Ferry—where before the hostilities, John had brought his wheat and corn to be ground into flour and meal, where he'd brought hardwood logs to be cut into boards for furniture. Harris's Ferry, now better known as Harris's Fort, had a stockade surrounding the store, the smithy, and cabins. The settlement's promising future as well as his own had been hanging in the balance for more than two years.

Riding ahead of him, Bob hollered over his shoulder. "Let's keep goin'. We could be home well before midnight."

"Bob." Toby emitted a weary sigh and reined his mount past John's. "The horses are tired, and we'd be goin' through the woods at night. The trace to the cove ain't marked that good."

Jackson came alongside John and called out, "We'll get an early start, Bob. Be home by midmornin.'"

The grieving father clamped his lips shut in resignation.

Once inside the gates and safe for the night, the full force of exhaustion settled into John's aching body. He'd had too many hard days in a row, and tomorrow would be worse yet.

After tending their horses and begging a supper of pork-flavored beans and fried potatoes from the militia cook, John and his three companions trudged to the blockhouse. There they laid out their bedrolls in a corner unused by the other militiamen. John noticed Toby looked as worn down as he felt himself. Hours of steady riding had taken its toll on the older man.

They eased down to the dirt floor and were starting to get comfortable when Bob regained his feet "It's stuffy in here. I'm gonna eat outside."

"The place does reek with the perfume of sweat and dirty stockings, that's for sure," Jackson quipped. They were the first lighthearted words he'd spoken since he and his father had delivered the bad news.

As Bob sauntered out, Toby lumbered up. "I better go with him. Don't want him getting no fool notions in his head—like takin' off without us." He followed his neighbor.

John watched after his friends, then, sitting cross-legged with the meal before him, he looked at Jackson. "Let's ask the blessing over the food." He bowed his head. "Father in heaven, thank You for the meal You've provided. Thank You that we reached here safely today. But mostly I want to thank You for good neighbors, men like Toby and Jackson Dunlap, who left their own family to Your safekeeping to come and fetch Bob. I pray You'll give Toby the words Bob needs most to hear. In Jesus' name. Amen."

John had barely dug into his food, when he became conscious of Jackson's gaze darting to him. The lad had something on his mind. "What is it, Jackson? What haven't you told us? Did something else happen we should know about?"

"In a manner of speakin."

John hoped none of his family had been injured.

"Me an' Robby both asked Lily to marry up with us."

John sat up straighter. The news came as no real surprise, since both young men had been eager for her hand. Still. . . "At the same time?"

" 'Course not." Jackson set down his spoon. "I asked her first; then the next day Robby did."

John maintained a placid expression, but this was tough to hear. "And?"

"She give us both the same answer. Said we all was supposed to pray about it. See who God wanted her to wed. And terrible as it is. . ." He glanced out the door, which had been left ajar. "Looks like God did answer. I guess what I'm sayin', sir, is I'd be plumb pleased if you'd give your blessin.'"

My blessing? John swallowed. He'd been wanting Lily for himself for months, even—God forgive him—before his wife passed away. And Jackson wanted his blessing as if he were Lily's father!

He swallowed again around his tightening throat. "I can't do that, son. I need to speak to her first, learn what's in her heart. She's a free woman now. She doesn't need my blessing." He took a healthy gulp of tea.

"She's always spoke real highly of you. Your blessin' would mean a lot." Jackson leaned forward, a nearby lantern reflecting the youthful eagerness in his dark eyes. "An' I want you to know I'd take real good care of her, buy her fancies an' such. I'd never lay a hand to her. I don't cotton to a man bullyin' a woman. 'Specially someone as sweet an' purty as her. When I joined the militia, all I thought about was goin' on a big adventure. But now all I want is to go home an' make a good life for her an' me."

The lad continued to stare at him, and John knew he ought to say something. "Going home, living our lives in peace again. . .that's what we all want." He reached over and patted Jackson's knee. "Eat up so we can get some sleep. We're going home in the morning." But sleep would likely be the last thing John would be able to do.

⌐⌐

With so many people crowded into the house since Edith had barricaded herself in the carpentry shop, the only peace one could get was before dawn. Lily sat quietly sipping her tea in a dining chair pulled close to the hearth while a number of MacBride and Randall children slept at the opposite end of the room.

She felt blessed to have Maggie MacBride and Millie Dunlap beside her. They were two of her favorite friends in the cove. She leaned toward them to whisper. "I expected the men to return last night. I woke at every little sound."

Millie's lips curved with a reassuring smile. "Only if Bob was at the fort and not out ranging when Toby and Jackson got there."

No one mentioned the always obvious possibility, *if* they made it.

Lily shifted her gaze back to the dancing flames. What if Bob was at the fort and John was not? The men wouldn't—couldn't—wait for him to return. John might not be with them. Her chest banded tight at the thought. She needed him here, now, more than ever.

"I pray the men come today," Maggie said quietly. "I don't think Edith will come out of that workshop till Bob gets here. I knew her takin' care of eight young'uns and a farm all by herself was getting the best of her. And with the ever'day threat of Injun attack. . ."

Millie darted a glance behind her at the slumbering children. "She was startin' to say some purty crazy things. An' now this. It's just too much for a body to take."

Maggie nodded. "She's gonna need a lot of extra love an' care. An' prayer."

Lily agreed. "Mercy, but I do wish she'd come out."

One of the sleeping children coughed, and Lily glanced over at the youngster before finishing her tea. "It's starting to get light. I'll go see if the hens have laid any eggs." Stepping quietly to the door, she plucked her heavy cloak from a hook and walked out into an icy mist.

Duke and the other dogs on the porch stood up, their tails swishing back and forth.

Lily untied them so they could take care of their morning business. She wouldn't be passing the carpentry shop, but still her gaze drifted to the shadowy building across the yard. The interior was dark, and no smoke issued from the iron stove inside. Edith must be freezing after locking herself inside with no more than a thin blanket around her shoulders. Lily sent yet another prayer aloft for her friend. *She needs Your care now more than ever, Father. Please look after her. And Lord, where is that joy You promised? And where is John? Is he not coming?*

The sight of the Randall children laughing and wrestling and slinging pillows with the other kids in the loft lifted everyone's spirits. The youngsters needed a few carefree moments before the afternoon's funeral service.

"Let's get them young'uns fed." Agnes MacBride set a platter of johnnycakes on the table to go with the new supply of sorghum molasses, then raised her voice. "A couple of you lads run an' fetch the families from the blockhouse."

"I'll go." Her eldest son, Michael, untangled himself from two little ones and came to his feet.

"I'll go with you." Matt went to get his musket racked high on the wall along with several other weapons.

"Don't forget your coats." Lily's reminder came seconds too late. The door slammed behind them.

"Come an' get it," Maggie called out.

The words were scarcely out of her mouth before the children clambered down the ladder and ran to one of the long tables, pushing and shoving to crowd in.

Lily scooped up the toddler, Laurie, and placed the little one on the lap of one of the twins. A ruckus sounded outside.

The dogs charged off the porch in a mad scramble, all barking at once.

Lily shot a glance to Millie. "Could it be the men this early?" She and half the household rushed out to the porch.

But the dogs hadn't gone in the direction of the lane. They were racing out back to the orchard instead! A high-pitched yelp came from one of them. Then another!

"Run!" Ian nudged the nearest children into motion. "Make for the blockhouse! Fast as ye can!"

The rest of the kids leaped from the porch, the older ones carrying the youngest. Lily and the other adults and lads charged back into the cabin for their weapons. Lily uncorked her powder horn in a frenzy and sprinkled some into the flashpan, then unhooked the ramrod and shoved the already-loaded paper cartridge wad more firmly into the barrel.

Noting that the others were already out the door, she regretted having taken that extra time. Without a second to waste, she flew off the porch and raced for the blockhouse as fast as her legs would take her.

Chilling screams and war cries pierced the air. Ominously close. The Indians must have already reached the stable! She didn't dare chance a look back.

Coming to the bridge, she caught up to Eva, who hobbled awkwardly as she ran. Not slowing, Lily grabbed the elderly woman's arm and dragged her along.

Within seconds they were past the creek undergrowth and onto the blockhouse clearing. *Out in the open!*

Deafening explosions came from both directions.

A bullet whizzed past Lily's ear.

The Indians were close! Too close!

"Hurry!" someone yelled from the door. "Hurry!"

Gasping for breath, Lily pulled Eva inside the split-log door as two bullets slammed into it.

Ian shoved it closed, and Richard dropped the heavy bar into place.

Cal shook his head. "From the number of muskets bein' fired, there must be fifteen or twenty of 'em out there. This is no small raidin' party." He headed for the ladder behind Richard. "Gotta get up top, make sure the boys don't waste their powder."

Glancing wildly around, Lily realized her two weren't among the children present. They had to be up above, *getting shot at!*

Eva's knees gave way. She started sinking out of Lily's grasp.

Millie caught hold of the sagging woman's other arm. "Are you all right, Mama?" She and Cissy took her from Lily and eased her down onto a sack slumped against a wall. "Talk to me," Millie urged, stooping before her.

The old woman's lined face was beet red. She shooed them away with a trembling hand. "Let me. . .catch. . .my breath."

"*Mama!*" one of the Randall twins wailed. "*We forgot Mama!*" She flew to the door.

Her heart sinking, Lily remembered that Edith was still out in the carpentry shop.

"Somebody has to go get her." The twin clawed at the heavy door.

Lily had to stop her. "You can't go out there, dear. You'll get shot."

"But what about Mama?" Tears streamed down Gracie's freckled face.

Taking hold of Gracie's shoulders, Lily turned the girl to face her. "With all of us running for the blockhouse, I doubt the Indians even suspect she's there."

The girl stared openmouthed as Lily's statement sunk in. She sniffed. "That's right. They're shootin' at us."

Lily nodded and eased her hold. "I'm going up top to help out now." She turned toward the ladder.

"Lily! You're bleeding!" Gracie pointed at her.

"What?" She quickly scanned her body.

"The back of your arm."

Propping her weapon against the wall, Lily tugged her sleeve around. It did have blood on it. . .and now that Gracie mentioned it, her arm started to hurt a bit. "Must've grazed me. Find a rag to wrap around it, would you?"

As the girl wrapped her arm, Lily saw that most of the young children were crowded at the back, whining and sniffing. Ruth had three little ones in her arms, nuzzling them and speaking in soft, comforting tones.

Lily arched her brows in wonder. Odd, now that the danger was actually upon them, with weapons firing from above and bullets splintering wood, Ruth's hysterics had vanished and she was admirably calm.

Lily snatched up her musket and hurried up the ladder. Seeing Matt and Luke down on the floor with other boys their age, loading weapons for the men and older lads, she nearly bawled with relief. She hunkered below the line of fire and scurried to Cal, crouched with only his musket, his hair and eyes above the half wall. "Cal?" She tapped him on the shoulder.

He sunk below and turned to her.

She leaned close to his ear, so as not to worry his son Henry, who was loading for him. "Edith's still in the carpentry shop."

"I know." Regret clouded his light brown eyes. "There's nothin' we can do about it." For a grim second or two longer, his gaze remained on Lily. Then he turned back.

Lily glanced around, counting more shooters than loaders. She dropped down beside Cal's son Sam as he rammed a shot and traded him her loaded musket for his. At fourteen, he was too young to be standing off a war party, but she knew the male in him would never allow her to swap places.

As she finished preparing Sam's musket, bullets flew across the watchtower from all directions. The blockhouse was surrounded! And no one had gone for help!

Sam fired and exchanged his spent weapon for the one Lily had finished preparing.

His father turned to him. "Did you get one of 'em?"

"I don't know for sure, Pa."

"Don't waste powder. Take sure shots."

Lily wondered if they had enough gunpowder to hold off the Indians.

Shortly, the shots coming from the war party within cover of the woods slowed to one or two every twenty or thirty seconds. They, too, were being frugal.

Across the deck, Richard tipped his head at Lily. "Don't appear as if they're gonna rush us, at least."

Cal gave a huff. "They'd be fools. They know they can bide their time. With no one knowin' we're bein attacked, they could hang around out there for days, till we run clean outta powder and food."

Ian looked from one to the other and back. "In the last couple months, we've killed seven of 'em. They're probably here for revenge."

Donald Randall hiked his chin. "Well, my pa's comin'. He'll know what to do—iff'n he don't ride into a trap."

And John? Now Lily didn't know whether or not to hope he was with the others. It was too much. All she wanted to do was cry, but she had to stay strong.

"Smoke!" Calvin raised up higher and pointed with his musket.

A shot whistled past him and he ducked.

Lily had to know. As she inched up cautiously and peeked over the edge, a bullet punched into the half-wall just below her. She hunkered back down. But she'd seen the evidence of destruction.

"It's comin' from the stable." Twelve-year-old Pete Dunlap's high-pitched voice rang out. "An' the loft's chock full of hay."

Lily stiffened. Her milk cow, Daisy, was still in there! And those savages would burn the other buildings as well.

And Edith!

Chapter 33

A thick wall of smoke roiled up beyond the trees lining the creek, eliminating all doubt. The Indians had set the buildings ablaze. Lily hadn't heard Edith screaming, but then with all the other noise and confusion. . .

Ian sat with Donald, holding the young man close as choking sobs wracked his body. For all he knew, his mother had either been hauled out by the Indians for some unspeakable manner of horrendous torture, or she was being burned alive inside, and he could do nothing to save her. None of them could.

Tears streamed down Matt's and Luke's faces as they witnessed their friend's grief. Their muskets stretched idle across their laps. Everyone up here knew.

Lily no longer tried to contain her own tears. These people were her dearest friends in the world, and like everyone else, she felt devastated and helpless.

"Ian." Cal tapped the old man's shoulder and spoke quietly. "I'm startin' to see smoke comin' from your place."

"Figures." Ian had never looked so old as when he eyed Cal over the top of Donald's drooping head.

"Mine'll be next." Richard gave a bitter laugh. "To think I made Ruthie stay here—for this."

Just then, a flaming arrow buried itself into a roof post.

As Richard stretched up to dislodge the thing and toss it off, a bullet grazed his cheek. He swiped at the blood with the back of his hand then took hold of his musket again.

Donald rubbed his red eyes and jerked free of Ian's grasp. Picking up his weapon, he slid the barrel across the railing. Mourning for his mother would have to wait.

John had expected to reach Beaver Cove earlier this morning. But a mile outside of Harris's Fort Bob's horse went lame, necessitating a return to the fort for a fresh mount. The weak sun would reach its zenith within the hour, but the day had yet to warm, and mist still dripped from the trees.

Anticipating a blazing hearth and a hot meal, he pulled off his tricorn and dumped the trapped water. The densely wooded trail had started to look familiar a few minutes back. He recognized the old lightning-struck oak and a small stream they'd crossed that fed into Beaver Creek. They'd reach Cal's place soon.

"You guys smell that?" Toby straightened in his saddle. "Smoke."

"We're getting close to home." Bob nudged his mount to a faster pace.

The Patterson clearing still lay some distance ahead when John's nerves bristled. The acrid smell floating toward them was too strong to be from a fireplace. Sounds of crackling and snapping grew louder by the second. Breaking out into the open, the evidence hit them full force. Every structure had been afire for some time. Roofs had already collapsed, and the slower-burning log walls smoldered black. The sight made him want to retch.

Gawking in shock, the others pulled out their weapons. But as they rode cautiously in, they could tell the Indians were long gone. Savages never lingered to revel in their destruction, just torched things and left as quickly as they'd come.

Toby reined alongside John. "Thank God, Cal and his family are at your place."

Bob spoke up, his tone raw with hatred. "There's more smoke to the south. They must'a got my place, too." He jammed his heels into his horse's flanks. "Come on."

With two miles separating the Patterson place from his own farmstead, John knew that even riding the animals hard, they wouldn't get to the blockhouse for twenty minutes, maybe thirty.

All too soon, they saw smoke coming from across the creek at Toby Dunlap's farm. John wondered why Richard and Cal let their property burn without running the savages off as they'd done before.

The group scarcely even slowed when they passed the smoldering, charred ruins of Bob Randall's place. From the meadow, the clear sky revealed a dense cloud filling the horizon to the south. Breathing came harder, and even the horses had to be urged onward. Had the Indians burned out the entire cove? The blockhouse?

It took all of John's better instincts not to charge full speed into the melee. He kneed his mount to the front and caught the reins of Bob's horse, pulling them to a stop, then turned to the others. "This has to be a larger war party. Let's not just ride in there like a bunch of idiots without a plan of attack."

A gunshot sounded from the south.

From the direction of the blockhouse.

⌇

Two more flaming arrows slammed into the roof.

Lily knew the men couldn't reach them without getting shot. But if the roof burned, it would collapse and crash down into the interior. They'd all be burned alive. Like Edith.

"Water!" Cal shouted. "Get buckets of water up here quick!"

Ignoring her aching arm, Lily scrambled to the ladder even as flames licked greedily at the top, spreading fast. "Water! We need water. Now!"

Another shot echoed through the woods.

The gunfire gave John a boost of hope. If someone was shooting, the blockhouse must still be standing. "Men, let's come up on the Indians from behind. Spread out. Make them think there are a lot more of us than there are. When we spot the devils, shoot your muskets, yell, and move before firing your pistols."

Jackson snorted. "An' chase the horses toward 'em to make more noise. Them savages'll think they're surrounded. They don't like fightin' if they don't got the upper hand."

Rage sharpened John's fear as he edged into position. If Lily had taken the boys away when he'd asked, he wouldn't be in such knots. He could wring her pretty neck for this.

Father God, You know I don't mean that. Keep them safe. Keep them all safe.

A feather bobbed up above the brush, moving stealthily. John moved from behind a tree to get a clear shot.

Jackson, further down, fired his weapon and gave a wild shout.

The Indian John had spotted sprang up.

John fired and hit his mark, and the painted savage crashed into some brambles.

Toby, at the rear, yelled and whipped the horses forward.

John hollered and moved as the enemy shot in his direction. Spotting the musket flash, he ripped his pistol from his belt and fired, then gave a wild yell and rolled away. He needed fifteen seconds to reload his musket and another five for his pistol.

A bullet crashed into a tree close to where he'd been seconds ago.

While he reloaded, a chilling scream followed another shot. Jackson had the best war cry.

The lad's fire was returned from two separate sources.

A musket report sounded from John's other side. Most likely Bob. Everyone knew not to shoot at once and give the enemy time to reload and charge them.

Weapon loaded, John crawled forward, passing the Indian he'd shot, sprawled facedown across a stickery bush.

A few yards ahead, another brave broke out of the undergrowth and ran off.

John fired. Missed.

The warrior never stopped. As three others popped up and sprinted after him, John berated himself for not having loaded his pistol, too.

Someone else shot at the fleeing savages and missed, but at least the marauders were on the run.

John gave a victory yell then crawled behind a tree and reloaded both weapons. He could still hear distant shots coming from the far side of the blockhouse clearing.

Crouching low, he hurried toward the building, gasping in shock when he saw flames licking up from the roof of the watchtower.

Toby came alongside. "God protect them!" he shouted and started forward.

John grabbed his pal's leg and yanked him back. "We have to stop the redskins on the other side first."

"Look!" Toby pointed. "I saw water bein' throwed on that fire. Our people are still up there."

A shot fired from the blockhouse.

An Indian fell into the clearing.

"Come on. We gotta scare those devils off." Skirting the cleared section, John led the way through the woods. Halfway around, he spotted a torch, the source of the flaming arrows. He fired.

It crashed to the ground, along with the warrior.

Another of John's comrades fired and hollered. John yelled with the others.

In a flurry of feathers and painted bodies, a dozen braves exposed themselves and raced to the west after the others. They were leaving at last!

John emptied his pistol at them then charged out of the trees toward the blockhouse, yelling and waving his musket overhead.

The structure's charred, sagging roof creaked and splintered then came crashing down. *Were the boys up there? And Lily?*

He had to get there before the fire reached below. Let everyone know it was safe. "Come out! Come out!"

He heard Bob and Jackson shouting as they emerged into the clearing. If only someone inside would hear them. Open the door.

Reaching the building, John banged on the door with the butt of his pistol. "Open up! It's safe! We're here!"

Screaming and crying erupted inside, and he heard the bar being raised. *Please let my family be there!*

Another section of the roof crashed down in flames.

The heavy door scraped inward. Frantic, John gave it a mighty shove, and people rushed out, crying and laughing.

Luke grabbed hold of him. Then Matt. He hauled them close. His boys were unharmed. *Thank You, God. Thank You. Thank You.*

But— John's heart pounded double-time. "Where's Lily? Is she all right?"

Matt lifted his head from John's shoulder. "Inside."

Why hadn't she come out? Didn't she know the roof was about to. . . ? Shoving his sons aside, John charged inside, where smoke was already drifting down through the cracks and filling the interior.

Then he saw her, kneeling with Cal beside a prone body.

Ian! The old man was conscious, but blood was staining the wad of cloth Lily pressed to his shoulder. Intent on her task, she had yet to look up.

"We had to drag him down the ladder," Cal explained.

John glanced up the length of the steps, where flames licked through a splintered board across the ladder hole. Reaching down, he took hold of Ian's arm. "Help me, Cal. We've got to get him out of here."

Lily's head jerked around. Her gaze met John's and held. She continued to press on Ian's wound while the men dragged him outside a safe distance away from the blockhouse. That's when John noticed the bandage on her arm. She'd been hurt, too.

As he and Cal gently laid Ian down, Maggie and Agnes dropped to their knees beside the old man, taking over from Lily.

"Isna' bad," the Scot assured his wife and daughter-in-law, but the strain on his face belied his brave words.

Neighbors crowded close, talking and crying and laughing at once.

"Can't abide gawkin," Ian said, wincing with pain. "Get the supplies outta the blockhouse b'fore they burn up."

As John took a step back, Jackson caught Lily—*his* Lily—away. The young man whisked her off the ground and hugged her to him.

Lily's wild gaze flew to John.

He didn't know if she was shocked by Jackson's aggression or was embarrassed that he'd seen her and Jackson together in such a familiar way. Fists clenching, he started toward them.

"Where's Edith?" Emerging from the blockhouse with a sack of grain over his shoulder, Bob searched frantically around. "Where's my wife?"

Edith! Lily pushed away from Jackson. "Let me down. Please. I need to go to Bob."

"He already knows about Robby." Frowning, Jackson lowered her to the ground.

"But not about Edith." She scanned the crowd for him.

Several neighbors had crowded around Ian. Ruth was tending the slash across Richard's cheek. Donald and Bob's other children stood frozen in place, wide-eyed as they stared at their father. Bob's gaze searched the area.

Lily hurried to John and took hold of his knotted fist. "Please, John. Bob's going to need you now."

His hand relaxed, and he wove his fingers through hers as she led him to his friend.

"Where's Edith?" Bob asked again.

Lily placed a hand on his shoulder and prayed for the right words. "I'm. . .so sorry, Bob. Edith locked herself in the carpentry shop with

Robby's casket and wouldn't come out for anyone. We need to go and see. . . ." Unable to finish, she bit her lip.

"*What?*" Bob wrenched away from John and latched on to Lily, his fingers digging into her arms. She flinched in pain. "*You left her to the Indians?*"

"The war party came on us all at once. We had to run for our lives. It wasn't until we were in the blockhouse being shot at that we realized she wasn't with us. Believe me, there are no words to describe how terribly helpless we all felt. I'm sorry. So very sorry."

John unfurled his friend's fingers from Lily's arms and took him in a firm hold. "Let's go across and find out what happened to her. The Indians might have dragged her away with them."

"Aye." Reason began to take hold. "Aye." The man dashed madly toward the bridge with John right behind him.

Although she dreaded what they were certain to find, Lily picked up her skirts and followed, uncaring that her arm burned and ached. She was more concerned about Bob and what he would have to face. She barely noticed that Donald, Matt, and Luke caught up with her.

On the other side of the creek, Lily saw that the springhouse and smokehouse, tucked in the trees near the creek, were untouched. Likely the Indians were saving them until they had time to empty the food stores. Climbing the rise, she passed the hog pen and noticed only one hog lay dead. The other three grown ones and their spring babies were still alive. The stable and corncrib, however, were nothing but charred jumbles. And just beyond. . .

Lily stopped in her tracks.

The carpentry shop still stood! Nearby, the roof of the cabin had burned and crashed in, and the interior still smoldered. But the shop appeared to be untouched!

Bob reached the structure and pounded on the door. "Edith! Edith! Are you in there?" He swung his musket up, butt first, and used it to bang harder.

Miracle of miracles, the door swung open. And there stood Edith, haggard and weary, her hair unbound and tangled.

Her husband gaped at her for a second, then pulled her into an embrace, kissing her and murmuring over and over in her ear. "I'll never leave you again. Never. I promise."

Lily stared at the couple in wonder, so overwhelmed by God's mercy, she broke into sobs.

John immediately enfolded her trembling body within his warm, strong arms.

She clung to him, weeping, until at last she was able to regain control of herself. As Matt and Luke moved in to hug her, too, her heart ached with joy.

When her shuddering breaths eased into more natural breathing, John held her away and searched deep into her eyes. "Now, tell me. Why on earth didn't you take the boys and leave here when I asked you to?"

Lily moistened her lips and swiped at her tears, then lowered her lashes. What could she say?

Chapter 34

John's gaze pierced Lily's soul as he stared at her, his features hard as granite. "How many times did I ask you, *implore* you, to leave Beaver Cove? Look around you, Lily. Everything you risked your life for, the lives of my sons for, it's nothing but ashes."

She had no words to speak in her defense. John had every right to be furious. With nothing to say for herself, her attention shifted to his youngest son. "Luke, run back to the blockhouse and spread the word that Edith is fine. There's a good lad."

"Yes, ma'am!" The boy trotted off, happy to be the bearer of good news on this tense day.

Reluctantly, Lily raised her lashes and peered up again at John. She opened her mouth to speak, but Matthew cut in.

"It ain't all her fault, Pa. The families had already decided to stay together in one place, to keep safe. Besides, you know it was me that refused to go anywheres."

His father pressed his lips together in a grim line.

Lily could tell he wasn't ready to forgive her. She was the one in charge. She should have compelled the boys to go away with her.

John's voice held a husky quality when he responded to Matt. "You two have no idea how I felt when we got to the valley and saw all the farmsteads on fire. I was so afraid I'd lost you, I could hardly breathe."

"We know how that feels." Matt raised his chin. "We watched our place burn up while we was trapped in the blockhouse. And we was sure Mrs. Randall was bein' burned alive—or worse."

Reminded that Bob and Edith stood but an arm's length away, Lily turned to them. "Edith, dear, I have to ask by what miracle you were saved?"

Edith, composed now, but dispirited, snuggled close to her husband and tried to smile. "Them savages was in such a hurry to get in on the turkey shoot over to the blockhouse, they just broke out a window here an' tossed in a couple of torches then took off. They didn't have an inklin' I was inside. I up an' threw them fire sticks right back out. That's them layin' over yonder." She pointed at two blackened lines marring the ground. "I was so worried for y'all, I never stopped prayin'."

Lily shook her head in wonder. "We never stopped praying for you, either." Moving to her friend's side, she took Edith's hands in hers—the woman who only this morning had been so beside herself with grief that she wouldn't leave her son's coffin.

"Bob tells me all my other young'uns are fine. That so?"

"Luke went to fetch them. Any minute now you'll be able to see for yourself." Sensing John's presence behind her, Lily bit down on the inside corner of her lip as he put his hand on her shoulder.

"What about you? Your arm, I mean."

For the few moments when she'd first caught a glimpse of him and then had to deal with his anger, she'd put thoughts of pain aside. But now it returned with all its biting and burning furor. Still, gazing into his eyes, she saw only concern in the blue depths, and it strengthened her. She ignored the discomfort, knowing the injury would be taken care of soon enough. " 'Tis a bit of a slice, I believe. I didn't even realize I'd been hit till I reached the blockhouse."

Matt chuckled and shook his head. "You should'a seen Lily come racin' in, draggin' poor ol' Eva behind her." Suddenly he grew serious as he searched past her with a frown. "Duke! Duke! Come, boy!" Waiting a second or two, he ran off whistling in the direction the dogs had gone earlier.

Lily looked back at John. "The dogs charged out to the orchard this morning, barking for all they're worth. They warned us in time, but we haven't seen them since. I'm afraid the Indians might have killed them."

John let out a resigned breath. "Guess I'd better go after Matt, then." Turning, he loped past their gutted, blackened house after his boy.

Lily couldn't help but appraise the destruction around her. Years of work she and John had put in, and so little had been spared. Whatever would he do now? What would any of them do?

⌒⌒

John strode back from the orchard with his arm about Matt's drooping shoulders. It seemed for every moment of joy, there was another of sadness. All three dogs lay dead, their bodies slashed by tomahawks and their throats cut. But Matt hadn't shed a tear. He set his jaw, his face hard with hatred.

Passing the unburned chicken coop, John wondered if the chickens would return to it this evening, considering the burnt stench coming from both sides—the stable across the barnyard and the house. He heaved a shuddering sigh. Hundreds of hours of labor gone in a morning.

The door to the root cellar near the smoldering log house remained intact. "Wait here. I want to check that out." He unlatched the door and swung it to the side, then climbed down the steep stairs into the shadowy, cave-like structure. His brows hiked at the sight of more canvas and jute sacks brimming with stores of fruits and vegetables than he'd ever seen it hold before.

"A lot of other families put their food down there, too," Matt called from above. "You should'a seen our hayloft. That's why the stable burned so fast. All that dry hay stuffed in. We been keepin' a lotta extra livestock here."

As John climbed back up, shouting and laughter reached him from out front.

Matt's sober face softened with a little smile. "Must be the Randall bunch. God gave 'em a miracle, for sure."

Rounding the corner of the rubble, John saw Bob's kids running pell-mell toward their mother. His gaze landed on Lily, who stepped away from the enthusiastic mob and started toward him. She looked from him to Matt and back, but said nothing.

"The dogs didn't make it," John said quietly.

Lily's eyes, soft with love, drifted to Matt. She reached out and brushed the hair from his brow. "Duke was a great dog, a true hero. He sacrificed his life to save us."

The boy's chin began to tremble, and he nodded. "He was the best." He sniffed. "Think folks'd mind if we buried him up on the rise beside Mama?"

She turned her beautiful, questioning eyes up to John.

"Why should anyone mind?" he asked.

"Yesterday the lads dug a grave for Robby up there. Ian also mentioned building a church on the hill after the trouble is over—providing you approve, of course."

John wasn't entirely certain he wanted to donate a patch of his hard-earned land to anyone. He tipped his head at Lily. "What do you think? That's quite a bit of property. Covers at least two or three acres."

She shrugged. "It could be used for a schoolhouse later, too. Think how handy that would be."

John couldn't help wishing she'd have said the church and school would be handy for *us*, but she was not his. Disappointment pulsed through him. He angled his head in thought. "Since we've been here, cash money has been so tight, I haven't been giving a tithe to the church, just helping folks out where the need happened to be. I suppose this could be my tithe."

A wistful smile spread across her lips. "I like the sound of that. A thank-you to the Almighty for saving us all here this day."

Standing before him with her golden hair every whichway, her day gown smudged and torn, and her delicate face streaked with dirt, Lily had never looked more beautiful. Drinking in the sight of the silver-eyed angel who had spent years of her own life caring for his loved ones, John gave a thoughtful nod. "Speaking of money, I haven't forgotten I've owed you two pounds since your indenturement contract ended. And extra, since you've stayed on since then to look after the boys."

Lily reached out a hand, then retracted it. "No. You're going to need every pence you have to rebuild. Mariah and my father sent me money from time to time during the last four years. I've more than enough already."

"But didn't it just burn with the house? The paper, the coins, they're probably melted into the rubble."

Her lips quirked into a half-smile. "Actually, with so many families living here, children running about and getting into things, I thought it best to bury it. My pouch is down in the cellar."

John realized that Lily could have bought back her papers and left Beaver Cove years ago, had she wanted to. Yet she'd stayed all that time. Hope came to life. Then he reminded himself it was for Susan and the children, not him. Even were he bold enough to ask her to marry him, how would she react to his betrayal of his wife's memory so soon? And what would the rest of the people of the cove think of him?

Looking over her shoulder, John spotted Jackson striding their way. His brash, young neighbor seemed certain Lily would marry him. If that were so, how would John deal with her living so close, knowing she could never be his?

"There you are, Lily." Jackson stopped behind her and straightened his shoulders, his expression rife with confidence.

She turned toward him. "Why, yes. Your timing couldn't be more perfect. The children are positively starved. We hadn't even had breakfast before the attack. Would you mind bringing up a ham from the smokehouse?"

"Uh. . .sure." He opened his mouth to say more, then clamped it shut and hastened off to do as she asked.

"Fast thinkin', Lily." Matt winked.

When she turned back to him and his son, John noticed a delicate tinge rise on her cheeks as she smiled at them. "Well, don't make a liar of me, Matthew. Run down to the cellar and bring up a dozen potatoes and a couple of those large squashes. And, John, would you see if you can salvage any pots and skillets from the hearth without getting burned in the process? Oh, and may I borrow your knife?"

"As you wish." He handed her his hunting knife and started around the smoldering remains of the kitchen, amazed at how his sweet, shy Lily had taken charge. With no effort at all, she'd dispatched all three of them to do her bidding. Another thought teased his consciousness. Considering Matt's remark, perhaps she wasn't quite as spoken for as Jackson Dunlap had led him to believe.

Surveying the confusion around him, John saw Ian's friends assisting the old man across the creek. His wound had been cauterized to stop the bleeding, and his wife had fashioned a sling for him. Maggie wasted no time getting her injured husband settled on a chair someone brought out from the workshop.

As aromas began wafting on the air from food cooking on open fires, Ian's wife insisted on seeing to Lily's arm. "Don't want no infection startin' in, you know," she said, clucking her tongue as she assessed the injury.

The older kids entertained the little ones near the well, and John gathered with the other men around Ian to plan the next move. He squatted down with Bob, his closest friend.

Richard Shaw still held a cloth to his cheek. He glanced at his friends and shrugged. "Still seepin' a bit. It'll stop soon 'nough."

"I believe the poker those wee womenfolk used on my shoulder's still hot." Ian's chuckle turned into a groan. Despite his pasty look, the Scot never lost his humor.

"Think I'll pass, if ya don't mind." Richard gave a one-sided grin.

"Wouldn't wanna scar up this purty face any more'n I have to."

"I don't think those savages'll tangle with the likes of us again anytime soon," Toby Dunlap said. "But what with winter breathin' down our necks, I don't see we have much choice but to send the women downriver to whatever family or friends'll take 'em in for a spell. Meanwhile, me an' Jackson'll stay here with our livestock an' get our place built back up."

"So ye plan on stayin'," Ian said thoughtfully. "I'd be obliged if ye'd look after our animals. With Pat still up at the fort an' me winged, we'll have to leave here for a while. Leastwise, till I'm fit again."

Cal met his gaze. "Would you mind takin' Nancy an' my young'uns down to Baltimore with you, Ian? I'll be stayin' here, too, with my oldest boy."

Bob kneaded his beard and focused his hazel eyes on John. "What d'ya say, my friend? You game? We could turn that workshop of yours into a barrack till we get some roofs up."

"You men really want to start all over?" John looked from one to another.

Bob shrugged. "I ain't got nothin' to go back to anyplace else. Took all I had to buy my piece of land here an' bring in my family. Donald'll stay with me, won't you lad?" He gave his second son, crouched on his other side, a hug.

"We built our places up from scratch the first time," Cal added. "Nothin' says we can't do it again. Fact is, it should be easier this time. Our fireplaces should still be good. An' think of all the clearin' an' fencin' we already done."

Richard eyed them with a bit of hesitance. "If we had some real assurance the redskins wouldn't be back, I'd stay around. I'm not sure I'll be able to convince Ruthie to come back till it's safe, otherwise."

John glanced over his shoulder at the women busily cooking over what were normally the washtub fires. Several of them, Lily included, slanted inquisitive glances his way. If he agreed to stay, he and the boys would be separated from her again. No, it would be just him and the children this time. Lily would be returning to her own family.

Disheartened, he turned his attention to the men grouped around him. "I'll stay. Me and my boys—if they want to. I came here to provide them with a future, and I intend to see it through."

"You mean you're gonna send all the womenfolk away?" Young Donald shot a plaintive look at Cissy Dunlap.

John started to smile. Then he saw Jackson lean past Richard to get a gander at Lily.

The young man rose to his feet. "If everything's settled, I'll—"

"It's not." John blurted out the words. He waited, watching until Jackson crouched down again. "There's still the matter of the rafts we'll need to build for transporting the women and children, to say nothing of supplies. They'll need as much as we can spare. We can build cabin shelters on the rafts and hire river men to take them from the mouth down the Susquehanna."

Toby nodded, his face set with determination. "Let's get started right after we eat. Shouldn't take more'n a day or two. I'm sure there must be wood we can salvage at the MacBride place."

"So, is that it?" Jackson stood up again. Without waiting for a response, he made a beeline straight for Lily.

Chapter 35

"Who do you think should say the words over our sweet Robby?" Agnes bent over a skillet to flip a sizzling ham slice, the steam adding roses to her cheeks. "Ian shouldn't have to climb that hill, wounded like he is."

Lily only heard her friend's comments on the edge of her consciousness as she tended another slice of meat. Jackson was heading straight for her.

Millie straightened, a stir spoon in her plump hand. "Toby's the next oldest here. I'll speak to him about it."

Edith, quiet once more, with her hair curls neatly brushed, moved closer to Millie and gave her a self-conscious hug. "I–I'm plumb sorry I went so crazy there for a spell. I just couldn't—"

As if he'd overheard and didn't want to intrude, Jackson stopped in his tracks.

Millie returned her friend's embrace with loving pats on the back. "We were grievin' right along with you. Now we're tickled to have you back. We were all prayin' for you."

Agnes stepped away from the fire, sincerity in her hazel eyes. "God answered our most fervent prayers. I shan't ever doubt Him again."

Lily knew she'd have to face Jackson any second, and though the answer to her friends' prayers had been obvious, Lily had yet to receive the direction she sought from God. The only thing she felt was dread every time she had to deal with Jackson, and now he was upon her again.

His glance swept the group, then focused on Lily. "Can I have a word with you?"

Mille gave her a nod. "Go ahead, dear. I'll watch your skillet."

"Thank you." Trying not to show her reluctance, she placed her spatula on one of the stones surrounding the fire pit with the reminder that Jackson's plump little mother was a sweet-natured woman no one would mind having for a mother-in-law.

Jackson led Lily away from the women at the cookfires, from the men still clustered at the woodshop, and away from the noisy children playing a game of drop the handkerchief. He steered her behind the tall hickory tree that had shaded many a Sabbath dinner last summer, then turned to her, his dark eyes intense.

She peered over her shoulder and caught John's steady gaze. What would he want her to say to Jackson?

"Lily." Jackson took her hands in his. "The men are gonna send all you women and young'uns away till we can get the cabins rebuilt. I can't wait no longer. I need your promise now. I need you to promise to return to me when I send for you."

Lord, what should I say? Please give me wisdom.

"I know your family'll try to persuade you to stay in Virginia with them. But like I said before, you belong here with us, with me. I know it, an' you know it." His grip tightened.

Be honest.

Had that come from God? How simple. . .yet somehow frightening. Lily eased her fingers from his and took a breath as she prayed for courage. Unsmiling, she looked him in the eye. "I'm afraid I cannot give you the answer you want, Jackson. I do not have the deep feelings for you that you profess to have for me. Nevertheless, I've honored your marriage proposal by praying for the Lord's leading, and He has not given me peace about making a commitment to you. You're a wonderful young man, and you deserve someone who can love you with her whole heart. That is not me. I am truly sorry to hurt you, but my answer must be no."

His demeanor hardened with confusion. "But I thought with Robby gone—"

"God never directed me to accept his proposal, either. And now the Lord is removing me from the cove altogether. Leaving here will be very hard for me. I shall miss all of you so very much."

He caught hold of her arm. "Then don't miss us. Marry me. I'll make you love me. Give me a chance."

Regarding him in silence, she stepped out of his grasp. "I must get back to work now."

As she turned away, Lily felt as if a huge weight had been lifted from her. She'd probably hurt Jackson, but he was young and would realize in time her refusal had been for the best. And even though it was inappropriate, she couldn't stop her lips from curling into a wondrous smile. The Lord had answered her. *Be honest.*

<hr />

John felt deflated as he watched Lily return to the cookfires wearing a happy smile.

She'd only covered half the distance when Matt broke away from the children's game circle and ran to her. John would have given anything to do the same and run to her, tell her not to marry Jackson, to marry him instead. But that was not possible.

Matt gave Lily a quick hug then ran back to the game, all smiles himself.

A frown knitted John's brow. He could've sworn his son didn't want her to marry that young man any more than *he* did. Matt must have decided her returning to the cove at any price was better than having her go to her sister's and never come back.

His gaze remained on Lily as Millie walked up to the men seated in a circle. "How are you feelin', Ian?"

The older man glanced down at his sheathed arm. "Me shoulder's still burnin' some, an' I'm weak as an ol' dishrag. But I dunna' want ye to be frettin'. I'll be fit again in a few weeks, Lord willin'."

"You know you'll be in all our prayers." Millie rested a hand on the back of his chair. "The reason I asked is because we're fixin' to take Robby up the hill after noonin'. We don't think you should hustle up that grade whilst you're feelin' poorly. I was wonderin' if maybe Toby could say the words over the boy."

Toby's brown eyes flared wide, and his face went almost as pale as Ian's. "I ain't no good at that sort of thing." He rubbed his balding head.

John scanned the group. None of them appeared willing to take on the chore. The cove had always relied on Grampa Mac to oversee all things religious.

"John had hisself a lot more schoolin' than the rest of us," Toby hedged. "He could read the words without stumblin' over 'em."

All eyes turned to him.

He felt panic begin to rise.

Bob's gaze was the most beseeching. "I'd be much obliged if you'd say the words over my son."

How could he let his best friend down? John smiled and nodded. "I've got my New Testament in my saddlebag. Maybe Ian will show me the passage to read."

"Don't mind a'tall, laddie."

"Well then, I'll go see if I can catch my horse." John stood to his feet.

"They all wandered in awhile ago," Cal said. "I had my boys put 'em in the pasture an' unsaddle 'em. Your gear should be hangin' over the fence."

"Thanks."

John left the men and started across the barnyard toward the pasture. On his way, he noticed Jackson striding fast for the creek, his head sagging. He didn't look like a man who'd just had his marriage proposal accepted.

Matt, still grinning from ear to ear, came running. "Where you off to, Pa?"

"Going after my Bible. For the funeral service."

The lad's smile faded. "I forgot about that. I sure am glad Lily ain't gonna marry up with that Jackson."

John slowed. "She told you that?" He let go of the breath he held.

"Yep. Now she won't haf'ta leave us."

Reining in his foolish joy, John wrapped an arm around his son. "Walk with me to the fence. We need to talk."

Once they reached his saddlebag and John removed the New Testament, he turned to Matt. "Son, the other men and I have decided it's best to send the women and children downriver while we rebuild. You're welcome to stay and help out, or you can go with them. But this you must understand. When Lily leaves here, the only logical place for her will be with her family. And once she reaches her sister Mariah's and gets some much-deserved pampering, I doubt she'll want to give up the luxuries of plantation life to come back to the hardships here. She's a lovely young woman, and she deserves the best."

"But she loves us."

John averted his gaze across the heat waves rising up from the stable, to where Lily was busy spreading out blankets from the blockhouse for sitting. So much of her hair had worked loose of its pins, she'd finally allowed it to hang free. The silky waves shimmered like molten gold in the sunlight with her movements. He had to will his eyes from the glorious sight. "Yes, she does. She loves you children very much." He laid a hand on Matt's shoulder. "And if you love her as much as you say you do, you should think about her and what's best for her." *As I am trying to do.*

Matt jerked away, his jaw set. "*We* are what's best for her. If you were around more, you'd know that." He wheeled away, leaving John gaping after him.

Obviously, Lily's leaving would be as hard on the boys as it was for him. With a defeated sigh, he started back to Ian. First things first. Right now he had a funeral service to prepare.

As John neared Ian, he saw the women in the distance handing the children whatever containers for food they could scrounge and sending them to the blankets. Lily chatted happily to each little one as she forked out pieces of fried ham. He drank in the sight of his beautiful Lily. . .loved by one and all.

Ian's voice brought him back to earth. "Hold on there, laddie, b'fore ye run into me."

John turned his head forward. "Sorry. My mind was somewhere else. On. . .the need for lots of trenchers and wooden spoons."

Ian's mouth twitched up at the corner. "An' furniture, I 'spect. An' mebbe a wife?"

John's breath caught. The old man knew exactly where his focus had been.

"Time's runnin' out, ye know, laddie. She'll be gone tomorrow."

"But. . .how. . . ?" His feelings couldn't have been so obvious. How many others were aware? He crouched down before Ian and spoke in a low tone. "You know it wouldn't be proper. Decent, I mean. It's barely two months ago that we buried my wife. Besides, Lily was entrusted to my care. I'm supposed to provide for her, not lust after her."

The Scot cocked a brow. "That all ye feel for her? Lust?"

"No, of course not. There are a thousand reasons to love her. All anyone has to do is look at her, be around her for any length of time, to know that. Her sister in Alexandria probably has several suitable men in mind for her already—men with the means to give her anything she wants."

"They canna' give her you or yer children."

John eyed him for several seconds. "What exactly are you saying?"

"That wee lass has been secretly moonin' over ye ever'time ye come home, just as ye do her. This *watchin' an' longin'* betwixt the two of ye has been goin' on for months now. I know ye've both tried to ignore those feelin's, but they're plain as the nose on yer face. Why do ye 'spose me Maggie insisted on stayin' at yer place that time?"

John felt heat rising up from his collar and climbing to his hairline. So those knowing looks Maggie had given him weren't merely his imagination. "Does anyone else suspect? Does Lily?"

He shrugged. "I canna' say. But even if folks did, ever'one knows what a fine wife an' mother she'd make ye. 'Twould be a perfect fit. Besides, nobody wants to lose her any more than you do. We've all come to love the lass. 'Specially those young lads of yours. They'd move heaven and earth for her if she asked them to."

It all sounded good, but John wasn't easily convinced. "But. . .so soon after Susan?"

Ian tipped his grizzled head. "All of us know the years of sufferin' yer whole family, includin' Lily, has been through. An' the way Susan loved ye, she wouldn't want ye to be lonely for the rest of yer life. Part of ye will always belong to her, but that don't mean there's no room in yer heart for another love. There's not one among us who wouldn't be pleasured by seein' yer family experience a season of nothin' but blessin's."

John couldn't believe what he was hearing. Then he remembered Dunlap, and gave a small huff through his nose. "No one, maybe, except Jackson."

"Lily doesn't love the lad, John. An' who would wish a loveless marriage on her after the selfless, lovin' care she gave Susan? Now, hand me that Bible. We need to take care of another piece of sad business now."

Chapter 36

Lily could not have been more impressed by John as he gave a heartfelt Bible reading over Robby's grave, then offered a prayer expounding the lad's qualities and expressing the sadness of everyone who'd known him. She could tell Bob and Edith felt comforted as they stood in a solemn cluster with their remaining children, drinking in his words. Even at this sorrowful moment, Lily sensed John's sincerity and the respect his neighbors had for him. He was a man whose faith never faltered despite his trials, who'd never wavered in his love for his wife through all the years of her illness. A man who had sacrificed two years of his life in the militia to keep the residents of Beaver Cove safe.

Throughout the graveside service, she reveled in the opportunity to gaze freely upon him without worrying that someone might notice. He stood tall and confident as his rich voice offered comfort to the mourners, and Lily feasted her eyes on his strong, handsome features, the square jaw that softened whenever he smiled, the compelling blue eyes that slanted downward when he was troubled, the nicely shaped lips that had once melded to hers in a heart-stopping kiss. Knowing she was gazing upon him for what could be the last time in her life, she memorized every feature, so she could draw upon those memories in the long years to come.

At the close of the service, he stayed behind to help cover the grave. As Lily walked down the hill with Matt and Luke, she thanked the Lord for another small blessing. Jackson Dunlap had not attended the gathering. After the noon meal, he and his dismal expression had ridden to Palmyra to fetch his brother Frank home. He would not be back until the morrow.

Reaching the bottom of the hill, Lily paused to let other families pass by. She tugged Luke's coat tighter about his neck against a sporadic, light mist that threatened rain. "I see your top button is missing."

"I got it here in my pocket."

"Splendid. I'll sew it on, then." She gave a light chuckle. "If I can find a needle." She paused, serious now. "Luke, will you be staying here with the men or leaving with me?"

He glanced beyond her, past the trees to the blackened rubble. "Wouldn't be right to leave." He smirked. "But when I look at the mess we gotta clean up, it sure is a temptin' thought."

"That it is." She tilted her head. "I'd gladly stay and help."

"You would?" His sky-blue eyes brightened.

Matt scowled. Always the more somber one of the two, his tone sounded almost angry when he spoke. "There's no place for you to stay. There'll barely be room in the carpentry shop for us men."

At the lad calling himself a man, Lily could hardly contain the smile tickling the corners of her mouth. But as the words settled in, so did a grievous sadness. She would be leaving the only family she'd known for the past four years, leaving Pennsylvania for Alexandria, Virginia. She'd sorely missed her sisters when they'd been torn apart on the Baltimore wharf back then, but that nearly forgotten pain wouldn't begin to compare with the parting facing her now. This one would be forever. And she wouldn't even get to say good-bye to Emma and Davy, her precious babies.

Her gaze drifted over her half-grown boys. "You're going to be such handsome men one day."

"Aren't we, though." Grinning, Luke hiked his chin and puffed out his chest.

Matt's expression, however, crumbled. He understood.

The moment needed lightening. "Tell you what, my fine lads. Let's go on a scavenger hunt. With this damp weather settling upon us, the embers should be dying out. Maybe I'll find my needles. I remember the exact spot where I left them."

Luke turned and took off, but not Matt. Almost as tall as Lily, he entwined his strong fingers in hers and looked up at her with sad azure eyes that were heart-melting replicas of his father's. "I'll never forget you, Lily. Never."

Lily cast a despondent look down at her hands and day gown. She was black with soot. While John and the other men went to the MacBrides' to build rafts, she'd been sorting through the rubble, salvaging whatever she could for the boys before the time came to leave.

Once again she thanked God that two of the families staying at the blockhouse had a supply of lye soap and a few other necessities. Ruth and Nancy had even offered clean clothes to Lily and the other women for their trip back to civilization. More of the Lord's tender mercies.

The scent of biscuits baking in the cast-iron dutch ovens drifted her way as she walked toward the well. The overcast sky was darkening as this longest of days drew to a close. Scouring the black from her hands, she noticed that two of the wagons had been rigged with canvas tents to keep out the rain. The men would have to sleep out in the cold until the women and little ones left. Small wonder they were in such haste to build those rafts. Toby voiced the opinion that if they didn't waste time, the conveyances would be finished as early as tomorrow afternoon.

La, how she dreaded leaving here.

Returning the piece of soap to a nearby log round, she picked up the drying rag and wiped her hands before joining Nancy and Agnes at the cookfires. "I'm going down to the cellar. Is there anything you need from there?"

"No, lass." Looking every bit as spent as Lily felt, Nancy brushed a strand of light blond hair out of her eyes.

Lily put fire to a piece of kindling to light her way in the dark cellar. "I'll be back in a few minutes."

Along the way, she snagged the shovel she'd been using earlier to sort through the ashes. The sooty handle dirtied her hands again, but she sighed and took it with her anyway. She should have completed this chore before washing up.

Down in the shadowy cavern, she lit the lantern hanging from the beam and began to dig. She'd saved twenty-four pounds of the monies sent her over the years. Twenty-four pounds. Rose had needed only four more pounds to satisfy Papa's creditors when she'd indentured herself to that unscrupulous sea captain. Lily could still remember the shock and sorrow she and the family had felt upon learning of Rose's actions. She also recalled not being able to bear the thought of her older sister sailing off to some faraway land alone, and so had done the same herself—as had Mariah, but for her own reasons.

The thought made Lily chuckle. Beautiful, headstrong Mariah eventually married her dream, a rich plantation owner—but not until the Lord taught her a few hard lessons.

With the ding of metal on metal, the shovel hit the small pewter container. Wedging it up with the lip of the tool, Lily reached down to get her *buried treasure*. Four pounds would be more than sufficient to see her safely to Mariah's. The remainder she'd leave for John. So much was needed here now.

Footfalls descended the steps. Lily swung around, and her heartbeat quickened.

John! Coming down here, in this secluded place!

He wore a peculiar expression. "Nancy said you were here."

"Yes." His nearness ignited a spark of awareness of her very smudged self, even though John's clothing was far blacker than hers. Collecting her thoughts, she held out the small round container. "I came for the money."

"The money," he said absently without looking at it. Regarding her without blinking, he inhaled. "I have something to say to you, and this is likely the only privacy we'll get."

"Quite true." The root cellar, with its abundant piles of sacks and baskets of food suddenly felt closed in. Airless. And John, scarcely two yards away, seemed to fill it with his presence. "I have something to say as well." She somehow managed to speak past her tight throat.

"You do?" He took a step forward.

"Yes. And I'll not accept your refusal."

He frowned, as if puzzled over her comment.

She cleared her throat. " 'Tis the money. I shall take only enough for my trip. The rest I'll leave with you. There are so many things that need to be purchased."

He took another step closer. "Lily. . ."

She waited a heartbeat. "Yes?"

"You've always been. . .a fine, honest—" He rolled his eyes. "That's not what I came to tell you."

Baffled, Lily wondered why he was fumbling so. He'd always been so sure of himself. She took a step toward him.

Be honest with him.

"Oh, but I couldn't."

"What?" John took her hand, the tenderness in his eyes stealing her breath.

Lily's cheeks flamed. She'd actually said the words out loud! "I. . . that is, the Lord—at least, I think it's the Lord—wants me to tell you something."

He tucked his chin in disbelief.

She put her free hand over her throbbing heart. " 'Tis not the first time I've heard from the Lord today, actually." She nibbled her lip, then filled her lungs and let the words pour out like water over a fall. "Considering everything, you'll probably think I'm horrid for saying it. . .but I cannot leave here with it unsaid. I love you, John. I do. With my whole heart. This love for you has been growing inside me for months, and no matter how I try, I cannot stop—"

In an instant she was in his arms, his lips on hers, his heart pounding against her own with the same wonder, the same incredible joy that radiated through her. When at last the kiss ended, her head was spinning and her knees weak.

What had just happened?

John's penetrating eyes glistened with moisture as he cupped her face in his palms. "Ian told me not to worry about what anyone else might think. He says it's a good thing—a gift from God—that we've grown to love one another. He doesn't believe anyone will condemn us, because it's right and good."

Lily was struggling to process John's words. Had he just told her he loved her?

Then suddenly, he eased her away. "No. It isn't right. It isn't right at all."

She felt as if her whole being started to cave in. " 'Tis Susan, is it not?"

"No." He shook his head. "Maybe it should be, but it's not. I'm being far too selfish. You deserve much more than I can offer you. You'll be going off to Mariah's tomorrow, and while you're there, I want you to remember what life was like before you came to the cove. I want you to see what life could be like for you again, in a place where every day isn't a struggle. I want—"

Lily pressed her fingers to his mouth to stop him. "And if I promise to do all of that, should I want to come back here afterward, will you stop me?"

He drew her hand away and kissed her palm, his gaze searching deep into her very soul. "If you still wish to return after you've spent at least three months with Mariah, I'll not stop you. But keep in mind, my love, the danger here is far from past. The Indians could attack Beaver Cove again."

"And you keep in mind this war cannot last forever." She reached up and slipped her arms about his neck.

He pulled back slightly. "By the way, what did the Lord say to you, exactly?"

"Oh, that." Her lips spread into a grin. "Not once, but twice today, He said it. The first time was when I spoke with Jackson. This time it was with you."

A frown drew John's brows together. "Surely He didn't have you tell Dunlap you loved him, too."

"No, silly." She laughed lightly. "The Lord said, 'Be honest.' "

"Honest, you say." Smiling, John drew her close again. "Then I reckon I'll have to be completely truthful with you. I absolutely love and adore you. . .sooty nose and all." Tipping her chin up with the edge of his finger, he lowered his head and kissed her once more.

━━

"Lily. . ." Luke reached out and caught her hand. "You are comin' back, aren't you?"

John tore his gaze from his son's hopeful expression. All around him, men were bidding tearful farewells to their wives and children on the ferry dock as their families boarded the three rafts. But Lily was all that mattered to John.

She raised her silky lashes to look at John over the lad's head, and those yearning gray eyes tore right through him.

One of them had to remain strong. He managed a curt nod.

She gave Luke a small smile. "Your papa made me promise not to make that decision until—"

"I know. Him an' you already told us how your other family wants you, too. But you love us best. I know you do."

The other promise John had exacted from her, not to tell his sons or the other people of the cove about the glorious confessions of love that had transpired between them in the cellar, pierced him to the core. He knew only too well that if the boys knew, they'd pressure Lily into making a commitment to return. If she did come back, he wanted it to be her decision, without regret.

He saw her lean close to Luke's ear and whisper something. *Please, Father, don't let her make a promise she may not keep.* Luke walked away with a disturbingly satisfied grin.

She then turned to Matt, who'd been waiting off to the side. Nearly as tall as Lily, he stood stiff as a ramrod, his expression beyond solemn.

Lily wrapped him in a hug. "My dear, dear Matt. You've been my rock for so long. I never could have gotten through these past two years without you. Thank you so very, very much." Easing him away slightly, she looked at his face. "Thank you for being the wonderful person you are. I'm ever so proud of you." Her gaze moved to his shaggy hair, and she ruffled it playfully with a smile. "My scissors are somewhere in the rubble. Find them. You still need a haircut."

Matt bucked his head away and smoothed down his brown thatch as he became serious again. "Come back to us," he said simply, his voice breaking. Turning, he bumped past John and bolted off.

John's heart wrenched at the sight of his son's shattered expression. He felt even worse when he looked back at Lily and saw her eyes brimming with tears. Stepping close, he took her hands in his. He couldn't afford to embrace her—he'd never find the strength to let go—or to kiss away the tear tracing a glistening path down her angelic face. The weight of all the things he wanted to say to her but didn't dare was like a chain about his heart. Mustering every ounce of fortitude he possessed, he cleared his throat. "Give my best regards to your sisters and Nate."

"Oh, yes. Nate." A delicate pink crested her cheeks. "That day when you found me, he saw us—well, you know." She moistened her lips.

Centering on those soft rosy temptations, John swallowed. "He sure did. The man knew about us even before we did. But you have to remember you've been pretty isolated here. Away from the rest of the world. There's so much more out—"

She rolled her eyes in frustration. "Will you stop? You needn't tell me again. I shall do as you say and consider the rest of the world. Not that I want to, but because you've asked it of me." She darted a quick glance around, then moved closer. "Take care of those boys. Especially Matt. He always tries too hard. . .and so do you. Take care, my love."

Those last whispered words turned John to mush. "Take care," he rasped, his voice husky. Then as Matt had done, he pivoted and hurried off the dock. Unable to watch her float away, possibly out of his life forever, he kept going.

Chapter 37

When Lily had escorted Emma and Davy to their grandparents' home in Philadelphia, she'd been amazed at how untouched by war the red brick city had been. But as she rode atop a wagon seat along the Potomac River toward Mariah's home, the expansive fields of the plantations and the opulence of the manors she passed left her awe-stricken. These aristocratic Virginia planters were far wealthier than she remembered. Even more breathtaking in this bare-tree month of November, a rainbow assortment of autumn leaves drifted placidly on the breeze as she and the driver passed beneath interlocking branches that created one glorious archway after another.

It seemed not even a whisper of the war had reached this place.

Lily knew that was not quite true. Mariah's husband, Colin, had been blinded in the first months of conflict, a full year and a half before Beaver Cove and the other settlements west of Reading ever suspected they were destined to be attacked in such vicious, wolf pack-like raids.

"Miss." The driver removed a hand from the reins and pointed. "We're coming up on the Barclay's Bay cutoff."

Lily glanced ahead to the oak-lined lane leading to the elegant manor house. She'd been here only once before—for Mariah's wedding—but the grand entrance was unmistakable. At least a dozen majestic trees graced either side of the driveway that circled a lovely fountain sitting like a diamond in the center of the expanse fronting the home.

" 'Twas such a blessing, Mr. Harris, meeting you at the Potomac ferry crossing. Otherwise I should have had to take the stage the rest of the way into Alexandria and arrange transport from there. You saved me hours, if not an entire day. I do thank you for your kindness."

The pleasant-faced gentleman guided the team onto Mariah's lane. "Nonsense, lass. For a spell now, you've provided me with the company of a lovely young miss, and it didn't put me out one whit." A jovial smile tweaked his bushy salt-and-pepper mustache.

Lily knew that as the proprietor of a general store in a small settlement farther west, above the falls, he had spoken truly. "Nevertheless, I deem it a pure blessing." She glanced ahead at the great white columns that graced the front porch and supported the balcony above. *Mariah, daughter of a mere tradesman, lived in this house of splendor.*

Mr. Harris reined his team to a halt and set the brake lever.

Lily's anticipation mounted.

Before the merchant had time to climb down and assist her, the front door opened, and a butler stepped out. Neatly attired in black and white, the tall African came to meet them. "If y'all's makin' a delivery, take yo' wagon on aroun' back. I'll fetch some boys to he'p y'all unload."

Mr. Harris chuckled. "The onliest thing I got to unload is this gal. Says she's kin to the mistress of the house."

The butler took a closer look at Lily.

She could tell he didn't recognize her. But then, she was still dressed in Nancy's homespun. "I'm Lily Harwood, Mariah's sister. I realize I'm not very presentable—"

The sudden patter of footsteps on the porch brought golden-haired Amy Barclay bounding down the steps. Taller now, and quite the lovely young maiden, she had obviously retained her youthful spirit. "Did I hear correctly? Is that you, Lily?" She turned to the butler. "Help her down, Benjamin." Then, whirling around in a rustle of buttercream flounces, she ran back up the steps and hollered into the door. "Mariah! It's your sister! She's here!"

Lily's heartbeat took up a staccato pace as Benjamin handed her down to the pebble drive. At any second, Mariah would emerge.

She'd barely circumvented the wagon when her beautiful sister came to the door, attired in a violet taffeta gown fit for a queen. But the smile she'd worn vanished as she halted where she stood. "Amy, I thought you said—*Lily? Is that you?*" With a most unladylike squeal, she grasped handfuls of her skirts and charged down the steps.

At her sister's enthusiastic welcome, emotion clogged Lily's throat. She could only manage a nod.

"Lily, Lily." Mariah drew her into a brief hug, then thrust her an arm's distance from herself and looked her up and down. "What on earth are you wearing? And your hands. . ." She picked one of them up. "They're rough and chapped. And your hair. Your complexion—why, you haven't even got a bonnet on for protection from the sun and the wind."

Lily could only shrug. "I suppose I should have taken the time to purchase more appropriate clothing, but—"

"Oh, bother." Mariah fluttered a hand as if details were of little consequence and gave her another quick hug. "You're here now. Everything else can be easily fixed. Come with me, and we'll get you in a nice warm bubble bath. And while you're soaking, you can tell me all about it." She barely paused for breath. "You do remember our darling Amy, don't you?" Flicking a glance at her young sister-in-law waiting on the veranda, she swept Lily up the steps toward the grand entry. "She's becoming quite the belle of the county, aren't you, dear?"

"So you keep sayin," Amy answered in her airy drawl as she traipsed after Mariah and Lily across the parquet floor toward the graceful staircase.

"Now, with you here, Lily, we'll certainly be the most popular home from here to Alexandria." She slanted a frown at her. "That is, once you've had a few milk baths to turn your skin soft and creamy again. Mother

Barclay has some simply marvelous oils and creams imported from the Orient."

Mariah's enthusiasm, the splendid sights. . . Lily could hardly take everything in.

Her sister stopped halfway up the stairs. "Whatever am I thinking? Amy, run down to the kitchen and tell them we need bathwater brought up right away." She smiled and placed a hand on Lily's shoulder. "I wasn't expecting you for at least another week. Your letter said Mr. Waldon would return after the first of November, remember? But this is ever so much better. We shall have more time to get you properly outfitted before your first ball."

"My ball?"

"Yes." On the top landing, Mariah stopped in the upstairs lounge area and turned to face Lily. "I sent out invitations last week. I want to launch you properly into our little society. There's no need for anyone to know about the rustic frontier life you've been leading, unless— Did you introduce yourself to anyone in Alexandria?"

"I never went there. At the ferry crossing, I accepted a ride from a merchant who lives somewhere above the falls."

"Splendid. Oh, and Rose will arrive in a few days. I asked her to come early. I'm so excited! You, Rose, and I together again. The three of us haven't been together since my wedding, and that was such a hectic time it hardly counts." She stopped prattling, and a slow smile graced her lips as she gazed at Lily a moment, then pulled her close and gave her a longer hug.

Lily basked in the feeling of being utterly safe and loved and cared for.

When Mariah stepped back, her violet eyes glistened as she smoothed a hand along Lily's cheek. "My baby sister is back where she belongs. God is so good."

～

No amount of protesting during the next two weeks would stop Mariah and Mistress Barclay from fussing over her. Since Mariah had yet to conceive a child—a sadness she mentioned only once—Lily soon realized she was their new plaything, the new dress-up doll. Amy, who'd always been more interested in horses than fashion, whispered that she was *monstrously relieved* that attention had been diverted away from her for a change.

Lily had every intention of returning to Beaver Cove and to John and her adopted family, but she hadn't managed to find the right words to placate her sister or the lady of the house. She did enjoy the pampering, the swish and rustle of costly fabrics, the scented soaps and perfumes, to say nothing of having someone swirl her hair into amazing styles. The corset, however, was another matter. She'd forgotten how binding those torturous contraptions could be, especially considering the delicious variety of food being served at every meal.

Then a most wonderful day arrived. Hearing laughter and loud talking downstairs, Lily peeked over the railing and saw that Rose had come. . . . Rose, the older sister who had mothered Lily since she was a tender four years of age. She and her two little ones had blown into this luxurious haven on a blustery mid-November day. Gasping with delight, Lily raced down the stairs to greet them, nearly tripping over the abundant petticoats she wasn't used to wearing.

She ran right to Rose, who was attired in a fashionable dove-gray traveling costume. Lily wondered if Mariah had provided the lovely clothing, since Rose, too, lived in the much simpler surroundings of a small farm.

After reveling in hugs and kisses and cooing over pretty little Jenny, now four and a half, and three-year-old Ethan Nathaniel, Lily realized how sorely she missed Emma and Davy. She glanced at Rose. "Did Nate come with you?"

Mariah answered for Rose. "When does he ever?"

Giving her middle sister a patient look, Rose almost said something, but instead turned to Amy. "Dearest, would you mind taking my darlings to the kitchen for something to eat? They've not had a bite since early this morning."

"We'd be delighted, won't we, dear?" Mistress Barclay swept forth in all her regal elegance and took Jenny's hand, while Amy latched on to

Ethan's. "It's been months since I've had a chance to fatten these little cherubs up. Mariah, why don't you take Rose upstairs to freshen up? I'll have Cook send up a tray for you all."

"Thank you," Rose and Lily said as one while the matron ushered the children toward the butlery entrance behind the staircase.

"I received a note from Nate the other day," Rose commented, accompanying her sisters up the stairs. "He and Robert hope to make it home for Christmas."

Lily gave her an understanding smile. "Waiting can be unbearably hard."

"Yes, but Nate's family does what they can to help Star and me with the farm. They've been a real blessing to us."

"That's how the people of Beaver Cove have been to me. Like a family."

"That's lovely, you two," Mariah piped in. "But now you're both with your *real* family at long last. There couldn't possibly be anything left to harvest, Rose, so I won't take no for an answer. You and the children will stay here with us until Nate comes home." Reaching the second floor, she caught both her sisters by the hand. "We shall have a marvelous time, just like when we were young. Remember how we used to talk about attending the grand balls in Bath's assembly rooms?"

Rose chuckled. "I believe that was your dream, sister-of-mine."

"My dream, your dream, it makes little difference. Lily's coming-out ball is next Saturday, and the whole of northern Virginia is going to meet and be enthralled by the daughters of Harwood House."

Rose erupted with her wonderful throaty laugh. "*The daughters of Harwood House!* What a clever way to put it."

"I thought you'd be pleased. It has such a resplendent ring to it." She hiked her perfect nose, then broke into giggles. "Come along to my dressing room. I believe I have just the gown to set off your eyes for supper this evening."

Mariah never ceased to amaze Lily. She'd always been the beauty of the family, but so much more, as well. She possessed supreme confidence in herself. During the past months Lily had begun to attain a measure of that elusive attribute. But she now realized it was a mere shadow of Mariah's.

Even take-charge Rose was simply following along and doing her bidding.

The deeper timbre of male voices drifted up from the entry below as Mariah's husband and father-in-law returned from a few days in Baltimore. With a joyous grin, Mariah ushered Lily and Rose into her bedchamber then left to greet the men.

At last Lily was alone with Rose. She gestured toward Mariah's blue damask chaise, and after her older sister sank onto it, Lily joined her, perching on the edge. There was so much to tell Rose about John. Lily hoped to make her understand the need to return to him.

Rose took Lily's hands in hers. "Baby sister, that missive I received from Nate also mentioned you'd almost been taken by Indians. Thank God you're here now and safe with us."

Lily nodded. "Truly, Rose, I'm thrilled to be here with you and Mariah. But I wish I were still at Beaver Cove."

Angling her head, Rose searched Lily's eyes. "Nate also mentioned he saw John Waldon kiss you *on the mouth* when he found you. And this was only weeks after his wife had gone to be with the Lord, was it not?"

Lily felt her cheeks flame. "He was profoundly glad to find me unharmed. As I said in prior letters, the Waldons treated me as if I were family."

"If 'twas merely a brotherly kiss, why are you blushing?"

Lily hadn't said a word to Mariah about her intention to return to the cove, because she didn't want to be harangued day and night. But she'd never kept anything from Rose. . .until now. "I was embarrassed. Nate thought there was much more to the kiss."

"Nate." A low laugh spilled from Rose. "Is it not amazing how much a man changes once he has womenfolk to protect?"

Or how closely a woman will guard a secret when she has a love to protect. Perhaps this wasn't the time to confide in Rose, after all.

Lily's spirits sank. Mariah was determined to find her a husband here among the wealthy Virginians. A coming-out ball, no less. Still, Lily knew she'd have to tell her sisters about her and John soon. . .and somehow make them understand.

Chapter 38

As always, the richly appointed dining room with its exquisite china and silverware impressed Lily as she entered with Rose and the Barclay family. She and the others were as richly attired as the furnishings, and even the food they'd be served would be worthy of the beautiful surroundings.

Everything flowed so graciously for these people, Lily mused. The women's hands were soft and white. No blisters or calluses ever marred them, no redness from lye soap. They'd never bent to cook over a hot hearth, washed a soiled dish, or boiled and scrubbed dirt and stains from worn work clothes. They'd never spent evenings at a spinning wheel or darning stockings, spent days behind a plow or in the stable helping a mother cow give birth. So why couldn't she embrace all Mariah wanted to offer?

Lily's gaze gravitated to Mariah and her strikingly handsome husband as he flawlessly assisted his wife into her seat. Only a small scar at his temple gave evidence to the battle wound that had blinded him. And with Mariah's impeccable taste, Lily surmised her sister had some dashing, refined gentleman picked out for her, as well.

From the head of the table, Mr. Barclay spoke down the lengthy expanse in his easy Virginia drawl. "Cora, my dear, Colin and I stopped by for a short visit with Victoria on our way home. She asked how your arrangements for the ball were comin'. She and Heather are both countin' the days."

Colin chuckled. "Tori's *simply devastated* that the fabric she ordered for her gown has not come. The poor, put-upon dear had to choose some *utterly dreadful* brocaded silk."

"Colin," his mother scolded, "you shouldn't belittle your sister. It's most important to maintain a certain standing among our friends. I'm quite proud of Victoria and the added grace and elegance she's brought to that household. I can say the same about Heather, also, since her marriage to Evan Greer."

Grace and elegance. Lily suppressed a smirk. The thought of any of her cove neighbors seeking a wife to add grace and elegance to his home was laughable. Those men chose capable wives, women who could work alongside them to build a home and a life together—and fight with them to save it, should need be.

Seated next to Lily, Rose nudged her with an elbow then turned to their host. "Mr. Barclay, did you perchance hear any news of the war while you were in Baltimore?"

"No, lass. With winter upon us, things should remain quiet until next spring."

Colin turned his vacant stare in Rose's general direction. "There was that one tidbit about the captured French soldier who got separated from the Indians he was supposedly leading, and they all disappeared on him." He gave a hearty laugh. "After a week of starving, the illustrious leader stumbled onto one of the forts along the Susquehanna and gave himself up."

Lily nodded. "Fort Henry."

"I believe so. Wasn't that where your Mr. Waldon was posted?"

"Yes. Did the Frenchman give any other information?"

Colin shook his head. "Just that he'd been dispatched from Fort

Duquesne with some thirty-odd Indians to harass the settlements along the frontier."

"Which they do quite viciously." Lily swept a glance around. "Once they sneak past the string of outposts on our side of the river, they separate into parties of five or six and attack lone farmsteads in sundry places, burning and murdering as they go."

"Rather ingenious, really," Colin admitted. "A small number can keep a much larger population on edge, wondering where they will strike next."

Lily knew that all too well. "Quite. They're rather successful at frightening settlers into abandoning their homes and leaving the area."

Mr. Barclay entered the conversation. "It's imperative that our forces take Fort Duquesne next spring and stop the supply of goods that buy the services of the Indian tribes."

"Will the British generals finally do that?" Lily met the older man's gaze.

A crystal bell rang at Mistress Barclay's end as the hostess signaled for the food. "Please. No more war talk at the dinner table."

"Quite right, my dear." Her husband cleared his throat. "How are your plans for the ball coming?"

How easy it was for these people to dismiss the war and any other unpleasantness, Lily thought bleakly.

"The Kinsales have sent their acceptance," Amy said.

Across the table, Mariah raised a meaningful eyebrow. "A reply we've been most anxiously waiting for, wouldn't you say, Amy?"

The young miss turned a becoming shade of pink, a sure sign of blossoming love.

At that moment, the butler and Pansy, the maid, brought in trays of delectable-smelling food. Everyone waited as the house servants carefully dished portions of ham and glazed vegetables on each person's china plate, then left as quietly as they'd come.

No passing of heaping bowls or platters around here, Lily thought.

"Let us give thanks." Mr. Barclay bowed his head. "Our gracious heavenly Father, we thank You for Your generosity and the bounty You provide. We pray for Your continued protection over Rose's husband and all those who are fighting to save our western frontiers. Please give our British generals the wisdom and fortitude to go forth next spring and end this threat to the settlers. We ask this in the name of Your precious Son, Jesus. Amen."

As Lily raised her head, she realized the wealthy people at this table made up a fine Christian family who cared about the plight of others. She also knew for a certainty that no matter how much they wanted her to be part of them, they were not her family. She didn't need three months to conclude her family lived 150 miles away in Beaver Cove. But how would she ever find a way to make her sisters understand she wanted to give up all this luxury and safety for a life of danger and hardship?

Be honest.

⌒

"Come and get it!" The call echoed over the incessant clatter of pounding, chopping, and sawing. John glanced down from the roof of the new MacBride cabin to see Edith Randall holding her woolen shawl close as she waved an arm over her head. The noon meal was ready.

The hardworking men were eating much better since a few of the womenfolk had returned to the valley, though most meals had to be consumed outside in the damp December weather at whichever farmstead they happened to be working. As Edith's smaller children ran toward the long tables set up in the yard, the menfolk ambled from their tasks at a slower, but no less eager, pace.

"I could eat a horse," Bob commented from the other side of the roof.

Pounding a peg through a shingle, John grinned at his friend. The Randall cabin had been the first one completed, since Edith feared her aging parents in Chestertown wouldn't be able to endure her rambunctious brood for long. She and the little ones had been back for almost a month now. Millie and Cissy Dunlap came soon after, Cissy being too enamored with young Donald to stay away.

An unbidden vision of Lily, smudged nose and all, gazing up at him with those bewitching silvery eyes made John's smile die as he crossed the sloping surface to the ladder. If only. . .

He stifled a heavy sigh. This last house would be finished by day's end, giving Pat and Ian's family time to return to the cove for Christmas and him and his boys time to reach Philadelphia. The Gilfords had extended an invitation to celebrate the holy days with them, and John hoped that would perk up Matt and Luke. Their hangdog expressions showed they missed Lily almost as much as he did.

Reaching the bottom rung, he saw Cal burying his hatchet in a stump where he'd been shaving shingles. John waited for his pal to catch up, then gave him a friendly slap on the back. "Almost through."

"All of us workin' together sure has helped things go faster." Cal pulled off his canvas gloves. "Still, it's hard to believe we've rebuilt five cabins and animal shelters in seven weeks."

John nodded. "Thank heaven for all the October rains. Without them, a lot more would've burned. We were able to reuse an amazing number of logs and boards. That was a blessing."

"Wish Nancy'd change her mind an' bring the young'uns back here when the MacBride women come. There hasn't been a sign of Indians anywhere below Blue Mountain since the attack on our cove."

"That's right. I forgot you and the MacBrides came here together."

"Aye. We all hail from Queenstown."

John picked a splinter from his palm as they strode along. "I doubt Richard and his family will come back even next spring. They might after the hostilities are over, though."

"That makes three families we've lost."

"I regret the loss of Richard Shaw the most. Young as he is, he worked hard to prove up his place. Maybe if their children had been a bit older. . ."

Cal chuckled. "Ruthie, too. That li'l missy could howl louder'n a pack of wolves when she got scared."

"Not my—" John caught himself before uttering Lily's name.

The aroma of roast pork drifted toward them before they reached the table, and John's stomach growled. His boys waved him to the place they'd saved between them.

"Mind hurryin' along?" Ian stood at the head of the table. "I need to say grace."

It was good to have the older man back, even without full use of his left arm. He'd returned last week, after Pat received a three-month furlough from Fort Henry.

John had hiked one leg over the bench when he heard a dog bark in the distance. Then another. Since all the dogs in the cove had been killed, he glanced across at Toby and his grown sons.

The other men all disengaged themselves from the benches, and John and Cal bolted for the muskets they'd left leaning against the cabin wall.

The unmistakable sound of hoofbeats came from the Swatara Creek trace. Before he was able to uncork the powder horn, John heard splashing in Beaver Creek. Whoever was coming would be here in seconds.

As three large dogs bounded into the MacBride clearing, John swung his weapon around to use as a club.

On the dogs' heels came riders and horses.

"Papa! Papa!"

John lowered his musket. Davy! And Emma! They were on the first horse!

And wonder of wonders—Lily!

Leaning the weapon back against the wall, he blinked hard and looked again. Lily rode right behind the children. She'd come back! And she'd brought his babies! He didn't know who to run to first.

Before he could decide, other riders leading packhorses stopped between him and his dear ones.

"Papa!"

Dodging around the animals, he found Lily already on the ground. He caught her to him and hurried to the children, but Matt and Luke were already lifting them down. In an instant he had his whole family in his arms. His heart nearly burst with joy amid the excited childish chatter as he kissed his clinging little Emmy, who looked so much like her sweet mother. Wiggly Davy was next. Then his beloved Lily.

"What's all this stuff?"

Matt's question drew John's attention from the sparkling gray eyes that held such promise. He set the little ones on the ground, noticing that there were two men and more than a dozen horses, most of which were loaded with goods.

Neighbors, all talking at once came to join the group.

Holding Lily against his side, John ambled over to the strangers. "You are most welcome. Thank you for escorting my family here."

"Only thanks we need is to share your grub," the huge backwoodsman with rough features said.

"Aye." His stubby partner gestured with his disheveled head at Lily. "Your missus insisted we start out a'fore first light this mornin'."

Ian spoke out. "Yer welcome to partake of our vittles. Ye rode in from the Susquehanna?"

"Yep." The first one eyed the food-laden table. "A crew of rivermen poled us an' all this truck up as far as the Swatara."

"The dogs, too?" Matt knelt down to pet one that was sniffing around his legs.

"Yep. Brung them mangy curs right along with us."

"Hey, they ain't mangy," Davy piped in.

Lily laughed. "No, they certainly aren't." She glanced at John. "If you don't mind, I thought we'd keep the female and let the Pattersons and MacBrides have the other two for watchdogs."

Davy puffed out his scrawny chest. "An' when Queenie has pups, I'll give 'em to whoever wants 'em."

"Except the prettiest one." Emma planted a fist on her waist. "I get to keep that one."

"Hey, folks," Edith called from the table. "Food's getting cold. Come on an' eat. We can catch up later."

Millie and her daughter had already set more places, and everyone found a spot to sit. John still couldn't let go of Lily. He couldn't believe she'd come back.

Directly across the table, Jackson looked at both of them, then grunted and offered a lopsided grin. "Ain't no never mind. Figgered as much. 'Sides, I got my eye on the sister of Frank's gal. Don't know why he didn't pick the purtier one."

Down the way, Millie wagged her salt-and-pepper head. "We're still talkin' about them German gals. I'm not sure I like the idea of you boys bringin' home wives that can't hardly speak English."

"Wait'll you see 'em, Ma." Frank angled his head toward her with a lovesick expression. "They got hair blonder than the sun an' eyes bluer'n the sky."

Ian's voice boomed along the length of the table as he looked straight at John and Lily. "Since we're on the subject of courtin', I reckon we'll be needin' us a weddin' today, soon as we finish the cabin."

Beside John, Lily stiffened slightly.

"Either that or our Miss Lily will be spendin' the night at the Randalls'."

John's mouth fell open. How could the old man be so crude?

"Well. . ." Lily relaxed against John again. "Since those Randall children are simply too noisy to abide, I suppose I have no choice."

Everyone laughed and started talking at once.

Amazed beyond words, John drew Lily's sweet self so close, he couldn't tell if it was his heart or hers beating with such incredulous joy.

Chapter 39

Is that the men coming?" Lily gasped the words over the happy chatter as Edith tightened the laces on the corset Mariah had insisted on sending.

Millie opened the bedroom door of the new Waldon cabin that still smelled of fresh-cut wood and peeked out. "Aye, they're ridin' in now."

Cissy and the twins tittered behind their hands as Cissy shook the wrinkles from the exquisite gown of brocaded emerald silk Lily would wear on this, her wedding day. Their eyes grew wide as they admired the white satin stomacher with its vertical row of tiny bows, an underskirt adorned with double flounces of fine lace edged with silver, and the dropped neckline with a matching flounce. "Even puffed sleeves," Cissy breathed.

"With lacy ruffles," Gracie added, hesitant even to touch the lovely creation.

"And satin bows to hold back the skirt," Patience said softly. "I've never seen such a beautiful gown."

"Thank you." Lily smiled at the threesome. "My sister insisted on having it made for me."

"This'll be the first weddin' in the cove, and mine'll be next," Cissy declared.

Overflowing with happiness, Lily wanted everyone to share it. "We shall start a new tradition. Every bride in Beaver Cove must wear this gown on her wedding day—should she choose to do so, of course."

"You mean it?" Holding the frock against herself, Cissy whirled around, fluttering out its glory as a dreamy expression lit her eyes.

"Of course." Lily bent to pick up a package from the bed and handed it to one of the twins. "Patience, would you please take this out to John and tell him it's my wedding gift to him? It's a new outfit, since all of his clothes were burned in the fire."

"Your sister must be very, very rich," Gracie said, regarding the trunk of new clothing they'd lugged into the room.

"Her husband's family is. They are also wonderfully generous people. When they heard of our sad plight, not only did they provide crates of clothes for everyone, but bed linens, quilts, kitchen towels, and fabric for curtains. And the other packhorses are loaded down with grain and corn to help feed our livestock this winter."

"I declare." Millie wagged her head in wonder. "It's a real blessin'. I brought some grain back with me, too, but not nearly enough. We figgered before winter was through, we'd have to butcher most of the animals."

Lily stepped into the gown's pool of silk and ruffles, and Edith drew it gently up so she could slip her arms into the sleeves. Then Edith tightened the back laces. "I've another bit of good news. Mr. Gilford, the children's grandfather, is sending a barge-load of bricks and slate shakes next spring, enough for a fireproof two-story house. So should the Indians ever come again, they won't be able to burn that one. We'll all be safe inside."

Straightening the generous skirt over the petticoats, Edith glanced up. "Bob tells me he don't think the Injuns'll be back. Ever'time they came here, they lost braves. They like easy pickin's."

"That's comforting." Lily gazed down at the ruffles and bows. "Mr.

Gilford says his friend, the governor, plans to pressure the British commander into capturing Fort Duquesne in the spring. If that happens, all our men will be able to come home for good."

"Mercy me. Wouldn't that be fine." Millie began arranging Lily's hair into fancy swirls and pinning them in place. "Then our husbands can get back to why we came here in the first place: makin' a future for us an' our young'uns."

Lily turned to her. "Speaking of the future, I brought another present for John he's sure to be thrilled with. . .a box filled with fancy hinges and drawer pulls for the furniture he'll be building for us all. I can hardly wait to see his face when he sees them."

Millie wrapped her arms around Lily and sighed. "I'd hoped you'd marry my Jackson, you know, but havin' you back, wedded to John, is almost as wonderful."

Lily returned the embrace. "And so is being back here with all of you. To be quite honest, I feared you wouldn't approve of our marrying so soon after Susan's passing."

"Not at all, dear. I think she would be the first to wish you happiness, you and John."

"Truly?" Lily's eyes misted over.

"Now, now," Edith scolded. "Stop the huggin'. We don't want to crush that gown."

Lily reached around and hugged the petite woman. "I'm simply too happy to care about the gown. I'm getting married today."

John flicked an imaginary piece of lint from his fine suit of clothes, feeling both dashing and thankful as he waited at the far end of the front room. His sons were attired in finery as well, the rich colors of their outfits making up for the lack of flowers for this winter wedding. Matt looked quite grown-up in sapphire, Luke in copper, and Davy in burgundy, all of which complemented John's café-au-lait frock coat and dark brown britches.

But where was Lily? He could hardly wait for her and Emma to emerge from the bedroom.

The guests, mostly men and their sons, fidgeted, too, as they sat on hastily set-up rows of benches, with Bob's daughters sprinkled about.

When John and the others first arrived from the MacBrides', his friends prevented him from going in to Lily. Bad luck, they'd said, though he couldn't imagine anything dimming the joy of this day. To think she loved him so much she'd chosen him over all the luxury that could've been hers. At long last, he'd have his life back, and so would his family.

He gazed again at his boys, flanking him on either side. They, too, watched for the door to open, knowing that from this day forth, laughter and good times would fill this home. Lily had a way of bringing such things with her.

The door cracked open.

John started forward, but Ian caught his shoulder from behind. He eased back on his heels. She was coming to him.

With a darling little giggle, Emma emerged and started past the rows of guests with practiced steps. She looked like a porcelain doll in a ruffled gown of gold silk, her red hair caught up at the crown with a matching satin bow and trailing down her back in ringlets. Her eyes fairly danced as she smiled up at him.

John bent to give his sweet daughter a kiss, then guided her beside him.

Next came Cissy in a fine gown of royal-blue taffeta that Lily undoubtedly had loaned her. Her head was bowed a little, and her shy smile was for no one but Donald.

An eternal moment later, out strolled Lily, and her glowing gaze met his and stayed there until she reached him. Looking every inch the angel she was, Lily made a breathtaking vision in emerald and white that John could hardly take in. Her hand trembled slightly as he took it in his, and he gave it an encouraging squeeze. When she looked up at him, all the love he felt for her was reflected in her eyes. What a gift she was. A gift from God.

Lily could hardly breathe for happiness. Lost in John's tender gaze, surrounded by well-wishing friends, she knew she would never forget this wondrous day. Ian's blunt but welcome words had laid the last of her fears and doubts to rest, and an indescribable sense of peace enfolded her as she looked up and met John's smile. The love they shared had been part of God's plan all along, and she knew the life they would build together would honor Him. Papa would be thankful to know that in coming to this new land, the Lord had blessed all three of his daughters with happiness and love. Rose first, then Mariah, and now His hand of blessing extended to Lily. Returning John's promise-filled smile with one of her own, she turned with him to face Ian and repeat the sacred vows that would bind them together for all time.

Author's Note

The area surrounding Blue Mountain in Pennsylvania continued to suffer random attacks in 1758 from Fort Duquesne, the southernmost French fort. In random raids, nine more people were killed, three captured, and three went missing. The fort's influence seriously waned during the year. The British naval blockade near the mouth of the St. Lawrence River stopped most of the flow of supplies and trade goods coming into Canada. Any goods that did trickle in were inflated in price and sold mostly around Quebec. None reached as far south as Fort Duquesne. Most of the Indians refused to fight without the payment of trade goods and returned to their villages.

In October 1758, the British command, along with representatives from Pennsylvania and New Jersey, invited the chiefs of thirteen tribes to a meeting. There the Treaty of Easton was signed. The Indians were given superior English trade goods in exchange for remaining neutral in New Jersey, Pennsylvania, and along a portion of the Ohio River for the remainder of the war. This brought peace to the region.

William Pitt in England was given charge of the war effort in North America. His directives changed the course of the war:

July 1758 – The British regulars and Colonial militias arrived by sea and laid siege to the French Fort Louisbourg at the mouth of the St. Lawrence River, defeating the French along with a number of their warships.

August 1758 – Lieutenant Colonel John Bradstreet defeated the French at Fort Frontenac at the east end of Lake Ontario with 150 British regulars and 2,850 colonials.

October 1758 – The Treaty of Easton (as mentioned above).

November 1758 – Only a small garrison of French was left at Fort Duquesne when they learned an English and Colonial force of six thousand was approaching. They abandoned and burned the fort.

July 1759 – The English and colonials captured Fort Niagara (La Belle Famille).

September 1759 – General James Wolf defeated General Louis Joseph Montcalm on the Plains of Abraham near Quebec City.

1762 – In the Treaty of Fontiubleau, France ceded Louisiana to Spain (an ally of England in the Seven Years' War, in which the French & Indian War was included, along with conflicts over colonies in India and Africa).

1763 – The Treaty of Paris ended the Seven Years' War. France traded all her possessions in North America for the lucrative sugar cane island of Guadeloupe.

Sally Laity has written both historical and contemporary novels, including a coauthored series for Tyndale House, nine Heartsong Romances, and twelve Barbour novellas. She considers it a joy to know that the Lord can touch other hearts through her stories. Her favorite pastimes include quilting for her church's Prayer Quilt Ministry and scrapbooking. She makes her home in the beautiful Tehachapi Mountains of Southern California with her husband of fifty years and enjoys being a grandma and great-grandma.

Widowed a few years ago, Dianna Crawford lives in California's Central Valley where she is active in her local church. Although she loves writing Christian historical fiction, her most gratifying blessings are her four daughters and their families. In her spare time she loves to paint and travel.

Dianna's first novel was published in the general market in 1992 under the pen name Elaine Crawford. She was pleased when it was nominated for Best First Book by Romance Writers of America. After publishing several works by that name, Dianna felt very blessed to be given the opportunity to write for the Christian market. A number of novels have followed. She and Sally Laity were honored when their third collaboration, The Tempering Blaze, resulted in another nomination, this one for Best Inspirational by Romance Writers of America.